THE DARK MAN

MARC SCHOOLEY

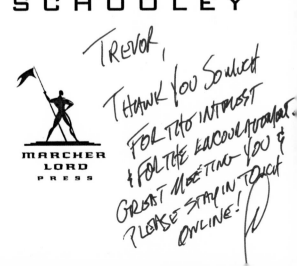

MARCHER
LORD
PRESS

Trevor,
Thank you so much
for the interest
& for the encouragement.
Great meeting you &
please stay in touch
online!

THE DARK MAN by Marc Schooley
Published by Marcher Lord Press
8345 Pepperridge Drive
Colorado Springs, CO 80920
www.marcherlordpress.com

MARCHER LORD PRESS and the MARCHER LORD PRESS logo are trademarks of Marcher Lord Press. Absence of ™ in connection with marks of Marcher Lord Press or other parties does not indicate an absence of trademark protection of those marks.

This is a work of fiction. Names, characters, places, and incidents are products of the author's imagination or are used fictitiously. Any similarity to actual people, organizations, and/or events is purely coincidental.

Cover Designer: Kirk DouPonce, Dog-Eared Design, www.dogeareddesign.com
Cover Illustrator: Kirk DouPonce
Creative Team: Jeff Gerke, Kristine Pratt

Library of Congress Cataloging-in-Publication Data
An application to register this book for cataloging has been filed with the Library of Congress.
International Standard Book Number: 978-0-9821049-3-4

Printed in the United States of America

For the Schooner, who loved the gospel,
in part because he knew the dark man

Acknowledgments

To UHCL Professor Craig White, the Captain, who, in true professorial spirit, forced me to walk the plank into the swirling and perilous waters of fiction.

To Donna Fleisher, who threw me a line when I was sinking.

And to Jeff Gerke, who grabbed the line, pulled me out, and then taught me how to swim.

ONE

The dark man was back.

Charles Graves fidgeted at the top of the staircase, keeping a wary eye on the man while attempting to eavesdrop on the ruckus developing below. It was a delicate balancing act.

The staircase wound around a spacious entry hall furnished with marble floors, luxurious antiques, portraits, and a gold chandelier with 121 bulbs. Thirty-two gold-inlaid steps led from the base of the staircase to the top step. Wooden eagles perched every five feet along the banister. The eagles' shadows soared across the wall opposite the banister in the light from the chandelier as if they were flying in formation.

The staircase culminated in a balcony, which fronted four rooms located above the entry hall of the Graves Mansion. One of these, the farthest from the staircase, belonged to Charles. The closest had belonged to his brother, Stephen.

Charles peeked through the woodworking adorning the balcony's railing. A forgetful, mechanically overproduced tune from the ASL meandered through the house, droning its way to the balcony. The singer alluded to something about the brotherhood of man. Charles did not understand the phrase.

Something crashed downstairs and the music stopped. They were arguing again.

Through the woodworking he watched the remains of his family's Approved Song List unit skid across the great white marble floor. It came to rest under the chandelier. Its ruins looked like an unfinished jigsaw puzzle.

The dark man was assembled at Charles's feet. Charles stole a quick glance. The dark man snickered at him like a ventriloquist's dummy.

Before he'd died, his grandfather had fashioned this woodblock puzzle for Charles. The puzzle consisted of a sunken oaken frame with raised sides two inches high. The frame enclosed an area of one square foot. His grandfather had sanded the oak meticulously, finishing the frame inside and out with a shiny lacquer.

The puzzle pieces were easily assembled blocks carved on all six sides. The sides represented facial features, hair, ears, foreheads, cheeks, and chins. Some pieces featured accessories such as glasses. Many emotions were represented as well, enhanced by the intricate carving of facial lines, muscular nuances, and distinguishing marks. Some eyes cried, some mouths laughed. The dark man's mouth usually sneered. The wood-block puzzle was a homemade, wooden version of Mr. Potato Head, with greater realism.

The dark man stared through hollow eyes—despite the fact that none of the eye pieces had been cut to appear hollow.

Charles supposed the combination of pieces that formed the dark man was special. His face was blemished from Charles having ripped him out of the frame or slammed him on the floor once too often. His hair was manicured, black, and parted in the middle. His lips were thin, yet full and red. The pieces tracing the dark man's outline were worn, creating an effect that appeared to suspend him within a fog of unknown origin.

"Get out!" Charles said to it.

With the nail of his left-hand ring finger Charles traced a jagged scar stretching across the left side of his face from cheekbone to lip. He overturned the dark man, spilling him onto the floor of the balcony. One of the dark man's plucked-out eyes stared up at Charles.

Charles righted the frame and began to refill it with different pieces. The tension escalated below.

"I don't care about that stupid ASL machine." His mother's voice rose from below. "And you used to not care!"

"Things are different now. Can't you see?" Charles's father said.

From the balcony, Charles peered down at his parents through an archway leading into an adjacent hall. They stood along the far side of a formal dining table embellished by an arrangement of white roses in an ornamental vase. His mother faced him, wearing an ankle-length red dress. She was partially obscured by his father, who leaned against the table with his back to Charles. Charles noticed the heart-shaped bald spot on the back of his father's head.

His mother grasped a remote control with red buttons in her right hand. "Different?" she said. "Here's something different." She pushed a red button.

The house erupted in sound. Charles thought this music was different from the ASL. It was raw and uncouth: *Can you expect a man that's rotten to the core to ever raise himself, to be anything more.*

His father's refined speech was easy to distinguish from the voice in the song. "Turn it off, Teresa." He seemed to be inching his way toward her.

Charles's mother pressed another red button. The music paused. "What happened to you, Cotton?" She hit Play again: *'Cause when I try it on my own You know I'm bound to lose.* Another pause.

"Nothing, baby. We have to fit in. Adapt. That's all."

"I don't want to fit in." Charles's mother mashed the red buttons again: *There's only one path a sinful man is ever gonna choose.*

"You have to quit. Give me that remote." Charles's father shuffled one foot nearer to Teresa.

"Don't come any closer," she said. Tears streamed. Her mascara bled. She ran her free hand through her hair, causing her bangs to tangle. She wiped the tears from her face, smearing her makeup. Her head fell to her chest. A stilted moan oozed from her mouth. It sounded like a whining cello.

Charles's father put both palms forward. "Okay, okay. Calm down." He was almost within reach.

The remote clicked twice. Between clicks the scraggly voice sang: *But when the Spirit touched my heart . . . .*

Charles's left hand arranged pieces in the oak frame, operating on its own volition. It removed two of the pieces from the frame. His hand searched for others to take their place. His eyes were fixed on the situation below. He saw his father nearing his mother. In the corner of his vision he noticed the outline of a face appear in the puzzle. It had his mother's hair.

Charles's mother backed two steps from his father. The archway leading into the dining room had not quite concealed her from his line of sight. Her moaning escalated to bawling. She tried to say, "I don't want to calm down." All Charles could make out was "I doe whaa cahhh dowww." She clicked twice: *And I called Jesus' name.*

"I've had enough," his father said. The heart-shaped bald spot blushed. "Teresa, I'm begging you. Please. I can still help you. Quick, they are coming."

No response, only clicks: *He saved the soul of a man in the sinners' hall of fame.*

His father rushed his mother. She tried to run, but he caught her before she took one step.

He took the remote from her hand and smashed it on the table. It exploded. One of the red buttons arced, striking the lip of the vase holding the roses. It caromed to the tabletop, spinning like a dime before it came to rest. It reminded Charles of tidilywinks.

Charles's father tossed the shattered remote. The pieces landed to the right of the wrecked ASL unit. More puzzle pieces, Charles thought. He looked down at his puzzle. His mother's nose appeared, followed by her mouth.

He refocused on his parents in time to see the roses and the vase bash into his father's forehead. His mother augmented the strike to the forehead with a kick to the groin. Charles's father slumped to the floor.

His mother darted around the far end of the table toward the entry hall. She disappeared from Charles's view as she completed the circuit. Seconds later, she came back into view, screaming for Charles at the top of her lungs, her red dress flowing over the table like a matador's cape.

The doorbell rang.

His mother's face came in all wrong in his puzzle tray. This was not the mother he normally saw there, the one who comforted him. This was someone else. Yet it was his mother.

His mother ran to the trashed ASL unit in full sprint. The doorbell ceased, giving way to pounding fists. His mother swiveled her head as she ran in an attempt to see through the door's beveled glass. Her left foot came down on the busted remote. She slipped like Ethel Merman on the banana peel in the last scene of *It's a Mad, Mad, Mad, Mad World*.

She hit the floor hard, then rested in a dying cockroach position. Her limbs shivered twice before falling to the floor.

The pounding at the door ceased. Charles saw two enormous shapes through the glass. They tried the door handle. The gold handle, shaped like a curly-Q, moved back and forth, slowly at first, then increasing in speed and urgency.

The door handle rattled like marbles in a cardboard box. Charles thought there were zombies at the door, faceless zombies that were not afraid of the sunlight outside. Hungry zombies.

The rattling seemed to awaken his mother. She rolled over and pushed herself to her feet. Her hands reached for the small of her back. She walked hunched over toward the staircase.

She reached the foot of the staircase when the door ruptured inward. The door jamb shattered, propelling shards of wood across the marble floor. The door shimmied open. Charles saw two massive shapes in the doorway. A burst of sunlight lit them from behind.

The men obscured the sun as they entered. With the light behind them Charles could not make out their features, but his mind conjured images of gaping mouths with rotted teeth and saliva dripping from the corner of zombie lips. The men scanned to their left. It seemed as though their heads rotated in unison.

Charles's father groaned on the floor. He rose to one knee. One hand was on his groin, the other wiping a tendril of blood descending his forehead. He tried to say something, but nothing intelligible came out.

Charles's mother climbed the stairs. She peeked back at the intruders, causing her foot to miss the third stair step. The instep of her shoe caught on the lip of the riser, sending her face-first into the seventh step. Her nose broke. Blood ejected from her nostrils in a violent spray.

"Mom!" Charles screamed.

The men rotated their heads back around. They moved toward Charles's mother at a deliberate pace.

Charles's mother clawed at the staircase. She climbed, nose broken, covered in blood, eyes filled with tears. She crawled up the stair steps by hands and knees. Halfway up, she paused. "Charles, don't forget." She gasped for air. "I'm your mother."

Charles saw the thing that was his mother crawling up the stairs. He felt a sudden urge to run to his room and hide in the closet. A picture of his mother screaming emerged in his puzzle.

Three-fourths of the way up, she appeared spent. "Charles, you have to remember. You have to."

She inhaled some of the blood from her nose. It wrenched out of her larynx in a ferocious hack. Her head whipped violently, spewing blood onto the wall. The stain resembled this inkblot thing he'd seen in a book. No, a rodent under the talons of one of the eagles' shadows. Behind her, the men were halfway up the stairway and closing.

She managed a last-ditch spurt at Charles. She lunged at him, a blood-soaked, screeching banshee.

Charles tried to escape to his room, but she caught him by his ankle. Blood spurted over his puzzle. A faint whiff of iron wafted through the air.

The banshee shrieked, struggling to breathe between each word. "You . . . have . . . to . . . *remember!*"

Charles compared the face of his mother with the blood-soaked puzzle. They were identical.

He broke free of her grip and ran for his room. The last two things he remembered were his mother's shrieks as the zombies dragged her away and the dark man's remaining eye winking at him from the floor of the balcony.

TWO

The year of Charles Graves's twenty-eighth birthday would be a bad year for the Creekside Baptist Church. The church currently conducted its leadership meetings at Creekside Lanes, a rundown bowling alley in Houston, Texas. Creekside Lanes was what the pros referred to as a dungeon.

Pastor Dean peered over the curve of his ball, his eyes studying the warped lane leading to the pins. What a hole, he thought. Dirty lanes, dirty floors, dirty bathrooms. This is not what I had in mind when I answered the call to ministry.

Behind him lounged the leadership of Creekside, two deacons and a trustee eating cheeseburgers. They were also not what Pastor Dean had envisioned when he'd answered the call. The deacons waited their turn in seats to the left of the scorer's table. The trustee monitored the score at the scorer's table. He had thin lips, droopy jowls, hair parted down the middle, and a double chin.

Pastor Dean lowered the ball to his chest, right above the Elvis logo on his T-shirt that read: The King Lives. Dean scooted toward the lane, slid to a stop, and followed through with the ball. He had no curve. The ball struck head on, leaving two pins he could pick up without much trouble. He twirled on one foot, achieving an about-face. He strolled to the ball return.

A deacon with cauliflower ears crossed his legs and folded his arms across his chest. On his bowling shirt were the words "Spare Me!" He pointed his thumb at the adjacent lane, indicating it was now empty. A foursome of teenagers was making its way to the checkout counter. "Pastor," he said, "I think we can talk now."

"You guys are going to keep on until Graves gets you," Pastor Dean said. He nodded at a custodian leaning on a mop near the restroom, just within earshot.

As if to validate the pastor's point, the custodian placed the mop in the mop-bucket wringer, grabbed the wringer's handle, and forced the handle downward. The wringer compressed the mop head, shooting dirty water through the sieve into the bucket. The custodian removed the mop and started to work on the tile fronting the bathroom door.

The cauliflower-eared deacon snorted. "You're paranoid, Dean. That, or you been readin' too many of them spy novels."

A selection from the ASL serenaded the churchmen from the bowling alley's PA system. The song's digital soullessness reminded Pastor Dean of their vulnerability. The world had somersaulted.

Pastor Dean held his hand over the air jet at the ball return. His ball exited the return chute propelled by a conveyor belt. The ball return rack was separated by a chrome median. The ball struck the median and stood suspended between the left and right side of the return rack as if it were trying to decide which way to go. Dean understood the ball's plight. It fell to the right of the median and rolled into the queue.

"Let me pick up this spare, then we'll get down to business." Dean knocked down the 5-8 combination for a spare. He returned from the lane with a swagger and motioned to a table a few paces past the bathroom in the alley's carpeted lobby. The table afforded a good view of both the front and side doors. It might give them a chance if there was trouble.

The church leaders filed over to the table like men leaving their armchairs for yard work. Ten lanes over, a couple of families were still bowling. The mop man moved into the bathroom, a short-order cook cleaned a grill, and the counter attendant checked receipts for the afternoon.

Dean commenced the meeting with a prayer. "Lord, we trust You in this time of need. Help us through this world that has turned over, amen."

Pastor Dean opened with a discussion of the needs of the exiled Creekside congregation. The bald-headed deacon bent over and fumbled through his ball bag. He extracted a hand-held computer.

"John, I thought I asked you not to bring that," Dean said.

"You're paranoid," the cauliflower-eared deacon said. "Ain't we been careful? I'm sick and tired of all this runnin' and hidin'."

"It's too hard for me to remember everything we talked about once we leave," the bald deacon said. "This way I can make notes. Besides, they could search my house while we're gone. Easier for them to do that, if you think about it."

Dean leaned back and placed his arms behind his head. "All I'm saying is that with Graves on the loose, we have to be extra careful. It's one thing if they get us. If they get that computer they will round up the entire church."

"What do you think our chances are in the long run?" the bald-headed deacon said.

The trustee leaned forward, tugging at his jowls. "What chances?"

"Of maintaining this charade. What do you think we've been doing all these months?" The bald headed-deacon's voice squeaked out the last sentence.

Pastor Dean noticed movement outside one of the side doors. He raised his arms, yawned, and glanced over his left shoulder at the other side door. All clear. His attention refocused on the meeting.

"What we've been doing is running around like a pack of sissies," the cauliflower-eared deacon said. "Drivin' twice through two neighborhoods before meeting to make sure we're not followed. Takin' Communion three at a time at someone's house. Havin' church in rundown warehouses—on Fridays. I tell you one thing, the apostle Paul never did nothin' like that."

"I think he escaped in a basket once," Pastor Dean said, "but let's get back on task."

The cauliflower-eared deacon snorted. The bald-headed deacon glanced across the three other men.

The trustee quit fondling his jowls and extended his hand toward the bald-headed deacon. "Could I see your gadget for a second? It looks pretty cool."

The bald-headed deacon sought the pastor's affirmation. Dean mumbled something and twisted to check the front door. When he turned back the trustee had taken the computer.

"Pretty nice gizmo you got here, John." The trustee set the computer down on the edge of the table in front of the bald-headed deacon. It was scrolled to a roster of the Creekside Baptist Church. "What is chance?" the trustee asked, his hand returning to his jowls. "Where does fate end and Providence begin? Regardless if it's fate, Providence, or the Cincinnati kid shuffling a deck of cards, the only thing that ever really happens is change."

"What on God's green earth are you talking about?" the cauliflower-eared deacon said.

Pastor Dean stared at the trustee. His mind could not solve the puzzle fast enough, but his eyes fixed on one piece of it. The pastor saw something he had not seen before. There seemed to be a faint scar running along the trustee's left cheek.

"Look how the world has changed around us." The trustee stood up, reaching his hands over his head, his fingers splayed. Dean followed the splayed fingers, trying to correlate the trustee's words with his weird behavior. His hollow eyes stared through them all. "The Spirit of the Lord will come upon you in power, and you will prophesy with them, and you will be changed into a different person. Once these signs are fulfilled, do whatever your hand finds to do, for God is with you."

This can't be, Pastor Dean thought.

"Incidentally," the trustee said, "you asked what your chances are. Frankly, your chances are zero." He reached one hand into his pocket and retrieved a transmitter. He pressed a button. "As for Charles Graves, I who speak to you am he."

With the other hand, the trustee grabbed his jowls, squeezed, and lifted. His face came off.

The bald-headed deacon squealed, springing out of his chair. His stomach bumped the table on the way up. The handheld computer fell to the floor, landing underneath the table next to a smeared streak of ketchup.

Pastor Dean shouted. "Run, John! And take that with you!" He pointed at the computer.

The cauliflower-eared deacon lunged at the trustee, bringing the table with him. He managed to grab the trustee by the waist. The trustee, the cauliflower-eared deacon, and the table ended up in a pile on the floor.

Noise in the bowling alley caught Pastor Dean's attention. The side doors opened, and uniformed officers poured through. Out front, police cruisers screeched to a halt, sirens blaring, blocking the door. Dean yelled at the bald deacon. "Hurry! Find a back door!"

The bald deacon grabbed the computer and ran across the carpeted lobby. He took a right turn into lane 23, past the scorer's table and ball return. Halfway down the lane he veered, adjusting his course diagonally toward the back of the building.

The front doors burst open. Policemen flooded in, guns drawn. The custodian ran out of the bathroom, dragging the mop behind him. The fry cook and counter attendant hit the deck.

On the carpet, Dean watched the cauliflower-eared deacon wrestling with Charles Graves, the very Charles Graves they thought they'd been avoiding all this time. Charles overpowered the deacon, rolled him over, and subdued him with a choke hold.

The bald-headed deacon reached the second to last lane before the police entered through the rear entrance. He squealed again, running back down the lane toward the entrance of the bowling alley. He ended up in front of one of the families who remained bowling. The family—a father, mother, and two daughters—stared at him, their mouths hanging open.

The deacon squealed at them like Peter Lorre. *"Help me, hide me. Do something to help me!"*

The family did nothing. The policemen tackled him.

Pastor Dean never moved from his chair. He placed his hands on his knees, palms up, signaling his willingness to go quietly. If you have to go, he thought, this is as exciting a way to do it as any.

Above, another selection from the ASL droned on.

Exhaust from the police cruisers floated in the air outside the front doors of the bowling alley as Charles stepped outside. An awning extending twenty feet from the building shielded the front doors. The overhang was suspended between the bowling alley and two columns on the opposite side. Between the columns, a bed of oleanders segregated the parking lot from the bowling alley entrance. The morning sun pounded the parking lot asphalt.

Charles stepped out from under the awning and into the parking lot to escape the exhaust fumes. The sun's glare assaulted his eyes. The air under the overhang was oppressive, yet he sensed it calling him. He stopped, spun around, and tried to focus on the shadow under the awning.

Besides the police cars, there were no vehicles under the awning. Yet Charles imagined cars in line waiting to pull up to the front door of the bowling alley. The car first in line under the overhang was his mother's BMW.

Charles concentrated, trying to remember. He imagined her behind the wheel, reaching into the backseat for her purse.

She brought the purse forward and set it in her lap. Her head bobbed and her lips mouthed the words to a song.

The passenger, a child, not quite a teen, said something. His mother gazed at the child. Charles remembered how much he missed that expression. She stared back down at the purse. One hand resumed rummaging. The other brushed the bangs out of her eyes.

His mother retrieved some cash from the bottom of the purse. She unhitched her seat belt and leaned over to hug the child. The child's head came over his mother's left shoulder as she hugged him. The child stared at Charles through the driver's side window. Charles was positive it was his own face he would see on the child.

It wasn't. It was his brother Stephen's face he saw. His brother's eyes opened, latching on to Charles like a sticker burr. The child strengthened his embrace on Charles's mother. His brother's face began to change. Blemishes appeared on his cheeks. His hair darkened and parted itself in the middle. The lips thinned and reddened. The eyes became hollow. It was now the dark man staring back at Charles. The dark man from his puzzle.

The thin lips parted. A voice in his mind spoke as the lips moved. "She's mine now," it said. "You wouldn't listen to me, and now she's mine."

Charles's mother released her embrace and turned around. Her face was a skull.

A wiry voice snapped Charles out of the daydream. "Would you sign this for me?" An officer held out the discarded trustee mask, retrieved from inside the bowling alley, for Charles to sign. "My son would appreciate it. His name is Randy."

Charles took the mask and pen from the officer, signed it, and handed it back without acknowledging the officer. The officer read what Charles wrote. It said: To Randy—one of the good guys. Charles Graves.

Charles shook his head as if to rattle out the daydream. Near the awning, officers milled around. Squad cars began to leave. The Approved TV news team appeared, and soon their people had cameras and microphones working the scene.

Richard Farris approached through the commotion. "Ingraham asked me to give you a ride."

"He must not want to see me," Charles said. He removed a one-shooter of synthetic whiskey from his front pocket and sucked it dry. He rubbed the tips of his fingers.

Richard Farris was a man women stared at the way cats stalk birds. He was six foot two, with textured, black hair sculpted onto his head. Charles didn't know where he shopped, but his clothes were immaculate. He took the detective's standard suit and tie to new heights. Charles could never quite pinpoint the material they were crafted from, but his suits seemed to flow like a river as he moved. Most likely Asian, Charles figured.

Farris claimed you could brush your teeth by the reflection in his polished shoes. Once, Charles dropped a pencil in the office to test Farris's claim. Stooping to retrieve the pencil, he determined Farris wasn't far off.

An assortment of exotic jewelry adorned Farris. It seemed he owned an inexhaustible supply. Silver bracelets, watch chains, tie-pins, cuff studs, rings. Farris even possessed enough mojo to pull off the occasional pearl. It was his signature play.

The first time Charles had noticed Farris's pearl necklace it was at an agency barbecue conducted in the spacious nature preserve maintained out the back doors of agency headquarters.

Farris had left enough of his button-down shirt open for the pearls to shine through. Charles had fixated on the pearls. He'd been forced to admit they were prepossessing, and upon later reflection, he did not think it had been the beer talking.

The remainder of features completing Farris's Adonis-like appearance were as would be predicted, all except for the nose. It seemed as thin as the pencil Charles had dropped for a closer shot of Farris's shoes, if not quite as long. The nostrils were so miniscule they were almost undetectable. Charles had studied them on more than one occasion. He found it difficult to ignore anytime Farris came around. The presence of that nose on this otherwise ideal specimen mesmerized Charles.

Charles shook his head again to clear his mind of Farris's nose. He took a step back and leaned on the front quarter panel of a police cruiser. As he shook his head, a waxy piece of makeup from his ruined disguise flew from his nose, landing six inches from Farris's perfectly shined shoes.

Farris regarded the wax as if it were a roach. "Whatever. You need to come. I think they have something for us."

"Great. My reward for this bust is getting to work with Ricky Farris. Wonderful." Charles rapped at the hood of the car with his fingernails, keeping an eye on Farris. Farris's hands coursed through the hair on the sides of his head.

He's the mother lode of manure, Charles thought. The way he wants his name pronounced: Fah-reese. What a jerk. Thank God for the nose. Or thank Charles Darwin. Thank someone. Without it, Richard Fah-reese would be insufferable. Charles wondered if there was such a thing as a reverse nose job. Probably not in a case this extreme. Farris had the money and the hubris to get one if there were.

"Wait here while I get my car." Farris meandered across the parking lot, stopping to issue a command to some officers.

Charles noticed the leadership of the Creekside Baptist Church emerge from behind the oleanders obscuring the awning's drive-through. The bald-headed deacon was still squealing, this time from what appeared to be a broken arm sustained when he'd been tackled by the police.

The cauliflower-eared deacon was cuffed behind, pacing to a patrol car. He walked with his head down, muttering. He displayed no concern for the Approved TV news cameras filming him. A uniformed officer opened the back door to the patrol car and guided his head as he entered the backseat.

Two officers escorted Pastor Dean. They came toward the car on which Charles was reclining. Pastor Dean halted and addressed the news cameras. "The King lives," he said. Charles figured it was his last sermon, at least in public.

After the brief address, two officers led Dean to the patrol car. One officer opened the back door of the cruiser.

Pastor Dean hesitated before getting in. He sought out Charles's eyes. "May God make His face to shine upon you, Charles Graves."

He backed into the cruiser and the officer shut the door behind him.

It figures Richard Fah-reese would own a Lotus, Charles thought. It was pearl white and streaking up I-45 so fast it probably resembled the double white lines painted along the breakdown lane. Farris had it up to 120 miles an hour, but all

Charles was concerned with was Farris's profile. How did those sunglasses stay perched on that nose?

Farris scaled back the volume from the approved radio station pumping out all the greats from the ASL. "What did you get your mother for Mother's Day?"

Charles felt the scar on his face flush. His hands clenched. His vision blurred. One day I'll break that nose, he promised himself.

He knows, Charles concluded. Somehow the cocky rat knows.

Charles's mother had been disposed of years ago, as efficiently as the remains of the ASL machine and remote that had been scooped up off the marble floor of Graves Mansion. One of them, or maybe both, had been placed in a waste hamper and shuttled off to the nearest government refuse center. Charles's father had kept it all off the books.

But somehow, Fah-reese knew.

Of course he knows. Guys like him always know. He's high enough in the organization. He has connections. He's got a messiah complex. He's the second coming of John Ingraham, and he hates you. Of course he knows. It's his business to know.

Charles fought through the anger by conjecturing whether they manufactured a Breathe Right strip to fit Farris's nose. He didn't know why his response here might be important, but he sensed it might. Farris must have a reason to gauge his emotional status.

"My mother left when I was a kid," Charles said. "I was raised by my dad mostly."

"Oh," Farris said.

Farris was good. Charles did not detect a hint of inquiry on his part.

"Been so long now I can barely remember. I was lucky to have my dad though."

Charles remembered isolated things: the way she used to pass his brother's room to come to his first, the way her voice floated across the great entry hall, how he used to hide in her dress as a child.

Twenty years had relegated most of these memories to the landfill of his mind. The most vivid memory he retained, and the one that came to mind when Farris mentioned Mother's Day, was the bloody, screaming banshee scaling the staircase. Deep down, however, he sensed he was supposed to remember more.

"Ever think of finding her?" Farris asked.

"She's dead."

"You could check the system." Farris didn't move a muscle.

Charles had expected more from Farris, but since they were a few exits from agency headquarters, he figured Farris was in a hurry. "You're a moron, Farris." Charles emphasized the standard pronunciation of Farris. "If I could, I wouldn't. It's too risky."

"I do it all the time." Farris glanced over at Charles and bent the corners of his mouth. "While you spend weeks running around in those ridiculous costumes, I do just as well right from my desk."

Charles realized for the first time he was not in the same league as Farris, trendy name or not. Though they had graduated into the organization through the same academy class, Farris was miles ahead of him. Any non-computer jockey who could hack the system at will without repercussion must have a truckload of influence, even up to Ingraham himself.

"Don't miss the exit," Charles said.

"When was the last time you saw me miss?"

Now that he thought about it, Charles couldn't think of a time.

THREE

Farris's reserved parking place in the front row of the agency's headquarters building was another reminder for Charles. They were peers in name only now, it seemed. He would have to contend with Farris as a superior.

Charles closed the door to the Lotus harder than necessary. It did not need the same coaxing as the door to his panel van. Another reminder.

The two men walked together toward the wooden revolving doors leading to the lobby of the headquarters building. Headquarters was a forty-story, onyx tower rising over the coastal plains between Houston and Galveston, about forty miles south of downtown Houston along I-45. Over the entryway were raised letters, each measuring three feet in height: Southeast Texas Reclamation Agency.

It was the end of May. The heat settled in like an uninvited guest. Charles remembered a sportswriter from New York describing Houston in June as hell. Hell would be here full force in a week. A terrible time for makeup, Charles thought. The humidity was already up and it was only mid-morning. Beads of sweat were forming on Charles's nose after twenty paces.

Farris appeared like a model on a runway. "You need to clean up before we go upstairs. I'll meet you in your dad's office in thirty minutes. I'm sure Ingraham will be there, so do something about your face."

Charles wiped the sweat from his nose. A handful of perspiration, mixed with powder, came off. "Cover me if I'm late."

They reached the revolving doors. Each one had enough glass set in its oak frame to allow visibility inside. Farris chose the right door and pushed his way through. Charles followed him, three cells behind.

The interior was polished chrome, walls, floors, and ceiling. The lobby was rectangular, stretching out to the right and left of the doors. Columns broke the monotony of the chrome walls. Cross-hatches on the floor traced a lattice-like pattern over the length and breadth of the lobby.

At the midpoint of the back wall was a seven-foot high metal door like what you might expect in a bomb shelter. It was the control gate to the remainder of the building. Through the door were all offices, elevators, and bathrooms.

A security desk was stationed to the right of the portal, ensconced in the wall behind a six-foot-by-three-foot pane of three-inch glass. Farris and Charles crossed the thirty feet to the window. Behind the glass Charles saw a man resembling Ed Asner monitoring video screens and colored lights.

Charles cleared his throat. "You there, Pete?"

Pete activated an intercom. "I seen you and Pinocchio comin'."

Farris peered through a one-square-foot beveled portion of the glass. A red light flashed in his eyes.

Behind the glass, Charles knew, a screen registered Farris's name, vital statistics, and organizational info. Pete glanced at it. "Open," he said.

The portal opened like a bank vault. Farris steeped through without a word. The portal closed.

"You better watch yourself around him," Charles said.

"At my age, what are they going to do?"

"I've seen people reclaimed for less," Charles said.

Pete's face changed, and he leaned forward across the desk to the glass. "Come closer." His breath fogged the glass. He took out a handkerchief and wiped it off. "I can't say too much over this system, but listen."

Pete gained nothing by leaning forward. The intercom was the same volume as it had been. Charles sensed he was trying to connect with him in some old-fashioned way. He pressed as close to the glass as he could.

"Listen," Pete said. "I'm old enough to remember the world 'fore it turned over. 'Fore we changed it for what we have now. It used to be a man knew what liberty was, what freedom was. My version of the change, coward that I was, was to end up changing my life for this box I sit in for fifty hours a week. It's not much difference from being reclaimed, I reckon. I've been in this box for fifty hours a week for thirty years now. I've paid the price for being quiet."

"But you have your life outside," Charles said. He peeked around to make sure no one was watching.

"Hang on a minute," Pete said. "Listen. I seen you comin' in here with your dad since you was a kid. You got no way to know what it was like before. Sometimes I think it started with cell phones and computers and stuff like that. People sort of forgot what it was like to be human. I'm old enough to remember, and if I had it to do over again, I would have traded all this time I've lived like this for a year or two of trying to make things right like they once was. It would be a fair trade."

"But your family?" Charles asked. "What about them?"

"My grandkids love the ASL—what does that tell you?" Pete said. "They got no idea. And it's all because when the world turned over, I changed the truth of God for a lie."

Charles's mind pulled like the left and right halves of his brain were caught in a Chinese finger trap. Pete had been a fixture in his life since Charles had accompanied his dad to work as a kid. When the fixtures malfunctioned in your home, you had to rip a wall out to repair them. Pete disappearing would be like ripping a wall out of his life.

"Pete, don't do anything crazy. I'll smooth that comment over with Farris. Don't do it again. You still have some good life ahead of you."

"I haven't had that for decades." Pete leaned away from the window.

"Hey," Charles said, "I think they're going to give me some time off since I closed the Creekside operation. I'll try to come by the house and see you. Until then, relax. Okay?"

"Yeah. All right."

Charles shuffled toward the steel door. He took a last look at Pete, staring through the beveled glass. The red light scanned his eyes.

"Open," Pete said. The portal opened. Charles stepped through.

• • •

Once through the portal, Charles made his way down an austere hallway constructed of the same chromium material as the lobby, only with less lighting. The hallway had always reminded him of a sewer without the smell. The walls seemed as though they would be damp to the touch, a slimy wetness, not at all disinfected. The tepid air was more oppressive than the hellish humidity outside.

Charles kept to the center of the hallway to avoid the walls, passing in and out of the shadows created by the spacing of the sparse overhead lighting. At uniform intervals along both sides of the hallway were doors with barely perceivable outlines—no handles and no windows. They were interrogation rooms, holding cells, prism therapy chambers—parlors for unwanted guests. Pretty soon they would be converted into storage rooms, he presumed.

Charles accessed the bathroom, as Farris had suggested. The bathroom had a row of urinals and stalls on the right and a mirror with three sinks on the left. A stifling smell of antiseptic hung in the air. Charles grabbed a paper towel and wiped a few drops of water off the sink. Otherwise, the bathroom was spotless.

His face was peppered with makeup and fragments of the trustee mask. A portion of jowl stuck to his neck, and some extra hairs, which Charles had added to his ears and eyebrows for effect. His hair was tussled from when he'd removed the mask.

Charles picked off the sizable portions of his used disguise, tossing them into a waste receptacle on his left. He had endured this process countless times, altering his image and restoring it. It was the only reason he kept this job. If he were required to work from the computer as Farris boasted, he would quit.

The reason was simple, he supposed. Disguising and un-disguising himself had always been an in-the-flesh version of his wood-block puzzle.

Charles engaged the faucet with hot and cold water at equal strength. Taking a liberal squirt of soap from the dispenser, he cupped his hands under the faucet, achieving a heaping lather of warm soapy water. He bent and brought his hands to his face. He felt himself being cleansed of the trustee. Charles brought a second cup of water to his face. The sink filled with powdery debris. Charles brought a third to his hair. It trickled down the sides of his head and the nape of his neck.

Charles reached for paper towels. He first dried his eyes, then his face, neck, and hair. He used his hands as a makeshift comb. Good enough, he thought.

He refilled his cupped hands with water until they were overflowing. He threw the water at the mirror, refusing to recognize his own emerging face, which now blurred and descended the glass like he was in a funhouse.

He'd read somewhere that mirrors were a corny author's device. A cheap way to describe a character's appearance with-out violating point of view, or some such drivel. But in Charles's mind, mirrors were a curse of civilization.

"Or at least my corner of it."

His voice echoed in the empty bathroom. He threw another cup of water at the glass, this time mixed with soap.

"I'll settle for wood blocks."

Charles ran a finger along his scar and remembered Pastor Dean's last-second recognition. I'll have to be more careful next time.

The scar had faded with time, but it was still his only truly distinguishing feature. He traced its course along his cheek and struggled to push it to the back of his mind. "At least you gave me something to remember you by."

When he removed the fake hairs from his ears and eyebrows, the metamorphosis back to Charles Graves was complete.

With the exception of the scar, Charles Graves was the most nondescript individual on the planet. Charles had worked hard to become so. People said that describing him was like trying to describe a brown 1982 Oldsmobile. His hair seemed fair when the light struck it just right, but it was dark at other times. He and his brother used to gamble for marbles as kids, using Charles's hair as a kind of three-card monte. They would guess: blond, brown, or black. His brother would then close his eyes and pull out a single strand of Charles's hair, winner take all.

Sparse facial hair grew on his cheeks and chin. Coupled with his soft skin, this facilitated disguising himself as either man or woman. The soft skin took well to makeup, and the generic quality of his pigmentation allowed him to mimic any skin tone with the appropriate base makeup. Charles always blamed his soft skin for augmenting the appearance of his scar.

His eyes were speckled, though he maintained a collection of contact lenses of every hue and color in his disguise kit. They defied classification. There was just a blank spot in the place on his national ID card where his eye color was supposed to be described.

He was medium build and height, not muscular but not emaciated. This frame allowed him to approximate any body type, male or female. The right clothes made him appear shorter. The right shoes created the illusion of height.

The difficulty in describing Charles Graves contributed to his reputation as a ghost. The sole way of identifying Charles in a lineup was to pick the only one who didn't resemble anyone.

Charles placed both hands over his face like a blind person feeling someone's appearance. The feeling reminded him of his wood-block puzzle when empty, with all the pieces out on the floor waiting to be inserted. What face was going to show up next? Who am I supposed to be? In his mind, the blocks began to arrange themselves.

As usual, it was the dark man who showed up.

Charles threw water on his face, dried off, and left the bathroom.

Charles entered the first-floor elevator. The elevator attendant, a faceless computer named FLORIS hidden in the false wood walls, asked for his destination.

"Forty," Charles said.

The voice-recognition software kicked in. "Thank you, Mr. Graves." FLORIS's voice was a monotone feminine voice, but pleasant.

The elevator ascended and opened to a suite covering the entire fortieth floor. Charles stepped out onto a plush tan carpet that massaged his feet through his shoes. He encountered an initial alcove—larger than most people's living rooms—that housed Cotton Graves's secretary. Selections from the ASL droned above. A modest sink, kitchenette, and bathroom were to his left. The suite opened up to his right.

Directly in front of him, the secretary sat behind a prudent but expensive desk almost to the back of the alcove. "How have you been, Charles? Congratulations. I heard the good news about Creekside." She pursed her lips and widened her eyes. "Your father is waiting for you in his office."

"Thanks, Sheila."

Charles passed through the alcove housing Sheila's desk To his right were two conference rooms, one with a fifty-square-foot screen displaying live satellite imagery of the greater Southeast Texas area. The agency maintained several satellites with both tracking and attack capability. As a child he had obsessed over finding his house on the screen. In a game of "getting warmer" or "getting colder," his dad would adjust the satellite tracking until Charles found the house.

He veered left, passing a spacious, unwalled lounge with couches, TVs, a billiards table, and a stocked bar. The place could satisfy VIPs at the Bellagio in Vegas. Past the lounge, the suite expanded into a single, open office, wrapping around the entire fortieth floor. His father's desk was at the far end of the suite. The suite had tinted glass windows from the floor to the ceiling. The view was breathtaking, both in its breadth and with the feeling of vertigo it engendered. It was like standing on the glass skywalk stretching out over the Grand Canyon.

The ASL faded as Charles crossed through the suite. A man could spend his whole life up here if he wanted. It was Howard Hughes-ish. The opulence of the suite, compared with some of the poor environments Charles had entered undercover on assignment, was striking. Immoral, perhaps.

Charles approached the far end of the suite. He saw his dad waiting there, along with Farris and three other men.

Though Charles's dad could see him coming from forty yards away, he waited until Charles was about ten feet from the desk before addressing him, and then he did so as if he had just noticed him. "Charles, hey-hey."

It wasn't superficial or forced, but Charles sensed some showmanship for the benefit of his dad's guests. "Hey, Dad. Good to see you."

His dad came around the desk and gave him a hug without showmanship. The rest of the group stood. His dad released him. "Let me introduce you. I believe you know Richard Farris already." His dad kept his right arm on Charles's back and motioned toward Farris with his left hand, palm up.

Charles inwardly cheered his dad's standard pronunciation of Farris's name. He nodded at Farris.

"Over here is Mr. Ingraham, Mr. Keesma, and Mr. Louis." He pronounced the first name In-gra-ham. Charles's dad gave each one the upturned palm. The men shook Charles's hand. Farris seemed as if he were attempting to hold in gas.

Charles slumped into a formal leather chair once his dad's guests reseated themselves. It was the expensive maroon type with oversized armrests and conspicuous brass studs. This office suite had been like a second home to Charles during his childhood. After his mother had "departed," he'd spent an increasing amount of time here. But on this day it shone with a special gleam.

Charles stared at the gold nameplate on his father's desk. It read:

Frank Cotton Graves
U.S. Senator
Director—Southeast Texas Operations

His dad opened the informal meeting. "Charles, Mr. Ingraham is the Director of National Affairs for the U.S. National Reclamation Project."

Ingraham reminded Charles of Orson Welles from his wine commercials days. Charles stood and shook Mr. Ingraham's hand again and, as an afterthought, shook the hands of his counterparts as well. This caused everyone to have to stand once more in mere formality. Charles noted the ridiculousness of the protocol. This time, Ingraham grimaced.

"Mr. Keesma and Mr. Louis are his deputies. First of all, son, I would like to express our pride in your latest accomplishment. The apprehension of the Creekside leadership, along with the database recovered in the operation, is a real tribute to your acumen as an agent."

Farris crossed his legs, his pant legs flowing like water. Charles's dad seemed to attach significance to the gesture. "You, along with Mr. Farris, have become the finest agents we have on staff here at Southeast Texas, and perhaps nationwide. You two are a genuine asset to your government."

Ingraham nodded with approval at both Farris and Charles. Charles accepted the praise, especially coming from his dad. But an uncomfortable feeling began creeping up on Charles. Something was not quite right here.

Charles's dad continued the informal congratulations speech. "And most importantly, Charles—excuse me a sec, Richard—you have developed into a fine young man. One I am proud to call my son."

Charles would have to lie to deny how good it felt hearing the praise. Yet his anxiety was growing. What is it? It's not Farris. I'm used to his nonsense. It's not Ingraham. Then a voice inside him said, It's Keesma and Louis.

Charles studied them closer. Had he seen them before?

In his mind's eye, the wood-block puzzled filled and emptied, filled and emptied, at a dizzying pace. Face after face came up and was erased. Finally, the puzzle locked on to a face resembling Keesma. It immediately erased and locked on to a face that was undeniably Louis.

Jumpin' George Romero. These were the zombies that had taken his mother away. Keesma and Louis are the undead. It was undeniably their faces Charles saw.

He felt the scar on his cheek heat up. He dug his nails into the armrests of the leather chair, fracturing one of his nails against one of the brass studs. His feet pressed against the floor with enough force to nearly raise the executive chair off the carpet.

But how could it be? It didn't fit. As he observed them sitting on either side of Ingraham, he imagined zombie heads rotating in unison, first to the left, then to the right. He imagined them growing until they blotted out everything else in the suite. It was them all right, but how?

"Charles and Richard," his dad said.

Charles snapped back to attention. Had he been too obvious staring at the men? He didn't think so.

His dad continued. "Today is a very important turning point for our operation. After monitoring your past efforts, Mr. Ingraham has selected you two as the point men for our most crucial operation to date."

Charles's dad grasped a remote control, pointing it at a freestanding screen perpendicular to the outer rim of windows. Outside, the sun continued its daily summer torment of Houston. From up here, folks on the ground resembled insects, scurrying about on their meaningless tasks.

His dad faced the screen, revealing his heart-shaped bald spot, which had fared well in its battle against time and elements. He clicked a button on the remote, reminding Charles of a day long ago when a remote had flown across the room and come to rest on the marble floor of Graves Mansion.

Charles half expected familiar text to appear on the screen:

How could a guy like me
    Ever turn the other cheek?
How could a good ol' boy
    Ever become one of the meek?
But when the Spirit touched my heart
    And I called Jesus' name.
He saved the soul
    Of a man
In the sinners' hall of fame.

Then perhaps the two men with Ingraham would arise like the undead and drag his dad out of the suite like a screaming banshee.

The wood-block puzzle shuffled again in his mind. The pieces arranged themselves into the dark man. He felt the dark man assuming control. His scar flushed. He fought to maintain his composure. How could these guys be here?

The actual text on the screen was:

OPERATION BELT BUCKLE

Farris crossed his legs the other way in an obvious pose of self-satisfaction. This allowed Charles to steady himself by focusing on his dislike for Farris. The nose knows. Think of the nose.

Ingraham laced his fingers in his lap and spoke. "Houston is the buckle of the Bible belt. Our operations have yielded significant results thus far in all sectors of the country."

Charles's dad, on cue, pressed the remote, displaying a map of the U.S., color coded by region. He pressed it again, forwarding to a graph detailing percentages of known unreclaimed Christian populations by region.

"We are well ahead of organizational projections, and, in a very real measure, you two are at the vanguard of this success. A full 87 percent of the U.S. population now at least nominally devotes itself to prism therapy—or, as we like to say in the organization, the Approved Spiritual System."

Charles's dad chuckled and clicked the remote again. A picture of a black man appeared on the screen. Underneath it were vital statistics:

> James Cleveland
> 6'2"—220 lbs.
> Age: 62
> African American. Brown eyes. Still wears glasses. Usually shaves head.
> Has identifying kidney-shaped birthmark below left ear.
> Walks with slight limp in left leg.
> Whereabouts: Houston, TX

"According to the latest departmental research," Ingraham said, "there remains but one thoroughly influential Christian leader at large in the country. James Cleveland. If we were to apprehend him—and you two *will* apprehend him—it will mark the end of the underground Christian resistance as we know it. This man is the only thing keeping it alive. We have reason to believe he is operating in and around downtown Houston."

The remote clicked. A map of downtown appeared.

"Why don't we cordon off downtown?" Farris pointed in the direction of the downtown skyline, clearly visible from the suite. "Catch him in the net?"

Charles's dad answered. "We are worried that when the Creekside news gets out, he will be especially careful. He could hole up downtown indefinitely."

"He still might try to get out," Farris said.

"We don't think he will," Ingraham said. "We think he will be expecting increased law enforcement and will lay low until the heat passes. There are literally thousands of homes, abandoned warehouses, businesses, schools, parks, sewers, and woods in and around downtown he could hide in. We can't check them all, so we have buttoned up the ship channel and put checkpoints on all avenues out to make sure he can't escape, along with any outgoing air travel. We believe the best way to root him out will be through espionage. That is why you two are here."

"Why not put his face on every public media outlet?" Farris asked.

Ingraham rearranged himself in the chair. "We have always considered it best to keep our operations under the radar. The less the public knows, the better. It helps to keep these law-breakers from soliciting sympathy, and it does not create martyrs in the public eye. Nothing better to fertilize a movement than the blood of martyrs."

"What's the plan?" Charles asked. He imagined throwing Keesma and Louis through the windows.

"First," Ingraham said, "we want you two to take three weeks off. Rest. Recharge. Then, Charles, you will go under-cover from this location." The screen changed, zooming in on downtown. A parking garage was highlighted. "Farris will operate from headquarters with computer support supplied by Julia Jenkins. After you handle this assignment, you both can expect a promotion and a long vacation."

"How do you know he is in Houston?" Farris asked.

"The initial scan from the computer retrieved from Creekside indicates he was there as late as yesterday. Since we immediately shut down all outgoing escape routes, we have to assume he is still there." Ingraham unlaced his fingers as if to indicate the meeting was over.

The men stood and shook hands for the third time. Farris, Ingraham, and the two deputies left. Charles's dad escorted them to the elevator.

Charles collapsed into the maroon executive chair and waited for his dad to return. Inside, the dark man raged.

FOUR

Beneath downtown Houston
a labyrinth of underground corridors serviced the city's business
community and downtown residents. The corridors connected
high-rises, facilitated shopping, housed stores and restaurants,
and even provided for a full-sized mall and underground
Hilton hotel. These corridors were accessed by flights of stairs
and escalators located at downtown stations marked by red,
diamond-shaped signs.

The tunnels' cinder block walls were painted an industrial
off-white. The floors were smooth concrete with yellow lines
painted next to the walls. The corridors were reminiscent of a
spotless parking garage, with excellent lighting and ample air-
conditioning.

Crowds moved through the corridors during working
hours, lunchtime, and evenings. The parking garage corridors
gave way to tiled floors and manicured walls in the business-

occupied sections of the tunnels, where people met and engaged in the same activities found aboveground.

At the end of one corridor, well traversed during the lunch and dinner hours, was a food court. The restaurants here could suit all but the most finicky of tastes. The last restaurant in line was named "Johnny Taco's," where sole proprietor Lars Wultman was struggling to stay afloat.

Past Johnny Taco's were three maintenance corridors, abandoned when the city maintenance department centralized its services between the mall and the Hilton hotel. One hundred feet down one of these dark and dusty corridors was an all-but-forgotten three-thousand-square-foot maintenance storeroom and workshop.

In the pitch-dark of the storeroom, a pair of knees met a filthy floor. The roar of the noontime lunch rush faded behind a foot of concrete wall fronted by cinder blocks. The Reverend James Cleveland imagined he was in the prison dungeon with the apostle Paul. Yet here in this forgotten storeroom beneath downtown Houston, a beautiful and wonderful thing happened.

The Reverend Cleveland was beginning to pray again.

He clasped his hands, not altogether comfortable in his new church home. This was not what he'd expected when he'd answered the call. He cried out to God, wondering why, after a lifetime of faith, God would forsake him. He began to sob for himself and for his family. His tears were lost in the dust and dirt of the floor.

He remembered once telling a woman in his congregation, Mrs. Cullins, that God does not answer the "why" question. She'd come to him in hysterics over the death of her husband. Her husband—thirty-eight, nonsmoker, nondrinker, athletic, running ten miles a week—had quit breathing one night in his sleep, leaving her with twelve-year-old twins to raise.

Cleveland, with ten years of pastoral experience at the time, had served her the customary biblical platitudes and spiritual clichés and dismissed her with a hug. Pressing matters were at hand: a sermon to write, a luncheon at the Rotary Club where he was to give an address, a building fund meeting. Besides, it was a perfect opportunity for his flock to get busy doing the work of Christ by caring for this woman.

Now that it was his family, he understood the woman's grief. It coiled around him like a serpent. And now, all alone in the dark under tons of concrete, he was asking God the why question.

As convicted as he was for his cavalier treatment of Mrs. Cullins's grief, he understood he had been right about one thing. God was not going to answer.

Cleveland whimpered. He slid from his knees to a prone position, lying facedown in the muck, wishing he could go back in time and speak to Mrs. Cullins. He wanted to tell her he knew how she felt. He wanted to tell her he was there for her. He wanted to weep with her.

He thought of his wife and daughter. He imagined the fear in their eyes as they were hauled away. He wondered if they were still alive. Why couldn't he have been there? Wasn't he a good and faithful servant?

Why are You abandoning Your Church, Lord? Where is Your strong right arm? The sword in Your mouth? Aren't You a mighty tower? ELI, ELI, LAMA SABACHTHANI? My God, my God, why hast thou forsaken me?

God was not answering the why question.

The Reverend James Cleveland realized he was shouting. He lay still for a few seconds, his sobs and tears subsiding. At least he would know soon if the room was soundproof. He rolled over onto his back and stared into the darkness.

Something approached. A voice began to speak to his spirit. It was difficult to understand at first. It was confusing, as if the voice's owner wasn't sure where Cleveland was. At length it found him.

Something pierced his spirit with claws. It began to rip at his soul. Two fiery eyes materialized out of the darkness a foot from his face. The eyes created a corona of light around the thing's skull.

The dark man revealed a row of teeth filed to points. He leaned forward, his nostrils touching the reverend's face. He snorted puffs of gas out of his nose, surrounding Cleveland in a putrid cloud.

Nearer and nearer the dark man came until Cleveland saw the pit of hell in his eyes. The eyes were so close now and so bright in the dark storeroom he saw nothing else. The eyes were oceans of despair.

The dark man hissed as he spoke. "Oh yessssssssss, they are there. They most assuredly are there. You know they are there. Look and see, Reverend. You can hear their cries. Their agony. And you weren't there to stop it." With each syllable a wisp of putrid smoke escaped his mouth.

Cleveland now saw Mrs. Cullins in the dark man's fiery eyes. She was with his wife and daughter, wailing like an animal caught in a trap. "Do you get it now, Reverend?" Mrs. Cullins shrieked. "Do you still want to talk to me? Explain grief to me? How does it feel, Reverend?"

The dark man sucked in all the putrid smoke and exhaled it onto Cleveland in one rancid blast. "Dost thou still retain thy integrity? Curse God and die!"

Cleveland wished the storeroom were not soundproof. He wished for the crowds outside to hear his wails. He wished they would break down the door and rescue him. He was left with nothing but his faith. He cried out for Jesus.

In the darkness of the abandoned storeroom, the Reverend Cleveland reached the end of his spiritual tether. No one acknowledged his cries. No crowds from the food court rushed in to save him. No God intervened in answer to his prayer.

His family was in a reclamation center, whereabouts unknown. His church was in disarray. They were strangers in the world, scattered throughout the provinces. The silence of God was worse than a hundred dark men with glowing eyes.

Cleveland sensed the dark man settling in.

"How many times did I try to tell you it wasn't real?" It hovered, the pointy teeth gleaming and fiery eyes still trained on Cleveland. "I told you fifty years ago all this hoopin' and hollerin' 'bout Jesus weren't nothin' but jive, man. Now look at ya. No family, no church, no life, no God. Wasn't ever nothin' but a white man's religion, sucker." The dark man licked his lips.

"I've gone along too far with Him now," Cleveland said. "Times weren't always bad. He's been there for me in the past."

The dark man switched off the fiery images in his eyes. Mrs. Cullins and the reverend's family disappeared. His voice became silky and smooth. "Reverend." The dark man said, then paused. "I don't think it's too late. You can walk out of this grimy old waller-hole, get you a taco, and go down to the reclamation center. The government's promised amnesty. With all the info you have, they would bend over backwards to set you up nice and pretty. Think of your wife. And your daughter— she's only thirty-seven. I'd bet it's not too late to save them. For a man your age, there's plenty of time to live a nice long life."

Cleveland considered this. Maybe he could save his daughter at least. He thought of her leaving the reclamation center, getting married, having kids, developing a career. The fantasy image grew. Soon she was listening to the ASL, watching Approved Television, captivated in its banality. Then he saw her practicing prism therapy. She sat in a circle with other young women chanting:

Green is the color of life. Green makes me feel alive.
    Green is mother earth.
Blue is the color of breath. Blue fills my soul with joy.
    Blue is father sky.

No, it would be better if she died in a reclamation center. His mind reached for a verse and found one: "For we have not followed cunningly devised fables, when we made known unto you the power and coming of our Lord Jesus Christ, but were eyewitnesses of his majesty. . . . We have also a more sure word of prophecy; whereunto ye do well that ye take heed, as unto a light that shineth in a dark place."

"Ah, so shines the word of God in a dark place," Cleveland said aloud. "Be gone, dark man."

The dark man did not respond. Suddenly Cleveland sensed a more sinister spirit in the room. He sat up. The hair on his arm stood at attention. The evil in the room was suffocating.

He prayed again in earnest. "Dear Lord, Your humble servant worships You for Your faithfulness and Your strong right arm. You, the Good Shepherd, protect Your flock. Thank You for restraining the dark man, but Lord, I think I need Your help again. There is something else in here."

Cleveland stood. No sound broke the silence of the storeroom. No light shone in this dark place. The evil presence was real. It was growing. Once again God was not answering.

He lost all feeling in his legs. He began to tremble, alone in the dark with this thing. He couldn't see it with his eyes, but he could sense its presence in his mind and spirit. For some reason, he remembered the story of Martin Luther throwing an inkwell at the devil. The inkwell struck the wall of Luther's cell, leaving a stain. He had been told the ink spot was still on the wall at Luther's monastery to this day.

A shaft of light forced its way into Cleveland's mind. Into the beam appeared the most gruesome sight he had ever seen. The figure reached at least eight feet tall and eight feet wide. It moved with the grace of a ballerina.

Its constantly changing form confused Cleveland. Its body had no set form, but was amorphous, molding itself into the likeness of mythical and real animals, inanimate objects, and things for which he had no prior conception. It was a fiery oven, a tombstone, a mushroom cloud, a giant disembodied eye, an undulating mass of such horridness he could not conceive it.

Cleveland gasped for air. The images changed at breakneck speed. The figure in Cleveland's mind seemed liquid the way it convoluted and changed, but the images it portrayed were crystal clear. Cleveland saw all that was evil: Hitler, Lenin, Jack the Ripper, werewolves, the dark man, pentagrams. He stared into the face of death itself.

The worst was the mouth. The mouth remained stationary as the changing images revolved around it. The mouth was bottomless, sucking the images down as water in a maelstrom. Cleveland felt his body being pulled toward the mouth as if he were about to tumble down an endless shaft. Flames glowed in the immeasurable distance.

A voice from the whirlpool mouth spoke to his mind. "Now that your God has shown He will not save you, curse Him and die!"

Cleveland braced himself.

"Curse Him and die!" The command seemed to echo not only in his mind, but also off the walls of the pitch-black storeroom.

The image displayed on the thing's body shifted to a Civil War battlefield. It was a scene of carnage. Dead bodies were strewn across the grass. Some were stacked in heaping piles. They stank. Some stared with blank eyes. Others cried in agony. Smoke rose from the battlefield in columns.

One of the soldiers rose. It approached Cleveland, limping on a gnarled left leg. The soldier had a mortal wound to the chest. A patch of blood widened across his battle vest.

The man wore a gray Confederate uniform. Cleveland noticed the soldier was black and wore glasses. He approached Cleveland with one outstretched arm. The soldier reached the envelope of the image, close enough to reach his outstretched arm into the time and space of Cleveland's mind.

Cleveland screamed. The soldier was himself.

His spiritual tether snapped. How easy it was to stand behind the pulpit and assault the hordes of hell. This is the real thing and I can't handle it. He shouted, "Lord Jesus, help me!"

He figured this was the defining moment of his ministry. If his years of faith were real, he would find out now.

Nothing happened. The image closed on him, folding his mind back in on itself. The mouth came nearer and nearer. It seemed to be savoring Cleveland's increasing horror. It dribbled a tepid, viscous fluid on Cleveland's chin.

"Red is the color of blood. Red makes me feel danger. Red is pain," it said, taunting Cleveland with the Prism Chant. "Black is the color of the grave. Black makes me feel lost. Black is death."

Cleveland drew himself up. "But the blood of Christ saves us from the grave."

In place of the horrid approaching mouth, a scripture appeared in his mind as clearly as if a Bible were suspended in front of him.

The Reverend James Cleveland lifted his eyes toward heaven as if he saw the glory of the Lord of Hosts. In his mind, the dark and dusty storeroom beamed with the light of a thousand suns as the ceiling gave way to the realm of the spirit world.

Cleveland spoke to the Lord, his voice quiet and stuttering. "I know that You can do all things. No plan of Yours can be thwarted. You asked, 'Who is this that obscures my counsel without knowledge?' Surely I spoke of things I did not understand, things too wonderful for me to know. You said, 'Listen now and I will speak; I will question you and you shall answer me.' My ears had heard of You, but now my eyes have seen You. Therefore I despise myself and repent in dust and ashes."

As Cleveland prayed, a beautiful and wonderful thing manifested itself in that forgotten storeroom, despite the evils of hell and the frailty of man. Cleveland felt the peace of Christ fill him to overflowing. He felt his hope enlarge like a sail filling with wind.

The dark thing in his mind was retreating. Its images were gone. Its mouth closed. It appeared as blank and hollow as

Cleveland knew its spirit must be. He thought he saw a twinge of fear in the thing as he continued piping out Scripture, now in his full sermon pitch.

With both hands raised he bellowed, hounding the image. "The Lord said: 'Who is this that darkens my counsel with words without knowledge? Brace yourself like a man; I will question you and you shall answer me.'"

Cleveland continued, towering over the image in his mind. "'Where were you when I laid the Earth's foundation? Tell me, if you understand. Who marked off its dimensions? Surely you know!'"

A million shrieks exited the image's mouth.

"'Who stretched a measuring line across it? On what were its footings set, or who laid its cornerstone—while the morning stars sang together and all the angels shouted for joy?'"

The fire was no longer shut up in his bones. Cleveland felt it escaping, as if he were consumed by the Holy Spirit, and it released upon his tormentor.

"'Who shut up the sea behind doors when it burst forth from the womb, when I made the clouds its garment and wrapped it in thick darkness? When I fixed limits for it and set its doors and bars in place, when I said, this far you may come and no farther; here is where your proud waves halt?'"

Cleveland's voice thundered, then grew quiet. The evil was gone. "There's two things I love," he said. "A good sermon and a captive audience." He now understood two other things as well. He was ready for whatever might come, and he understood one reason why God allowed certain evils to exist.

He thanked God for deliverance and his renewed faith. Taste and see that the Lord is good, he thought.

Now the Reverend James Cleveland had his own inkwell experience.

Come to think of it, a Johnny Taco did sound pretty good. Cleveland brushed himself off and felt his way through the dark. As he touched the door with his hands, the dark man spoke. "I'm still here, Reverend. I'm considerably more tenacious than those others."

"I know you are," Cleveland said. "But I got your number. Go on now, git. Ya hear!"

Frank Cotton Graves escorted Ingraham, Farris, and the two deputies to the elevator. It was waiting for them when they arrived. Slow day at the office, Cotton thought.

He started back to his desk, pausing long enough to tell Sheila to take the rest of the day off. He gave her a hug. She rubbed his calf with the bottom of her right foot as he hugged her.

Cotton was in as good a mood as he could remember for quite some time. Creekside was a success, Charles had performed admirably, and Ingraham was pleased. Things were good for Cotton Graves. He whistled as he returned to Charles.

But he sensed something wrong as soon as he sat down behind his desk. "What is it, Charles?"

"You're pathetic," Charles said. "I can't believe what I just saw."

Charles was breathing hard, his scar flushed against his soft skin. It also seemed like Charles was carrying on a second conversation in his mind. Every second or two Charles's head would twitch and his eyes would roll up as if he were arguing with someone.

Cotton's mind jumped into hyperdrive, searching for the reason for Charles's anger. Was it Ingraham? Shouldn't be. Is he over-tired? Stressed out from Creekside? It had been months and months of work, after all. Maybe it's Farris. I know he doesn't care much for that pompous jerk.

Cotton chose between Cotton the Father and Cotton the Politician. On account of the anger he saw in Charles, he chose the latter. "What's on your mind, Charles?"

"How could you let those two goons in here after what they did?" The volume of Charles's voice was rising.

"What goons?" Cotton used the remote to turn off the screen displaying the Belt Buckle information.

"Don't lie to me. You know who I am talking about."

Cotton the Politician kicked in a higher gear. "I understand you are angry. It's pretty obvious. But I honestly do not know what you are mad about. Why don't you back up and tell me what is upsetting you."

"Keesma and Louis."

Cotton noticed Charles scrutinizing his face. Cotton had no idea what he was upset about. He hoped his face said the same.

"Are you telling me you don't know?"

"I don't, Charles." Cotton the Father took over. "Why don't you explain it to me? Maybe I can help."

"Those are the two guys that dragged my mother down the stairs and out of the house." Charles readjusted himself in the executive chair.

Cotton felt like George Foreman had socked him square in the jaw. He wrestled for words. He stuttered and stammered. "Charles, you have to believe me. I had no idea."

"I don't know that I do. I have always half-blamed you for that day. This makes it worse. You have to admit it looks bad.

The same two guys that hauled off Mom are sitting in your office."

Cotton noticed the anger in Charles giving way. That's good, he thought. This may end okay after all. "Think back," Cotton said, "if you can. I know it hurts, but try for a second. First of all, remember that I was trying to convince your mother to not be so obstinate. She was so stubborn. She wouldn't listen to me."

Charles nodded. His head twitched again.

"Secondly," Cotton said, "remember that I never got a good look at the men. Your mother brained me with that vase and floored me with a kick. I was half-conscious with blood running down my face and into my eyes. It all happened so fast. They were gone before I ever recovered enough to do or see anything. You have to remember, Charles."

Charles twitched. It worried Cotton, but then Charles came back.

"Now that you put it that way, it makes better sense," Charles said. "But you never did anything about it. Nothing."

"Yes, I did."

"What?"

"I don't want to talk about it." Cotton rubbed his bald spot and placed his hands on his desk.

"Why not?"

"Don't worry about it."

"But it's my mother we're talking about," Charles said. "I have a right to know."

"The same way I have a right to know about your brother?" This came from neither Cotton the Diplomat nor Cotton the Father. This came from Cotton the Fighter. Cotton the Fighter expected Charles to leap over the desk and hit him.

Instead, Charles sobbed. "I can't believe you said that. I was just a kid." His speech came out blurred through the tears.

Watching Charles sob and try to talk was like watching Teresa all those years ago. He remembered how she'd said "I doe whaa cahhh dowww" on that terrible day. With two family members gone, it was a miracle he and Charles were even reasonably close, or even that Charles hadn't killed himself. How have we held this together all this time?

Father Cotton arose from his chair, walked around the desk, and put his arms around Charles. Charles accepted the hug. He wept until his eyes were dry.

Cotton whispered in his ear. "I apologize for bringing up your brother. It was wrong of me. But I also want you to know that I did try to help your mom. I did. I loved her. I am not perfect, son. That's why I mentioned Stephen. Not that it's a good excuse. I guess I wanted you to know I hurt too. Way more than you know. Call me a coward. Call me whatever you think fits. But don't say I didn't try, and never say I didn't love your mother and your brother."

"I believe you, Dad," Charles said. "I believe you."

"Thank you, Charles. Now, listen to me. What is past is past. We only have each other. We have to stick together. It's a miracle we have made it this far, but somehow we have. Just a little further to go now. Remember, your mother would want it this way."

Charles had been holding tight on to Cotton, but after that last line he released his hold ever so slightly. Cotton noticed but did not ascribe any meaning to it. He was happy to have navigated another crisis with his son.

He formed a mental note to inspect Keesma's and Louis's files.

FIVE

"Six please, FLORIS," Charles said.

"Thank you, Mr. Graves." Monotone, but pleasant.

"You married, FLORIS?" Charles said.

"I do not recognize the command, Mr. Graves. Please restate your request."

Charles thought if he could have transferred FLORIS's programming into Lisa, his last girlfriend, they might still be together. *Lisa probably wished I could be programmed into someone too, anyone but this ghost that I am.* He supposed it might be difficult to maintain a relationship with someone who was everyone but no one. Everyman, but no man.

"Six, FLORIS."

"Thank you, Mr. Graves."

The elevator doors parted, revealing a labyrinth of gray cubicles populating the cube farm that filled the sixth floor. On the outer rim of the floor were genuine offices, each with a door and a window revealing the view outside. Charles's office was in the back, next to Farris's. It overlooked the nature preserve. Farris owned a corner office with a view to the preserve on one side and a view to I-45 on the other.

The cube walls were six feet tall, blocking the view across the office. Each aisle displayed a cube map, listing the names of the cube occupants along the aisle. The cubes were arranged in blocks of four, with a crossing aisle after every second cube. Charles had vivid memories of hiding from his dad in this maze of cubes.

He stepped out of the elevator and reported to a desk obstructing the first line of cubicles. The sixth floor office guard saw Charles coming. He tensed up tight as a board in his chair at the security desk.

"How's my favorite hall monitor today?" Charles asked. He grabbed a pen from the guard's chest pocket, flipping it into the air with his right hand and catching it with his left.

The guard pushed up his glasses and shuffled his papers. "Just sign the register, Graves."

Charles tossed the pen back onto the desk. "How come they won't give you one of those fancy eye-reader machines?"

"I can't wait 'til Fah-rees gets promoted upstairs. You'll be stuck in this hole for years." The guard's eyes lit up. "Oh, that's gonna be sweet."

Not after I catch Cleveland, Charles thought. Farris can stay here and play with his computer.

"I think you missed your Dale Carnegie training last week." Charles walked past the guard before he could respond. He was thinking about Julia.

Charles wound his way to Julia's cube, three aisles across to the right, four cube-squares down. The genius of the entire operation stuck in a cube. I'll get her out of here too.

Charles unfolded a chair and sat down behind the woman working at her computer. He leaned back on two legs, balancing against the cube wall, underneath a sign that read: You do not compute.

Julia Jenkins whirled around in her chair, stopping it in front of Charles with her feet. Russet hair flapped across her face before cascading down to her shoulder blades, flowing like a Richard Farris suit. Her posture caused her to appear taller than she was, whether standing or sitting. The perceived height accentuated an athletic frame, toned but not muscular. She exuded austerity, but with an obsolete attractiveness that persevered without cosmetics.

Julia's eyes maintained a bullish stare, as if she were constantly surrounded by matadors. She gestured directly when talking with graceful yet incisive hands. Her manner was tentatively authoritative, as if she were constantly questioning herself and subsequently justifying her contentions and decisions. She wore a dark bodysuit under a jacket, dark slacks, and flats.

"I've been waiting all day for you. What took you so long? I've been wanting to congratulate you for Creekside." Julia pulled Charles off the cubicle wall and gave him a hug. She embraced him longer than standard-hug duration.

"I couldn't have done it without you, Julia," Charles said. "You are absolutely the best. No one like you, not here, not anywhere."

He leaned forward in his chair, cupping the back of Julia's neck with his left hand. Her eyes intensified, as if he were waving a red cape in front of her. With his right hand he slid a wrapped package into her lap. "I want you to have this. It's sort of a thank-you for all your help. Don't open it 'til I leave."

"Is this why you were late getting here? Thank you!" She gave him another longer-than-usual hug, squeezing his neck with her arms. Her head hung over his left shoulder.

Charles flinched. Julia hanging over his shoulder reminded him of his vision outside the bowling alley. He expected to see a skull on Julia's shoulders when the hugging was through.

Julia released him. "What's wrong?"

"Nothing. I hurt my back wrestling with one of the deacons during the—"

"Charles, I know when you lie."

Charles focused on her eyes, being careful as he spoke not to allow his eyes to wander. "Let me give you a hint. If you think I'm lying, I'm not. 'Cause if I were, you wouldn't know it."

"Oh yeah, how could I forget. The big secret-agent-disguise-man thing. What's wrong?"

"Do you mind if I tell you some other time? I'm worn out."

Julia relaxed her features. "Sure, no problem. I'll wait."

She's the best. "Okay," he said, "here's the news. I was late because I was forced to ride with Farris—"

"Oooooh, I can't stand that ridiculous clown," Julia said.

"Actually, he got me here earlier the way he drives. But we got called to a meeting upstairs right when we got here."

"And every phone in the world was out of order?"

"I wanted to save the best for last." Charles felt the cube walls closing in, much like when his mother would tuck him in at night.

"And did you?" Julia asked.

Charles savored her response like melted ice cream at the bottom of the bowl. "I'm pretty sure." He reached for her hands in an awkward lurch. They were draped around the package.

"Julia," Charles said.

"Not here." She pointed a thumb over the cube wall. "Let's wait for a better place."

Charles nodded. "You're the best."

A few seconds passed. "Well, tell me the news," she said.

"I am going after Cleveland."

She inhaled sharply. "James Cleveland? The reverend? Charles, that's great! Tell me I'm on the team."

"You are. I'm the point man. You're on computer. Farris is backup from the office. They are giving me three weeks off. After that, we start. I need the rest. I feel beat up inside."

"Yeah, you need it. Will you call me and tell me what is wrong? I mean, if all the phones aren't out of order?"

"You can count on it," Charles said. "Let me go and get some rest. Thanks again. I mean it."

Her fingers traced the edges of the package in her lap. "You're welcome, Charles."

Charles fought the urge to say more. He left her cube and wound his way out of the maze.

Julia opened the package the second she thought Charles was gone for good. In it, she found a twelve-inch replica of Mr. Spock with one word printed on the figurine's base: Logic.

This man understands me, she thought. What a rare quality in a man. He has his issues, no doubt about it, but he understands me and he appreciates me. You could do a lot worse, Julia.

She positioned Mr. Spock front and center on her desk. At least the Approved Television List was allowed to keep some decent shows.

She felt the rustle of someone intimately familiar. It spoke without sound. *He was lucky, Girly-Girl. Use your brain, not your heart. He heard you mention* Star Trek, *that's all. He is trained to notice such things, you know.*

But it's not Spock that counts here—it's the word. He knew. He knows me.

What other word would they put under Spock: comedian?

Julia ordered a détente. She dug into Charles's package. There were two items remaining.

One was a card. She put it to the side so she could concentrate on it later. The other was individually wrapped. She opened it slowly at first, gaining speed as she tugged at the wrapping paper. She paused as the hall monitor passed her cube.

It was a nice box. She was afraid to open it, but she conquered her fear. Inside, she found a string of pearls.

"Ugh," she said. "Who does he think I am, Richard Farris?"

I told you he was lucky. Doesn't know you that well after all, does he?

Détente was finished.

Yes, he does. He doesn't see me often dressed up outside of work, that's all. How would he know? The one person who would wear these at work is Farris. Besides, they are very nice. Any woman would understand the gratitude behind them. And more, as far as that goes.

If you are going to take his side no matter what, then you are following your heart. And you and I both know that's a mistake.

We'll see about that, won't we?

Julia put the pearls back in the box. She opened the card. It was plain white. It said: Sometimes a partner has a horse, sometimes a cape. Mine has a computer and is both the smartest and best person I know. Love, Charles.

Told you . . .

Inside the card was a slip of paper folded and taped to the card. Julia unfolded the note. It appeared hastily written.

> Dear Julia,
>
> I don't know who else to talk to. You are the only one I trust, and the only one I think can help me. This stuff is embarrassing and hard to talk about.
>
> I don't know what is wrong with me, but I think maybe a good place to start would be the fact that I lost my mother and brother when I was young. I carry around this constant pain and confusion with me. Half the time I am not even sure of who I am, which is pretty funny I guess considering I am a "master of disguise." :-)
>
> Except most of the time it is not very funny having to live it. One of the reasons I enjoy my job so much is that for long periods of time I can become someone else. Sometimes during these jobs, I can almost forget all these faces that follow me around.
>
> Then there's my dad. (I am taking a big chance trusting you with this—tear this letter up when you are done. If it got out I would be in big trouble.) I am not sure of him, although he seems to care about me. I have never been sure if his version of things is exactly 100% true.

But worst of all, if things could be worse (and I can't believe I am about to tell you this, but I HAVE to tell someone and there is no one else to tell. No, let me restate that. It's not that there is no one else, it's that you are the only one I trust). As if things could be worse, I have to tell you that I have been haunted by something since I was a child. I don't know how to explain it—just take my word for it. I see his face sometimes. Sometimes I can feel him. Sometimes I hear him. Anyway, it is not pleasant, and I have to tell someone.

I'll call you after I rest a little. I am going to try and sleep for 24 hours straight.

I am now debating whether I should tear this note up. I don't want you to think I am a freak! I am not suicidal or violent. I just need someone to talk to. If this weirds you out too much, forget I said anything. You don't have to answer if you don't want to.

OK, I think I am going to put this note in the card after all. Probably the worst decision I have made in a long time (and that's bad!).

You are absolutely the very best and I am so grateful to have you around.

Charles Graves

The voice in Julia's mind fired a parting shot. "You were saying?"

• • •

Two weeks after the Creekside bust and his meeting with Ingraham, Cotton Graves, and Charles, Richard Farris lounged in a steamy bubble bath. The tub was more similar to a hot tub than a bathtub, which was fitting for his upscale loft. Though it was thirty floors in the air, the loft was not far from where the Reverend Cleveland had established his temporary sanctuary beneath the streets of Houston.

Although it covered only half of the thirtieth floor, the loft in many ways reminded Farris of Cotton Graves's office on the fortieth floor of the headquarters building. The other half was owned by an aging sports legend Farris detested. The two shared one hallway leading to the elevator. Their doors were staggered so as not to be directly across from one another. Farris had installed a mother-of-pearl-inlaid door purchased from a specialty designer.

Inside, his loft was carpeted pearl white throughout. It was one open room with no walls, save for the bathroom. At the far end of the room, beyond a sliding glass door, was a balcony. The balcony overhung from the loft a good ten feet, with marble railings four feet high. A bust of Julius Caesar was fixed on the marble railing, keeping watch over the city. From the balcony, a two-foot ledge spread to the corners of the building, wrapping around the building to an identical balcony at back of his neighbor's loft.

The tinted windows stretching around the entire loft began about waist high over sculpted brick. With the balcony and ledge, it was a blend of old and modern construction.

The view from Farris's loft was worth the lease. To the left was most of downtown. Straight out from the balcony was the agency headquarters building. Farris envisioned one day splitting time between his loft and the fortieth floor office suite occupied by Cotton Graves.

An odor of incense filled the loft. Farris was watching the Approved News from his tub. He sat with his feet on the rail of the tub with his back pressed against a water-jet.

The loft computer spoke to him. "You have an incoming call, sir."

Farris reached his manicured hand reached for the remote. "Identify the caller."

"A Mr. Keesma, sir," the loft said.

"Audio," Farris said, "no visual." The loft channeled the incoming call to Farris through speakers concealed in the ceiling.

"Fah-reese here."

"Hello, Richard. It's Karl Keesma. It's been awhile since the meeting and Mr. Ingraham wanted me to give you a call."

That's because you're a trained donkey, Farris thought. "Great. What's on your mind?"

"He wanted me to make sure you know we consider you to be the owner of this upcoming operation. That its success or failure depends on you."

As if I didn't already know that. This guy must be reading from notes or something. Upcoming operation. He couldn't talk like that on his own if you handed him a thesaurus. What a boob. Why does Ingraham keep these incompetents around? Because a guy like me is too threatening. Better play it cool for now.

"Thank you, Mr. Keesma. Please inform Mr. Ingraham that Belt Buckle is my highest priority." He scrolled through channels on the video screen as he talked.

"Have you met with Charles Graves yet to strategize?" Keesma asked.

Opportunity comes a knockin'. "Not yet, Karl. He needed some time off after Creekside. In fact . . . Well, may I speak frankly?"

"Of course, Richard," Keesma said. "That's why we're here."

That's not why you're here, but that's beside the point. I'll explain that to you at a later date. Farris hesitated, waiting until what he thought was the right time to speak. "I want you to know I am a team player all the way and will do whatever it takes for the benefit of the organization. But I have to say, and I trust I may speak with the utmost assurance of confidentiality—"

"You can. I promise."

"I have always been, uh, hmm, concerned with Charles Graves. Don't get me wrong: he is gifted in some respects. But his past worries me. Sometimes I get the distinct impression he is, uh, unstable, even paranoid. I know he resents me, for example."

"We are aware of Graves's problems. That is part of the reason for this call. I am glad you brought this up. It makes it a lot easier. I can see now why Mr. Ingraham has so much faith in you."

What a patsy. "Thanks, Keesma. What's the other reason, if I may ask?"

"This is top secret. Mr. Ingraham wants you to know we are unsure not only about Charles Graves but about his father: Cotton. The senator has a spotless record and all, but the thing with his wife and now Charles. Mr. Ingraham wants to be cautious. That is why he wants you to know that behind everything, he considers you to be in charge down in Houston."

Bingo. All too easy. "Karl, please relay to Mr. Ingraham that I hear him loud and clear and that we see eye to eye."

"I will do that right away. I want to remind you this operation has to succeed."

Farris shifted in the tub, splashing the water. "Have you ever seen me miss?"

"I guess that's why Mr. Ingraham has you in charge down there."

"While you're at it, Karl, inform Mr. Ingraham I will track down Charles right away. He's hard to find sometimes, ya' know. We'll get started working on Belt Buckle."

"Roger. Thanks, Richard,"

Did he say Roger? What an idiot. "Yeah, thanks," Farris said. "Audio off."

"Nothin' to it, the way I do it," Farris said aloud. He rested his head on the rim of the tub and instructed the loft to dim the lights. He shut his eyes, thinking about how he would rearrange Cotton Graves's office.

Charles owned a red brick house in the country fourteen miles to the southwest of headquarters. It lay down a dirt path known to the locals as Old Bones Lane. The house sat off the main road a half-mile on fifteen acres of land. The path wound through oaks, pines, tallows, and dense underbrush, concealing the house from the main road. It was said that Old Bones Lane cut through an Indian burial ground, though the best evidence of this was talk at the local feed store and the periodic tale of ghost sightings.

Charles bought the house furnished and had not changed anything since. The house had hardwood floors, three rooms, and a kitchen. His lone improvement was to hang comforters over the windows to allow him to sleep during the day.

He sat in a wicker chair on the front porch watching the sun set over the trees. The time off had been productive in the sleep department so far. But it had been a disaster in the mental health department. He was becoming a well-rested, energized loon.

I should call Julia again. When I am around her, the voices go away. Staying out here alone is not good.

Charles walked inside to his bedroom and instructed the house phone to connect him with Julia. When the house phone was unable to locate her, he sat down on the bed and left her a message. "It's Charles. Call me. Bye."

He sprawled on the bed waiting for her to call. He drifted before plunging into a deep sleep.

Somewhere beneath his consciousness a phone rang. But the world was turning over and over and he was running from it. Faster and faster it came, gaining on him.

He realized the world was an immense bowling ball charging down a bowling alley. A wild-eyed Pastor Dean stood at the end of the lane, screaming: *"Yes, Charles, the world turned over. It turned over, but it kept rolling. And now it's rolling over you!"*

Charles saw the polished wood of the lane beneath his feet. He attempted to jump off the lane, but the gutters became boundless chasms writhing like serpents. He sprinted for the end of the lane, only to discover that the pins were giants. One pin was the cauliflower-eared deacon. Charles begged it for help.

"Spare me," the cauliflower-eared deacon said.

Two other pins wobbled toward him with circling red rings around their necks. The pins' heads rotated to the right and left. It was Keesma and Louis, arms outstretched as they advanced.

Charles thought he heard Farris behind the pins. "The ball won't miss, Charles. Have you ever seen me miss?"

Charles wheeled around, sliding on the lane's oily surface. He ducked Keesma's arms and scampered toward the ball, which had progressed three-fourths of the way down the lane. It was accelerating.

The finger holes in the ball ignited with crimson light. With the ball's rotation, the crimson holes seemed to hover in one place as the ball rolled. The ball bore down on Charles. As it reached him, he realized it was the dark man's eyes staring at him.

Charles leapt to his left as the ball reached him. He narrowly escaped, gaining traction on the oily surface at the last second. The ball crashed into the pins, vaporizing Keesma and Louis and jettisoning the cauliflower-eared deacon two lanes over. The ball and the rest of the pins disappeared into the backstop.

Charles's leap propelled him to the edge of the lane, where he balanced on the edge of the gutter, arms spread as if he were mimicking an airplane. For an instant he thought he was safe, but the writhing of the gutter sent him sprawling into the darkness.

It seemed he fell for hours. He watched the light from the bowling alley above him fade. It receded as if a door were slowly closing. Then it was gone. Charles stood at the bottom of the chasm, wide-eyed in the dark.

He stood motionless, wishing for his wood-block puzzle. He imagined the smell of the oak frame, the textured feel of the pieces. In his mind, he saw the pieces assembling into faces. Charles's spine relaxed. His head cleared. The sweet elixir of sleep poured into him.

A woman's voice startled him. Adrenaline shot into his veins. "Julia?"

The woman was sobbing. Why would Julia be crying?

The sobbing echoed all around him. A thousand needles pricked at his heart. The sobbing was desolate, forlorn, forsaken.

"Why, Charles? Why?"

"Why what?" Charles's words entered the chasm like an antelope creeping down to crocodile-infested waters for a drink. "Who are you?"

"Why, Charles? Why?"

Charles's puzzle arranged itself in his mind. It was the face of his mother. Tears smeared her makeup.

"Mother?" At a distance through the darkness, he saw her. She was suspended in midair, sitting with her legs crossed under her. She was searching for him. Her image grew as it neared him.

"*Mother!*"

The image behaved as though it heard his voice but could not locate the source. "Charles, is that you? Are you there?"

"*Here! Over here!*"

The image was still thirty feet away. "Charles, I can't see you."

"I can see you, Mom. You are as beautiful as I remember. I love you. I miss you."

His mother burst out in a new round of tears. "Remember. Remember? I asked you to remember. I pleaded for you to remember. My last words to you were to remember. But you forgot." She struggled to get the last word out through her tears.

Charles's gut exploded. He remembered now. He remembered his mother clawing her way up the thirty-two gold-inlaid stair steps. "You . . . have . . . to . . . *remember!*" she had said.

He called for her. Now the image responded as if it knew the location of his voice. The image stood and walked toward him. Its footfalls were heavy on the floor: clop, clop, clop, clop.

The wood-block puzzle in Charles's mind began to rearrange itself. He screamed. "*No!*"

The approaching image changed with the blocks. The smeared makeup became blemishes, the lips thinned, the tears became a haunting grin.

"You knew all along it wasn't her," the dark man said.

"No!" Charles said. "It was her. I remembered." He clenched his fists. He felt his scar flushing in the darkness.

"You miserable fool. When are you going to learn? These disguises you wear, you wear them because you hate yourself. You detest yourself. You loathe yourself."

"Not as much as I hate you," Charles said.

The image of the dark man drew closer. "If you hate me so much, why do you keep calling me back? Hmmmmm?" The dark man drew close with his hollow eyes.

Then Charles did something that surprised even himself. He reared back with all his might and swung at the dark man, connecting squarely with his nose. His fist sailed clear through the apparition.

The dark man ridiculed the vanity of Charles's strike. He caressed the tip of Charles's nose with a fingertip. Charles's head split with a brilliant light of pain.

"Ah, that hurts," Charles said.

"Of course it does," the dark man said.

"Who are you?" Charles asked. "Tell me that one thing. That's all I ask."

"Like you don't know," the dark man said. "Now go to sleep and forget, my friend."

The dark man walked off. Clop, clop, clop, clop.

SIX

The legend of Old Bones Lane seemed real enough to Julia. She left Houston before sundown, hoping to arrive at Charles's place before dark. She failed.

She exited the main highway onto the dirt path, halting at the tree line. The trees draped over the path, producing the appearance of a long cave. A country darkness saturated the air.

Do you want to do this? You could turn around and go home. No harm, no foul. Are you even sure this is his place?

She stared at Old Bones Lane, thinking of Ichabod Crane riding home on Halloween night.

You girly-girl. It's the same as it is when it's light outside. It just happens to be dark. There's no such thing as whatever it is you think you are afraid of right now. Aren't you a naturalist? It's time for your beliefs to match your actions.

She consulted the GPS unit in her dashboard. "This has to be it." She edged forward, right inside the tree line. The overgrowth engulfed the hood of her car.

Are you sure he's even here? He didn't answer when you called. If he is here, maybe he wants to be alone. It's a valid point. She stared at the gear shift indicator as if she wanted it to give her a sign. It didn't.

Okay, Girly-Girl. That *point* is easily dispatched. If he is not here, you will know it when you get to the house. Then you can go home and quit worrying. Simple logic: if not A, then Non-A.

Julia willed herself to inch the car forward. As the car crept along, rocks from the dirt path crackled under the tires. Julia kept an eye on the rearview mirror, watching the opening to the outside world closing.

Having common sense does not make one a girly-girl. Logic is great and all, but this situation calls for intuition, something girly-girls are stocked up on. And the drums of intuition are beating a clear signal: *do not go in there.* Did you forget the letter he wrote you? Sure, he might need your help and all. Sure, he might not be the raving psycho who wrote that letter. But how 'bout let's do this at a nice, comfortable, public restaurant instead of out here in *the middle of nowhere?*

If darkness is your thing, we could even pick a restaurant where they serve by romantic candlelight. Table for two please, waiter. How about a nice cozy booth in the corner?

The path ahead jogged to the left. She knew that if she took that left, her line of sight behind her would disappear. It had the feel of the point of no return. Julia pressed the brake. She flipped the interior light on to touch a button on the GPS in the pretense of making sure this was the right location.

With the light on, the world outside vanished. Because of the headlights, she saw forward with no difficulty, but the side and back windows blanked out. There could be anything out there, she thought. It could see me, but I couldn't see it.

About the most dangerous animal in Southeast Texas is a cow, Girly-Girl.

Or a man. One who writes cryptic letters. Maybe he's a psycho killer who posts pictures of victims all over his house. Maybe he keeps souvenirs of them. Maybe he has fifteen acres of land in the middle of nowhere so no one hears when he tortures his victims, or knows when he locks them in cages, or finds them when he buries their remains.

Julia turned off the light, expecting a gruesome face to appear inches from the driver's-side window.

"Enough," she said. "This is simple." She explored the center console for a coin. She found one suitable. "Heads, I go forward. Tails, I go back."

You will *not* flip a coin, Girly-Girl. He is not crazy—well, he's not the killer kind of crazy—and he needs you. And you trust him. Admit it. You do. You are not afraid of him in the least. He needs you now. How do you know that? Let's not think about that . . . .

"You're right," Julia said. "You usually are. That's why I get Spock as a present."

You loved that present, and rightly so. Plus, didn't you get that other one as well? Did the girly-girl present scare you? Make you feel uncomfortable? Don't worry. I'll work that out for you when I explain to you why you know he needs you now.

"Got it," Julia said.

One more thing, GG—you are an officer of the law. There is a gun on your hip and you know how to use it better than three Charles Graveses. Cheer up.

Julia drove to the end of the dirt path. It was a long half-mile, but by the time she reached the house she was not a girly-girl. "I'm glad for Spock instead of McCoy."

You'll be Kirk before long.

"Enough."

Julia killed the engine and listened. The soft hum of locusts.

She stepped out of the car, shut the door, and walked to the house. The lights were out. The locusts paused for a few seconds then resumed their humming. At the front door she raised a fist to knock, but paused. Why am I so worried about him?

The letter.

She placed a palm on the door. With her other hand she turned the knob. It rotated. She pushed. The door creaked open.

"Charles?" She raised her voice a few decibels. "Charles, are you home?"

No answer.

The locusts paused again. Julia took two steps into the house. No pictures of victims, no souvenirs, no walls covered with newspaper clippings. He could use a housekeeper though. She took four steps across the hardwood floor: clop, clop, clop, clop.

A voice sounded from the back room. She froze, her hand moving to the grip of her pistol.

He's talking in his sleep. He's having a dream.

She took four more steps to the door of the bedroom: clop, clop, clop, clop.

Charles sat up in bed, staring. "Who's there?"

"Julia."

"You came," Charles said, his voice wavering.

"What were you dreaming about?" Julia asked. She tried to measure his facial expressions in the dark.

Charles swung his legs over the side of the bed. He wiped his face in the sheet then let the sheet fall to his lap. "I'm not sure. I wish I could remember. I think I was supposed to remember something, but I can't."

Julia stepped toward him. Her shoe struck a bottle, sending it clanking across the hardwood floor. It smacked Charles's nightstand and ricocheted back to Charles's feet. It revolved four times before coming to rest.

"Have you been drinking?" she asked.

"Not like I want to. And not for a few days. One sure sounds good about now, don'tcha think?"

"I've had better offers," she said. "You wanna go for a drive or something?"

"Sounds good. I know a good place where we can talk if you want."

Forty-five minutes later they were staring up at the night sky from the hood of Julia's car, parked down a gravel path in a field bordering Houston Hobby airport.

"Here comes one!" Charles said. "Hang on!"

The ground began to tremble. The car began to tremble. The warmth from the engine engulfed Julia through the hood. As the trembling increased, the warmth worked its way into her back, giving her a shiver. Her toes curled.

Then it happened. *WHOOOOOOOOOOOOOOOOOOSH.* A jumbo jet passed overhead, filling the sky, blocking the night from her view. The jet's engines were so loud Julia thought they were going to suck her up into the sky. For three seconds she forgot everything.

The jet touched down on the runway. Julia watched the landing by peering through a chain-link fence in front of the parked car.

"I want another one!" Julia said. "How long 'til the next one comes?"

"This time of night, every five or ten minutes." Charles was lying lengthways across the hood of the car on the driver's side. Julia was along the passenger's side. The runway beacons flashed on and off, casting an intermittent amber light across Charles's face. On. Off. On. Off. When they were off, he resembled a boy. When they were on, a man.

"How did you know about this place?" Julia asked.

"I used to come out here to get away," Charles said. "Haven't been here in a while. I fly planes and stuff too, so it suits me."

"You come out here to think?"

"Yeah, or not to."

Not to is more like it. It's too loud for logic. A bit too muggy, as well. "What are you thinking now?"

"I'm thinking how stupid I feel for writing that letter. Correction. Not for writing it—for giving it to you."

"Is that what was bothering you in the office the other day?"

"That was part of it."

"What was the other part?"

He propped himself up on an elbow. "I don't know if I can talk about it."

He seems like he's carrying a load. That's a good sign, better than being crazy, so don't scare him off.

"Let me ask you something," Julia said. "Is it because you can't talk about it or because you don't trust me?"

Charles turned his head to the left and to the right. "I think I trust you, Julia. But the truth is you're it. You're the only one. And I can't stand holding this in anymore. Does that make sense?"

Why do men have such trouble expressing their feelings? It's illogical—what irony. Julia started to speak, but she hesitated. She propped herself up on an elbow, facing him. She placed her free arm on his shoulder.

Be careful, Girly-Girl. What he's about to tell you, if he does, ain't your run-of-the-mill feelings. Better buckle up.

"You can trust me. I promise," she said. "Besides, I sure don't mind being the only one."

"Okay, I'll try then. But first, here comes another one."

They lay back down flat on the hood, waiting for the approaching jet. After a minute or so, it came.

WHOOOOOOOOOOOOOOOOOOOOOOOOOOOOSH!

To Julia, it felt like the crashing of a thousand waves on the shore all at once. It was cleansing. The vibrations from the jet engines touched her deep inside. *I could lie here all night,* she thought.

Their eyes met and Charles spoke. "Outside the bowling alley after the Creekside takedown, I saw my brother giving my mother a hug in her car." Charles looked down at his feet.

"I know it wasn't real. They've both been dead for twenty years. But it seemed so real at the time. He was hugging her the way you hugged me in the office. It shook me up, that's all."

"I had no idea," Julia said.

"Of course not. You are a jewel."

Julia winced at the pun, but figured it was unintentional. Her high school sweetheart had called her Jewels. The luster had since faded from the nickname.

I'm pretty sure that worn-out pick-up lines are the last thing on his mind, Girly-Girl.

"Tell me as much as you can, Charles. About the letter too."

Charles raised up, looked backward over the top of the car, and then turned back to Julia. "My brother died an unnatural death, and I think my parents always blamed me for it. I never felt like I had made it up to them, no matter how good I did. Plus, he was my older brother, so I figure my parents think they got robbed of him and stuck with me. My mother was taken away right after that."

Julia resisted the melodramatic and hackneyed responses flooding her mind. They spilled over into her response somewhat anyway. "That would be devastating to an adult," Julia said, "but to a child? I can't even imagine."

"I know. That's the conventional wisdom, but it doesn't apply here. This is not one of those 'he's screwed up because of a traumatic childhood' things. I have my issues, but I cope pretty well with the loss of my mom and my brother, considering. And yes, I realize I spend half my life pretending to be someone else, and the other half drinking, but cut me some slack. I think I have done okay under the circumstances."

"I do too. I can't even imagine."

Be careful, Julia thought. You are getting close. And be quiet. He's finally talking.

"I always figured I couldn't change what happened, so I better try to forget it and do better with the here and now. But that's always a problem because my dad reminds me about the past all the time. I don't mean he says things about it. What I mean is that I've had this nagging feeling since I started with the agency that he was in on it somehow. Maybe not on purpose, but involved anyhow.

"He did a good job convincing me as a kid. I suppose that's because all we had was each other. But now, I'm not so sure. Also, right before I came to see you that day, in that meeting were the two guys that took my mother away. I couldn't believe it. Dad denied it, and was pretty convincing too, but I don't know. What are the odds?"

"Where did they take your mother?" Julia asked.

"I don't know, probably to a reclamation center. She's dead. That's all that matters. I don't like to think about it."

"Charles," she said softly, "could I give you a hug now without it hurting you?"

"I think so," Charles said.

Julia reached over and hugged him. She held him lightly at first, then pulled him tighter. They lay there for a minute without moving.

WHOOOOOOOOOOOOOOOOOOOOOOOOOOOSH!

Julia pulled even closer. The car trembled with the roar of the jet engines. Julia felt a solitary tear slide down Charles's cheek. She spoke in his ear, not knowing if he could hear her. "It's going to work out, Charles. I know that sounds trite, but somehow I know. It's going to work out. Everything works out."

The roar subsided. Julia's mind fired back up.

Okay, do you want to be a replacement for the mother he lost? It will always be this way. You playing the mother—him playing the child. Is that what you want?

Hang on a sec. It's true that he has some issues. He is a man, you know. Comes with the territory. They all got 'em. This one more than others perhaps, but every one of them wants to be mothered from time to time. And think about it this way: as a child, this man lost his brother, his mother, and now has a father he can't trust. As an adult he is responsible, successful, and caring. This man is a genuine, bona-fide rock. Granite, not sedimentary. He's a foundation to build upon. If he can play the hand life dealt him, he can handle anything. Just a thought.

She released Charles. Back on their elbows, their eyes met again.

"I feel better. Thanks," Charles said. "Can I tell you one more thing? This one is the worst."

"Please do."

"You won't think I'm crazy?"

"Well, if you told me you were in love with Richard Farris I would."

Charles paused long enough to pretend the joke was funny. "Okay, then. Promise me you will stop me if you think I am getting too weird."

"I will. I promise."

Charles looked around as if he were waiting for the next plane to come. He looked back to Julia and held his hands out, thumbs at 90-degree angles, to form a square. "When I was a kid, I had a wood-block puzzle. Still have it. It had pieces that made faces and stuff. You could flip blocks to different sides and create just about any face or expression you wanted. I played with that thing for hours on end.

"Here's the deal. There was one face that came up a lot. I don't know how, but I kept finding myself arranging the blocks so that his was the face looking at me. I called him the dark man, but I don't know his name or if he even has one. Whatever. He haunted me. But here's the really strange part: he haunts me now. Still. I see him everywhere. In the mirror when I'm shaving, in the rearview mirror when I'm driving, and sometimes in dreams.

"But even when I don't see him, I feel him. He is always there. He calls to me. He taunts me. But sometimes he helps me. If I could have my choice of anything, I would like to find out who he is and get rid of him. He makes me so tired."

Uh-huh, Julia thought. Where does that leave you, missy? And what does that mean: if he could have his choice of anything? Kinda leaves you on the outs, doesn't it?

Shut up. This man is pouring his heart out. Trusting you. That's what you wanted, isn't it? What you asked him for?

"Charles, I believe you," Julia said. "I can't tell you what it means or who he is, but I believe you. I promise you this though: if you will let me, I'll try to help you find him and get rid of him."

Julia saw Charles's uncolored eyes staring at her. They pulsated with the runway beacons, alternating from hollow, serpent eyes to eyes full of endurance. "Lie down," Charles said. "There's another one coming."

You're in it now, Girly-Girl.

Julia closed her eyes and allowed the roar to take over.

• • •

Charles chewed four aspirin into a fine powder and swallowed. "Should get something with more kick," he said to no one. "Four aspirin's no match for three weeks on the bottle."

He stood outside the front of his home in the morning light, taking inventory. The doors of his van were wide open, as if he were displaying it at a car show. It was white, resembling any of a thousand vans on the streets of Houston. The van's audio blared an aggressive, non-ASL tune.

Inside were the tools of his trade. Charles collected disguise paraphernalia to a neurotic extent, mostly at taxpayers' expense. His van was a mobile Smithsonian of disguise.

"Music off," he said. The country air became quiet, except for the hum of the locusts not ready to call it a night. Charles pressed his temples with the palms of his hands. Three weeks go by in such a hurry.

Sometimes that happens when you self-medicate. Should have spent more time with Julia. And Pete. Forgot about him, didn't you? Another benefit of self-medication.

"Great. Phone."

"Yes, Mr. Graves," the van answered.

"Connect me to Pete Redding."

Charles clambered into the back of the van. He unfastened a locker labeled "Ears." Inside were around a hundred preformed ears and assorted ear disguise kits.

"Pete Redding located," the van said. "Connecting . . . "

"Charles," Pete said over the audio, "you all right? Thought you might drop by."

"No excuses: I forgot. Give me a pardon on that one. You at home or at work?"

"At work."

"Oh. I wanted to see if I could drop by on my way out. Guess not." Charles inspected the ear locker. He shut it and switched his attention to the hair locker.

"No worries. I know you got a lot goin' on. Come see me after you're done doin' whatever it is you're doin'. You know where I'll be."

"Thanks, Pete," Charles said. "Phone off."

Charles shut the hair locker.

"He could have called me."

Charles shut the back doors, then the side, then leaned over the bucket seats and shut the driver's and passenger's doors, shutting himself inside. "Climate, seventy-two. Music, soft."

Thirty minutes later, Charles climbed out the van's side door. His face was grizzled. His hair was a scraggly, stringy, white. Seven days' growth of whiskers protruded from his cheeks and chin at weird angles. His eyes were bloodshot. One ear featured a nick of flesh cut out of it. On his left forearm was a tattoo of an eagle. He wore a faded army-green jumpsuit, worn through in several places. On his feet were a set of ruined boots, one with the heel missing. The whiskers concealed his scar.

Charles practiced walking with an all but imperceptible limp. One more thing would complete the disguise. He lay down in the driveway and rolled in the dust three or four revolutions. He stood up and brushed himself off.

Now it's perfect. I was right about one thing: me and Farris ain't in the same league, all right. That pansy couldn't spot me from Ingraham.

Charles opened the driver's door and entered. A wooden chest sat on the passenger floorboard. He unlatched the cover and opened the chest. He reached in, retrieved his wood-block puzzle, and placed it on the passenger bucket seat. He picked up the chest and put it between the bucket seats where he could reach the pieces. He raised the passenger seat armrest so he could access the puzzle without interference.

"Ignition," he said. The van started. "Drive." The transmission slipped into drive. He took his foot off the brake and the van eased onto the dirt path leading down Old Bones Lane. "Music," he said. "'Faces,' by Lester Hollingsworth."

"That selection is not on the ASL," the van said.

"Override code 25878-22B14-33."

As Lester started to sing and Charles drove the van through Old Bones Lane, his right hand began to shuffle pieces in the wood-block puzzle.

By the time Charles reached the interstate, Julia's face had appeared in the wood-block puzzle. He crossed under an overpass, turned left, and accelerated toward the entrance ramp.

He traced the outline of her face as he merged onto the freeway. "Phone. Julia Jenkins. Music off."

"Yes, Mr. Graves," the van said. A family car passed him. The parents and two kids were sunburned and looked worn. Probably returning from a day at Galveston Beach.

"Hello, Charles," Julia said. Charles perceived her voice as arising from her picture in the puzzle. "Hang on. I'm locating you on my screen."

Charles smiled at the thought of her looking over him from on high, both from her cube at the agency and through her satellite link. His own guardian angel.

"You're on Interstate 45," she said. "Forty-four-point-six miles south of downtown. Twelve hundred fifty-eight feet past the Primrose feeder entrance. Traveling at fifty-two-point-six-three miles per hour. Give me three seconds and I will have satellite video. Three, two, one, gotcha. How are you doing?"

"Good now that you're with me."

"What's your disguise?" Julia asked.

"Can't tell you, but you wouldn't recognize me."

"I bet I would," Julia said.

"This call may be monitored to ensure quality service," Charles said. Julia shuffled on the line. "So," Charles said, "where am I going?"

"Parking garage. Downtown. Thirty-four-twenty-four Main. Fifth floor, space number five-two-six. I've got a space prepaid for six months—it better not take that long—and there is a unit stationed across the street with twenty-four-hour surveillance on your van. Farris is operating primarily from his loft, so he will always be just minutes away. That's about it. I believe we're ready to go."

"Have I ever told you that you are absolutely the best?"

"Not enough," Julia said. "And Charles, please watch yourself. I'm worried."

"Don't be afraid. What's the worst that can happen?"

SEVEN

Charles signed off the phone. He pulled the audio/GPS tracking device out of his phony left ear and put it in the breast pocket of his jumpsuit.

Fifty-two-point-six-three miles an hour was a leisurely pace to downtown. The traffic rocketed past him as if people had someplace to get to in a hurry. Charles dumped the contents of the wood-puzzle into the wooden chest. His right hand resumed its work rebuilding the puzzle.

Charles watched the scenery go by. The world has turned over. Pete said so. Dean said so. I've heard that stupid phrase my whole life. What does it mean? That it changed? Big deal. Everything is always changing. An hour ago you were Charles Graves, now you're a deadbeat.

But the more things change, the more they stay the same. Oh yeah, good one. Truck out the tired clichés, why don't you?

I can put on these disguises for the rest of my life, but it won't change the fact that Stephen's dead. It won't change the fact my mother's dead. Some things can't turn over.

It won't change the fact Julia must think I'm nuts. She's been real good about it, especially with the letter. But she has to be wondering if she wouldn't be better off with someone normal.

But if everyone is always changing, how can anyone be normal?

No wonder I drink. With all these voices, I'm lucky it's not worse. Too bad I can't change my brain out with the disguise.

Farris doesn't change. He's always a jerk.

Yeah, and your mother didn't change, and you know where she ended up. Your dad changed, and now y'all are doing well.

Well is a relative term.

Yeah, and *relative* means changing.

"That's enough of all that," Charles said aloud. "What a freak show. I wonder how long I was out?"

He passed under the 610 interchange, a few miles from downtown. He checked traffic in the rearview mirror, then peeked at his puzzle. A set of hollow eyes gawked back at him. Charles refocused on the highway.

"What do you want?" Charles asked.

"I don't change," the dark man said. "Been here pretty-as-you-please for a long while, eh, Chuck?"

"I told Julia about you," Charles said.

"I heard you. Am I supposed to be intimidated? Should I go running to my mommy? Oh, pardon me."

"One day I'll kill you," Charles said. "One day."

"Yeah, whatever. You are a menace, that's for sure. People close to you do end up dead. It's just never me. You're a loser.

You're weak. You're worthless. You know it too. And you also know that's another thing that won't change. And I'll make sure Julia knows it before it's done too, just like I did with Lisa."

Charles floored the van. He ripped the rearview mirror off the windshield and threw it backward. It shattered against the back door, landing on a locker marked "Noses." Shards of mirror scattered across the back of the van.

Charles dumped the wood-block puzzle into the chest. The hollow eyes flashed before fading out. The van was up to 110 miles an hour. He swerved, missing a pack of Harley Davidsons cruising ahead of him. He let off the gas, braking to a normal speed.

The bikers sped up alongside him. The head rider took one look through the window and backed off, saluting Charles as he passed.

Charles felt the tracking device vibrate in his breast pocket. She's always there when I need her. He stuck the device back into his ear.

"Yes, I'm fine," he said. He took the Scott Street Exit into downtown, noticing the police cordon on the outgoing side of the freeway. "Thanks for being there again. Have I told you that you are absolutely the best? Gotta go."

Ten minutes later he pulled into the parking garage. It reminded him of a mausoleum. Inside, two attendants were sweeping the concrete drive with floor brooms. A third attendant handed him a ticket and waved him on.

Charles took a left onto a circular drive that wound around and around, higher and higher in the parking garage. He entered the fifth floor and found space 526. He touched the nose of the van to the waist-high concrete wall girding floor five.

"Park. Cut engine."

The van shut down. "Good-bye, Julia. See you soon," Charles said. He removed the device and placed it back in his pocket.

He exited the van and descended into the depths of the city.

Ten days is a long time to go without a shower, Charles thought. Charles was more scraggly and dirty than when he'd first donned the disguise. The Texas summer heat augmented his disguise, adding a pungent funk to his increasingly realistic costume.

He sat on a sidewalk in the center of downtown with an empty tin can in front of him. The beggar business was not very good these days. Neither was the Belt Buckle business. The crowds passed him by as if he were part of the pavement.

The crowds were steady all day. Heavier in the morning, at lunch, and at quitting time. Charles sat on a makeshift cardboard mat that bottlenecked the crowd somewhat as it passed. He was surrounded by concrete, granite, asphalt, and skyscrapers. The vehicle traffic increased and decreased on the same schedule as the pedestrian crowds. The automobile and bus fumes hung in the air like Michael Jordan.

Ten days is longer to go without booze. Charles's fingers itched. He rubbed the tips of his fingers vigorously, the friction failing to relieve the urge. He scratched them against the rough pavement of the sidewalk. No relief.

A convenience store sign across the street blinked on and off. Open. Open. Open. Charles reached for his pockets. There was no cash. He was good enough to steal and not get caught. Was he bad enough, though? His itching fingers said Yes.

The urge worked up from his gut, through his heart, and out his fingers. It left his mind somehow detached, drifting like a cloud. The booze, or something even stronger perhaps, would stop that. It would ground him.

Besides, drunkenness would put the master's stroke to his disguise. Nothing like professionalism. Gotta give them taxpayers their money's worth.

Drinking was better than prism therapy, at any rate. Green is the color of life. Green makes me feel alive. Green is mother earth. Nonsense. Green is the color of margaritas. Margaritas make me feel alive. White is the color of Russians. Black too.

Charles reclined with his back flat against the pavement, staring at the clouds floating across the sky. It would be something to be a cloud. Float through life. Follow the wind. Rain on someone when you were in a bad mood. Throw lightning at them if you were in a very bad mood. Send a tornado if you hated them.

From his viewpoint, the skyscrapers were bony, pointed fingers aching to clutch the clouds. Somehow the clouds always slipped through. Farris was probably in one of those bony fingers right now: his loft. Seemed like Farris was always sniffing around.

It's good to be a cloud. Speaking of slipping through, I wonder if there's news on Cleveland.

Charles rolled over and feigned sleep on a sheet of cardboard, not that anyone noticed. "Julia, you there?" It's the middle of the day—she oughta be.

A brief pause. "Yeah, of course. What's up? You shouldn't break silence."

"I know the rules, Spock. There's just nothin' out here. Besides, if somebody sees a homeless guy talkin' to himself, it just helps the disguise. Listen, are they still sure Cleveland's here?"

"They moved the cordon in toward downtown a mile. This morning they nabbed one of his lieutenants trying to slip through. He talked, without too much persuasion. He didn't know too much, but we're pretty sure Cleveland is still in or around downtown. Are you eating and getting any rest?"

"I get a bunk, dinner, and breakfast at the homeless shelter when I want. It'll hold me over. I've heard a lot of covert gospel in the last few nights. I can't believe these folks are still at it when they know it will get them reclaimed. I've heard Jesus this and Jesus that, sin and salvation, more Jesus, forgiveness of sin. I may be dressed like a cripple, but I don't need no crutch."

Charles thought of the blinking convenience store sign and the offer of release from the urge it promised. His fingers itched.

"I know," Julia said. "Unbelievable."

"That's what will get Cleveland before it's over. These Christians can't help doing what they think is right or trying to share their faith, in public or not. They're so stupid that way."

CLANG. The empty can in front of him teetered and tottered before coming to rest. Must be a whole handful of change, Charles thought. A good customer. Maybe business is picking up. From his feigned sleeping position, he eyed his customer.

He was a well-dressed donor. Three-piece suit, nice shoes. He was wearing a hat and sunglasses, so Charles could not make a positive ID, but the rest of the profile seemed to fit the description. African American. Tall, over six feet. Despite the hat, he appeared to be bald or very closely shaved. Older, definitely over fifty, probably a bit older than that. Hard to say for sure with the crowd, but it appeared the man was limping. Charles could not pinpoint the kidney-shaped birthmark.

He sat up, attempting to thank his donor, but it was too late. The man was already down the sidewalk a piece.

"I got a prospect, Julia," Charles said. "Signing off for now. I am not comfortable with the wheel in the sky."

"Charles, no!" Julia said. "You can't go off the grid. I need you to stay in communic—"

"Bye. I love you." Charles stood. No one in the passing crowd took notice.

To his left, he saw the donor making his way to the corner. He removed the tracking device from his ear. He surveyed the scene as he blended in to the pedestrian traffic moving to his right. He settled in behind a woman carrying an open purse.

The purse was unzipped. It opened and closed in time with her gait. He thought with luck he could make it.

Timing her footfalls just right, he pitched the tracking device into her purse. It rattled around the top, scooted across a mirror, and dropped to the bottom.

Perfect.

Charles slinked behind a concrete pillar that jutted out from the skyscraper's base. From here, he had a good view to the corner with little chance of detection. The donor stood at the corner, waiting. Periodically he scanned the crowd of pedestrians behind him. Charles's pulse spiked.

The donor took a left and disappeared behind the corner of the building. Charles counted thirty seconds.

Bingo!

Charles spotted a man at the corner on the opposite side of the street, dressed much like the man Charles was tailing: head fully covered by a hat, dark sunglasses, three-piece suit. But it was his behavior that raised Charles's suspicions. The man scanned the pedestrians in an all-too-resolute manner. The light changed, but he remained standing at the corner.

Charles ducked behind the pillar. The reflection from the windows across the street gave him an idea of the light changes. He waited through a cycle of the lights before peering around again.

The man was still at the corner. He waited for one more light change. When the pedestrians began to cross, he took a left behind the corner of the building, walking in the direction of the donor.

Will there be a third? Yes or no, Charles. Will there be a third?

"Not at this corner," he said. He slipped around the pillar, resuming his limp. If there is a third I might be able to fool him, but I can't go too slow or I may lose the first two.

He reached the corner of the building and promptly sat on the sidewalk. He removed a mirror from his jumpsuit. He held it around the corner, ankle-high. No sentry.

He put the mirror back and stood. He dared a peek around the corner. At the end of the block, the two men stood together at the corner, surrounded by a crowd of pedestrians. The traffic on the street in front of them raced by. When the light changed, the donor crossed. His accomplice remained behind.

Instead of trailing the men directly, Charles crossed the street to the opposite side from where the sentry now stood. He ran to the end of the block across the street from the donor's accomplice, ducking behind cars as he ran.

From his corner, he saw the donor making his way down the next block. The donor stopped halfway, propping himself against a building. He took out a book, pretending to read. Charles figured he was scanning the crowds over the spine of the book. Charles noticed he was checking across the street as well as to the right and left of the side he was standing on. *This will be a tough tail. At least if I get caught, I won't have to worry about getting roughed up. Stupid Christians.*

The accomplice crossed the street in the direction of the donor and passed him without a nod. The accomplice reached the corner and stopped. The donor put his book away and began walking. They repeated this technique for three blocks.

Charles tailed from across the street. *If they see me now, will they recognize me as following them? I don't think so. All the same, don't get seen.*

After the third block, the donor took a left. Charles had to wait until the accomplice vacated the corner, passed by the donor midway down the block, and reached the next corner. This forced him to cross the street twice in order to stay on the opposite side from the two men. *These guys were good.*

The donor, at the block's midpoint, was scanning over his book again in between passing pedestrians. Charles completed the first crossing behind a couple holding hands. The second crossing was easier. A bus shielded him as he crossed.

By the time he gained the opposite side of the street, the donor had moved on. Charles followed the men in the same cautious manner down two more blocks and a left turn. Then the donor took a right at the corner. He was heading to Charles's side of the street.

Charles considered his options. The building to his side offered no hiding places. He could not enter it. Guards stood at the entrance, checking ID badges. He could try and run for the corner he came from, but the donor was already halfway across and the accomplice was scanning his side of the street from the opposite corner.

Look for the diamond sign on a door, you moron, the dark man said. You can hide at the foot of the stairs. You will be able to see them pass if they are doubling back.

"What do you care?" Charles said.

Let's just say I am an interested party.

Charles saw a large, red diamond marking the entrance to the stairs and escalators leading underground. He sprinted for it, ducking undercover right as the donor reached the corner. Charles took the stairs two at a time. At the bottom, he knelt, staring back up at the street.

A minute passed. Then two.

Patience, Charles.

Shut up. Charles saw the donor at the stairway entrance. He appeared to be waiting. They're coming down.

Where would you be without me? The dark man sounded pleased with himself.

Charles weighed his options. Stairs in one direction, a fifty-foot corridor in the other. "I hate stairs." He ran down the corridor.

The corridor opened into a food court. Charles slowed to a brisk walk. To his left he saw two police officers drinking coffee outside a café named Ground Zero. He veered right, hoping they didn't notice. With this disguise on, they'll run me in for sure. I need to hide.

He kept his head down and kept walking. Heads turned and eyes locked in on him. At the center of the court was an ice cream to-go parlor surrounded by palm trees. To its right were three waste receptacles. He trudged to the receptacles.

As soon as he touched the first waste receptacle, the tension left the food court. Heads turned back around, eyes quit staring. There was no sign of the donor or the accomplice. He lifted one of the receptacles and walked toward the back of the food court.

Past a place called Johnny Taco's he saw three dark corridors. He chose the middle one and carried the trash can into the darkness. As much as the world turns over, as much it stays the same. Give a bum a trash can, and no one pays him any mind.

Julia looked at the Spock figurine above her computer monitor in her cube. Wheel in the sky. Wheel in the sky. It has to be a reference to the satellite link.

No it doesn't, thought Julia's girly-girl side. Use intuition on this one, not logic.

Julia watched the Charles's movements as the GPS tracked him on her computer screen. His beacon had showed movement for two blocks. Now it was stationary on the third floor of the Carolina building.

"What are you doing, Charles? What's in the Carolina building? What's the wheel in the sky?"

Girly-Girl has a point. You can search for anagrams with the letters from "wheel in the sky" all you want, but this is not a logic problem. He's not logical, and that last outburst signifies he's worried. He wanted you to know in case something bad happened to him.

It was sweet, though.

Yeah, I have to admit that it was. But if something goes wrong here, they will be playing those transmissions over and over, and you will have some uncomfortable explaining to do. This has the potential to be very bad.

"Wheel in the sky," she said. "Ezekiel? Nah. Journey? I doubt it."

Relax, Girly-Girl thought. It'll come to you.

"You go into Johnny Taco's and order a drink," Cleveland said. He and one of his elders strolled across the food court. The officers at Ground Zero didn't notice them as they passed. "I'll go ahead on in. Loiter outside Johnny's for a minute or two. When no one is watching, come on down the hall."

The two men picked their way through the food court. When they reached the end, the elder entered Johnny Taco's.

Cleveland milled around outside, waiting for the right instant. When it came, he ducked down the hall. "Just something not right about all this runnin' and hidin'," he said.

At the end of the hall, he let himself into the abandoned storeroom. The light was already on. Three more members of Cleveland's church were present, two men and a woman. The woman reminded Cleveland of Mrs. Cullins. One of the men wore a red cap with an embroidered cougar on it.

"How do you like the room?" Cleveland asked.

Cougar spoke up. "It'll do. I don't know how you do it, Reverend."

"I got lots of friends in maintenance." Cleveland stepped forward and gave each person a hug.

"Reverend," Cougar said, "I wish you would rethink this whole thing. I know you're dead set, but this is pushing our luck. Why can't we lay low for a while?"

"There's no luck where God is involved," Cleveland said.

"Amen!" the Cullins look-alike said.

"I know, Reverend," Cougar said. "All I am saying is we could lay low for a while. Take it easy. Live to fight another day. We think they nabbed Ray this morning. No tellin' what he has told them."

"Not about this place," Cleveland said. "I didn't pass the word to y'all about this place 'til a few hours ago."

"But what about Graves?" the other member said. His ears twitched as he spoke.

As if to accentuate the comment, the Reverend's elder entered the room. In his hands were a Johnny Supreme and a plastic cup with the Johnny Taco's logo. "Anybody want some?" he said.

Everyone declined. Cleveland swiped at the dust on the floor with his shoe. His voice rose. "I don't care about the danger. They are going to get us sooner or later if we keep this up. As far as this room is concerned, we will use it for a week or two then rotate to another one, just like we always do."

Cleveland surveyed his little flock in the dim light of the workroom. "What we need to do in these dark times is continue to do what God has told us to do. God is still in control, no matter if there were a thousand Charles Graveses running around. Do you remember what happened when Elisha asked God to open his servant's eyes? There was a heavenly host all around them. We would see the same thing around us if our eyes were opened."

"Amen, Reverend," the Mrs. Cullins look-alike said.

"I'm preaching the gospel tonight, right here." Cleveland pointed at the dirty floor. "Get the church and as many unsaved as you can find in here. Be safe, but get them in here. We should be fine. If not? I would rather preach the gospel in chains than not at all."

"You could get reclaimed, though," Cougar said. "Where would that leave us?"

"Being in the company of Peter and Paul is not that bad," Cleveland said. He stepped toward Cougar and placed his hands on his shoulders. "They may kill me before this is all over. It may be God's will. When and if they do, you four will need to step up. Until that time gets here, I will be praying God gives you strength when that hour comes."

The Mrs. Cullins look-alike put both hands to her chest. Cleveland embraced her. He tried to squeeze his understanding into her through the hug. "Listen, dear, there is a reason for the evil in this world. Believe me, I have seen it. However you cut it, it's a small price to pay to be close to God."

"Amen, Reverend," she said.

The five souls in the dusty storeroom beneath downtown Houston gathered together, hand in hand.

"One more thing before we pray," Cleveland said. "Pray for Charles Graves. I know what you all think, but he's still a man, and he ain't out of the reach of God. I even hope he comes tonight. If anyone needs it, he does. Saul was a destroyer of God's children before he was Paul."

He smiled that smile that only pastors can smile.

EIGHT

"What else is in the sky besides satellites?" Julia said.

Clouds, birds, airplanes, helicopters. Uh ... UFOs. Missiles, rainbows.

Hang on, Girly-Girl.

Why? I thought we agreed to use intuition on this one.

What I agreed to was trusting your intuition to know that he meant more than the obvious satellite reference. Logic, however, will solve the puzzle.

He loves that wood puzzle thing doesn't he?

Yes, he does. Now focus. What's the context in which he delivered the puzzle to you?

He was downtown, sitting on the sidewalk.

Good. Now analyze the statement within its context.

What do you mean?

I mean if you were sitting on the sidewalk downtown, what would you see in the sky.

The sun?

Probably only at noon. Now why would that be?

Because it's blocked by the buildings?

Good. And what is another name for the buildings downtown?

Skyscrapers!

Precisely. I think the odds are pretty good that's what he meant by the sky. It fits better than anything else so far. Let's take it out for a drive and see how it performs. What kind of wheel is in a skyscraper?

I saw this restaurant one time that rotated. It was at the top of a tower. What do you think?

Hmm. Not promising. Can't make a link to it. Any other ideas?

Wheel: the lowest possible straight in poker. Prehistoric invention. Boethius's wheel of fortune. Roulette. *The Price is Right.* A big-shot, a cartwheel, a wagon-wheel. A style of offense in basketball . . .

Girly-Girl, think Orson Wells.

"*The Third Man,*" Julia said. "It's gotta be!"

Julia thought of Orson Wells sitting across from Joseph Cotton, attempting to justify his evil actions.

Where were they sitting, Girly-Girl?

On a Ferris wheel!

Code broken, GG.

"Of course! Farris! Sitting in his loft looking down on Charles. The wheel in the sky." She stared at Spock. "What do I do now?"

Nothing, GG. Just wait.

• • •

From the darkness of the corridor, Charles saw the donor part with his accomplice at Johnny Taco's. After waiting a minute, the donor disappeared down the dark hall to Charles's right. The accomplice ordered something from Johnny's and carried it with him on his way to joining the donor.

Sometime later, two men and a woman he did not recognize exited from the corridor ahead of the donor and his accomplice. Charles had almost walked down the corridor right into the donor's friends.

As it was, he waited thirty minutes after the donor left before investigating. He thought about trailing the donor but decided against it. This was where they'd all been headed.

Charles found the door at the end of the corridor without incident. He tried the door. Unlocked. He paused. Why would they leave it unlocked? Maybe there is someone still inside. No. It's been long enough. They are either very trusting or don't want a locked door drawing attention. Maybe this room is so old the lock is broken, or maybe since they have to sneak in, they don't want it locked. Not everyone could have a key. Nobody knows about this old hallway, judging by the dirt and trash.

It doesn't matter. Go in.

He found a light switch right inside the door and flipped it on. Just your basic abandoned maintenance room doubling as a sanctuary for a church in exile. Workbenches and tables had been dismantled and were leaning against the wall on the far side of the room, next to some storage rooms or utility closets and a chain-link bullpen that extended two yards from the wall. There were holes in the floor where the tables and benches had been fastened.

The room was covered in what appeared to be years of dust, dirt, and trash. It was orders of magnitude times nastier than the hallway on the first floor of the agency, but to Charles it was simply dirty, not sinister like that hallway. The room was stale, but the air didn't stink, except for perhaps a faint hint of lubricant.

I wonder how the electricity gets paid. Someone from the city is in on it, no doubt. He closed the door. Charles figured it could hold a hundred or two hundred people easy. Makes for a granddaddy of a bust, he thought.

A makeshift pulpit was erected at the head of the room, about thirty paces from the door where he stood. Two wooden beams leaned against the wall behind the pulpit. Charles saw they were notched to fit together for a cross come service time. If those people were Cleveland's leadership team and they just had a meeting here, I'll bet they'll come back with two hundred people for a service. He felt for the transmitter he'd used on Creekside. Get ready, old pal. You'll have to squawk loud to get through these walls.

Had it been a mistake to ditch the GPS? Probably not. If I set this transmitter off at the beginning of the service, there will be plenty of time for the troops to arrive. And if Farris knew I was here now, he'd be poking his ridiculous nose around, messing things up. Farris nosing around—gotta love it.

"All I need now is a good hiding place," Charles said.

He saw in the back an old-fashioned air conditioning condenser. There was a fair amount of trash in front of it. Bags and bags worth. Enough to hide a horse. Charles crossed the room and rearranged the trash around the condenser. The arrangement allowed a place for him to lie down without being seen. Yet he could see out from several vantage points through portals in the trash.

That'll do.

He stepped out of the trash and returned to the light switch. He took a mental picture of the back of the room toward the condenser in order to be able to find it in the dark. He noticed where he'd disturbed the dust in the room. It did not resemble footprints, but someone cognizant of such things might be able to detect an intruder. *Can't do anything about it. If I tried, it would be more obvious than it is now. You're trained to notice such things, they aren't. Quit worrying. And, oh yeah, they won't beat you up if they find you.*

Charles cut the light and walked straight at the condenser in the dark. He crossed the room, trying to not stir up any more dust. When he estimated he was three-fourths of the way across, he slowed, walking with his arms in front. He found the trash and felt his way around to his hiding place.

He was fast asleep in ten minutes.

"Julia, Fah-reese here. Any news on Charles?"

Julia snapped herself to attention. The wheel was spinning. "Hi, Richard. How are you?"

"Well. Thanks. Here at the loft. Thought I might drop down to street level and have a look at things. Where's Charles at?"

What do I do? What do I do? What do I d—

Chill, Girly-Girl. That's the first thing.

Julia held her breath and studied the GPS screen. "He's on Hamilton Street between Third and Fourth."

"If that's the case, I should be able to spot him from the window. Hang on a minute. I'll grab my field glasses."

Think, Julia, think. He won't see him and you know it. What then?

"I don't see a whole lot," Farris said. "There are a few folks down there, but no one who looks like Charles."

"How would you know whom to look for?"

"I don't, but there's not many people down there, and none of them are acting like a plant."

"That's a good thing," Julia said.

"I suppose."

Gamble time, Girly-Girl. "You could go down and observe firsthand."

"I could," Farris said, "but I have a better idea. Why don't you give me a rundown on his whereabouts today?"

"Okay." Julia felt her mind starting to swim. Hold on. Got to be cool. "He was stationary on Hamilton all morning, then loitered outside the Caroline building for four hours, then to his present location." I hope he buys it. I won't have an answer if he asks if he entered the Caroline.

"Why wasn't I notified?" Farris asked.

Sometimes aggression works best, GG. He won't expect it. I promise.

"They were standard movements, Farris. What do you want me to do, call you every time he blows his nose? My standard operating procedure is to influence the operation as little as possible."

Silence from Farris's end. Julia hoped logic girl was right.

I'm right, GG. Right as rain. As usual. My being right is your real standard operating procedure. SOP, as we say in the biz.

"I'm going downstairs," Farris said. "I want a complete movement analysis on my desk in the morning, SOP or not."

"Will do," Julia said.

No, you won't, GG.

Charles dreamt. He floated in the darkness of the storeroom like a spirit. He saw himself sleeping behind the condenser.

His spirit floated through the wall of the storeroom out into the food court. It floated past Johnny Taco's, past a restaurant called the Chicken Ranch, and past Ground Zero. It floated through the corridor and up the stairs. At the top of the stairs, a preteen boy with hollow eyes stood waving.

Charles floated through the red diamond entrance where the boy had been and hovered over the street outside. Everywhere the world had turned over. And everywhere he saw people oblivious to the change.

Pedestrians rushed to and fro. Cars accelerated to red lights. People talked endlessly on cell phones, saying nothing. It was a unified, meaningless cacophony. Everyone is in a hurry, but they have nowhere to go. Why would you speed to a red light?

What's the meaning of it all? Hurry to grow up. Hurry to graduate from school. Hurry to get a job. Hurry to raise a family. Hurry to retire. Hurry to die. What's the point?

Charles floated upward. He drifted past Farris's balcony. Farris was busy slaughtering a pig underneath the bust of Caesar. The blood from the hog filled the balcony, spilling over the sides in a crimson waterfall. Farris bowed in front of the bust. Crowds stood below on the pavement, cheering madly, dancing in the red rain of swine blood.

Charles floated on. He left downtown behind, the revelry of the crowd still ringing in his ears.

An unknown force propelled him forward. Soon, he recognized beneath him a part of town he hadn't seen since he'd been a child. He fought to reverse course. He fought to change course. But he was not strong enough.

He was descending on Graves Mansion. His spirit passed through the roof and alit at the top of the gold-inlaid stairway. *No. Anything but this. Please.* The staircase extended itself until it was thirty floors high.

He hovered in front of his brother. They stared eye to eye. His brother began to teeter-totter like Charles's donation can after a donation. Unlike the can, however, Charles's brother toppled over. He fell and fell. Charles felt a ripping sensation on his left cheek.

He watched his brother splatter the marble floor at the base of the stairs.

Wake up, you ninny, the dark man said. It's time to go to work.

Charles jerked to consciousness. He was not alone in Reverend Cleveland's underground sanctuary. He rubbed his eyes. His stomach growled. He sought his nearest pre-formed peephole.

There must be three hundred people in here. How did they do it? What a gutsy move. Stupid, but gutsy.

What time is it? How long did I sleep? He felt for the transmitter. It was in his right hip pocket. He took it out and thought to call in the troops. Not yet, Charles. Not yet.

The lights were on. The congregation was mingling. Charles switched to a different viewing portal and saw two more entering. A man with a red cap stood at the door. He closed it after the two entered.

Five minutes passed. The man with the red cap opened the door to let another congregant enter. He shut the door and gestured with his hand.

The lights shut off. In the pitch black, a single voice began to sing. It reminded Charles of a lullaby his mother used to sing to put him to sleep. The congregation joined in the singing. The room erupted in song. The hair stood up on Charles's arms. They sang for fifteen minutes. It was hypnotic.

The singing ended and the room fell silent. The dark man whispered in Charles's ear. We got 'em now. This is huge. Let's see. So far we got 'em on illegal assembly and songs not on the ASL. We'll get 'em all. Farris don't have nothin' on us now.

Ssssh, Charles said. I gotta make sure Cleveland is here.

In the dark, a lone voice cried out. "The Lord is in His holy temple. Let all the earth keep silence before Him."

Dead silence. After what seemed a localized eternity in the dark, a single floodlight suspended from the wall behind the makeshift podium clicked on. The man with the red cap stepped into the light. He took off the cap and laid it on the floor. "One announcement tonight. We will meet again next week. Your cell leader will inform you of the time and location. Thank you."

During the announcement, Charles stood. Staying behind his wall of trash he moved to the side of the condenser, where there was a better view.

There won't be a meeting next week, the dark man said.

Charles stared at the light. It formed a halo on the pulpit. It was so bright in the dark room that everything else faded in front of the last row of congregants. An imposing silhouette stepped behind the pulpit and into the light. Charles could not distinguish the face. It was the outline of a man in the light. It must be Cleveland, he thought. He retrieved the transmitter from his pocket.

Now, said the dark man. Now!

Hang on a minute, Charles said. Let me make sure.

The man who might or might not be Reverend James Cleveland began his sermon. "Tradition tells us that the apostle Peter was crucified upside down on a cross because he considered himself unworthy to die as Christ did. All the apostles, save John the Revelator, died horrible deaths because they refused to bury the gospel in the earthen vessels of their bodies. They refused to place a bushel over the light and life they found in Jesus Christ our Lord. I ask you then: why today have we become frightened of the gospel?"

"Amen, Reverend!" a voice said. A host of amens followed.

The silhouette moved around the pulpit toward the congregation. The silhouette grew as it came closer. Charles stood on a wooden box to get a better view.

The reverend's voice somehow got bigger. "I repeat. Why then today have we become frightened of the gospel? Many even here in our midst consider their temporal security worth more than the lost receiving the blessed news of our most holy and beautiful Savior, who forever reigns in glory."

With the flood lamp on and about three hundred people in the room, the air grew thick and heavy. The silhouette took out a handkerchief and wiped its brow.

The preacher's voice was nearing sermon pitch. "Stephen was stoned for the love of Christ. His last words echo throughout all of eternity: 'Lord, do not hold this sin against them.' Yet we continue to be a clan of closed-mouth men."

The room fell silent. Charles placed his thumb on the transmitter button. It's got to be him. But I'll give it a minute or two. Someone is bound to yell "Amen, Cleveland." Why did he have to mention Stephen? His brother's name.

Again, the silhouette wiped its brow. "Many of you fear not your God who is a consuming fire. You fear not the devil and his demons. You even fear not the pit of eternal damnation in hellfire. You have let it be known that you fear the long arm of the law known as Charles Graves. Yes, I have heard the rumors. Yes, I have heard that he is combing the city searching for us.

"Well, brothers and sisters, tonight I want to pretend that Charles Graves is here tonight. I want you to think: if he were here tonight, what would we say to him? What should we say to him? Tonight I am bringing my gospel message to Charles Graves."

Charles's mouth hung open. He stared at the light as if in a trance.

It's just superb oratory, Charles. Get hold of yourself, the dark man said.

This was the Reverend James Cleveland. He knew it now. He no longer needed someone to confirm it for him. This voice, this presence, this was why his father and the entire government feared this man.

Cleveland transitioned from the introductory section of his sermon. He was gathering steam. His voice thundered. "My God is the great King of kings and Lord of lords. He is the Alpha and Omega, the Holy One of Israel, and the fairest of ten thousand. He is the almighty Majesty who reigns in glory. *'Where were you, Charles Graves, when I laid the earth's foundations?'* says the Lord of life."

Sweat broke out on Charles's brow.

"*Do you have an arm like God's, Charles Graves, and can your voice thunder like His? Then adorn yourself with glory and splendor, and clothe yourself in honor and majesty. Crush the wicked where they stand. 'Then I Myself,' says the Lord God Almighty, 'will admit to you that your own right hand can save you.'*"

Charles felt his legs grow weak.

"Charles Graves," the reverend said, "your own right hand cannot save you."

Charles stared at his right hand in the dark. His hand loosened. The transmitter fell softly into the trash on the floor.

It's impossible. He can't be talking to me. It's a coincidence.

He thought there was another voice in his head now, but it was faint, as if it were behind a wall. On the other side of that wall, the dark man clawed to get through.

Charles stepped out from behind his blind. He needed to get out of this room. Now. He had to escape this pit of darkness. Maybe he could sneak out and lock the door behind him. Charles started toward the door, trying not to draw attention to himself. At least the room was still dark.

The Reverend stepped forward out of the light where he could no longer be seen. His voice calmed. His words were more controlled. Charles heard the preacher's voice. He knew it to be Cleveland, yet it seemed to be a higher voice calling.

"No, Charles, you cannot save yourself. You are a man of a thousand faces, Charles Graves. You are a man of disguise because you do not know who you are. You don't know your own soul. You are an actor on a stage who plays a thousand roles yet is lost when he leaves the theater."

Charles froze. The light was now all that he saw. His eyes fixed on it.

A muffled and distant voice called to him. It was the dark man. He screamed at the top of his lungs. *You fool! You fool!* He screamed over and over. He was locked in a padded cell.

For the first time in his life, Charles forgot the dark man. The light flooded his entire consciousness, his entire being.

"Charles, you cannot save yourself, nor can any earthly being. However, there is one, and only one, whose sandals we are not fit to untie, who loves you and died for you."

Cleveland remained silent for a few seconds.

It was the longest four seconds of Charles's life, longer than his mother scaling the Graves Mansion staircase, longer than his brother descending them. He was being drawn into this light in the darkness of this abandoned storeroom beneath the heart of the city. It was beautiful to his eyes. He crept nearer. It was irresistible.

"The one whose sandals we are not fit to untie is here tonight, Charles. He is our beautiful Savior, who came to Earth to live and die as an ordinary man. He alone is able to save you, Charles. You, and every other person in this room tonight."

Charles felt his throat swell. He crept nearer. Whatever this was, whatever James Cleveland was saying, Charles knew he needed it. It was as if he were finally hearing the thing he'd been waiting to hear his entire life.

"He is your God and Savior. With Him, Charles, you need no disguise. He knows the deepest reaches of your soul. There is no hiding from Him. Nor should you hide, for in Him is life, and life everlasting. Take off the mask, Charles. Take on the robe of life. He bore your sins on the Cross and died that you might live. If you would cling to Him. Exchange your mask for the love of Christ, Charles Graves."

Charles's eyes let loose with tears. He pushed his way toward the light, flinging himself at it. He reached the reverend, throwing himself on the floor. He cried. "My God, forgive me."

The room was dead silent save for the weeping of Charles Graves. It was the Reverend James Cleveland who spoke first. "He is just and faithful, forgiving all those who call upon His name. What is your name, my friend?"

Charles gazed up from the floor, tears streaming down his cheeks. "Charles Graves."

"You're way too old to be Charl—" The reverend caught himself in mid-sentence.

The Lord was in His holy temple.

NINE

After a full hour's worth of singing and another hour for the congregation to trickle out, only Cleveland and Charles remained. They sat together at the foot of the pulpit. The work lights were on. Cleveland examined the miracle sitting next to him, amazed at God's endless, mysterious ways.

"The Lord is truly amazing," Cleveland said. "You're right up there with the Red Sea and floating axe heads."

"I'm in shock. I can't believe it happened to me," Charles said. "The funny thing is, I know it's real. I don't know how I know. I just know. I know tonight that Christ found me." Charles tried to cry, but he was all out of tears.

Cleveland gave Charles a good Christian hug. For the next thirty minutes he prayed with, and mostly for, Charles.

After the prayer, Cleveland broke the silence. "Charles, if you don't mind me asking: how did you know we were down here?"

"It's my business to know," Charles said. "If you don't mind me asking, how did you know to preach to me?"

"That's the power of God, Charles. He knows everything. Sometimes, like tonight for example, He chooses to remind us." Cleveland locked Charles with a hard look. "Charles, I detest being a sucker. For all I know you could be as good an actor as you are at disguising yourself. But I believe you because I know the power and beauty of God, and I understand the call of His gospel."

"And maybe because I didn't sic the agency on you and your entire church tonight?"

"I guess you've got a point," Cleveland said.

"If you don't believe me, check behind the A/C condenser. You'll find the transmitter."

"I believe you, Charles."

"Reverend, I have so many questions."

"I'm sure you do. But not now. We both need rest, so let's go get some. God might be getting busy."

Charles did not understand what Cleveland meant by God getting busy. "Tell me when and where to meet you. I've got something to take care of."

"You're in trouble, ain't ya?" Cleveland asked.

"No more than you."

Cleveland stared at the filthy bum that was Charles Graves. "All right. Let's go for broke." He gave Charles directions to where he could meet him. "Two hours, tops."

"What can I do to repay you?" Charles asked.

"The same thing you can do to earn God's grace, Charles: nothing."

Charles shook his head. "I don't understand it. It's amazing that God remembered me, Reverend." At the word *remember,* an image of his mother flashed in Charles's mind.

"That's His business, Charles."

Charles crawled along the waist-high concrete wall girding floor five of the parking garage and walked toward where his van sat parked in spot 526. He felt the eyes of the police surveillance team peering over the wall, watching for him, even now in the wee hours of the morning. If they'd spotted him, they would've moved to contact him by now. The van was three spots ahead.

Charles reached the front bumper of the van, which was nosed to the wall. He went prone and wedged himself through the narrow gap created by the van's front tire and the wall, rotating to his back as he made the turn under the van. His knees creaked as he executed the turn, then the pressure released as his legs came through the gap. He was face up, staring at the undercarriage of the van. It was inches from his face.

By inching along, Charles reached the rear of the van. His head emerged first, then his arms. He grabbed the bumper and pulled out, crouching.

He cracked the van's back door open, just enough to allow him to crawl through. He shut the door behind. He sat in the rear, satisfied the surveillance crew hadn't seen him and was unable to peer this far into the back of the van. If they hadn't noticed him yet, he was safe.

Charles began preparing a new costume. This one needed to fool the guards at the parking garage entrance. From there it was a sprint into the darkness before the surveillance team could warn the agency to track him via satellite or mobilize a ground unit.

Charles froze. A metallic sound. Something was rattling in the van, like a horde of six-inch long cockroaches trapped in a box. The sound came from the front of the van.

He peered into the passenger seat. The wooden chest. His puzzle pieces were calling him from the chest. Charles prostrated himself and crawled to the front of the van like a reverent man consulting an oracle.

He tipped the chest. Pieces scattered like roaches, then assembled inches in front of his face as if the roaches has discovered a pile of sugar. At first Charles saw the undercarriage of the van. Then his father's face appeared.

It was Frank Cotton Graves, no doubt about it, but without the oak frame the pieces were slightly disjointed, with cracks scattered throughout the image. The cracks seemed incongruous for a politician. Cotton spoke, and the van exploded with mystic light.

"Unacceptable, Charles," Cotton said. "Unacceptable."

"I . . . couldn't help it," Charles said. "It was real."

"Seems real," Cotton said. "Seems real. It'll seem not so real in the morning. A few days later, it'll seem even less real. Weeks down the line, it'll seem like the dream that it is. Let it go."

"I can't. It was too real."

"No, it wasn't. You were tired and stressed. It was an emotional reaction, nothing more."

The light emanating from the image intensified, blinding Charles. In his blindness, Charles heard the roaches at work again. He felt one crawl across his hand. Charles swatted at his chest, bruising himself in an attempt to get the roaches off. Then he could see again.

The new image was of a decayed head, more gruesome than the skull he had seen in his mother's car outside the bowling alley. The cracks in the image added to the effect, creating wrinkles in the thing's face. The light was gone from the image, and Charles thought roaches really were crawling around the grotesque head.

His mother's voice came from the monstrosity. "Charles, it was real. You remembered. Don't let anyone tell you any different."

"No," Charles said. He covered his face with his hands. "No. I can't stand the thought of you like this."

"I'm in a much better place, Charles. Don't worry for me."

With his hands over his face, her voice sounded sweet, just like he remembered. Charles dared a look back between his fingers. His mother was back to normal. He saw the hint of a red dress around the base of her neck.

"Mom?"

"Yes, Charles. I don't have much time, so listen. You remembered. Don't you see? Your whole life has been going in the wrong direction until now. Not just the drunkenness, but the whole misguided thing. The rush into meaninglessness and madness. That's over now. What happened to you is real. It happened to me a long time ago, and it happened to millions of others. You'll come to see this in time. For now, just hang on. As time goes by, it'll become clearer to you."

"Mom, I—"

"No, Charles, there's nothing you can do for me. I want you to listen to Cleveland. Listen to what he says. The meaning of your new life will be clear soon enough."

"*Mother!*"

The image began to turn back. His mother's soft skin began to fade, harden. The cracks returned. The death mask returned.

Charles shut his face in his hands before the transformation was complete.

"Are you really going to fall for all that?" Charles saw the light of the puzzle return through his fingers. Cotton was back. "Do you have any idea what havoc this 'new life' is going to cause for you, and probably us?"

Charles rolled to his back on the floor of the van. "Would you please turn out that stupid light before we get caught?"

"They can't see it. I wish they could. If I thought it would do any good, I'd turn it up higher."

"I guess it's a good thing you can't work the horn and the headlights," Charles said.

"Son—"

"Forget it, Dad. I'm going ahead with this. At least for a while. We'll see who's right. If I get over it in a week or so like you said, no worries. We'll see. I'll come find you soon either way."

The light subsided in the van. Charles imagined his mother smiling on the dark roof of the van. She seemed to float for a moment before disappearing.

"The headlong 'rush into madness,' or away from it. Hard to tell," Charles said. "We'll see."

As the sun came up, Charles arrived at the safe house Cleveland had told him about in the storeroom. Charles saw the Reverend Cleveland wearing slippers, red warm-up pants, and a T-shirt with a picture of Bum Phillips on it. Cleveland was motioning him to pull in. Charles pulled his van onto a shell driveway lined by hedges leading to a garage. Charles pulled in the garage, and Cleveland closed the door behind him.

The garage was attached by an enclosed walkway to a one-story house. The house had tan siding and a new roof. Two poodles patrolled the front yard, which featured a layered flower garden enclosed by a waist-high chain-link fence. Two oaks stood in the front yard ten feet apart. They were ringed by stones with red mulch covering the base of the trees. He was in Houston's Third Ward, a hair southeast of downtown.

Ingraham was right. There must be at least a thousand places to hide in Houston's inner loop. Charles got out of the van. "It's perfect."

"We have several like it, and plenty of non-residences as well," Cleveland said. "The church ain't done. It's in hiding."

"It's gone underground," Charles said.

"Technically, no," Cleveland said. "The visible church is on the run, perhaps, but the invisible church is alive and well. This ain't the first time."

"You've got a lot of teaching to do," Charles said.

"Maybe, but not now. First we need some grub and some rest. And you, my friend, need a shower. Your disguise is a little too authentic."

The two men stepped out of the garage into the walkway leading to the house. The walkway was enclosed, with two sky-lights, windows, and a concrete path between two beds of dirt with no plants. Charles paused.

Cleveland took two more steps before stopping. "What?"

Charles peered out at the street through a window in the walkway. There was no traffic on the street. "Are there people here?"

"Sure. Why?"

"I'm worried they might not like me so much."

Cleveland smiled that smile that only pastors can smile. "Yeah, I git ya. Do you know who the apostle Paul was?"

"The Damascus Road guy, right?"

"Right," Cleveland said. "And before that?"

"Hmm, not real sure."

"His name was Saul, and he was a persecutor of the church. Had guys executed and stuff. After he saw the light and met Christ on the Damascus Road, his life changed and he became one of the greatest of the apostles. Problem was, the Christians didn't trust him at first. Even the other apostles were afraid of him. But once they saw the Spirit at work in him, they accepted him as a brother."

Charles thought about Paul and the light on the Damascus Road. He saw himself in the abandoned storeroom being drawn to an all-consuming light. He thought about Christ.

"It'll be that way for you too," Cleveland said. "They will not trust you at first, but when they see the Spirit at work, that'll change."

Charles shuffled. "Do you have a Bible story for every situation?"

"Would you trust a book that didn't? Would God's Word to man not?" He tilted his head. "Don't get me started preaching now."

One of the poodles in the front yard barked. Both men looked outside but saw nothing. Charles refocused his attention back on Cleveland, but he sensed another presence nearby.

And that's all they are, Charles: stories, the dark man said. Remember that. Your mom used to tell them to you. They were stories then, they are stories now. You think because you saw a light and heard some good oratory something changed? Well, something changed all right, and I'll even admit it's your life that changed. But not for the better, you moron. The world has turned over and you should have rolled with it. Now it's about to roll over you. That's the change coming. And all the stories in the world can't change that.

"What's wrong, Charles?" Cleveland took a step toward Charles.

I thought you were locked away, Charles thought. I thought you were gone.

You would think that, the dark man said. I'll be here for a lonnnnnnnnnng time. You'll never get rid of me.

Charles took Cleveland's outstretched hand. "I'm fine. Just had a visit from an old friend of mine. I thought he was gone. I'd like to ask you about him, but right now I like your eat, clean up, and sleep plan."

"Let's go in then," Cleveland said. "And you can let me do the talking. At least at first."

Yeah, let's go in, the dark man said.

Cleveland led Charles to the end of the walkway and rapped three times on the door to the house. It opened outward toward the men. Twin barrels of a shotgun appeared and pointed at Charles. Cleveland's initial thought was "I ain't marryin' him."

"How many times have I told you to get rid of that thing," Cleveland said. "If Christ comes back, will He find faith on the earth?"

"It ain't loaded," a voice said.

"Then why you got it out?" Cleveland's voice was at half-sermon volume.

"I don't trust him."

"You think he trusts you with that scatter-gun starin' at him?" Cleveland took the barrel of the gun and pulled it away. He cracked open the gun. It was not loaded. "Come on in, Charles."

The two men entered the house. Cleveland shut the door and turned on the light. It was a comfortable, lived-in house with tile floors, wood-paneled walls, and plenty of used furniture. There was a kitchen to the left, a living room to the right, and a hall leading to two bedrooms straight ahead. A cat lounged on the back of a brown leather couch in the living room. The house smelled of potpourri.

The woman took two steps backward toward the kitchen. She was African American, middle-aged, with hard features on a soft face, and straight black shoulder-length hair with gray streaks. She wore a pink bathrobe with an LS monogram, and pink slippers to match. Her toes stuck out of the oval holes at the end of the slippers. Her big toenail was missing on her right foot.

Cleveland motioned to Charles. "This is Charles Graves."

Charles stuck out his right hand.

"I know you didn't bring no Charles Graves into my house." The woman shifted her weight to the left and put up her right hand.

Cleveland continued as if he didn't notice. "Charles, this is Lasanya. Sounds like the food, but it ain't."

Lasanya stood pat. "He stinks."

All things considered, this is going better than I figured, Cleveland thought. We'll have won her over soon. The rest will be easy. Lasanya will see to that.

"That's why you are going to let him borrow your shower," he said aloud. "Then we'll cook some breakfast, eat it, and go to sleep."

"This look like some kind of boardin' house to you?" Lasanya said.

"'And she brought forth her firstborn son, and wrapped him in swaddling clothes, and laid him in a manger; because there was no room for them in the inn,'" Cleveland said.

"You got one of them stories for everything, don't you?" Lasanya glared at Charles and pointed at Cleveland. "You're lucky he's here. I'd a kilt you dead."

"The gun wasn't loaded," Charles said.

"I'd a beat you over the head with it. Look at you. You just a rundown bum. Why's everyone so scared a' you?"

Charles pulled half of his face off. "How's that for starters?"

Lasanya screeched. She pulled off one pink slipper and slapped Cleveland on the chest. "Why you wanna bring this thing in my house?" She glared back at Charles. "Do that again."

Charles pulled off some more of his face and both ears. Lasanya screeched again, this time with a hint of pleasure. She disappeared into the kitchen. Charles gestured a "that oughta do it" sign to Cleveland. Lasanya returned with a wet rag. She caressed Charles's face with the rag. It removed days' worth of grime, dirt, and dried sweat along with Charles's makeup. Lasanya returned for a second wet cloth, this time making sure it was doused in warm water.

She continued to wipe Charles's face. She stopped when the scar became visible. "Oh, baby." She caressed the scar with two long fingers. "Man who got a scar like that gots a story to tell, maybe more than one. Got some pain too." Her eyes welled up. "You come on over and sit down," she said. "Lasanya's gonna fix you something good to eat."

This is way better than I imagined, Cleveland thought. Won't be nothin' to it now. Lasanya has a lot of discernment too. Makes me think I was right about him. Yes, Lord, forgive me. I doubted. Lead the way, though. I don't know what to do from here.

Cleveland led Charles to the bathroom. "Tomorrow, we baptize you. For now, take a shower."

When Charles returned, breakfast was ready. When they finished eating, Cleveland took the couch and Charles took a spare room. They slept. Cleveland did not dream.

I wanted to get nine holes in before dark, Frank Cotton Graves thought. What could Ingraham want this late in the afternoon? And what is he doing in Houston?

Cotton swiveled in his chair. He could not count the hours he gazed out the window. The nature preserve behind the agency looked like a heavily wooded fairway. He embraced the view like a lost love.

Or like a long departed spouse? That qualifies as lost love, doesn't it, Cotton? You ought to jump out that window, you coward, instead of staring out of it. This is a blood view. You paid for it with Teresa.

Quit. Guilt is no good, Cotton. You tried. You know you tried. She wouldn't listen to reason. She did not have to do what she did. If she believed all that Christian stuff, she should have been a submissive wife. Then she would still be here.

Cotton watched a flock of seagulls heading toward Galveston. To be free, he thought.

But you are free. Free because someone else paid the fare. Is that what they meant by "love your wife as Christ loved the church"? Didn't think so, Cotton. And think what it's done to Charles. With Stephen gone, you should have at least cared for Charles more. He's a wreck.

But I did care for Charles. Spent most of my waking hours caring for him. You have to admit that considering all he's been through, he's pretty successful. Ask Sheila how much time I have spent with him, or at least worrying and caring for him.

Why don't we ask Teresa?

Shut up!

That must be it, Cotton thought. Ingraham must want to talk about Charles. Is he dead? I wonder what's—

"Cotton," Sheila said, "your visitor called. He's in the elevator."

Cotton lifted his feet and pushed the glass. His chair spun around. "Send him over when he gets here."

"Are you upset, Cotton?" Sheila twirled a lock of her hair right above the shoulder.

"Nothing I can't handle." He maneuvered the chair up to the desk and sat up straight.

TEN

John Ingraham sat across the desk from Frank Cotton Graves. It was 3:30 in the afternoon.

"John, how are you?" Cotton said. "I have to admit, this is an unexpected visit. Can't be a good sign."

Ingraham leaned over and picked up Graves's nameplate. He spun it around a couple of times, replacing it on the desk facedown. "Cotton, please allow me to talk to you as a friend for a minute or two. Unofficially," Ingraham said. "I fear this will not be pleasant."

"By all means," Cotton said. He sat forward with his elbows on the desk, one hand over the other, supporting his chin.

Diplomatic or direct? he thought.

Diplomatic of course, you fool. Don't trust that friend routine. Men do not become national directors by being friendly. I know that's what they teach in orientations and management classes, but you know better. He's an older version of Farris.

And get your face prepared. What he is about to say may tax your emotions. Don't let it show. Start him out with something like this:

"I suppose this is serious," Cotton said aloud. "I cannot conceive of a pleasant reason for you to return to Houston so abruptly."

Ingraham did not move. His line of sight was anchored to Cotton's face. "There is a serious problem with Belt Buckle. After these many years serving together, I wanted to tell you in person."

Here it comes. Brace your face.

"I have ordered Keesma and Louis to Houston. They are already on the scene." Ingraham maintained his stare. His eyes hardly blinked.

Cotton felt the eyes boring into his mind. Better alter the playing field. "John," he said, "I am on the team. You know that. Whatever this is—and again I am prepared for the worst—I am on the team. Tell me, Charles is dead, isn't he? That's it, isn't it? It couldn't be anything else. How did it happen?"

"In a sense perhaps," Ingraham said. "Cotton, it seems Charles has disappeared. We are all very concerned."

Concerned with yourselves, maybe. Charles, what's happened? "Disappeared? What happened?"

"We're not sure. As I mentioned, Keesma and Louis are already on the scene. I have ordered Farris to assume control of the operation immediately."

"Absolutely," Cotton said. "The operation must be run by the book, like any other. No question about that. I am behind you all the way. If that's what you came all the way down here to find out, then I can set your mind at ease." Cotton let his face sink down into his palms.

"I am pleased to hear you say that," Ingraham said.

"Do we have any idea about Charles? Is there any trace? Any idea?"

Ingraham returned Cotton's nameplate to its upright position. "This may be difficult for you to hear, Cotton."

You don't know difficult, pal. First a child, then a spouse, now an adult child. You don't know difficult, pardner. I'm going to break down right here in front of the national director. Yippee-kai-yay.

"Try me," Cotton said.

"We have reason to believe Charles has defected."

Cotton felt his jaw drop. Defected? To China. That's impossible. He didn't have his passport on him.

For the first time, Ingraham let his eyes wander from Cotton's face. He looked at his watch. "We think it was sometime early this morning. That affords him a day's head start."

Head start? To China? Of course not. To where then?

Get a hold of yourself, Cotton. Consider the bright side. You're so surprised you don't have to put on an act for Ingraham. Think now. Think fast.

Cotton sighed and leaned back in his chair. It creaked. It was a slight creak, but it creaked. He rubbed the brass buttons on the armrest, then brought his hands together at his chin, with two fingers reaching up past his lips. "Level with me, John. What is happening?"

Ingraham hesitated. "Our best estimate is that he has thrown in with James Cleveland. We cannot be certain, but our squad surveilling the parking garage recorded his van exiting the garage."

"That's impossible. Guards were stationed at all exits."

"You forget who *we* are dealing with. What we think is that Charles snuck in through the back of the garage, somehow got into his van, arranged a disguise to mimic one of the outside agents, and exited the garage as if it were one of them taking the van out for some legit reason. By the time we mobilized, the van had disappeared."

He said who we are dealing with. That's good for you, Cotton. He thinks you are on the team, at least for now. It's bad for Charles though. What is wrong with that boy? His mother's genes of course. What to do? It's decision time again. Or is diplomacy still in order?

"Maybe he needed a break," Cotton said, as if trying to make sense of it—which he was. "Maybe he started Belt Buckle too soon after Creekside. He wouldn't be the first to crack on assignment."

"Perhaps, but the evidence doesn't seem to indicate psychological issues. Julia Jenkins prepared a tracking analysis of his GPS coordinates for the time in question. She determined he planted his GPS tracking device on a downtown office worker to throw us off the trail. We found the device in the woman's purse. She was unaware of its presence."

"I'm not following the logic," Cotton said.

"His last words were 'I've got a prospect.' We believe he made contact with Cleveland. Hours later, he retrieved his van and fled. Cleveland has vanished as well. It is not an ironclad case, but we have to proceed on the basis a defection has taken place.

"Maybe it will end up as a false alarm. However, if Charles has indeed defected, think of the problems he could cause for us with his abilities. Not to mention what it would do to embolden our enemies if they thought the great Charles Graves was no longer hunting them—that he was now on their side. Cotton, he could already have Cleveland through the cordon and on his way to anywhere in the country."

"That would be a disaster," Cotton said. "I can't imagine Charles doing this."

Yes, you can. Like mother, like son. You can believe it because you have always half-expected it. That encounter with Keesma and Louis didn't help matters much either. It might have sent him over the edge. You'd better brace your face again. The thrilling conclusion of the Ingraham episode is approaching, and you are going to supply the cliffhanger.

"What is, is," Ingraham said. "We have a go-forward plan in place. I do not intend to give you details. Listen to me, Cotton. Listen very carefully. Here is the deal. It is nonnegotiable."

"I'm listening."

"I am not giving you the details because of your relation to Charles. We expect him to make contact with you sooner or later. The less you know, the better. If we handle it in this manner, we will not be forced to suspect you. Your job in the operation from here on is a limited one. You will assist us in any way possible, when and only when we request it.

"With your knowledge of Charles, you may be able to decipher his actions at a crucial juncture. We will have you under house arrest, here at the agency, with constant monitoring. This is because we know you are not involved, Cotton. So, in exchange for your assistance and silence, you will retire at the end of this operation. You will be given a sizeable nest egg and full accommodations. It's a great deal, Cotton. Please be smart enough to realize that."

"Haven't I always?" Cotton said.

"Besides," Ingraham said with a shrug, "it may all be a false alarm."

"I am getting the feeling it's not," Cotton said. "One thing, though: can Sheila stay on as my secretary during this portion of the operation?"

Ingraham bellowed. "I knew there was a reason I liked you, Cotton." Ingraham shook Cotton's hand and left the office.

Cotton twirled in his chair, embracing the view like a lost love.

Julia Jenkins passed John Ingraham on her way out the wooden revolving doors.

Outside, the air was muggy although the shadows were advancing against the daylight. An isolated thundercloud rumbled in the distance. She glanced over at it but did not feel threatened. What caught her eye, however, was a jet descending to Houston Hobby Airport. The jet was silent at its distance, yet she imagined its roar consuming her. It worked its way in through her fingertips, up her arms, into her chest, and at last throughout her entire body. She shivered in the heat as she walked toward her car.

I don't understand, Charles. Why did you do it? What got into you?

She reached the first row of cars, pausing for two men in a Cadillac to pass by. It was muggier in the parking lot. Heat rose from the concrete. Her car was five rows back.

You do not compute, Charles. Did you get hold of some booze out there on the streets, or something worse? Did you check out because of the guilt? Because of the pain of loss? Was it that dark man guy? Did he do this to you? We were so close. Now you're gone, and I've stuck my neck out for you by lying to Farris. Thanks.

She passed another couple of rows.

I know you get tired of me butting in, GG, but it seems to me he was coherent and logical when he checked out. Yep, I used the "L" word: logic. Charles wears a lot of disguises. This time maybe he disguised himself as logical. Hard to believe, I know, but Mr. Charles may be totin' more gray matter than he has let on.

"*Ugh!*" Julia said. "If this keeps up I may be the one handing out weird letters." She passed another row of cars.

For example, he did use the other L word when he signed off. No, not "logic," GG—the other one, the big kahuna L word. Now that could mean he was planning to kill himself, that he was planning to disappear, or that he was on to something. Plus, didn't he give you that nifty puzzle there at the end? Not exactly crazy man stuff. My money's on Charles. Something's up, GG. Get ready.

She crossed the last row leading to her car.

Real quick then, GG. Remember back at Old Bones Lane when I told you I would explain to you why you knew that he needed you then? It's that L word thing. You have it for him— and I don't mean logic. I didn't think you were ready to hear it then, but you are now. You have to be ready now. 'Cause it's here. You know he needs you. You know he'll be around. And you also know you need him. Search your heart, Girly-Girl. Tell me I'm wrong.

You're not. You seldom are. It's that L thing. Logic.

Thanks, GG. Now get ready. There's a change a comin'. Your life is about to turn over.

Julia unlocked her car and slid behind the wheel. She backed out of her space, left the parking lot, and started toward home.

After ten minutes of driving, the computer broke the silence. "Incoming from Richard Farris."

Julia could tell the computer voice recognition was having difficulty pronouncing Farris's name, as if it were confused. It came out garbled, halfway between Farris and Fah-reese.

"Pompous pearl boy." She blushed as she remembered a time she'd blurted out a more descriptive epithet when she'd thought the audio was off. It had cost her her first professional job. Apparently the boss did not appreciate being exposed in front of the corporate stockholders. But here she was at a much better job, and the events in motion were getting interesting in a hurry.

"Audio on," she said.

"Juuuuleeeee," Farris said.

"Yes, Richard." She pulled under the overpass and headed for the entrance ramp to I-45.

"Nice job on the GPS report," Farris said. "Ingraham put me in charge now that Charles has disappeared. Keesma, Louis, and I—well, Keesma and Louis—are canvassing downtown, questioning pedestrians to see if anyone spotted Charles on the street. He's got a pretty good head start, but we'll catch up to him."

If you're so worried about everyone knowing you're in charge, why don't you hang a forty-foot sign from your balcony? "He'll be tough to catch, I think."

"Nah. He'll make a mistake," Farris said. "By the way, I need copies of the digital files from the last correspondence before he defected. Do you have them?"

Oh, no. He knows. He knows I doctored them. Why else would he want the digitals?

Stop it, Girly-Girl. Settle down. He doesn't know. He won't know. You are the best at what you do. Relax. "Sure. They're at headquarters. I can get them for you." Julia accelerated onto the freeway in front of an eighteen-wheeler.

"Why don't you just bring them by my loft? We should be done on the streets once it gets dark. The crowds are dying down. How about around eight-thirty or nine? I could order dinner in."

"I like men, Farris," Julia said. She achieved a triple lane change across I-45. Ouch. Did I say that? Yep. Audio was on too. Better start preparing for job number three.

"The type that dresses up in costumes, I imagine," he said. "No problem. I have to drop by headquarters to meet with Ingraham tomorrow. Have it ready in the morning. I am interested in it. Fah-reese out."

"Audio off," Julia said.

You better hope you did a good job on that file.

You did, GG. Go home and get some sleep now. I have a feeling you're going to need it. *I like men.* That was a classic. Worth the job too.

Julia accelerated. Things were picking up.

Charles awoke in the dark. He sat up in a strange bed, searching for something to grab hold of. A ceiling fan circled overhead.

He rolled out of the bed. The tiled floor was cool to his feet. He surveyed the room for his clothes but saw none. Van, garage, clothes. The images were disconnected but at length formed a picture in his mind. He rubbed his face.

Charles peered out the door of the spare room and saw no one in the hallway. A faint light shone from the living room, but there was no sound. They're asleep. I can make it.

Charles navigated the hallway and crossed the tiled floor without making a sound. A clock ticked in the kitchen. Charles thought about the ticking clock rather than wondering why Cleveland was not on the couch. He grabbed the doorknob to the door leading to the walkway and turned it. The door gave way and he stepped into the walkway.

Right into where Lasanya and Cleveland stood talking. Charles was in nothing but his underwear. They both looked at him.

Lasanya broke the silence. "You as white as a ghost."

Cleveland laughed with so much force the poodles began to bark in the front yard.

"I'll just get some things," Charles said. He continued on into the garage.

"Is that what y'all were so afraid of?" Lasanya said.

Charles reentered the house in shorts and a T-shirt, holding his wood-block puzzle. Cleveland sat on the couch, drinking a soda, with his feet on a worn coffee table. Lasanya was firing up the stove.

Charles sat in a recliner opposite the couch. "What now?"

"We eat," Cleveland said. "I've been praying on the 'what now' and haven't gotten an answer yet."

"Is that your storybook?" Charles pointed at a Bible on the coffee table.

"Ain't gonna be no blasphemin' in my house, Charles," Lasanya said.

"No offense meant, ma'am," Charles said. He set the wood-block puzzle down on the table.

"That don't mean none was taken," Lasanya said.

Charles sensed she was playing with him.

Cleveland picked up the Bible. "This one's for you," he said. "I figure we need to go over some things before I baptize you."

He handed Charles the Bible. Cleveland opened another Bible and set it on the coffee table in front of him. "Open yours, Charles."

Charles opened his Bible. Cleveland thumbed through it upside down until he reached the Gospel of John. He opened his to the same page. "In the beginning was the Word."

Sometime later, Lasanya entered the living room carrying chicken fried steak and mashed potatoes. She set a glass of milk next to Charles. "Y'all eat up now. You're fixin' to get your 'what now' and you'll need your strength."

"We just ate, didn't we?" Charles asked.

Cleveland raised his eyes from his Bible. "You were asleep for about fourteen hours, Charles."

"What time is it?"

"About eleven-thirty," Cleveland said. "Lunchtime."

Charles sliced the steak into bite-sized pieces. He mixed a piece with a bite of mashed potato, dipped it into some white gravy, and ate. It was delicious. He wanted an excuse to eat and not talk. "How do we know what to do from here?"

Cleveland focused his attention back to the Bible. They had been working through the Gospel of John. "We have the work of the church for starters," he said, "but listen to this."

He read, "'These things have I spoken unto you, that my joy might remain in you, and that your joy might be full. This is my commandment, That ye love one another, as I have loved you. Greater love hath no man than this, that a man lay down his life for his friends. Ye are my friends, if ye do whatsoever I command you. Henceforth I call you not servants; for the servant knoweth not what his lord doeth: but I have called you friends; for all things that I have heard of my Father I have made known unto you. Ye have not chosen me, but I have chosen you, and ordained you, that ye should go and bring forth fruit, and that your fruit should remain; that whatsoever ye shall ask of the Father in my name, he may give it you.'

"Doesn't sound like a story, does it?" Cleveland said.

Charles shook his head.

"Sounds like to me we are ordained to bring forth fruit," Cleveland said. "That's Christianese for 'good works,' in case you were wondering."

"Y'all will know soon enough," Lasanya said.

Charles finished his plate and pushed it to the side. "Excellent, Lasanya."

Lasanya came in and cleared their plates.

"Charles," Cleveland said, "tell me why you are carrying this puzzle around."

Charles reclined in the chair, stared at the ceiling, and told Cleveland about his childhood. The words came out sounding like FLORIS the elevator attendant. After a five- or ten-minute monologue, Charles sat up and twirled the puzzle toward Cleveland. "This is the dark man."

Charles caught his breath. The dark man had grown wrinkles since he had seen him last. They were faint, undistinguished crow's feet, but they were there. What's happened, my old friend?

Don't cry for me, Charles, the dark man said. I'll be here when the keg floats. You and I go together like spring and baseball. In this world of change, one thing's constant: wherever you are, I'll be. The world can turn over a thousand times and I'll be right there with you. Comforting, isn't it?

"What is it, Charles?" Cleveland asked.

Charles refocused on Cleveland. "You wouldn't believe me if I told you."

"Try me."

Charles reached down and ran his fingers over the dark man's face. He spoke a little. Then he spoke a little more. He told Cleveland about how the dark man had haunted him as long as he could remember. He told how he scared him. How sometimes the dark man spoke to him. How at other times he gave him strength and resolve. He told Cleveland how he hated the dark man yet couldn't imagine life without him. Then he told Cleveland about the last time he saw his mother and how the dark man had been there, staring up at him.

"I would love to know who he is," Charles said. "I'd like to know why he follows me. What he wants."

"I'm sure the Book's got a story for that too," Cleveland said. "The Christian has three main enemies, Charles Graves: the world, the flesh, and the devil. When you come along in your studies, I'll explain it to you."

"I want to know now."

"You keep reading and you will."

Charles pressed Cleveland for an answer.

"Trust me, Charles: don't rush it. It will confuse you right now. Next thing you know, you will be wanting me to explain the Revelation to you."

"Now that you mention it," Charles said. But Cleveland was not to be cracked, at least not now.

I'll explain it to you, the dark man said.

"Go away," Charles said.

"Is he talking to you?" Cleveland asked.

"Yep."

"If it's that bad, maybe we can address it tomorrow. Right now, I'm tired, and we still have a baptism to take care of."

"Now?"

"Yes, now. But first, I want to share something with you. The story you shared about your mother broke my heart all over again. I want you to know that I know how bad it hurts." Cleveland reached over and took Charles's hand. "I want you to know that I am here day or night for you."

Charles tore his hands loose. "How could you know?" He stood. "This is what I hate about all this religion. You couldn't know how it feels. How bad it hurts. How it feels having your guts torn out every day. How booze and dope stop it by making you pass out. How could you know?"

The dark man eyed Charles from the puzzle. Lasanya peeked around the corner of the kitchen. The house grew silent.

"Charles," Cleveland said, "my wife and daughter were reclaimed ten days ago."

Charles's mind sputtered, coughed, lurched forward, and stalled. He sat back down. "Please forgive me."

"Nah," Cleveland said, "it was your dark man talking. We'll take care of him soon enough."

Charles put his face in his hands. "I don't understand how God could forgive a guy like me."

"That means you understand it," Cleveland said. "Let's get some rest. I have a funny feeling we are close to the 'what now.' But first, baptism."

Cleveland led Charles into the bathroom. Cleveland prayed with Charles while Lasanya filled the tub. It was barely big enough to dunk Charles.

"If your tub were any smaller, Lasanya, we'd have to be Presbyterian," Cleveland said.

He stood over the tub with Charles. "Charles Graves, I baptize you in the name of the Father, in the name of the Son, and in the name of the Holy Spirit."

Charles submerged. Barely, but he went under.

ELEVEN

Mid-morning the next day, Richard Farris walked through the parking lot of the Southeast Texas Reclamation Agency. The sun was in full force. Farris wore sunglasses only a touch smaller than Elton John's to combat the glare. His overconfident walk was almost a parody approaching the revolving doors.

A man carrying a briefcase exited the revolving door. "Good morning, Mr. Fah-reese."

Farris nodded. The man passed by on his way to the parking lot. "Hey," Farris called.

The man stopped and looked back over his shoulder.

"I don't like Fah-reese anymore. Call me Farris. Fah-reese is pretentious, pompous even, if I do say so myself."

"Whatever you say, Mr. Farris." The man crossed the drive and entered the parking lot.

Farris entered through the revolving door. The lobby was bustling with activity. A group of five agents was huddled on the left, taking direction from a senior officer. On Farris's right, two other agents were arguing with a delivery driver over the contents of a box. A line had formed in front of Pete's window.

From across the lobby, a female agent called to him. "Back early, Richard? How did it go?" Her voice echoed in the lobby, drawing considerable attention to him.

He eased his way over to her. "It seems early," he said. "Always does when you come through those doors."

The girl was pretty. She stepped in closer. He could smell her perfume. It reminded him of a girl who sat next to him in high school geometry class. She'd chewed gum like a cow and copied off him during test time.

The woman lowered her voice. "Maybe we could *leave* early through those doors tonight." She squinted at him. "Are you warm, Richard?" She reached up to feel his brow.

Farris intercepted the hand and brought it to his lips for a quick kiss. "Not at all, my dear," he said, pulling her hand back down to her side. "It's good to see you."

"Tonight, then?"

"Make it seven-thirty. Call me at the loft. I'll come get you."

The woman headed for the revolving door. "See you."

Farris walked to the line for Pete's window. The line had dwindled to three. He checked his reflection. Hair? Perfect. Clothes? So-so. Nose? When was it ever good? The sunglasses help, though. I'll leave them on. Cool, Daddy-O.

Farris waited. The guy in front of him offered to let him to go ahead. Farris refused. He noticed sweat was beginning to form on his brow. He needed to hurry. The man in front finished with Pete and entered the portal. The portal closed.

Farris stepped up to the window.

"Well, Jiminy Cricket, what have we got here?" Pete said.

Farris did not reply. He faced the beveled glass and removed his sunglasses. The red light scanned his eyes. He replaced the sunglasses.

Pete's eyes went wide. He looked from the monitor to Farris and back again. His bottom lip began to quiver. His eyes darted around the lobby, then landed again on Farris. Farris who wasn't Farris.

"My fault for missing you before I left," Charles said.

"Pinocchio's ghost, Charles! What you doing?" Pete said. "I just want to know one thing: is it that important that you get in? You know what will happen if they find out I let you through."

"It is that important, Pete. I will explain why later. Right now, you can see I am in a hurry. It won't be too long before they figure out I'm here."

"You won't be able to explain it to me. They'll lock me up for this."

"Trust me," Charles said. "You were right. The world has turned over."

"Trust you," Pete said.

"Would it help if I told you I can't stand the ASL?" Charles checked over his shoulder at the lobby. So far, he was safe.

"Open," Pete said. The portal opened. Pete's shoulders slumped. He looked almost lifeless. "What's the difference between being locked up in here and somewhere else? Promise me one thing."

"What's that?"

"You'll beat Farris."

"God willing," Charles said. "Now you promise me one thing."

"What?"

"Never call yourself a coward anymore."

Pete's lip began to quiver again. He sat up straighter. "Thanks, Charles. Now hurry."

"Welcome to the team," Charles said.

He entered the portal.

The portal closed behind him.

If this doesn't work, this will be a real short adventure. The elevator door shut. Charles pulled a mouthpiece out of his suit pocket and inserted it into his mouth. He spoke one word. "Six."

Without hesitation FLORIS responded, "Thank you, Mr. Farris."

Charles put the mouthpiece back in his pocket. Too easy. I'm surprised Farris hadn't had his name reprogrammed to Fah-reese. Halfway home.

The elevator doors opened. Charles stepped out and resumed the pompous walk to the hall monitor's desk.

"Mr. Fah-reese," the hall monitor said, "it's good to see you." The hall monitor seemed starstruck. "It's been awhile for you, Mr. Fah-reese. I hope everything is all right."

Charles scrunched his lips and hunched his shoulders. The less said, the better. This guy idolizes Farris. He'll be used to Farris being a haughty jerk. Charles paused long enough to sign the register. After signing, he walked past the monitor without a word.

He counted ten steps before it came. "Mr. Fah-reese?"

Charles stopped. Is it the suit or the nose? That nose could only be duplicated by a miracle, and Cleveland didn't seem up to the task. The sunglasses helped some. Or is it the suit? Thank God preachers like to keep a nice suit around. It's not Fah-reese worthy, but nobody should notice with just a glance. His girl-friend hadn't in the lobby.

He shot a quick glance at the suit leg cuffs. Due to Cleveland's height, Lasanya took the cuffs in to simulate Farris's shorter stature. One of the stitches had unraveled on the right cuff. Very un-Fah-reese-like. I must have kicked it walking in. Nothing to do now but face the music. At least it's ASL music.

He turned to face the music. A vision of the hall monitor doing the Irish river-dance and singing folk ballads caused him to snicker. He converted it into a Fah-reese sneer.

"It's Graves you're here for, isn't it?" the hall monitor asked. "I mean, there's been rumors."

Charles stifled his relief. He remained silent. He sensed the monitor was uneasy with Farris. Gotta play this one right. I may get busted, but not by this guy. I have to say something, though. Silence won't work.

Charles walked off. With his back to the monitor, he called out in a low, but authoritative voice. "Top secret." He contin-ued to walk.

"Yes, sir, Mr. Fah-reese," the hall monitor said. "Yes, sir. I hope you get him."

Charles entered the cube maze to find Julia.

• • •

"Yes, for the second and last time: you and Keesma stay downtown. I am pulling into HQ now. I'll get the disk from Julia Jenkins and be back at my loft in under an hour. Later."

Farris pulled into his reserved spot and killed the Lotus. He was out of the car and across the drive in nothing flat, fine suit flowing in the morning sun.

A female agent exited the revolving door. "Good morning, Mr. Fah-reese."

"Yeah." Farris entered the building and sauntered to Pete's window.

Julia saw Farris in a mirror she kept on her desk. Nothin' like a mirror in a cube—standard issue, mandatory. What does he want? Another shot at a date?

Then it hit her: he's here for the disk. Option one: give him the phony. It's got the same info, but it's specially prepared. Option two: the doctored one. Option one is safer if they don't run a scan. Option two is safer if they do. What's it gonna be, girl, one or two?

Julia reached in a desk drawer and brought out disk number two.

Good girl. To thine own self be true.

Shakespeare is not on the Approved Reading List.

So what?

Julia handed the disk over her head.

"I don't want that," a voice said. "I need to talk to you." The voice was soft, kind, and trying not to be heard in the next cube.

What in the world does he want? Is he trying to apologize for that pass he made at me? Does Farris have a soft side?

No, Girly-Girl, he doesn't. At least not that you'll ever see. He probably cracks like a sidewalk over a tree root when he's alone, but you'll never see it. Something else is happening here. Something big. Because something is not right about that voice, and yet it is as right as rain. Turn around, GG, and get ready to be a big girl. He's gonna need you. He always has.

Pete watched Farris approach the beveled glass. Here we go, Pete thought. I'm gonna make the big time at last. And there's no better way to do it than getting all the way into Pinocchio's kitchen. I think I'll cook a grand slam breakfast while I'm in there too.

The red laser scanned Farris's eyes. He walked to the portal. Nothing happened. Farris walked back to the window.

"How you doin', Mr. P?" Pete took a gulp of soda.

"Open the door," Farris said.

"I forgot how," Pete said. His face lit up. "I know, let me consult my user's manual. I'll have it, uh, un-closed in a jiffy."

"*Open the door!*"

"I'm gettin' to it. I'm gettin' to it," Pete said. "You know, Farris, if you would tell a few lies, that nose of yours might grow out some."

Farris stepped back three paces, pulled his gun, and put four slugs in the window. Three bullets lodged in the glass in front of Pete's forehead. The fourth ricocheted off the glass, hit the lobby's ceiling, bounced off the back wall, and landed three feet to Farris's right. The sound was loud in Pete's box—it must've sounded like cannons in the lobby.

A door at the far end of the lobby burst open. Blue-coated security agents poured out with firearms drawn. Farris dropped his gun and lifted his hands.

The guards closed in on Farris. They recognized him, lowered their weapons, and gathered around him.

A short guard with a moustache spoke. "Mr. Fah-reese. What's going on?"

"Open Pete's office," he said. "I am being refused entrance for no reason."

The guard questioned Pete with his eyes.

Pete thought he might get out of this yet. He increased the volume on the intercom. "Farris went nuts and started shooting. Beats me why. Almost gave me a heart attack when those bullets went in the glass."

The guard turned back to Farris. "What's all the shooting about?"

"Let me explain something to you," Farris said to the guard. "Open the door now. Something is wrong here, and I need in immediately. Open the door now or I will have each one of you, your families, and your pets reclaimed with your friend Pete there."

"Pete, what's up?" the guard said. "This is Richard Fah-reese. Did you refuse to open the door?"

So much for getting out of it. Charles, I hope you know what you are doing. You've got about one more minute before they break in. So get after it, whatever it is.

"I don't know how, Kevin," Pete said.

Farris, hands still in the air, nodded at the door. The guard motioned to two of the other guards. They unlocked the door leading to Pete's office.

Farris pushed the mustached guard out of his way and ran to Pete's office. He entered ahead of the two other guards. Pete didn't move.

Farris grabbed the back of Pete's chair and flung it. The chair toppled over. Pete grabbed for the desk but missed. He toppled with the chair, hitting his head on the floor. His hands flailed as he fell. His right one caught a counter behind him, breaking two of the bones in his wrist. He did not make a sound.

"Cuff him," Farris said.

"He's hurt," one guard said.

"Cuff him."

Farris found a manual override and opened the portal. He made it halfway back to the office door before returning to Pete's console.

Pete cried out when the guards cuffed him. His wrist felt like a spike was being driven through it.

Farris righted the chair and scanned back through Pete's activity screen for what he'd been doing over the last hour. His eyes narrowed when Charles's name appeared on the electronic register. He spun around and kicked Pete in the ribs. One snapped. Pete moaned.

Farris ran for the office door. He steamrolled the mustached guard, who was trying to enter the door at the same time he was leaving. He gave the guard quick instructions. "Wait two minutes and then sound the general alarm. Close all exits. Two minutes."

From the lobby floor the guard nodded. "Two minutes," he said.

Farris sprinted through the portal.

• • •

Julia studied the face. It was too Farris-like not to be Farris. Yet something was not right. It was the nose. The nose was too big.

Just to be sure, she continued the conversation. "What do you need to talk about?"

The person who might be Farris entered the cube, crouching below Julia's "You do not compute" sign. He balanced himself with his left hand on the floor beneath his knees. He whispered. "Julia, it's Charles. I need a favor. It's a big one."

Part of her had known it. "So you disappear into nowhere, don't call me, then show up here needing my help?"

"Not now, Julia," Charles said. "I don't have much time."

"Why shouldn't I report you?" She tried to force her face into a frown. "I mean, this is asking a lot coming here like this. You must be in trouble, and you're going to get me in trouble too. I can't believe you told me you loved me right before you disappeared."

"Come meet me after work," Charles said. "I'll have time to explain it then."

You are about to ruin your whole life, Julia. Is it worth it?

Of course not. Never has been. Millions of women through the ages have made that choice and lived to regret it, Girly-Girl. On the other hand, what life are you worried about losing? Your job does not resemble a career. Not without Charles, it doesn't. And he sure has driven the wheels off of your promotion, unless you were thinking of promoting yourself to Farris's loft.

Well, for starters, I enjoy not having to be on the run, hiding night and day hoping to not get reclaimed.

You don't know for sure that's the case.

You're right, I don't know for sure. But what else could his disappearance and sudden reappearance as Richard Farris mean?

You won't be reclaimed for talking to him. Maybe reprimanded. Fired perhaps. But not reclaimed. You haven't done anything.

Yet.

"Julia," Charles said, "what's the matter?"

Julia stared at the Spock figurine. "Nothing, Charles. Everything. This is so sudden. You, right here in front of me out of nowhere, asking me to risk everything."

"Trust me," Charles said.

Oh, ho! Here we go with the trust routine. That line should be a starter pistol for women. Get out, Julia, *now*.

You haven't heard what he wants yet.

So what? This can only end badly for me.

"Julia," Charles said, "this is what I need you to do."

"Six, FLORIS," Farris said.

"I already show you on six, Mr. Farris."

"Well, I'm not. Take me to six."

"My programming will not allow for that," FLORIS said. "You may state your override code if you wish."

"Farris, 838-88WFR-77127."

"Authorizing."

Farris paced back and forth in the elevator. He consulted his watch. The alarm would sound in one minute.

"Thank you, Mr. Farris."

"Get on with it!"

"I do not understand the command."

"*Six!*"

"Thank you, Mr. Farris."

"There's no way I can do that," Julia said. "No way."

"They'll never know," Charles said. "You are way good enough to hide it from them. They'll never know."

Julia's chest swelled. "You're right about that, but it's not the point. I can't do that."

You've done it before. You've been all through the system backward and forward. It's easy. They won't catch you and you know it. So why wouldn't you do it?

Because it's presumptuous of him to show up here and assume that I would do it. That's why.

Good point, GG.

"Are you sure you won't?" Charles asked.

"I'm sure."

Charles stood up, leaned over, and hugged Julia. "That's my girl," he said. "I shouldn't have put you in this position. I don't know what came over me. I gotta go."

He's hugging me as if it's the last time, Julia thought. Her insides melted. Her throat clammed up. She imagined the roar of a plane in the distance. "Charles—"

"Not now. This doesn't change anything. The whole world can turn over and we won't change." He released her and turned to leave.

Julia poked her head out of the cube. Charles stepped out into the hall, only to run into Richard Farris. Farris was on a dead run down the aisle. Julia saw Farris's eyes double when he saw his likeness emerge from the cube.

The general alarm sounded. Sirens blared on every floor. Red lights flashed. Farris reached for his gun as he ran down the aisle. His hand came back empty. She saw Farris study his empty hand.

Charles stepped forward with his left foot and connected his right fist to Farris's nose. Julia heard Farris's nose crack in two above the siren. Farris wailed and stumbled back into the adjacent cube, landing on the lap of Julia's cube-mate. Both hands clutched his nose. Julia's cube-mate screamed.

Charles hollered back at Julia. "Cleveland hasn't taught me to turn the other cheek yet." He extended the hand that broke Farris's nose. "Come on. If they catch us you can claim you were trying to stop me."

Or that you forced me, she thought.

You are not considering this, are you? You're playing, right?

See how alive he is. With him is life. Here are cubes and Farrises—or would that be Farrisi? Of course I'm going. Think of the airplanes. *Whoooosh.*

It's not logical.

I know, but neither is working in a cube for the next twenty-five years. Besides, you are the one who told me about the other L word. And about getting ready to help him. Remember all that.

Sure, but—

Then help me.

I guess I'll have to.

Julia took Charles's hand.

• • •

Charles jerked Julia out of the cube. They ran away from Farris, hand in hand, to the end of the cube aisle.

"We have to get to the stairwell," Charles said. "Hurry!"

They reached the end of the row and took a left between the cubes and the outer offices. Charles swung Julia around the corner as if they were on a skating rink. It was about one hundred feet to the end of the row of outer offices, where Charles's and Farris's offices were. Across from Charles's office was the stairwell.

The general alarm had flushed people from their cubes and offices. The hallway was filled with people. Charles dodged and weaved, all the while holding Julia's hand. One woman darted out into the hall ahead of them. Charles lifted their hands over her at the last second. Their hands swooshed through the woman's hair.

Another man got caught between their interlocked arms as if they were playing Red Rover. He backpedaled, trying to keep up with them before catching his left heel on the tip of his right wing-tipped dress shoe. He tumbled in a perfect backward somersault, stood, and ran the opposite way.

The world is turning over, Charles thought.

Forty feet from the stairwell two guards raced around the corner in Charles's and Julia's direction. Charles forgot he was still disguised as Farris.

"Mr. Farris, what's happening?"

He recovered quickly. "Uh, there's a man loose with a gun at the end of the aisle!" Charles pointed down to the end of the row. The guards drew their weapons and took off toward the spot Charles had indicated. With all the chaos people must not think. There must be a hundred armed agents on this floor alone who are trained to eliminate gunmen.

Charles and Julia arrived at the stairwell. The guards were halfway down the row.

Farris appeared at the corner where Charles and Julia made the left turn. He yelled at the guards and pointed toward Charles.

The guards leapt for cover, figuring Farris for the gunman. Farris indeed seemed like a crazed killer. His face, hands, and shirt were soiled red from his broken nose. He was staggering forward, screaming, wild-eyed.

He's tougher than I thought. We are not out of this yet.

Charles felt the stairwell door handle. Please be unlocked. Does the system lock the doors automatically? No, you don't lock the doors during a fire. But it's not a fire. There's a madman on the loose.

Charles felt the door give way. He patted the back of Julia's head. "How are you doing?"

"I'm fine," she said. "Don't stop now."

He pushed her into the doorway. Down the aisle, the guards restrained Farris. That won't last long, but it may give us enough time. He entered the stairwell behind Julia.

They reached the first stairs leading down, Julia in the lead and Charles following. There were a few agents descending the stairwell, but most seemed to have gravitated to Farris and the guards.

Charles grabbed Julia. "Hang on."

The stairway writhed. It contorted and swayed. Charles felt his stomach churn. His vision blurred. He grabbed a handrail.

"What are you doing?" Julia said. "Let's go!" Her voice echoed in the stairwell.

Julia's face began to change. Her head bloated out to twice its size, then deflated into place. The eyes inflated then popped. Her hair fell out and regrew. It was his brother.

Charles saw himself at the top of the gold-inlaid stairway at Graves Mansion. He felt his consciousness slipping. His brother was dressed up in Julia's clothes. He stared back at him from the top step. His brother pulled Julia's gun out of her holster and pointed it at him. His brother grinned. "Not this time," he said.

The dark man's voice screamed in Charles's head. "Now! Do it!"

Charles let go of the railing. He fainted. Everything faded.

TWELVE

"Freeze," the first guard said. He positioned himself half inside one of the outer office doors. He pointed his gun at Farris.

"You idiots!" Farris said. "He's getting away." He pointed down the hallway. Farris shook his hands. Blood sprayed against the gray cubicle wall next to him.

The guards looked at each other, then back at Farris.

"Look at me," Farris said. "I'm the real Fah-reese. I'm the one that is injured. That's Charles Graves. He broke my nose. Do I have a gun, you idiots?" Farris showed his empty holster.

The guards came out from under cover. They approached Farris with caution. "Excuse me, Mr. Fah-reese," the second guard said.

"Shut up and give me that gun," Farris said.

"Regulations state I am not allowed to surrender my firearm to—"

"Don't quote me regs—I wrote 'em." Farris took the guard's gun. He flipped the gun around and cold-cocked the guard with the butt of the gun. The guard's knees buckled. He fell back against the cube and slid to the floor.

Farris addressed the first guard. "They don't write rules for nothin', you blue-coated buffoon. Let's go."

Farris led the other guard toward the stairwell at a run.

Julia was holding Charles in her arms when he awoke. She saw his eyes dart side to side and up and down.

"You caught me," he said.

"Of course I did."

Charles grabbed the back of her head and gave her a deep kiss.

She accepted at first, then pulled away. "Not now," she said. "They're coming. We have to go."

Men.

They ran the stairs apace. At the bottom of the stairwell were two doors. One led outside, the other led to the first floor offices. Charles tried the outside door. It was locked.

They must have shut down all the outside exits, Julia thought.

Upstairs, a stairwell door opened and slammed against a wall. The sound reverberated throughout the stairwell. Farris.

Julia grabbed Charles and pulled him to the inside door. She tried the handle. It was locked.

Plan B, Girly-Girl. Time to give him up. You can still save yourself.

Charles grabbed her and pulled her up the stairway, taking two steps at a time. Above, Julia saw Farris and a guard descending the stairway. She figured Charles was heading for the second floor stairwell door. It was going to be tight.

They reached the stairwell door two flights ahead of Farris and the guard. Charles tried the door. It opened. They entered.

The floor was empty. Evacuated. Charles pulled her into an outer office three doors down. He shut the door behind them.

Not too late for plan B. They will find you for sure in here.

The stairwell door crashed open.

Silence.

The office door three doors down opened. Julia heard rustling.

Two doors down opened.

One door down.

She pulled her gun and pointed it at Charles. His jaw dropped.

It has to be this way. There is no other way out. No fear, GG. What else are you going to do?

She yelled. "Farris, it's Julia. In here. I've got him."

No guilt. No worries. You have no other choice, GG. Be strong. Be steady. It will all be over soon.

Julia opened the door with her left hand. Charles backed up to the window. Farris peered in, then entered, gun drawn. The guard followed a step behind.

Farris looked at Julia, then over at Charles. Julia saw his mind working at an accelerated pace.

He's about spent, GG. Note the blood. He has to be on his last leg. Dangerous like a cornered dog. Make him feel at ease.

Give him credit. He's a jerk, but he's a tough jerk. Gotta respect him for that.

"He forced me down here," she said, "but I got the drop on him when we came in here to hide."

Farris watched her eyes. "Nicely done. This is going to be good for you." He took a step toward her. "Now hand me the gun."

Nice and easy. You're almost there, GG.

Julia flipped the gun over butt-first and held it out toward Farris. "I'm glad you made it down here," she said. "This was closer than I like."

Farris grinned. "I'm always right on time, Jewels." He took the gun.

"So's this," she said. She lunged forward and shoved the palm of her hand into Farris's bloody nose with a fierce, compact jab.

Farris blacked out. His body fell limp to the floor.

Ooh. That had to hurt.

The guard raised his gun. Julia was under his arm in a flash with her back to the guard. She stood, with his wrist in her hand palm up and his elbow on her shoulder. She pulled down on the wrist as she lifted her shoulder. The elbow creaked.

The guard dropped the gun. "Stop! Stop! I give!"

She released the pressure slightly but held on. "Charles, get the guns."

Charles got the guns.

Julia spun the guard around, removed his restraints from his belt, and cuffed him to a desk handle. "It'll do," she said. "Charles, break the window."

Charles put one gun in the inside coat pocket of his suit and handed the other two to Julia. She holstered hers and stuffed the other into the belt of her pants.

Charles lifted a chair and threw it at the window. It bounced off.

Julia rolled her eyes, drew her pistol, and obliterated the window. "No time to waste. Roll when you hit the ground." She holstered the gun, stepped onto a credenza in front of the window, and jumped out.

Charles followed.

Charles hit the ground rolling. When he came up, Julia was making her way to the side of the building. Some woman, he thought. The agency sirens blared through the broken window. Charles could hear response vehicles arriving at the front of the agency. Two agency gunships roared overhead. Charles guessed that the building's occupants would be exiting out the front and side doors.

He spoke softly so as not to draw attention. "Julia!" He waved for her to follow. He pointed to the nature preserve and ran. Julia followed.

It was about fifty yards to the tree line. If they could make it without being spotted, they might make it out. What a miracle. If we can get out of this, anything might happen. Yeah, anything. Julia will shoot you for ruining her life. The miracle will be her not hating you over this.

They reached the tree line without pursuit. The two stopped inside the cover of the trees to catch their breath. Charles saw no one, yet.

"What now?" Julia stood straight, barely breathing.

Charles put his hands on his knees. He kept an eye on the clearing. "We still need to hurry. They will be on our trail."

"Do you know how to get out of here?"

"Sure, I used to play here as a kid. Follow me."

Julia hesitated. "I want to finish something first." She walked to Charles, pulled his hands off his knees, and put them around her neck.

"I don't deserve you," he said.

"We'll see about that." She kissed him.

Fifteen minutes later they were a half-mile deep into the preserve. Charles led her to a dirt path where a station wagon sat waiting. Behind the wheel sat a Hispanic man in a jumpsuit and a fishing hat.

Charles loaded Julia into the backseat and hopped into the front. "Let's go before they get wise to us. Julia, put these on." He handed her a set of overalls, tennis shoes, and a T-shirt. He removed his suit coat and threw it out the window along with Farris's face.

The driver started the station wagon and pulled onto the dirt path. Five minutes later they were on a back road heading toward Houston. They were three fishermen returning from Galveston.

"Julia," Charles said, "this is the Reverend James Cleveland. Reverend Cleveland, meet Julia Jenkins."

On the fortieth floor of the Southeast Texas Reclamation Agency, Frank Cotton Graves took in the view, trying to tune out the alarm, along with his troubles. He walked to the window overlooking the nature preserve and saw two figures bolting for the tree line.

"Well, what do you know about that?" He thought about reporting it. "Nah," he said. "I'm on house arrest. They'll contact me. I'm supposed to sit here."

He returned to his desk and sat in his chair with his feet propped up on the glass.

Farris stepped out through the revolving doors in front of the agency headquarters. He saw agents loading Pete into a patrol car. Headed for a reclamation center, most likely. Pete's breathing seemed labored, his sides heaving. He held his left ribs with his right hand.

The sunlight stabbed Farris's head. Blood seeped through a heavy bandage over his shattered nose.

Farris walked to Pete. "You shouldn't have done that, old man."

Pete struggled to breathe. "Hey, Farris. You tryin' out for the circus?"

Farris didn't get it.

"I seen you got a clown nose on and all." Pete worked up enough air to cackle.

Farris knocked two of Pete's teeth out and walked off. The show has only begun, old man, and I don't miss.

"The Reverend Cleveland, masquerading as a Hispanic fisherman?" Julia said. "Charles, what have you done to me?"

"Pleased to meet you, Julia." Cleveland extended his oversized right hand into the backseat.

Julia considered it before turning her head and staring out the window. She nibbled at her thumbnail.

Charles grabbed the headrest of his seat and rotated to face her. "I didn't mean for it to end up this way."

Oh, but it did, Charles. Now I'm part of the Charles Graves Traveling Circus. "I can't believe you risked my life, Charles. Maybe you wanted to ruin yours, but mine?"

"Julia, I never would have intentionally put you in harm's way. You know that. I meant to get that data from you and then disappear out of there without you. But I hadn't expected Farris to show up. It wasn't supposed to go down like that." Charles shifted in the front seat until both of his knees were on the seat cushion. "We can stop the car right now and let you out if you want. You can still claim I forced you."

Out the window, Julia saw a field of cows grazing. "I think that detail where I rammed my palm into Farris's nose and cuffed the guard pretty much ruins that option. What do you think?" Julia lips parted, then spread. "I have to admit it felt good, Charles."

That's because you have been spending your life like those cows you're passing. Not much different from being in a cube, except you know it and cows don't. That makes it worse.

Yeah, but that is only one side of the coin. Working in the cube provides for lots of free time, provides for your own home, pays for all the other things that make your life full.

And those are?

I like my life, thank you very much. You are not going to convince me otherwise. You forget there is a whole world of starving, dying people out there. Besides, I could have a family one day.

Gonna be awhile now. You're a featured performer in the traveling circus.

Cleveland came to a T in the road and stopped. He nudged Charles in the ribs.

Charles pointed left. "This will take us to 288. From there we can get to Lasanya's."

"What about the cordon?" Cleveland asked.

"Berry patch," Charles said. "You saw how easy it was to get through on the way out here. I doubt they will have it up much longer. I'll fix myself on the way and maybe cook up something for Julia."

"Julia," Cleveland said, "if you don't mind my saying—"

You should be ashamed of yourself, GG. He's a nice man, even if he is a Mother Goose. Don't you think you ought to fix that?

Well maybe, but no matter how nice he seems, he did have a part in what Charles did to me today.

You don't know that for sure. He might have argued against it.

He's driving the car.

Good point.

Julia interrupted Cleveland. "Before you finish whatever is it you were going to say, let me apologize first and shake your hand. That was rude."

"Never thought twice about it, ma'am," Cleveland said, shaking her hand. "I can imagine what is going through your mind right now."

"What did you want to say?" Julia asked.

"I was going to suggest you forgive us, mainly Charles, for what happened today. What's done is done. You see, when God starts moving—"

"Don't start with the religion stuff."

"Julia," Charles said.

"No, Charles. I said No."

Cleveland flashed the pastor's smile.

Watch out for this one, GG. Yeah, he's nice. Yeah, it feels comfortable to be around him. Yeah, you've known him thirty minutes and you feel something. That's the spell. It has already mesmerized Charles. It's the sideshow at the traveling circus. Step right up, folks. Come on in. See the Great Cleveland explain the mysteries of the universe. No thank you.

Cleveland drove under two old oaks leaning over the two-lane farm to market road they were on. "Hold on a minute, ma'am," he said. "I just said when God starts moving." Cleveland did not use the preacher's standard Gawwyud pronunciation.

Okay, then. Do we want to engage in some logical discourse?

Sounds like fun.

"The whole concept of your God is illogical," Julia said, "not to mention how you would even know or prove He is moving."

Cleveland pushed his considerable bulk back into the chair. She saw his eyes through the rear viewmirror. The eyes were like a warm blanket on a cool evening. "You didn't know electricity made the light come on when you were a kid," Cleveland said.

"Actually, I did," Julia said.

"Somehow by listening to you, I believe that," Cleveland said. "But you didn't know how the electrons worked to produce the electricity that caused the light. How's that?"

"If by kid you mean three or four, fair enough," Julia said. She saw Charles working on something in the front seat. Clown costumes for the traveling circus, no doubt.

"Knowing God is moving is like knowing that electricity causes the light," Cleveland said. "When you see certain things happening, you know it's God behind them."

Julia blew air through her lips. "Nice analogy," she said, "but logically, you have no way to connect the activity of God to the activity of electricity. If I stick my finger in an electrical socket, I will get a shock. Show me a God-socket, and I'll be in the front row of your church every Sunday."

"You won't say that after you have met Him," Cleveland said.

"Experience is the mother of illusion," Julia said.

Cleveland tapped Charles's shoulder. The car was nearing a freeway interchange.

Charles motioned to the right with one hand and resumed his work. "I think they will be searching south for us. You haven't noticed any agency gunships have you?"

Julia glanced out at the sky. "Not one."

Cleveland entered an entrance ramp onto Interstate 288 toward downtown Houston.

"Here," Charles said, "put this on." He handed her a mask that was a twin to the one Cleveland was wearing. "Not my best work, but it will get us home. I reckon they are not checking that closely. Tuck your hair up into it. Julia took the mask and Charles began working on himself.

"Julia," Cleveland said, "one more thing. I can already tell you are way smarter than me, so humor me. Where does this logic of yours come from?"

Julia avoided the eyes in the mirror. "It's a brute fact of the universe."

"I was kind of hoping you would say something like that," Cleveland said.

Julia rolled down the window and spit. The car was fifty yards down the road by the time it hit the pavement.

• • •

Cleveland slowed the car to a stop, the tenth car in line to the cordon. Two policemen were busy checking the first car in line.

From the front seat of the wagon, Charles could make the officers out in the fading light. They wore leather boots with three-inch heels, gray, tight-knit pants, leather jackets, motor-cycle helmets, and sunglasses. They were monoliths. They reminded Charles of the policeman who stopped Vivian Leigh in Alfred Hitchcock's *Psycho*. They wore holstered firearms and billy clubs.

The interstate had been fitted with tollbooths to facilitate the cordon, squeezing the traffic down to two lanes. Temporary structures serving as barracks blocked the remainder of the highway, which was patrolled by armed guards. An agency gunship sat on a concrete heliport constructed to the right of the breakdown lane.

Charles rubbed his forearms together to rid himself of an itch. "Relax. Act like you are tired from fishing all day." At the front of the cordon, the first car in line pulled off. Charles guessed they had ten minutes to wait.

"And you do this for a living?" Cleveland said. "I don't see how you do it."

"Seems to me you've been hiding a lot lately, Reverend," Charles said. The car in front pulled off. An elderly woman alone in the next car was waved through.

Cleveland rolled down his window. "What if they ask—"

"Too late to think," Charles said. "Act. Act like you know what you are doing."

"Can I act like I'm asleep?" Julia asked.

"Nah," Charles said. "It will make them want to wake you up."

More cars were waved on. Cleveland pulled up, second in line.

Charles watched the officers. Two young women occupied the car in front. One officer was on each side of the car, flirting with the girls. Charles thought it was a lecherous type of flirtation, not good-natured fun. He also thought he saw an emblem of a prism on one officer's boot.

"We may have picked the wrong day to be Hispanic," Charles said.

"Been a lot of wrong days for minorities," Cleveland said. "I can act natural on that one."

"Speak in your normal voice," Charles said. "Trying to mimic an accent will draw suspicion."

The officers waved the girls through the cordon. The one on Cleveland's side motioned them ahead. Cleveland eased the station wagon forward.

The officer on Charles's side noted the license plate and logged it into a handheld computer. He started toward Charles along the passenger side of the car. Charles stared forward, motionless.

The officer on Cleveland's side worked his way toward Cleveland's open window, dragging his gloved hand along the hood. His index finger traced the groove formed by the hood and quarter panel. He paused at the base of the windshield to examine the registration and inspection tags.

The officer placed both hands on Cleveland's door and peered in. "Gonna need tags next month."

The second officer tapped on Charles's window with his billy club. Charles lowered his window.

"Yes, sir, officer," Cleveland said.

"License," the first officer said.

Cleveland reached above the sun visor, producing the license. He handed it to the officer.

"You have got to be kidding me," the first officer said.

The second officer rose from Charles's window, looking across the top of the wagon at his partner. His right hand moved to his gun.

Charles used this unsupervised time to gather himself. What was unbelievable? What was wrong with the ID? This was supposed to be easy. These were no run-of-the-mill cordon officers. The billy club in the officer's hand must be a foot and a half long, but it resembled a conductor's baton in the officer's mammoth hand. This is not good, Charles thought.

"Tucker," the first officer said, "you'll never believe this. He flipped the license across the hood to the second officer.

The second officer scooped up the license. He read the license and slapped his club against his left leg.

Charles felt himself sinking. He checked the rearview mirror. Julia was squirming.

"Get out of the car," the first officer said.

Cleveland lifted his eyebrows, opened the door, and got out.

"Put your hands on the hood."

Cleveland obeyed.

The officer on Charles's side flipped the license back over to his partner. He stared back at Charles. "Sit tight, boy."

The first officer grabbed the license and held it in front of Cleveland. "So your name is Jesus Carpenter?" he asked. "Jesus Carpenter? I don't know whether to laugh or throw up."

"That would be Hay-soos," Cleveland said. "My dad was a plant worker with a third-grade education. My mother came across the border and didn't speak a word of English. I learned fightin' as a young 'un."

Cleveland was cool under pressure. Cool enough to be an agent.

The officer rubbed his nose with the palm of his hand. "What's your zodiac sign?" the officer asked.

"Sagittarius, not that I take much stock in it," Cleveland said.

The officer studied the license.

Charles's officer jerked his head down toward a buzzer at his belt. After a hesitation, he removed a phone and answered it. A few seconds later he was on the opposite side of the wagon conferring with the first officer.

"Get back in the car, Jesus," the first officer said. He handed Cleveland the license. "Y'all get on down the road."

The second officer stammered. "You sure?"

"Yeah," the first officer said. "Those saps couldn't break into an old folks home."

Charles noticed the first officer point to a car further back in line. Cleveland entered the wagon and drove off.

"I don't believe it," Julia said.

"Me neither," Charles said. "You lie real well for a preacher."

"Some of it ain't that far from the truth," Cleveland said. "I'll be asking forgiveness for the rest."

"That's not what I meant," Julia said. "I can't believe they let us go."

Cleveland gave her the eyes in the rearview mirror. "That's your first zap of God's electricity. A small one. Not a socket.

More like touching your tongue between the posts of a battery."

"I couldn't make out the call they got on the phone," Charles said.

"They got a hot call to detain any car carrying two men and a woman. They thought they saw one a few cars back. Told us to go on."

"Amazing," Julia said.

"No," Cleveland said. "Electricity."

THIRTEEN

"Hey, baby," Farris said.

"Hey." The voice maintained an edge, but Farris could tell it wanted to be nice. "I called you like you said. Hope you don't mind me calling you on your car phone."

"I wouldn't have answered it if I minded." The Lotus hopped into overdrive. Farris's mind followed suit. *Why is she calling me? When did I talk to her? And what did I tell her? Do I have a date tonight?*

No. You have been working on Julia, unsuccessfully.

What could it be then?

You did have an impersonator at work today.

Charles. Oh well, I guess I should thank him. Company sounds pretty good.

"Hey, baby," Farris said. "I guess you heard what a day it was today at HQ. Give me a pass on being late. I've got a couple of stops to make. Why don't you come to the loft around nine? I'll meet you downstairs in the lobby."

"Sounds good. See you at nine."

Farris caressed the bandage on his broken nose.

The station wagon cruised up Highway 288. Downtown was illuminated in the twilight. Charles stared through the windshield at the high-rises.

The speed of life was accelerating. Day and night came on each other's heels as if they were chasing each other. In his mind, Charles saw his wood-block puzzle changing faces.

He lifted his arms and stretched off a yawn. His bleary eyes landed on one particular building downtown. "Julia," he said, "that thing I asked you to do—"

"I said no, Charles," Julia said. "Although it doesn't matter much now."

Charles twisted in the front seat to face her. "You left the disks in your cube, didn't you?"

Julia muttered under her breath. She placed her face in her hands. "Yes. How stupid."

Charles took her wrists and pulled her hands to his face. Her palms were warm. He rested his cheeks in them. "Since you left the disks there, it won't matter much doing the other. Think about it."

"We can't go back to HQ," she said.

Charles let go of her left hand and pointed back over his shoulder at downtown. "There's another way."

Her gaze fixed on downtown like it was a kaleidoscope.

"I see where this is goin'," Cleveland said. "Y'all don't have to do this."

"Yes, I think we do," Charles said. "I don't know why. Maybe I feel the electricity. I don't know."

"What if Farris is home?" Julia asked.

"We come back when he's gone."

Julia unfastened her seat belt and sat up, inches from Charles's face. She placed her left palm back on his cheek and pressed in. "Maybe."

Julia's intensity radiated into Charles's cheeks through her palms. She may be stronger than Cleveland, he thought. The wood-block puzzle in his mind arranged itself into Julia's face. It was beautiful. It was neo-classical in its strength and austerity.

"One thing, though," she said. "I need to know why it's so important."

"Cleveland's family got reclaimed," Charles said. "I might still have time to save them."

Julia found Cleveland's eyes in the rearview.

"You don't have to do this, Julia," Cleveland said.

She smiled kindly. "Yes, I do."

At the mother-of-pearl inlaid door to Farris's loft, Julia watched Charles insert his voice-modifier and command the apartment to open. The apartment computer complied, greeting Charles as Mr. Fah-reese. Julia followed Charles inside.

Her stomach plummeted to the pavement thirty floors below. This was nerve-wracking. It was bad enough that, with Charles sounding like Farris and them now entering Farris's apartment, she had a stabbing fear that she had accompanied the real Farris back to the loft.

Julia scanned the loft. *Pompous Pearl Boy's been at it again. Pearl this, pearl white that. This place is clammy.*

The computer that had to be Farris's remote link to HQ was easy enough to find in the open loft. Julia sat down in front of the terminal and zoned in.

"Mr. Fah-reese," the apartment computer said, "you left the front door cracked."

"Acceptable," Charles said in Farris's voice.

Julia hacked in to the HQ mainframe. The computer clock read 8:47. "Farris is one of a kind. His password is kool_moe_ dee. Can you believe?" Her fingers picked up speed on the key-board. "I can camouflage my entry so he won't know we were here."

"Can you reprogram the apartment computer as well?"

"To do what?"

"To not let him know we've been here, or *are* here, if it comes to that."

"With enough time. How much time do you think we have?"

"You're early."

"I know, baby," Farris said. "Are you disappointed?"

"Of course not. Oh! What happened to your face?"

"Line of duty, baby. Tough day. How about stayin' in at the loft tonight?"

"That was the idea. Let's go."

• • •

Julia's posture stiffened. "I'm almost there! A few more minutes."

Charles used the computer screen as an excuse to lean over Julia. She eased into him, pulling his neck to her shoulder. Charles whispered in her ear. She released him and returned to the keyboard.

"Hurry it up if you can," Charles said. "I'll be back in a minute."

"Where are you going?"

"Just keep working."

Charles trundled over to a kitchenette area that doubled as Farris's bar. He scanned the available liquors. The closer he looked, the more he realized the amount of booze stocked in Farris's bar. The tips of his fingers tingled. For show, Charles thought. For show and the occasional date. Think, Charles— which bottle is the right one?

"What are you doing over there, Charles?" Julia asked.

"Nothing. Keep going."

The wood-block puzzle clicked in his mind. It was his old nemesis. I bet it tastes good, Charles. One nip might calm your nerves.

Shut up, I don't have to listen to you anymore.

Whatever. Don't believe everything that preacher says. Or your little honey, either. By the way, it's the one at the bottom with the fancy glasswork. See how it's pulled out some? Ah, Charles. What would you do without me?

A blinking sign that read "pick me" would not have made the bottle more conspicuous. Charles twirled a hand as if to say "When he's right, he's right."

Charles removed a pouch no larger than four square inches from a pocket sewn into the inner lining of his shirt. He unfolded the pouch, revealing a syringe, needles, and several plastic packets containing liquids. He inserted the needle into the syringe and plunged it into one of the packets, drawing solution from the package into the syringe.

Charles poked the cork of the wine bottle, taking care not to move the bottle as he worked. He squirted, then dismantled the syringe, replacing it in the pouch and the pouch into his pocket.

"How is it coming over there?" Charles asked.

"Charles, you are not going to believe this. I don't know how to tell you—"

Charles managed one step toward Julia before the elevator bell chimed in the hallway.

"Computer, close door," Charles said. The apartment door clicked shut. "Julia, shut down. It has to be now!"

"One minute! I need one minute!"

"Now, Julia!" Charles ran to her. Julia's fingers blurred like spokes in a spinning bicycle wheel. "Now!"

Julia hit the enter key and verbally commanded the computer to shut down. A dark patch began as a tiny square in the middle and grew until it eclipsed the entire screen.

Charles lifted her out of the chair and carried her halfway to the balcony.

"I can't, Charles."

"No time to think." Charles opened the balcony door and thrust Julia into the night air.

• • •

Farris leaned against the apartment door trying to kiss his date. The bandage on his nose complicated matters.

"Baby," she said, "let me doctor you up first. I'll run you a hot bubble bath. I know how much you like that."

"All right then." He did not renew his attempts. "Apartment. Open."

Charles perched on the ledge spanning the perimeter of Farris's loft, facing the balcony. Julia was still on the balcony, facing him. Both of her hands were in his, resting on the balcony railing. Charles risked a quick glance through the window at the loft's front door. It was slowly opening. He figured they had seconds left.

"Come on, Julia," he said. "The ledge is wide enough for you too."

"I can't. It's too high."

"You can. You have to."

"I can't feel my legs," Julia said. "Let me go, Charles."

Charles found Julia's eyes. They reminded him of a logic term she used when she argued: special pleading.

I fall in love, and here I am standing on a ledge thirty stories in the air. The saga continues.

"I don't have good luck with balconies," Charles said. He released Julia's hands. He thrust his own underneath her armpits and pulled. With her weight above him, he managed to pull her over the railing to her waist without much effort.

Julia teetered on the railing. "Okay, stop. I'll come. Let me do it myself."

Her tone made it sound like she was talking about removing a splinter. Then the apartment computer responded to Farris's open door command.

"Too late." Charles yanked Julia across the balcony railing like it was a conveyor belt. Charles took a step forward, embraced her in a bear hug, and pulled her off the railing. He hoped the ledge would hold.

It did. He set her down. "Duck!"

She went down onto her knees, below the window, obscured by the wall.

Charles sat down, facing her. "We have to get around the corner to be out of sight, in case they come out onto the balcony." He began shimmying backward on his rear end, pushing with his feet. Julia crawled on all fours toward him.

Inside, the lights dimmed.

Charles reached the corner.

Julia was close behind. She grabbed his feet. "Let's go back in. You can handle him." She looked briefly over the edge to the traffic thirty stories below. "I'm scared."

"He'll shoot us."

Charles managed a glimpse over his shoulder. There was no corner piece to the ledge. Instead, the ledge quit even with the corner, and resumed again on the other side of the building. He'd have to turn the corner with nothing below him but thirty floors of air.

He backed up to the edge, straightening up as he did. He rotated toward the wall, grasping in vain for a handhold on the ledge around the corner. He reached for it and found it with his right hand. He ventured a peek around the corner, pressing as hard as he could against the side of the building. A cool breeze greeted him.

"Can you make it?" Julia asked.

Charles thought he detected hope in her voice. Hope that he couldn't reach. She was probably hoping they would have to go back. "I can make it, easy," Charles said. "Let go of my feet."

Without thinking, he stretched out flat around the corner, stomach over the break in the ledge, grabbing the ledge as far down as he could with his hands He pulled. His body slinked around the corner. It met the ledge at his waist. He dangled waist high, legs flailing below the ledge. He pulled himself up and forward onto the ledge around the corner.

The balcony floodlight came on behind them, casting a pale light into the darkness. The balcony door rattled open. The sound of soft jazz filled escaped the loft.

I hate the ASL, Charles thought.

Charles crawled a few feet forward, got up on his hands and knees, and looked back. Julia was straddling the corner, one foot on each ledge, the break in the ledge beneath her. A gust of wind cast her hair in all directions. Her face resembled an Edvard Munch painting.

Charles peeked over the sculpted brick surrounding Farris's loft. He saw two figures moving out the balcony sliding glass door.

"Come on! Now!" Charles said.

Julia pushed with her left foot, let go of the corner, and fell to the ledge. She landed hard on her right shoulder. Charles reached to steady her.

Julia turned toward him, her eyes almost closed. "Step right up, folks," she said. "See the death-defying high wire act in the Charles Graves Traveling Circus."

• • •

Frank Cotton Graves rested alone in the dark of his office suite. He reclined in his executive chair, stripped down to his boxer shorts, feet propped on the window. He swiveled back and forth, alternating his view from the lights of downtown to the traffic on I-45.

You are a senator. They can't keep you locked up here indefinitely.

Cotton rotated the seat toward downtown. A senator is not what it used to be, my friend. Ingraham can pretty much do whatever he chooses. You're right, though, they won't keep you up here forever.

A swivel back toward I-45. His mind began to recognize it was wavering back and forth as well.

I didn't think so. No matter who they are, they can't keep me up here without cause.

Swivel. There are worse things than being up here. But you are right: eventually someone would wonder. That could be a week, though. Two, maybe. A month.

I have friends. They would notice.

Friends? Really. Who?

Charles would notice. We have come together lately.

Charles is preoccupied, in case you haven't noticed. Even if he wasn't, he blames you for Teresa. Deep down, you know he does. There's something worse though.

What's that?

You are correct that they won't keep you up here indefinitely. They have a definite plan to resolve this situation, if you know what I mean.

They wouldn't. I'm a senator.

They would. They can. And they have.

You have a week. Two at most. Sooner if they catch Charles. You'd better unpack that patented Cotton Graves survival kit. Time's a-wastin'.

I don't believe it.

What rat ever does before the trap snaps shut? Get with it, Cotton—you're smarter than this.

Cotton stopped swiveling the chair. He thought long into the night about Charles, Teresa, Stephen, and himself. But he mainly thought about plane crashes, car wrecks, and headlines about the tragic death of a senator. When he fell asleep, the traffic on I-45 was gone.

"How long do we have to stay out here?" Julia asked. "I'm cold."

Charles felt Julia roll to her side. They were lying on their backs, head to head.

"We can shimmy along to the apartment on the other side if you want," Charles said, "and take our chances sneaking through."

"What if the balcony is locked?"

"Who locks their balcony door on the thirtieth floor?"

Julia reached behind her and slapped Charles's head.

"Hey," Charles protested. "Anyway, I kinda like this. How else are we going to have time alone?"

"I don't want to think about that right now, Charles."

"Okay, then. Think about the airplanes. This reminds me of that night."

"Me too." Julia ran her fingers through his hair. "Charles, I need to talk to you about something I found on Farris's computer."

"Not right this second, Julia. I want this time with you."

Charles grabbed her hand and held it. Charles wished he could freeze time, but time seemed to be balancing on a ledge as well. He stared up at the night sky, hoping for an airplane to cruise overhead, the vibrations coursing through their bodies.

What Charles got was the night sky, stars, and a cloud floating above the skyscraper. It was enough.

A few days ago you were on the pavement below, disguised in rags. Since then your world has somersaulted. Now you are on a thirtieth-floor balcony, professing faith in Christ, and holding hands with the woman you love. What's next?

"You alright, Charles?" Julia asked.

He squeezed her hand. "I don't know what's going to happen, Julia. I just want you to know I love you, no matter what. And I despise myself for bringing all this trouble on you."

"We'll find a way," Julia said. "I love you too."

He closed his eyes. It was cool in the night air. When he reopened his eyes there was a silhouette in the window above him.

FOURTEEN

Charles's mind processed the murky silhouette. At first he thought it must be Farris. But the woodblock puzzle kicked in without warning. Charles realized his consciousness was receding. He reached for it. It fled to a corner of his mind as murky as the image above him. In a matter of seconds it was submerged, replaced by the wood-block puzzle.

The puzzle arranged itself. The dark man spoke to Charles through the silhouette at the window.

Nice work! How's the penthouse suite? Cold, I would imagine. The dark man accepted a glass from another silhouette in the loft. The dark man's companion was shapely. Cheers!

Charles stared at him from the ledge. The hollow eyes. How could his eyes still look so hollow at night through tinted windows?

Because I see through you, Charles, the dark man said. Now listen up. Close like. You could have been in here with this. The dark man ran a finger along his companion's cheek. In here. In other words, warm, comfortable, satisfied, on the top of the world. Instead, you traded all of this, plus more, for some foolish crusade. All over one moment's weakness when you were exhausted from tracking Cleveland. Now you're on some quixotic adventure. And that girl who likes logic instead of lingerie. Come on. You're killin' me.

Charles flapped his jaws like a dog with a glob of peanut butter in its mouth. I tried your way. My whole life I tried your way. Where did it get me? A dead brother. A dead mother. A dad who barely tolerates me. No family of my own. No real friends. I'm a drunk who lives by himself in the middle of nowhere. *That's* your way. That's what I got for listening to you.

No, Charles, the dark man said. Listen, I brought you through all those times. I saved you from them. I was there for you. Who else was? We were about to cash in, you and I. But I carried you through. Then you threw it away.

You're a liar. Get out. Let me talk to Julia. The dark man's eyes flared. Charles thought he saw the loft light up and fall dark again.

Have it your way, but I will take you with me one way or another.

The dark man shoved his hands against the glass.

Despite the distance between them, Charles felt himself pushed toward the edge of the ledge.

The dark man's image decomposed in the glass. First the outline of his silhouette became hazy, losing definition and contour. Then the image became smoky. Then it dissipated. The glass held the image suspended in the darkness for a split-second. Then it dropped out of sight. Charles thought he heard a crash.

He tried to reel in his consciousness from the murky pool in the back of his mind. Meanwhile, he felt for the edge of the ledge. What he felt was the underside of the ledge. He figured he must be hanging halfway off.

His eyes were drawn to a pinhole of light shining from the high-rise across the street. The pinhole began in the middle of one particular window and grew. Within seconds the entire window filled with light. The spreading light was impeded by the window frame. It pooled inside the frame until the whole window was full of light. The light began to change colors. The rectangular window colored itself.

The window frame was not stout enough to curtail the tide of light. Light began to spill over the frame like water over the sides of an overflowing tub. The windows filled and overflowed, filled and overflowed. Before long, Charles saw forty colored blocks on the skyscraper across the street.

It's a giant wood-block puzzle.

The blocks began to arrange themselves. All across the face of the building they shuffled, spun, gyrated, and blinked. In an instant, they stopped.

Charles tried to shield his eyes from the titanic face staring back at him. He wasn't sure he could shield his eyes or even if it were his eyes that were seeing the face. It was the face of his brother, Stephen.

"Time for me to return a favor, bro," Stephen said.

The building across the street trembled. The ground quaked. The building shimmied and shuddered under the strain of a gigantic lurch. A fire escape mounted on the side of the building wrenched free. The bolts mounting the fire escape to the wall shot out, puncturing windows on Charles's skyscraper across the street. Glass cascaded to the pavement. A flowerpot fell from the third level of the fire escape and shattered. The fire escape moaned and creaked, loosening years of rust and lethargy.

"I feel like the tin man," Stephen said.

The fire escape pulled free from the ground floor of the building up to the thirtieth floor, which formed Stephen's shoulder. It raised its lower half, bending in the middle as if mimicking an elbow. It snaked around the side of the building, rotating in front of Stephen as if he were getting acquainted with his new limb. The fire escape squealed with every movement.

The tip of the fire escape changed first. To Charles it seemed as if magic dust were falling from the sky over the metal of the fire escape. The dust worked its way from the tip of the fire escape, where Stephen was admiring his hand, to the shoulder still connected to the building. Where the dust passed over, metal transformed to flesh. Stephen formed a fist with his new hand and flexed the muscles of his new appendage.

The arm extended across the street to where Charles and Julia rested on the ledge. Stephen reached an index finger toward Charles and caressed his head.

"How're ya doin', my brother?" Stephen said. "I bet you got a scar there on your cheek. Can't see it real well from here. You got makeup on, sissy boy?"

"Sissy boy, hmm," Charles said. "Last time I checked, I was the man here, weenie boy."

Stephen dropped his new arm thirty floors, making a fist as it fell. The fist pounded into the street. The buildings shook, car alarms sounded, and a bell tower three streets over clanged.

"Yep, haven't changed," Charles said. "You always were a weenie boy."

"Sissy boy."

"Weenie."

Stephen raised his arm. Charles watched it sail upward from the street. The hand rose until it hovered over him. Stephen opened the mammoth hand and rested it on Charles.

"I miss you, Stephen. Big brother," Charles said. "All this time and I miss you. I can't believe what happened."

"Get over it, sissy boy."

"I can't."

"Then come with me." Stephen lowered his hand and moved it to the edge of the ledge in front of Charles. With the slow swoop downward, the hand distributed magic dust all the way down to the pavement below.

Charles watched the dust do its thing. It sailed in updrafts. It zigged and zagged, did curly-Qs and loop-de-loops. It colored the night with whites and golds and browns. The dust recreated a thirty-floor-high version of the Graves Mansion staircase, complete with gold-inlaid steps and wood-carved images of eagles. It was perfect in every detail. Charles could almost discern the marble floor beginning to form at street level.

"Is it real?" he asked.

"Seeing is believing," Stephen said. "Come on down."

Charles reached out with his hand and fondled the top step. It felt real. It felt right. It felt good. He ran his finger along the gold inlay. It was cool to the touch, just as he remembered. He strained to hear. Music was wafting up the staircase from downstairs.

He noticed something else. The music was the only sound. There was no screaming or fighting. No yelling or name-calling.

"Stephen. Is she there? Please tell me she is there and she is all right. I don't hear any fighting. Maybe we could all be together again. And be happy?"

"Come on down, Charles," Stephen said. "We're waiting for you."

Charles thought he saw the tail end of a red dress pass over the white marble floor far below. It seemed to glide across the floor. It's her. I can almost smell her.

The Graves Mansion chandelier burst into light. To Charles it seemed like the creation of the universe.

"Hurry up, Charles. I can only hold it so long. Let's go."

"Coming," Charles said.

Charles lay on his side, lengthwise along the ledge, facing the drop. Julia lay behind him, her head even with his shoulders.

"Charles, come back. I can't hold on much longer." Julia tucked both her hands into Charles's back pockets. To Julia it seemed that Charles had entered an epileptic shock without the spasms. He was babbling, reaching over the ledge with both hands.

If he goes over, he'll take you with him.

Let him go then.

No way, GG. You can manage this. First things first, though. Take your hands out of his pockets. That way if he goes, you don't.

Julia hesitated. She removed her hands. Charles slid closer to the edge.

Lie with your back against the wall and see if you can roll him over away from the edge.

Julia shimmied forward so his head was even with hers. She grabbed Charles's right shoulder and pulled. Charles slid back an inch, no more.

I can't do it.

You will do it.

Charles stopped reaching and rolled his head over toward Julia. His hair was wild in the breeze. His speech was rapid, but senseless. His face was covered with dirt and bird droppings from the ledge. His eyes were zombiesque. In the dim light of the ledge, they seemed hollow.

It's not him, GG. It's that dark thing he was telling you about. Worry with it later. Right now, you've got to get him away from the edge. Given what you just found on Farris's computer, he's got to live.

Charles rolled his head back over and recommenced his reaching. Julia pulled on his shoulder again. Charles's body raised up about six inches before dropping back. The senseless babbling continued.

One more time, GG. This time pull like it's a tug-of-war. Wimpy-chick time's over.

Julia lifted with everything she had. Charles again raised up about six inches and dropped back down.

You've got to pull harder, GG.

Shut up! Can't you see I am pulling as hard as I can? I thought you were the logical one. This is not going to work. I should try something else.

Julia climbed on top of Charles. She figured the added weight might keep him steady for a minute or two. As she climbed on, she caught a glimpse over the ledge. The height was repulsive. Her guts wanted to slither out of her body and slink off into the night. She put her head to the left of his, away from the drop.

Julia stroked Charles's hair with her right hand and in vain searched for a handhold with her left. She whispered into his ear, aware it was all for nothing. "I'm here, Charles. Hold on." Julia caressed Charles's head where his hair met the back of his neck. "Come back, Charles. Cleveland is waiting for us."

Charles reached again for the staircase. If he could get a good grip on one of the steps, he thought he could pull himself down to where his brother and mother were waiting. He stretched and grasped a gold-inlaid step. He pulled. He felt himself slide forward.

One more and you should be there, he thought. Charles strained to reach the next step. It was close, real close. His fingers found it and tightened.

A sneaker came down on his fingers. The pressure was firm but gentle. Charles looked up.

It was Cleveland in his fishing outfit. "You sure you want to do that?" Cleveland asked.

"It's beautiful," Charles said. "My mother—"

"Is dead," Cleveland said. "You can't go to her that way." Cleveland eased up on Charles's fingers. "I won't stop you, though, if you want to."

How did he get here? If he walked up, the gold staircase must be real.

Something moved behind Cleveland. It began behind Stephen's building across the street. It was picking up speed. It was a giant fist—aiming for Cleveland. Charles saw his brother's twisted snarl and eyes burning through Cleveland.

"Over here, Charles," Cleveland said. "This false staircase of yours is not Jacob's ladder. Now c'mon!"

The fist was halfway across the street and gaining speed. Charles saw the veins popping out of his brother's arm, the muscles undulating, the hairs bristling. The last thing Charles noticed before the fist struck was its dirty thumbnail.

The fist slammed into Cleveland full on. It was three times bigger than Cleveland, and it hit with the force of a volcanic blast.

All of downtown seemed to shake. The concussion blew out the windows across the street. Stephen's image shattered, plunging to the street below. Charles saw fragments of his brother falling. Charles grabbed for his brother but came up empty. The last thing he saw was his brother's mouth. It was screaming. *No!* Stephen's mouth shattered on the pavement below, glass shrapnel flinging in every direction.

The fist exploded into a fireworks display of magic dust. The dust shot out from Cleveland's back in all directions, lit up in an array of color, exploded one last time, and disappeared.

The fire escape fell thirty floors to the street. It creaked and moaned all the way down and exploded on the pavement not far from where Stephen's mouth had landed. The shock detached the shoulder end of the fire escape from the building, which plunged to the ground onto a parked garbage truck, flattening it. The fire escape rolled over, letting out one last wail as if it were glad to be dying. Then its twisted metal corpse lay silent.

Cleveland smiled that kind of smile that only pastors know. "The forces of darkness seem invincible in our world. More so when we focus on the reclamation centers, the evil, our troubles. But in the spiritual world, you get to see how darkness is no match for God. Remember that when you get back. Remember the real Jacob's ladder."

Charles watched Cleveland and the staircase fade away. The stairs lit up a final time and disappeared. Below, down on the street where the staircase ended, he thought saw someone waving a flashlight overhead in an attempt to signal him.

Charles came to himself. He realized he was hanging over the edge of the ledge, thirty stories high. He flailed for a handhold.

"Easy, Charles," Julia said. "I've got you."

"Thanks for not letting go," Charles said.

"I couldn't pull you up." Julia covered her eyes with her hands. "I was so scared. You were so heavy."

"No, you did fine," Charles said. "Come here." He reached to pull her close but she resisted. Charles noticed how close he was to the edge. "Ah. Maybe I should come to you."

Charles scooted away from the edge. He rose up on his elbow and gave her a kiss. A long one. She responded. He stroked the back of her head. For one long minute, in the cool night air, thirty floors up, Charles thought the world was flat.

Julia released him. "I love you."

"You're the best thing that ever happened to me."

Movement behind Julia caught Charles's eye.

It was Farris. He was clawing at the window. He tried to scream, but no sound came out.

The clawing was brief. Farris pasted his hands against the window above his head, as if trying to hold on. He slobbered on the window and began to sink. His eyes followed Charles as they sank. About halfway down to the window's base, the eyes closed. Farris fell to the floor.

"Time to go," Charles said.

Julia sat up in alarm, watching Farris's slide. "What happened to him?"

"Oh, I spiked his wine bottle. He'll sleep for hours." Charles looked at Julia. She favored her shoulder a bit. "Do you think you can make it back?"

"Do I have a choice?" Julia said.

Seconds later they were back in the loft. Farris was slumped by the window. His date was passed out on the floor by the computer. Charles noted the open bottle. "Thanks, man," he said.

No problem, the dark man said. Always there for you.

"Who are you talking to?" Julia asked as she checked Farris's pockets.

"Myself. Forget it."

"Why do you think Farris was at the window?"

"Probably knew we were here somewhere. Felt the dope and knew something was up."

"We're lucky he didn't set off an alarm or call HQ then."

"Maybe." Charles walked across the loft toward Julia. "He's not the type though. More likely, he was trying to shoot us. Did you get everything you needed from the computer?"

"I did. And I still need to talk to you about what I found."

"Let's get out of here first."

Ten minutes later they were back in the station wagon with Cleveland. Cleveland put the car in gear.

Charles noticed a flashlight on the dash. "Cleveland, what is Jacob's ladder?"

• • •

Charles grabbed a chair for himself and pulled it up to the plastic table on Lasanya's back porch. Cleveland was already seated at it, and Julia was inside taking a shower.

The backyard was eight parts dirt, two parts grass. Two large oaks, mirroring the two in front, blocked most of the sunlight during daylight hours, which stunted the grass. The poodles ruined most of the rest in a figure-eight track they had carved around the trees. What grass was left grew along the fence line. Clouds filled the night sky. A glow from Lasanya's bedroom window afforded a dim light out on the patio.

"So tell me," Cleveland said.

"All I know is she got it," Charles said. "Wait until she gets out of the shower."

"Well, I wasn't gonna bust in on her," Cleveland said.

Charles leaned over the table toward Cleveland. "Hey, I know how bad you want to know about your family. I do too. Will you do me a favor though? Right now we have ten minutes or so. I was thinking you could explain the dark man to me. You promised."

Cleveland peeled a piece of duct tape off the table, rolled it up, and flicked it into the yard. "You gonna believe it if I tell you?"

"Any reason I shouldn't?"

"Funny you should say that." Cleveland leaned forward and retrieved a pocket-sized New Testament out of his pants. The cover was tattered. It resembled a shred of lettuce. "Gideons—gotta love 'em. Got this when I was back in school. There is still a force of 'em in this town. I'll introduce you sometime."

"I thought we got all of them," Charles said.

"Not hardly." Cleveland spread the New Testament open on the table.

Charles repositioned himself next to Cleveland. He popped his knuckles and rubbed his forehead.

"You all right?" Cleveland asked.

"Yeah." Charles tried to sit up straight.

Are you? You've been waiting for this for as long as you can remember, and now you don't know whether to be excited or sick. You're finally going to get to know. Quit being such a sissy.

Cleveland began to read aloud from his Bible. He kept his voice low in the night. "Are ye also without understanding? Do not ye yet understand—"

"No. I don't," Charles said. He felt the wood-block puzzle warming up.

Cleveland raised his head and stuck Charles with his eyes. "Do you want me to do this or not?"

Charles retreated into the backrest of the chair.

Cleveland read again. "That whatsoever entereth in at the mouth goeth into the belly, and is cast out in the draught? But those things which proceed out of the mouth come forth from the heart; and they defile the man. For out of the heart proceed evil thoughts, murders, adulteries, fornications, thefts, false witness, blasphemies: these are the things which defile a man."

Charles pondered the archaic words as they rolled off Cleveland's tongue. They were just settling into a cozy part of his mind when Charles noticed the dark man sitting in Julia's chair. He was wearing a Hawaiian shirt and a Panama hat.

Don't be a sap, the dark man said.

"I want to know," Charles said.

"Listen to what I am reading then," Cleveland said. "You with me here?"

"Yeah. I'm with you."

Who's been with you all this time? the dark man said. It wasn't him that showed you the right bottle back there in Farris's loft. That was me. The dark man pointed at Cleveland and then at himself to emphasize the point.

Charles put a finger to his lips.

You already know who I am, the dark man said.

Cleveland held the Bible up and pointed at the passage. "I love the Word of God. Cuts deep, don't it? Cuts true too."

Charles refocused on Cleveland. He's answering you, Charles. Try to listen.

Cleveland's gaze was kind. "The evil ain't all outside you, Charles. The worst of it, as far as a man is concerned, is inside."

"You're going to tell me I've got a demon inside me, aren't you?" Charles tried not to sneer. "Want me to turn my head all the way around for you?"

Cleveland guffawed. "You ain't got no demon, boy."

"I don't?" Charles blinked at him. "Well, that's good, right?"

"Charles Graves, if you had a demon we'd a-dealt with that a long time before now. No, son, what you got is something much less exotic. But just as evil."

He tilted his head. "Charles, you call this thing inside you your dark man. Well, look: we're all of us born with 'a dark man' inside us. Listen to what the apostle Paul says: 'That ye put off concerning the former conversation the old man, which is corrupt according to the deceitful lusts; and be renewed in the spirit of your mind; and that ye put on the new man, which after God is created in righteousness and true holiness.'"

Cleveland shut the Bible and placed it on the table. "What that is saying, Charles, is that your dark man is your sin nature. It's 'the old man' Paul was talking about. That's why he's always there. That's why he knows you so well."

The dark man lifted his shoulders and opened his hands, showing Charles his palms. *Told you we was tight.*

Charles descended into the maelstrom of his past. It made some sense, what Cleveland was saying. The dark man was the me-first voice in his mind. He was the go-to guy, the "I know it all" and "look at me now" guy.

"You're sure he's not the devil?" Charles remembered how the dark man had rejoiced when his brother had fallen.

"I'm sure," Cleveland said. "He's the devil's friend and the devil's pawn, but he ain't the devil."

"Does he—"

The screen door leading to the porch swung open. Julia stepped through, dressed in one of Lasanya's robes. The screen door's hinges creaked as it shut. Julia sat down in the empty chair.

Charles watched Julia sit on the dark man. He swelled with her weight like a balloon full of air. Then he popped, first at the head, then the rest of him, and disintegrated into the night.

Could Julia have a dark woman? It's not possible. But if what Cleveland says is true, everyone has one. How come she doesn't see hers? He thought to ask Cleveland about this later. Several other questions leapt to the front of his mind, but he beat them back to focus on Julia. The dark man would have to wait.

"Feel better?" he asked.

"Much, thanks. I needed that." Julia tightened the belt holding the robe together.

"I can't wait no longer," Cleveland said. He laced his fingers together.

"Okay." Julia grabbed Cleveland's hands. "I found them. They are at Reclamation Center Three. There's still time. Not much, but there is still time."

"How much?" Cleveland asked.

"A week at most. Maybe a day or two."

"That's not right," Charles said. "Can't be. They'll use them for bait. I'll bet anything on it."

"All I can tell you is what I found in Farris's computer, Charles," Julia said. "That's what it said."

Cleveland unlaced his fingers and placed his face in his hands. A muffled sound came out. "Is there anything we can do, Charles?"

Where's the dark man when you need him? Charles winced, thinking he might reappear at the mention of his name. I need a good lie about now. Odds of infiltrating a reclamation center and breaking someone out: one in a million. Odds of rescuing Cleveland's wife and daughter: one in a billion. Tell him the truth.

"Can't be done," Charles said. "Forget it."

The screen door squeaked open. Lasanya came out backward, pushing the door with her rear end. She turned around once clear of the door and set a tray of sandwiches and chips down on the table. In her other hand was a pitcher of tea and three glasses, which she set on the table. She flicked an oak leaf from the table before returning inside.

"I'm gonna try," Cleveland said. "I don't have a choice."

"Hang on a second," Julia said. "There's more." She turned in her chair so that she faced Charles. She placed her hands on his.

A tingling seemed to jump out of Julia and into his fingertips. But booze was the last thing on his mind.

"Charles," she said, "don't be mad at me, please."

Charles shifted in his chair. Cleveland put his hands down and leaned in.

"I don't know why I did it," Julia said, "but while I was in Farris's computer, I decided to, you know, uh . . . " She swallowed.

"Just say it," Charles said. "I won't be mad."

"I don't even know why I thought about it. Maybe because I worry so much about you. It was hard to find too. Out of the way, in an ancient file. I don't know how to tell you this, Charles."

"Just say it."

She looked into his eyes. "Your mother is still alive."

FIFTEEN

Frank Cotton Graves spied the digital clock on the media center where they had briefed Charles and Farris on Operation Belt Buckle. It read 2:30 a.m.

"Belt Buckle? Ha!" he said. "I think someone's pants fell down."

Cotton was on his knees, caressing a column in the corner of the suite. His fingertips fondled the plaster, tracing a three-foot-square concealed door near the base of the column.

Where will you go?

Anywhere but here. Can't trust this place anymore.

You've got no place and no one to go to.

I've got money and connections. What else do I need? I'll vanish like the 2007 Mets.

Cotton pricked his finger on a spur of plaster. He grabbed it with his other hand and squeezed. "No way to do this cleanly."

He reached into his slacks and extracted a pocketknife, which he opened. The blade locked into place with a click. Cotton plunged the blade into the column. It sunk in a half-inch, four feet from the floor. Cotton pulled the blade down. It left a gash in the column about six inches long until the blade caught on a metal plate.

He pulled the blade out and reinserted it an inch below the plate. He fished for a second or two. The blade found a crease in the plaster and sank in. Cotton pulled hard to the right. The blade exposed a slit in the plaster that ran to the edge of the column. Cotton removed the blade, reversed it, and ran it to the other side of the column. He repeated the activity vertically along the sides of the column.

I guess being an old-timer has its advantages, he thought.

Cotton felt the slits in the column. He stuck the knife in the top slit and pushed up, grimacing. The door wavered, but did not budge. The knife blade snapped at its casing under the strain. Cotton's hand followed through upward from the force of the break. The plaster worked his knuckles like sandpaper, some of the spurs ripping the skin off in chunks. He cried out in the loneliness of the suite.

Cotton crossed the suite, leaving a trail of blood droplets on the floor. He sought a supply closet to the left of Sheila's desk. He entered and fumbled around in the dark. A few minutes later, he returned with a screwdriver and a first aid kit.

Cotton sat on Sheila's desk to bandage his hand. He detected a faint reminder of her perfume. I should at least leave her a note. He did.

Back at the column, Cotton forced the screwdriver into the slit. He put his palms underneath the head of the screwdriver and forced his weight up. The door groaned, squeaked, and spit rust and plaster out at Cotton. He felt it give way. It protested one last time, then fell with force against a shin. Cotton clenched his teeth.

He swept his gaze around to absorb one last impression of the suite. Some corners of it were dark now, but his memories from the long years here filled in the pieces. "Good-bye, lady." He sat down and inserted his legs into the hole.

On the far side of the hollow column, his feet felt a ladder. The tube was not much wider than his body.

Get the screwdriver and pull the door shut. That may buy you an extra few minutes. You may need them.

Can I get the door below open?

How would I know? Get going. You've got nothing to lose.

I am losing everything, in case you didn't realize it.

In case you didn't notice, you already lost it. Now get going.

Cotton reached back out the door with one arm and fumbled around for the screwdriver. His hand lit upon the plastic handle and pulled it in. He dropped it into a pants pocket. The door was too bulky to lift back into place so he just left it on the floor.

Cotton descended. The ladder was sturdy. It was also dirty. He imagined himself exiting the tube covered in grime from head to foot. The tube was stifling. His sweat poured from a combination of stuffiness and exertion.

He descended carefully: foot, hand, foot, hand, foot, hand, foot, hand. The monotony of the descent was a distant third to the heat and the darkness. Foot, hand, foot, hand.

Ten minutes later, Cotton's foot found empty space and he almost fell. He found himself hanging by his left hand, his heart pounding with adrenaline.

Thank goodness it wasn't the right hand. You might have fallen.

Pull yourself up before you do.

Cotton pulled himself up. He clung to the ladder like insecurity on a seventh-grader.

What now? Go up, I guess. Why did the ladder end? Doesn't make sense.

Do you smoke, Cotton?

Yes.

Then take out your lighter and light it.

Good idea. If I can pry myself off this ladder.

Cotton fired the lighter. Because of the closeness of the tube, he could not see very well below. He tried holding the lighter down by his side, but it didn't help. The light was blinding in the darkness. Cotton coughed. He inhaled some of the rust and grime from the ladder and sides of the tube.

Put it away and get out the screwdriver.

Why?

I have a feeling.

Cotton obeyed. Now what?

Drop it.

He dropped the screwdriver.

Nothing. No sound. No nothing.

That's impossible.

I know. What now?

How long have you been climbing?

I haven't. I've been descending.

Shut up. How long?

I don't know.

Long enough. Jump.

No way.

Do it.

No.

Cotton let loose of the ladder.

One of Lasanya's poodles propped itself up by its front paws on the armrest of Charles's chair. It licked tears off his cheek. Charles put a hand around the back of the dog's neck, pulled it close, then shooed it away.

What a life I lead, Charles thought. "Thank you. I don't know how I can—"

"You don't need to," Julia said. "I had a feeling, that's all. It was a couple of keystrokes. I didn't do anything."

"You've done everything," Charles said. "Thanks."

"Electricity," Cleveland said. "That's what this is. Can you feel it? Awesome, ain't it?"

"No, what it was, was an encrypted database and someone who knows how to hack it," Julia said. "The only electricity was the moving electron type, fully accounted for by natural law."

Cleveland poured a glass of tea, added sugar, and stirred. "'Verily, verily, I say unto thee, except a man be born again, he cannot see the kingdom of God.' Those Calvinists might have gotten it right after all." Cleveland took a sip of his tea. "Use that logic of yours, girl. Look at what's going on. Can all this be meaningless coincidence? Or are you gonna watch the Red Sea part and not believe?"

Julia pointed at Charles. "All I know is that I fell in love with him, he fell in love with your gospel, and you are fugitive." Julia reached over and grabbed a potato chip. "One of the more charming fugitives we been after, though. I'll give you that."

"All *I* know," Charles said, "is that for the first time in my life I feel like I have a purpose." He felt tears coming again. He took a second to tamp them down. "I spent years feeling guilty for my brother, years missing my mother, years dancing around my dad, years wearing a mask. Now," he said, looking at Julia, "I have you. At least, I hope I—"

"You do."

Charles smiled wetly. "I met the right reverend here, I got saved, and I found out my mother is alive. I don't know what is going to happen, but I feel the purpose. I feel something behind it all. I feel alive and hopeful for the first time in a very long time. I guess that's God, huh, Reverend?"

Cleveland nodded, a huge grin on his face.

"With the whole world after us, who knows what's gonna happen?" Charles said. "But no matter what happens, it is great knowing there is a purpose behind it, rather than it all being just . . . people drifting around through life with masks on."

"Wonderful for you, Charles," Julia said. "You found your purpose. Great. But I felt like I had meaning in my life already. A good job, maybe a family someday. Now it's gone. I'm thrilled for you, but what about mine? It's ruined."

Cleveland raised a preachin' finger. "Julia, when the Spirit of—"

"Hang on a minute, Reverend," Charles said. "Uh, I don't think that will work right this second."

Charles turned to face Julia. "I hate myself for what I've done to you, Julia. I do. It seems like everyone close to me gets caught in a whirlpool and flushed into the sewer, with the exception of my dad perhaps. Julia, what has happened to you bothers me. *Bad.*" Charles emphasized the word by throwing his hands out in front of him. "But maybe, just maybe, things are changing. Maybe we will actually get away with all of this. Maybe that's the purpose."

Charles leaned over the table to place one hand on her hand and his other hand over his heart. "I promise you this, Julia: if we get away with what we are about to do, I'll take you far away from here and make that purpose of yours come true. We could find a good life somewhere. I promise."

Julia looked at their hands together on the table. "Charles . . . ? What are 'we' about to do?"

"I'm gonna get my wife and daughter," Cleveland said.

Charles spun on him. "No, you're not, Pastor. *I* am going to get your family. You and Julia are going to get my mother."

Cleveland and Julia started to speak at once.

"Trust me, you two," Charles said. "You're both masters of what you do. But at this part, I'm the expert."

Cleveland and Julia shot a quick glance at each other.

"As long as it is quick, I guess," Cleveland said.

"Tonight, we rest. Tomorrow morning, we plan," Charles said. "We move out tomorrow night." He stood up. "Let's get some sleep. We're going to need it." He motioned for Julia and Cleveland to go inside. Charles sat back down.

"What are you doing?" Julia asked.

Charles looked up into the black sky. "I can't believe she's alive."

Frank Cotton Graves landed with a soft thud. His feet hit the floor of the tube before he could finish hollering "Geronimo!" The end of the ladder had been four feet above the bottom of the tube.

Cotton fired the lighter again and found the screwdriver resting on a mound of painters' drop cloths. To his right was the door leading outside.

There was a latch on the door Cotton killed the lighter and worked the latch. It was rusty, but with minimal effort Cotton was able to open it. The door fell open. Outside, he saw the manicured agency lawn. And beyond it, the nature preserve.

The feel of the outside air on his face reminded him of younger days. He bolted out the door, joints crackling like a popcorn popper. In ten minutes he was deep into the woods.

By mid-morning the sun had crept high enough to gain direct access into Farris's loft. The light shot down from the sky, penetrated the tinted windows, crossed over the computer where Julia's fingerprints were imprinted on the keyboard, cruised over a sofa, and landed on Farris's exposed face. It burrowed through his eyelids.

Farris was chasing a freight train. He ran, as fast as one can run in a dream, down the middle of the tracks, catching the wooden crossties with the balls of his feet. He was a hundred yards from the caboose. The caboose was constructed with the traditional back porch and railing. From the railing hung presidential red, white, and blue bunting. Farris saw Charles and Cleveland in top hats, dancing the tango from one end of the porch to another.

Farris's left foot came down on gravel that had spilled over onto one of the crossties. It acted as marbles. Farris did a remarkable job of balancing initially, then fell face forward onto the tracks.

The effect was a ruined suit and limitless pain in his nose. He propped himself up on his knees and brushed himself off, finding a set of pinholes in one sleeve. His dream tortured him with the thought that this was the last suit in the world, and now it was ruined.

The train's brakes squealed and Farris forgot his suit altogether. The train stopped almost in place and generated a cloud of dust that enveloped it. Farris wondered how a train could generate a cloud of dust.

From inside the cloud came the sounds of dreams, those that cannot be reproduced in the waking world. Farris recognized it as the train's whistle, yet he realized it was more. It was a tearing sound, a hypersonic but audible reconfiguration. It was the sound of reconstitution.

The light was the first thing to emerge from the dust cloud. It pierced the cloud and traveled over the intervening space in a single ray, two feet in diameter. It struck him in the face.

Blinded, Farris stood. The light tracked him, remaining on his face.

It's the engine, Farris thought. Somehow the train reversed itself. It's coming for me!

The light dimmed as, back in Farris's loft, a cloud eclipsed the sun.

The face of the engine poked out from the dust cloud. It was now an antique locomotive. The headlight and a cowcatcher emerged. The cowcatcher spoke—in Charles's voice.

"You missed," it said. "I thought you never missed."

Over the distance, Farris imagined the cowcatcher's breath smelled like steam and oil. "This one doesn't count as a miss," he said. "You sucker-punched me. What were you after?"

"Secret things."

"The world has turned over, Charles," Farris said.

The light switched off. The cowcatcher receded into the cloud. When it reemerged the engine was charging toward Farris at full steam.

The locomotive chassis was still intact, but the iron wheels had become the hooves of a bull. The light morphed into an enormous nose, ejecting smoke and fire from two pulsating nostrils. Gargantuan horns grew out from the sides of the engine, spewing steam and smoke from their tips.

The bull's head was the face of Charles Graves. Farris understood this on a primal level because the face was nondescript and ever-changing. Farris was hard-pressed to describe it. Charles's reputation as a ghost was intact. Sometimes the face was the trustee of the Creekside Baptist Church. It was alternatively a vagabond, Julia Jenkins, Ingraham, the Reverend Cleveland, Cotton Graves, an inexplicable man with slick hair, thin lips, and hollow eyes, and a thousand other of Charles's disguises over the years.

Throughout its changing assortment of faces, it focused on Farris. He experienced a flicker of honest self-disclosure. He saw his own face. Immediately, Farris doused the image. Surely Charles had incorporated that pompous grin, those greedy eyes, and that freakish nose from his own envy of the great Richard Fah-reese.

The bull stopped, reared up on its hind legs, snorted, and crashed back down. The ground shook when it landed. The tracks to either side of Farris undulated like waves with the shock of the bull's impact with the ground.

When the bull lurched forward again, Farris saw a medallion around its neck. The medallion swung back and forth like the pendulum on a grandfather clock. It was a timepiece. The hands were moving backward, turning back time.

Now someone was riding the bull. It was Cleveland. He was dressed as a dime-store cowboy. He wore riding gloves. One hand was wrapped in a rope slung around the bull's neck, the other waved above his head for balance. Farris figured he had eight seconds before the bull ran him down. "I should have stayed in Wisconsin."

He removed his pistol and put three slugs into the bull's forehead. The bull crashed at his feet without a sound.

"I don't miss." He holstered the pistol.

Three rays of light shot out from the bullet holes in the bull's head. The light hurt Farris's eyes. He turned from the light—and found himself nose to nose with a train conductor.

"Message for you, sir," the conductor said, holding out a card. "From a Mr. Keesma."

Farris took the card and opened it. It read: Phone.

Back in the loft, Farris wrestled with consciousness. He held one hand out to block the sun. The other pushed against the floor.

The loft informed him a Mr. Keesma was calling.

Farris decided his head needed both hands more than he needed to stand. He put his back to the wall and both hands to his head, avoiding his nose.

"Audio," he said. "No visual."

The audio crackled to life. "Mr. Fah-reese," Keesma said, "we have a problem."

"Speak," Farris said.

"Senator Graves broke out last night. They found an open escape hatch around 8:30 this morning. His car is still in its parking space, so they think he is on foot."

"Get Louis and meet me at HQ in two hours."

"We're already there."

"Good. Then even you two idiots can't mess that one up. We are operating out of HQ full-time until this is settled. Audio off."

Farris crawled toward the medicine cabinet.

Charles sprung out of the bed in the back room. Outside, the sun had not yet fallen below the horizon, but it was losing its grip. The half-light increased Charles's disorientation. He heard an argument escalating in the front of Lasanya's home. He forced his feet into the pants legs. Seconds later he scuttled down the hall to the den. The poodles barked in the back yard.

When he entered the den, he saw two men arguing with Cleveland and Julia. One of the men had oversized gray side-burns growing on bulging cheeks. He pressed his finger in Cleveland's chest. The other man resembled Friar Tuck. He stood next to sideburns man, across from Julia.

"You in or out?" Sideburns said.

"Out," Cleveland said. "Definitely out. Gurdy Morrison, the church has no business with violence."

Gurdy forced his words through a sneer. "The church? Who're you kiddin'? You ain't got no church, just a bunch of scared, hidin' mice. And they're smokin' y'all out in droves." Gurdy pleaded with Cleveland. "We got to strike, Reverend. Hit 'em hard. Turn the world over for real."

"God does not condone His children acting that way," Cleveland said. "This is a time for faith, not violence. Joseph was sold into slavery. Daniel was a faithful subject. Even Jesus refused to strike against the injustice of His day. Instead, He came to do the will of His father. We need to wait for God. This thing you are planning, it's—"

"Shut up with that faith stuff," Gurdy said. "We'll hit them so hard that people will rise up from every city in the country. Revolution's in the air. It ain't got nothing to do with faith. You folks were all such talkers in your marches and protests, but now that the real war is here, y'all ain't nothin' but a bunch of prayers, talkers, and hiders. You make me sick. The church. Please."

"What—"

"I said shut up, Reverend." Gurdy leaned toward Cleveland's face. "A word of this out of your mouth and you ain't safe no more." He removed his finger from Cleveland's chest and motioned to his partner. "Let's go."

"You can't do this," Julia said.

"You one of them agents, ain'tcha?" the man said. "We can—"

Charles entered the den bare from the waist up, hair mussed. "You can what?"

Gurdy squinted at Charles. His face twisted itself in a circle as if he were trying to ratchet the gears of his mind. "That him, Cleveland?"

Cleveland produced a noncommittal gesture.

"We're leavin'."

The two men slinked out the door. The door clicked shut, leaving the house silent except for the howling of the poodles on the back porch. Outside, the twilight deepened.

Julia marched to her purse, which was propped against the armrest of the couch. She extracted her pistol. "We can't let them go." She started back for the door.

Cleveland took a step toward her. "Whoa, girl. What are you thinking? We can let them go. Remember what we're about to do. We can't be shootin' people just before we do this. Besides, we can try and catch up with them later. You guys are good at tracking folks, right?"

Charles moved to Julia and Cleveland, who were facing each other. He placed his left hand on the back of Julia's neck and his right hand on the back of Cleveland's neck. He imagined a Three Stooges maneuver with their heads and wondered why the Stooges were not on the approved TV list. "Fill me in," Charles said.

The sound of car doors came from the drive. The car's engine attempted to turn over. On the second attempt it finally did. The car backed out of the drive, paused, and took off down the street.

Julia spoke. "They're planning to set something off downtown. Soon. A week at the outside. Could be a bomb. Could be something worse. They claim they have Novichok agent stockpiled. Can't be, though. Not them. No way. They could do something, though." She glared at Cleveland. "And he let them walk out."

"This week just keeps gettin' better." Charles released Cleveland and Julia, rubbing the tips of his fingers against his thumbs. Settle down, fingers, he thought. If this keeps up, you might get all the booze you want. He sat down on the couch and rubbed his fingers along its grainy seams in methodic strokes. "You know where they are headed?"

"I know where they stay," Cleveland said. "Can't say how long they will stay there, or if they will even go back there."

"Well, it's not our first problem," Charles said. "We can try to do something about it, but—"

"Charles," Julia said, "We have to do something. We don't have a choice in this."

"I do," Charles said. "I haven't seen my mother in twenty years. I thought she was dead. She's first." He held a hand out to her. "Come here."

Julia relinquished the death grip on her gun. She dropped it in the purse and sat down next to Charles. He put an arm around her.

Did you notice how she takes all that booze lust away from you? She does it without trying. She sits down beside you. Poof, all gone.

Charles noticed his fingers were not rubbing the skin off of themselves anymore. He caressed Julia's hair with subtle down-strokes. "I'll figure something out. Don't worry. First, though, it's Cleveland's family and my mother." Charles traced the contour of Julia's face with his fingertips. He addressed Cleveland. "Do you have a secure phone?"

"I do," Cleveland said, pacing in two-step turnarounds. "Can't use it here, though."

"Right," Charles said. "Now sit down so I can explain what we are doing. It's close to dark. We need to leave soon."

Cleveland found a seat on Charles's left.

"Okay," Charles said, "we eat, I fix us up with disguises, and we move out in three hours. No later. I am going to make the shift change at the reclamation center at 11:00. There I will find your wife and daughter and get them out. You two are going at the same time to get my mother. I'll tell you how on the way."

"Absolutely not," Cleveland said. "I am going for my family. There's no debate about this."

Charles let go of Julia. The dark man welled up inside. Charles worked to keep him under control. He placed one hand on Cleveland's knee. "I'll leave the preaching to you, but leave the intrigue to me. I need you to do what I say. Please. And the first thing I need you to do is line up a new safe house. It needs to be ready by the time we leave so we can drop my van off on the way."

"Charles," Julia said, "what about those men?"

"I've already got a plan working."

Cleveland groaned. "Well . . . you're the boss, Charles. But I ain't goin' no further until we pray about this."

SIXTEEN

"So we're all set then," Charles said from the front seat. It doesn't matter though. This is a fool's errand. Charles fiddled with two pieces from his wood-block puzzle stowed away in his pants pocket.

Cleveland affirmed Charles without taking his eyes off the road. The station wagon he drove crossed under the NASA Parkway overpass, going south down I-45. Cleveland maneuvered around an eighteen-wheeler and settled back into the center lane.

"What about the bombing plot, Charles?" Julia asked. "You said you had a plan."

Charles straightened a badge pinned to his shirt. "I do. Give me the phone."

Cleveland reached into the wagon's center console and brought out an old-style cell phone. He handed it to Charles.

"Haven't seen one like this in a while," Charles said.

"That's why it's secure." Cleveland slapped at a mosquito buzzing around the windshield. It evaded his fingers and bounced along the windshield toward Charles.

Charles pressed the green button on the phone and it lit up to the first nine notes of Amazing Grace. "ASL?" The green display light of the phone displayed: Hello, it's 10:30 PM.

"I quit the ASL when they threw Sam Cooke off," Cleveland said. "Never did get that one."

"'A Change Is Gonna Come,'" Julia said from the backseat. Her fingers tapped away at a laptop keyboard.

"It came, all right," Cleveland said, "The church sure didn't know what was happening when it got itself entangled in politics. On both sides of the aisle."

Charles dialed in a number. The phone rang.

The clicking of Julia's fingers on the laptop paused. "I don't agree with it, but in a way the ASL serves you right for all the censorship the church performed over the years."

Cleveland sighed. "You're right. Somewhere along the line the church forgot its mission and started focusing on the world instead of changing people's hearts with the gospel." Cleveland flashed the pastor's eyes at Julia. "You interested in hearing the gospel?"

Julia redirected her attention at the laptop. "Got too many other things to deal with right now."

Someone answered the phone.

"Dad," Charles said. "I need your help. Gotta scoop for you."

"You're the scoop, Charles," Frank Cotton Graves said.

Charles pulled on the visor of the hat he wore. "You're kidding."

"No, I'm serious," Cotton said. "I think they aim to kill me. Where are you?"

"I don't trust you enough to answer that," Charles said. Nor do I trust you enough to tell you about Mom. "You got wheels?"

"I do. I am not alone out here, you know. I can help you."

"Maybe, if this is not a setup. It could be they let you go so they could follow you, or you could even be in on it. Look, if you want to help, do this. There's a club called La Rosa Blanca right around St. Charles and Capitol, or maybe Dowling. There's a pair of trolls operating there. The leader has obnoxious white sideburns. You can't miss this guy. His name is Gurdy Morrison and he runs with a sidekick. Stake them out until I get back in touch with you."

Charles watched another overpass approach. "If your whole breakout thing is a setup, then have Farris get over there with a team and round these guys up. We think they are going to blow something up or unleash something nasty in downtown within a week. Maybe as soon as a couple of days."

"Yeah," Cotton said. "I think the La Rosa is across from a Mexican restaurant I used to eat at. I'll go over and check it out. If I see anything requiring immediate attention, I'll get Farris on the horn. Otherwise, I'll wait for your call."

"Thanks. I'll call you in a couple of hours. And Dad, be careful."

"I will, Charles. Thanks. We have a lot to talk about."

"I know. Bye." Charles terminated the call. "Feel better now, Julia?" Charles looked to the backseat.

"How would I feel better? What did you talk about? Anyway, I'm still not sure what we are doing here."

"Dad's on the case, and he's probably got half the agency trailing him."

Julia shook her head and continued tapping on the laptop.

"There's the exit." Charles pointed with one hand and put the phone back in the console with the other. The console lid slammed shut with a thwack.

Cleveland steered the car off the freeway. Ten minutes later, Cleveland stopped the car behind a copse of trees. A hundred yards ahead through thick forest stood a fifteen-foot concrete wall.

"You know what to do, then," Charles said. "Everything on time. I'll give you fifteen minutes before I go in."

"Got it," Cleveland said. "God is with us."

"Yeah," Charles said. "Electricity." Charles reached over the seat and grabbed Julia's hand. "Love you."

Charles stepped out and shut the door. This will never work, he thought. I must be crazy letting her go.

Charles watched the station wagon pull off. He took mental notes of his surroundings. The trees would shield him until it was time to make the hike to the gate of the reclamation holding center. He took a minute to take in the night. It was playful: a light breeze, birds, crickets, and a clear sky crowded with stars. Unfortunately, the mosquitoes were crashing the party.

Charles saw the wagon's brake lights turn red. The back door flew open and Julia exited at a run toward him.

She leapt at him from three feet away, landing in his arms, her legs wrapping around his waist. Charles spun her around in circles.

She found his ear with her lips. "If this is the last time I see you, Charles Graves, I want you to know you mean everything to me. I don't care about all this, only you. When this is over, we are going away. Far away. I love you. Be careful."

• • •

Mexico is calling, Cotton Graves thought. Calling your name like a child in the night.

Except you still have one child left and he just called you. Literally.

Cotton turned right on St. Charles and slowed the car. He passed under a street lamp that was an oasis of light in an otherwise dark neighborhood. The side of his car read "Texas Taxi Co." At the end of the street he saw a sign with cursive letters spelling out La Rosa Blanca.

"What a hole."

Cotton made a left at the corner. On his left was a side view of La Rosa Blanca. He figured it had once been a home and had long ago been converted into a bar. A newer section had been added to the back of the house. Cotton wondered why a Great Dane with a white flower in its mouth was painted on the side of the addition.

He found the rear parking entrance and pulled in. He backed the cab into a nook beside a dumpster and under what appeared in the darkness to be a willow tree. Cotton cut the engine and killed the lights. The parking lot was full, but he figured no one would pay attention to a cab until much later.

"I love my boss! I love my job!"

Thirty minutes after Charles finished his call to Cotton, Farris swallowed three aspirin and chased them with a sip of coffee. His face throbbed if he moved hastily, but otherwise he felt well, all things considered. He propped his feet up on his desk at the agency. But blood began rushing to his head, so he thought better of it.

It was dark outside his office window, and a skeleton crew manned the agency.

Keesma and Louis sat across his desk. Keesma sat with his hands on his lap, staring ahead. Louis was half asleep. He let a yawn escape.

"You're not worried about Graves, Mr. Fah-reese?" Keesma asked.

"Not particularly."

"You don't think Mr. Ingraham's gonna be mad when he calls?"

"Nope."

"I—"

"Shut up, Keesma."

The office computer chimed in. "Mr. Fah-reese, your conference is ready."

"Video on," Farris said.

Ingraham appeared on Farris's office wall monitor. His bulk filled the screen. Keesma and Louis snapped to attention. Farris drained his coffee. He crushed the coffee cup and threw it at the trash.

"Mr. Ingraham," Farris emphasized In-gra-ham. "Thanks for joining us for this brief."

"Sure, Farris, make it short," Ingraham said. "Do you have any good news? The reports I received are not favorable."

"No luck with Charles Graves yet, but we figured a man with his talents would be difficult to locate." Farris paused to allow the office computer to improve the quality of Ingraham's image on the screen. "No luck with Cleveland or the girl either. We believe all three are still together and still in the city."

"What about Cotton Graves? We were informed he escaped."

"That is confirmed. I practically left the front door unlocked for him."

Ingraham paused. He looked at Farris cannily. "Why?"

Farris maximized a preselected screen on his desk computer. "We had him fitted with a GPS. He is not aware of it. Here is his present location." Farris pressed a button and an enhanced satellite image appeared, showing Cotton Graves's infrared signature in the parking lot of La Rosa Blanca.

"We believe he will lead us to Charles and the other two," Farris said.

"And he doesn't know about the plant?" Ingraham asked.

"Doubtful. We used a new product implanted orally. He drank it at dinner last night. The bug burrows into the small intestine but is small enough not to cause discomfort. It should give us a one-week surveillance window."

"Do you have a surveillance team in place?"

"We do. We have one-minute or less response capability. We also know he received a call around 10:30. We suspect it was from Charles. The translation was garbled, but we are working on deciphering it. We maintain a high level of confidence it was Charles."

Ingraham's eyebrows went up a millimeter. "Sounds like things are progressing. Keep me posted. You may be moving to the top floor, Farris."

"That's where I belong, sir. We'll have this closed down within a week. Video off." The screen went blank.

"I can't believe you talk to him like that," Keesma said.

Farris lit a cigarette. "I wouldn't recommend you try it."

"I thought smoking was against the law."

"It is." Farris blew out a plume of smoke. Farris thought the cloud resembled a face, but he couldn't decide whose it was.

• • •

"That has to be it," Julia said. The countryside reminded her of her trip to Old Bones Lane.

"Better be, or we will miss the timing," Cleveland said.

Cleveland pulled the station wagon off the farm to market road and into a field of high grass. The section of grass the car pushed down popped back up again behind the station wagon, creating a visual barrier on all sides. Cleveland cut the head-lights and drove about a half-mile further into the field.

"Far enough," Julia said.

Cleveland cut the motor.

"Wish me luck," Julia said.

"There's no such thing," Cleveland said. He gave Julia the pastor's eyes.

I wish he would quit doing that. Julia pulled the door handle and pushed the door. The door budged a few inches. "The weeds are too thick." She rolled the window down. The weeds pushed their way into the car. Three grasshoppers jumped in. One lodged in Julia's hair. She fought with herself to get it out.

"Pull the door closed and shut the window," Cleveland said. "And hang on."

He fired up the engine and put the wagon in reverse. Cleveland executed half of a three-point turn, bringing the wagon sideways across the weeds they had weakened driving in.

Julia was able to open the door. She noticed the weeds rising from the path where they had been trampled by the wagon. It reminded her of *The Day of the Triffids*.

"This path will be difficult to follow back in the dark," she said. "You will need to drive straight that way, so get your bearings. I'll be back as fast as I can." Julia leaned over into the backseat and hit a button on her laptop. She brought the laptop from the rear and placed it on the passenger's seat. "Time's started."

Julia stepped out of the car. She reached back in for a supply pack Charles had outfitted for her from his van, which was now parked at the new safe house. She slung the strap around her neck and plunged into the high grass.

Three steps into the weeds she lost sight of Cleveland and the car. She picked a piece of straw from her hair and took another step into darkness.

On Charles's walk from the trees to the gate, the dark man came to him. Why are you doing this?

Charles continued walking along the asphalt road that ran along the front of Reclamation Center Three. Up ahead on his right was the fifteen-foot concrete wall. To his left was a field of scrub grass. Straddling the asphalt road was a ditch. It reeked of mud and sewage. Charles had stepped in it coming out of the trees. His foot felt wet and he hoped it was not too noticeable on his uniform.

Charles felt his badge and straightened his officer's cap. He wore the standard issue blue reclamation center officer's uniform, tapered with a stripe down each side. The uniform featured a thick belt and black shoes. On his face he wore a thin moustache and a cleft chin.

Why am I doing it? I'm doing it because I have to. Cleveland's family is in there.

The dark man countered. No, you don't. Think about your own future for a change. Julia, perhaps? Mexico? You have enough money between the two of you to live well for a long, long time.

Julia and Cleveland are going after my mother. I have to do my part to see her again. Do you know how long it's been since I saw her? I can't imagine what it will be like. All this time I've thought she was dead.

You mean the woman who is responsible for all the trouble in your life? It started when she flipped out when you were a kid. Following cults, breaking the law, destroying your family. For God's sake, she's responsible for your brother's death. Without her, none of that would have happened.

That's not true!

Sure it is. Was your family in an uproar over anything else? No. And here's another thing: despite all of that, you still had a pretty good life cooked up for yourself before her influence from your childhood caused you to throw it all away over Cleveland and his fancy rhetoric.

No. That was real. I felt it. I know it.

Real in the sense that you did it, maybe. But it will wear off. Trust me. A week or two more of this and you will see the light, all right. It's a lie, old pal. Just a worn-out old story. Don't let it ruin your life. You should have listened to your dad.

Oh, yeah. The one that put her away. No thanks.

No, wrong again. The one that saved her. Despite all she did to your family, he saved her. How else could she still be alive?

Charles shook some grass off his damp shoe, then twisted it around, checking to make sure it was presentable. I don't know and I don't care. I am still going to get her. You know what?

Cleveland told me about you. That's the other thing. After all this time, now I know who you are.

Who I am? You know who I am. I'm the one who is looking out for you, as always.

Charles passed the corner of the wall. The gate was fifty yards ahead.

Julia's field of vision was restricted to about three inches. This is worse than Old Bones Lane.

She kept one hand straight out and another in front of her face to shield her eyes. The weeds surrounded her as if she were hiding between coats in a closet. She had to concentrate on mashing the next step down in front of the last to keep from walking in a circle.

How far have I come? Ten steps, twenty? How far should it be to the fence? If I veer only a degree, I could miss it altogether and end up in the next county.

Then count your steps from here, GG. If you go over fifty, you're in trouble.

Would that be fifty big steps or small?

Either.

How will I find my way back?

The weeds will give you good cover. Plow through until you come to the crease created by the car. And hope you are not being chased.

Julia counted three steps.

Do you think Charles's mother will be crazy after all this time?

I doubt it. She probably has a pretty good life out here, all things considered. But be prepared just in case.

I'm scared.

There's no room for that, GG.

Still . . .

Julia counted six.

At least Cleveland is here. I like him.

Faith is the enemy of reason, GG. Don't fall for that sideshow. Get this over with and get out. Charles will come out from under Cleveland's religious spell if you can get him away.

Julia counted twelve.

She knelt down in the tall weeds, her throat tightening, her cheeks beginning to shudder.

Don't you do it, GG.

What in the world am I doing?

Think Mexico. Be strong. It's the only way out now.

Julia adjusted the pack on her shoulder. A piece of straw poked her in the rear. She reached back and snapped a whole clump in two.

That's what you needed, GG. If I could have kicked you there, I would have. This foxhole is populated by an atheist.

Charles fiddled with the wood-block pieces in his pocket as he approached the gate. The gate was a stainless steel portal, eight feet high, four feet wide, flush with the concrete wall. It appeared to emit a pale luminescence in the darkness in contrast with the concrete walls. At right was the standard eye-reader. It was much like the portal inside the agency lobby, except that this one built into the side of a prison.

Let's see if you got it right, Julia. He inserted his head into the reader and let the laser operate. A display panel beneath the scanner flashed on. It read: Quentin Murphy. The portal opened.

He entered the portal into a dimly lit, fifty-foot long interior hallway terminating at the Reclamation Holding Center Three Guard Complex. The portal closed behind him as he marched down the hall. It was like walking through the barrel of a rifle.

Good work so far, J. You oughta be cuttin' that fence about now.

The hallway terminated at a second portal. Charles approached it. A two-way monitor illuminated on his left. A reclamation guard with sunken cheeks appeared on the screen.

"What's up, Murph?" the guard said. "You ain't on tonight."

"Yeah, I am," Charles said. "Check the roll."

The guard stared at Charles before swiveling his head to the left. Charles saw him manipulating buttons. The guard's face returned. "I guess you are. That's weird. I checked that schedule when I got here."

"Late addition," Charles said. "It was me or Jimmy, I guess."

"I guess," the guard said. "Things bein' the way they are and all."

Two for two, J, Charles thought. Good job. Halfway to four.

"What's that in your pocket?" the guard asked.

Pocket. What's in my pocket? His hands instinctively searched his pockets. His right found nothing. His left fumbled with the puzzle pieces. Stall, Charles, Stall. "What do you mean?"

"The scanner shows two objects in your left pocket."

"They're paperweights." Paperweights? Charles, you moron.

"We ain't got no paper in here," the guard said. His sunken cheeks seemed to fill out.

"They're a present for a couple of the crew," Charles said. "They're novelties."

"Let me see 'em," the guard said.

Charles removed the pieces from his pocket. He held them up. They were eyes. The guard's head grew in the monitor.

The eyes on the pieces flashed to life. At once they were searching to and fro, pupils growing in the dim light of the hallway and closing in the light of the monitor. The dark man was back.

Admit it, he said. You need me now, don't you? All that talk of Cleveland, but when it's crunch time who's there for you? Me. And . . . paperweights? I taught you better than that. Now pay attention and I'll get you out of here. You are no good to me dead. Are you listening?

Yes.

"All right, Murph, come on in," the guard said.

The portal opened.

Let me handle this next part, the dark man said. Charles put the pieces back in his pocket and stepped through the portal.

SEVENTEEN

Julia counted thirty-two. If this goes on much longer the timing will be all off.

Julia looked straight up into the sky, searching for light from the compound. Nothing but stars.

Julia counted thirty-six and her right foot found space. She jerked it back. Kneeling, she parted the weeds. A three-foot-wide strip of manicured grass formed a boundary in front of a ten-foot high chain link fence. The fence was topped with razor wire.

Remaining in the cover of the weeds, she ventured a glance at the compound. The fence formed a square perimeter with fifty-yard sides around a solitary house set in the middle. Was Charles's mother in there? She had better be. The house appeared to be thirty yards from the fence from all sides as far as she could see. As it turned out, she had wandered off course by several yards. She was almost to the back corner of the fence. Still, not too bad, considering.

So far so good, GG. The plot and schematics seem to be reliable.

The yard appeared well groomed. A lush St. Augustine carpet surrounded the house, which reminded Julia of a commonplace rural home. The compound was dark.

Julia focused on the side of the house. It sat up on cinder blocks, forming a crawlspace beneath. She studied the outline of the house, from eave to eave, corners down the sides, bottom corner across to bottom corner. She didn't see what she was searching for.

Julia fumbled through the pack and extracted a set of night-vision glasses. She trained the glasses on the house and resumed her search. She saw moldy siding, a rain gutter, an open window.

Hurry, GG. The timing needs to be right for Charles.

A foot below the eave, a third of the way from the end of the house, she spotted a translucent rectangle not much larger than 1 x 2 inches. Bingo. Motion sensors.

She placed the glasses back in the pack, swapping them for an instrument resembling a miniature camera mounted on a tripod.

Julia armed the unit, which responded with a whir. Keeping it inside the line of weeds, she aimed its lens at the rectangle, peering through an eyepiece in the back of the unit. The unit communicated with Julia through the eyepiece: Locking . . . locking . . . locking . . . locked.

The unit flashed green in Julia's eye, and the whirring discontinued. With great care she pushed the unit outside the line of weeds, lowering it to the ground. The unit self-adjusted its lens to maintain contact with the rectangle. Julia fixed the tripod's legs into the ground. Then she stood, ready to approach the fence.

Not so fast, GG. Think cross-perimeter.

Julia considered the fence line to her right. If there were a motion sensor mounted on the inside of the fence, she would not be able to detect it until it was too late. To her left, there was only a short section of fence remaining. But there it was. The sensor was at the top, left-hand corner of the fence.

She repeated the procedure with a second unit.

Julia bolted from the weeds to the grass boundary beside the fence. She dropped to her knees and placed the pack on the ground to her left. From it she took a set of insulated gloves and a spool of wire. She shoved her hands into the gloves and attached the wire to a link at the bottom of the fence. The wire lit up red.

That's what I call electricity, Cleveland.

She negotiated the wire through an unbroken series of links in a five-foot high semicircle, terminating in a bottom link about three feet to the right of where she started. When attached, the wire registered green.

Julia reached into the pack for cutters. She cut a hole in the fence beneath the arc created by the wire. She ripped out the cut portion of the fence and threw it in the weeds behind her.

At that moment Julia noticed two things. Her watch spelled "TIME" in green letters and a guard came around the corner of the house.

A dog followed at his heels.

• • •

Through the portal, Charles encountered another hallway. This one was shorter, twenty-feet long perhaps, with prism emblems adorning the walls. It terminated in another portal. To Charles's left was the guard room. The guard room was small and confined, not much bigger than a cinema ticket booth. A door allowed access and a window cut into the hallway afforded visibility to the guards.

Charles checked his watch. It was nearly time.

"Buzz me through." Charles kept walking toward the portal at the end of the hallway.

"Can't do that, Murph," the sunken faced guard said. He spoke through a mouthpiece in the window.

Charles halted halfway along the length of the guard window. He faced the guard.

"New regs," the guard said. "Gotta check everyone. No matter who."

Charles ripped the Quentin Murphy badge off of his uniform and slammed it against the window in front of the guard's face. The window was too thick to shudder, but the guard did all the same.

"Can't help it, Murph," the guard said. "Things bein' the way they are and all. Got special orders to check everyone for masks and disguises."

"Check me all you want when I get my first round done. I'm almost late as it is."

"Murph, the new regs—"

Charles leapt at the window, thrusting his face as close to the guard's as possible without smearing makeup on the window. Charles felt the dark man take over. "*I said, buzz me in,*" he shouted. "*Who does this look like to you? How many times have you sat with me in that control room with that stupid look on your face, you—*"

"Hey, Murph, settle down. It's just the new regs."

Charles grabbed the hair on both sides of his head, jerking wildly to the sides. *"How's that, you fool? Now buzz me in!"*

"Okay, Murph, okay. Settle down. I'll buzz you in."

Charles collected himself and took a couple of steps to the door.

"Man, is Patty giving you a hard time at the house or something?" the guard asked.

"It's Michelle, moron. And my two kids are Nate and Candice. And, yes, they are."

The portal began to open. Charles waited for it to clear. He stepped through and it closed behind him.

Charles entered a hallway flanked by cells on either side. The cell doors appeared to be fashioned of thick glass. The only light was a weak, deep fluorescent blue escaping from some of the cells. The cells were narrow, about six feet across, and receded about fifteen feet back from the doors. The deep blue light faded into darkness as the cells receded, making it difficult to see the back walls clearly. The first two cells were apparently empty.

The cellblock was frigid. Charles rubbed his arms to combat the chill. There were ten cells on either side, and the unlit ceiling stopped about three feet above Charles's head.

Charles detected a medicinal smell in the hallway. It reminded him of scalpels and medical scissors, of syringes and forceps. Despite the utter silence, Charles thought he heard the clanging of metal instruments. He took a step. His footfall clicked, echoing in the hallway.

You forgot to thank me for getting you through, Charles, the dark man said.

Shut up, Charles said.

I—

No, I mean it. Shut up.

Charles stood facing the second cell on the left. A tripod rose from the center of the cell. A mechanical claw at the apex of the tripod held a mounted prism that emitted a deep blue, pulsing ray.

The room's occupant was a male inmate restrained by a porcelain shaft extending from the back wall of the cell. The shaft culminated in a porcelain semi-sphere attached to the back of the occupant's head by a strap running around his face below the nose. The occupant's feet were strapped to the floor, his arms stretched out, attached to the walls. It looked like the person was spread-eagle and freefalling from a great height

The prism's beam aimed at the man's eyes. The ray pulsated in escalating and de-escalating rhythmic bursts. The man's lips moved with the rhythm of the prism.

Charles could not hear through the glass door of the cell, but he could imagine the droning voice in his head: Blue is the color of breath. Blue fills my soul with joy. Blue is father sky.

At the end of each prism burst sequence, the blue ray dissipated. The prism then discharged a black jolt of energy into the man's skull. Whenever the black ray hit, the man's face contorted into an expression resembling a hyena. Charles assumed he was cackling.

Charles witnessed two repetitions of the blue prism before it repeated the process with a green ray. The hallway assumed the faint hue of green in place of the blue. Charles could all but hear "the green voice" in his mind: Green is the color of life. Green makes me feel alive. Green is mother earth.

Charles left the occupant to his fate, thoughts of his mother and Cleveland's wife and daughter passing through his mind.

He passed two empty cells before halting in front of another one.

Inside, by the light of a green prism, two men in white coats operated on a prisoner secured to what reminded Charles of a dentist's chair. Every portion of the prisoner's body was restrained—the head by a claw suspended from the ceiling.

The men were attempting to implant a crystalline object into the person's forehead. The prisoner writhed in agony, struggling against the restraints, but no screams escaped the glass cell door. Charles was not certain if the prisoner was male or female because its face had been removed. It looked as if it were wearing a porcelain mask. A featureless mime behind noise-proof glass.

The hallway darkened then switched to blue as Charles staggered back against the cell door on the opposite side of the hallway. The doctors continued their operation on the faceless creature. Charles averted his gaze by turning and leaning on the cell door he had backed into. His head leaned on his forearm, which rested against the glass of the cell.

Charles swiped his forearm across his eyes and tried to focus on his mission. When he gazed into the cell door in front of him, a creature was staring back at him an inch from the glass. It stood as motionless as a zombie, its mouth a gaping pit, its eyes black and hollow. A tiny aperture in its forehead glowed blue in tandem with the pulsating of the prisms. It also had no face.

Charles scrambled away from the glass, his hands over his face. "It can't be. No. It's impossible. It can't be."

Charles reached the end of the hallway and collapsed in the corner beneath the laser scanner. His hands searched every crevasse and corner of his own face. "It can't be."

Do you have a hole in your head, Charles? the dark man said. The hallway light switched to green.

Charles did not respond. His hands kept their track around and across his face.

Your forehead, Charles, the dark man said. Is there a hole in your forehead?

The tips of Charles's fingers searched his forehead. No, I don't think so. He wasn't certain. It seemed like there might be a bump in the middle of his forehead. Funny how he hadn't noticed it before. Maybe a scar had grown over the wound.

You don't have a hole in your head because they haven't done this to you. Quit the sissy-stuff and get on with it.

That was me in the cell, Charles said. You saw it.

It's gonna be you in the cell if you don't get up, the dark man said. Julia too, and Cleveland. Your mom. Cleveland's daughter and wife. Get up.

Charles felt the prism therapy in his mind again. Green is the color of life. Green makes me feel alive. Green is mother earth. Blue is the color of breath. Blue fills my soul with joy. Blue is father sky.

Get up, the dark man said

A concentrated pulse grew within his consciousness and overpowered the prism therapy. It was a new poem. It repeated itself until the greens and blues faded to black: Black is the color of power. Black makes me feel strong. Black is the dark man.

Charles stood up and engaged the laser scanner. The portal opened. He stepped through.

• • •

The portal led to another bank of cells running 90 degrees left from the experiment chambers. Down this cellblock ran a twenty-five-foot-wide walkway marked with parallel yellow lines painted three feet from the cells. The cells were recessed behind thick oval glass. Charles estimated fifty cells on each side of the walkway: even-numbered cells to the right, odd to the left. The numbers were spelled out in red block letters.

The ceiling rose three floors above the walkway. There were two floors of cells above the ground floor. Elevated platforms provided access to cells on the upper floors. Belt-high metal railings skirted the platforms. The lights were dim upstairs, and Charles couldn't be sure, but it appeared that all current inmates were housed in the bottom floor cells, which were all lit.

Somewhere in this room the Reverend James Cleveland's wife and daughter waited. Or so Charles prayed.

Polished wax shone from the floor. Charles's shoes clicked against black tile as he walked. The clicks echoed through the chamber. Charles took inventory of the cell occupants as he passed.

A contingent of guards stood at intervals along the cell-block. Charles noticed their uniforms were green, which he assumed was a lesser rank. This was confirmed as the guards all saluted him as he passed. Yet they never ventured eye contact. Charles counted six guards in all.

Which one is going to try and be the hero?

It's guard number two on the left, the dark man said.

Charles realized this was the only guard who had attempted eye contact.

The silence was remarkable. Charles figured the cells were soundproof. Some of the occupants beat on the glass, yet no sound exited. Most occupants reclined against the back walls of the cells or paced back and forth. Some rooms contained multiple occupants. Some were singles. The only audible sound was the click, click, click of Charles's shoes.

By cells 25 and 26 there was no trace of Cleveland's wife and daughter.

Julia was not certain of what to do first. She sat stunned, wondering if the guard would spot her.

The watch was now blinking in bold, fluorescent green letters: TIME, TIME, TIME. Julia pulled two items from the pack—a gun and a transmitter.

She popped open a cover on the transmitter first. She pressed a button on it and tossed it back into the pack. Good luck, Charles.

There's no such thing as luck, Julia. Good determinism, maybe. Good causality, good philosophic necessity. Anything but good providence.

She pointed the gun at the guard and searched for his neck through a telescopic site. She squeezed the trigger. The gun fired a dart with a squirting sound.

The guard reached for his neck as if to swat a mosquito. He managed two steps forward and one back before he sank to the St. Augustine.

The dog's ears perked up. It sniffed the air and licked the guard's face. Julia put a dart in the dog's neck.

Julia shouldered the pack, crawled through the hole, and sprinted for the side of the house.

• • •

Cleveland saw the transmitter on the dash of the station wagon light up. It startled him. He reached over to the passenger seat and grabbed the laptop, adjusting it so that the screen faced him. It had gone to power-saving mode.

Cleveland mashed buttons with both hands. The laptop woke up and defaulted to its lock-out function. It requested username and password.

Cleveland stared at the laptop, his jaw dropping. He twirled his hands around each other in circles. Think. Think. Think. Cleveland couldn't think.

Pictures of his daughter and wife raced through his mind. Without this laptop, he would never see them again. Their faces retreated from view as images of them enduring atrocities took their place.

Cleveland scrambled halfway over the driver's seat, scanning the backseat for assistance. He rummaged through clothes and papers. He tossed aside a Bible after fanning its pages. He fell back into the driver's seat. He scanned the dashboard and the passenger's seat. Nothing.

"Not this way, Lord. Please."

Cleveland closed his eyes, calmed himself, and prayed. When he opened his eyes, he inspected the laptop. He tilted it back, exposing the seat beneath it. There was a note underneath, hidden when he swiveled the laptop to face him. On it were Julia's password and username.

"Thank You, Lord!"

Cleveland typed the username and password and hit the enter button. The screen blinked. It reported entry of an unrecognizable user ID and password. It requested him to check the information and try again. Cleveland did.

The laptop blinked. Unrecognizable.

"If I do this wrong again, it may lock me out for good."

Cleveland stared at the screen as if its instructions were written in Russian. He checked Julia's note again to make sure he had entered the correct info. He had entered the info correctly, he thought.

Cleveland pulled the note from underneath the laptop, lifted it to his face, and read it again to be sure. Underneath the password and user ID Julia had included further instructions the laptop had obscured. The note said to enter the instructions verbally.

Cleveland did so. The laptop unlocked, revealing a red rectangle with one word within its borders: Enter.

Cleveland placed his index finger over the return button of Julia's laptop. "God be with you, Charles. I hope I'm not too late."

He pressed the button.

After an hour in the back parking lot of La Rosa Blanca, Cotton Graves felt like a sandbag holding back a flood. *I don't see how Charles does this.*

The parking lot was full of cars now. Muted soca drifted from the club, spiking in volume when the occasional barhop exited the back door to dispense of empty bottles, dead soldiers in a war of attrition. There was always more booze than drunks to drink it.

Cotton felt himself nod. He had climbed out of the car twice to revive himself already. As the night wore on, he became more and more afraid to get out. The crowd entering the club had become increasingly rough.

This is an odd place for a couple of trolls to be hiding. Then again, maybe not. Maybe this is what trolls do.

Cotton fished a phone out of his pocket and attempted to call Charles. No answer.

This is not smart, Cotton. You should be on a private jet out of the country. Get your money from the bank and get out. Someone will recognize you sooner or later.

Cotton tossed the phone onto the dash of the taxi. No can do, Jack. I owe it to the boy.

Not anymore. He made a weird choice. He's an outlaw now.

So am I.

That's because of him. If he would have done right by everything you did for him, you would be in your suite right now—with Sheila.

There are thousands of Sheilas in South America. A million in Asia. Get on the plane.

So what you are saying is I shouldn't worry about these trolls and their plan to blow up downtown?

You are catching on. What's Houston done for you? Let it blow up the same way it blew your family up. Let those trolls spread some disease through the city like they injected Teresa with that religion pestilence. What do you owe them? Nothing. The world has turned over. You need to as well.

I am a senator.

You were a senator. More like Ingraham's pawn now. Soon to be Farris's pawn.

Cotton's debate with himself led him further inward. Before long, he was snoring.

EIGHTEEN

Click, click, click, click. Charles halted in front of cells 28 and 29. The two guards posted at cells 44 and 45 remained at attention and did not acknowledge his presence. Charles felt guard number two's eyes on his back.

Charles noticed a man in cell 30 beating on the glass. No sound escaped the cell. Charles's mind conjured up an old movie poster he'd seen as a kid. There was a caption he could not remember, but it entered his mind as "In Reclamation Center Three, no one can hear you scream." Charles wondered if that old movie was on the Approved Motion Picture List.

A peculiar noise emanated from one of the upper levels. The sound was a tapping noise, the type of ringing produced by metal on metal.

The guards seemed oblivious to the clanging, which should have been impossible in the morgue-like cellblock. Charles figured he could chance a glance at the upper levels, even with guard number two's eyes on his back. He was, after all, a superior making rounds.

Charles saw a figure on the third level. The figure was on his left, outside cell 33. The person was not much taller than the rails lining the catwalk that led to the third-level cells. The figure wore a black garment with a shawl wrapped around its head. It was beating something metal against the railing.

Cling! Cling! Cling!

The cellblock resounded with the clanging. It became droning in its monotony yet ordered in its intent. Each new rap faded away, following after the one that had come before.

To Charles it was a demented church bell bonging out the Reclamation Center Three death march. He fought to keep his hands at his side and away from his ears. Why weren't the guards reacting to this?

Cling! Cling! Cling!

Charles lowered himself into the dark man well once again. The descent was effortless. His left hand clasped the woodblock pieces in his pocket as eagerly as smokers grab cigarettes after a cross-country flight. He caressed them. He thanked them for being there.

You rang? the dark man said.

I guess I did.

Good man. There's hope for you yet.

I don't know how "good" I am, but what now? Why am I seeing this? Why am I hearing it?

One psychologist might call it unresolved guilt. Another might call it repressed emotion. Cognitive personality disorder from all your disguises? Traumatic disjunction? Pick the psychobabble flavor of the month. I say you're nuts.

Cling!

The figure began to remove the shawl from its head. It performed this as a one-handed operation. The other hand grasped the metal object, which Charles now identified as a gun.

"Do you see it?" Charles said aloud. He hoped the guards did not hear him. He took two steps forward to make it appear as if he were inspecting something. The man in cell 30 kept beating on the glass.

Let's just say I know who it is, the dark man said.

You gonna fill me in?

You'll know soon enough.

Charles watched the shawl unravel. As the dark man had predicted, he knew who it was before the shawl came off.

The shawl dropped from the figure, slithered across the railing, and floated down from the third level. It wound through the cellblock sky like a smoky snake. It slunk back and forth in thirty-foot arcs, gaining speed in straightaways, slowing for turns. At one point the arc swept out so far Charles thought it might plummet down right on guard number two.

The smoky serpent shawl was as dark as smoke from an oil fire. It obscured the red block letters of cell 33 on one pass, creating red snake-eyes that glared at Charles. The shawl completed three more passes and came to rest across the yellow caution line running the length of the cellblock. It coiled and hissed at Charles, then melted into the floor.

He felt for the scar on his cheek. Some of his makeup rubbed off on his hand.

The figure called from the third floor. "Look at me, Charles. *Look at me!*" He pounded the gun on the railing in unison with his words.

Should I look? Charles asked.

Why? You know who it is, right?

Yes. It's Stephen.

Let him come down here if he wants to talk, the dark man said.

The pounding of the gun continued. "Do you know what it feels like to fall, Charles? It's about thirty-two steps to where I am up here. Do you want a demonstration? A reminder?"

Forget him, the dark man said. The jerk deserved it.

But he was my brother, Charles said.

Half of your family was crazy.

The pounding ceased. After ten seconds, Charles figured his latest installment of madness had passed. He forced his eyes upward.

Stephen had climbed through the railing and was leaning out into space, his hands holding the middle rail behind him. The gun was in his mouth. Stephen let go of the rail with one hand and fell forward, grabbing the rail with the other hand only just in time. He alternated hands like this, teetering back and forth. Charles remembered Stephen playing this game from the Graves Mansion balcony.

Charles stretched both hands toward Stephen as if to catch him.

Stephen quit teetering. He released both hands, bent down, and jumped upward. He spread his hands and extended his chest. His feet came together, forming a decent swan dive. Stephen's body hung in midair right over Charles. Then it plunged toward the cellblock floor.

What a fool, the dark man said.

Charles braced for the impact. It never came.

As Stephen was about to create a mess with his impact on the floor not far from where the shawl had landed, the cellblock erupted.

The overhead lighting shut off, replaced by red strobe lights. A warble arose outside the cellblock. A repeating alarm inside the cellblock sounded. It reminded Charles of the sound contestants received when they missed an answer on a game show. He pondered why game shows appeared on the Approved TV List.

The cell doors opened. The man in cell 30 beat at the air a couple of times, not noticing that the door had slid aside. Then he stopped, staring at his hands. He burst out of the cell chanting. "The British are coming! The British are coming!"

Charles saw the guards moving in stop-motion animation in the flashing red light. He did the math in his head: approximately one hundred prisoners, exactly six guards.

Thank you, Reverend Cleveland. Perfect timing.

The dark man screamed. Take off the uniform. Now!

Charles obeyed without hesitation. His hat and shirt tumbled to the floor, along with half of his face.

The cellblock flooded with prisoners. How long before reinforcements arrived? A minute? Two, tops.

Cleveland's wife and daughter have to be ahead of you, the dark man said. You haven't seen them yet.

Charles trudged forward, dodging prisoners as they exited their cells. With half of his facial disguise hanging off, he looked like the undead from a George Romero flick in the flashing red light. In only his undershirt and pants, the cell block was that much colder.

Two gunshots came from behind. Charles swiveled and saw guard number two swarmed by prisoners. The feeling of guard number two's eyes on him dissipated.

The two guards in front of him cornered themselves in cell 43, guns drawn. A horde of prisoners hid along the sides of the cell. The guards called to Charles as he passed.

By cells 44 and 45, Charles had still not found Cleveland's wife or daughter. He kept to the center of the cellblock walkway, checking to the left and right as he passed each cell pair. In cell 46 he saw two women huddled in the corner. The cell door was open but they hadn't come out.

He sprinted to the cell. "Mrs. Cleveland?"

The woman and her adult daughter shrunk against the back wall when Charles entered the cell. They were dressed in two-piece reclamation center uniforms with prism emblems over their hearts. The uniforms alternated white and pink in the light of the flashing red alarm.

Mrs. Cleveland was almost as tall as James. She was thin, with matted hair most likely from her protracted stay in the cell. Charles felt a pang of guilt when he thought how Cleveland's daughter might look outside of a reclamation center. She was tall, shapely, with dreadlocks dyed a reddish-blonde reaching halfway down her back.

Charles figured he resembled a ghoul in the flashing red light. He stepped halfway into the cell, picking off portions of his facial disguise. "James sent me here to get you." He repeated it in a louder voice to compensate for the alarm.

In one flash of the light she was against the wall with her daughter. In the next she was standing. In a third she leapt into Charles's arms. The effect of it stunned him.

Mrs. Cleveland tossed her head back. "Electricity!"

"Not if we don't move fast," Charles said. "Get your daughter."

• • •

Julia crossed the fenced compound and reached the side of the house without incident. She set her pack down and approached the unconscious guard, who was facedown in the St. Augustine. Julia pulled the dart from his neck and tossed it underneath the house. The guard's pulse was slow but steady.

She rolled him onto his back. A search of the pockets yielded nothing of value. She rolled the guard over twice more. He was now on his back next to the crawlspace under the house. Julia pushed him under. She did the same with the dog.

She went to her pack and withdrew a flashlight, a pistol, and a laser. She tucked the pistol in the front of her belt. She guessed she had five or ten minutes at most before the guard was missed.

She sunk to the grass and rolled over on her back beside the house. The lawn smelled freshly cut and was cool to the touch. She pushed with her feet, forcing her head into the crawlspace under the house.

There was a foot or so clearance below the flooring of the house. Julia felt the dirt and grime of the crawlspace latch on to her hair, back, and arms as she pushed herself through. She clenched her teeth and pushed harder.

Once her whole body entered the crawlspace, she could raise her knees a half-foot or so. She propelled herself with a truncated backstroke, arms to the side. The dirt was cool but dry.

She felt the dirt working its way down her collar like fingers groping her back. She flailed her hands through the dirt in an attempt to expedite her movement. She tried a wriggle maneuver in lieu of lifting her knees. No improvement.

You're about ten feet in, GG. About ten more to go. Keep your nerve.

The dirt had managed to get its cool fingers to her lower back. It was worse than the thought of Farris touching her there. She wriggled again, trying to scratch the sensation away.

Her hair matted in the back. She raised her head as best she could and shook it. Dirt fell in clumps from her hair, some of it cascading down the back of her collar. One clump rolled down the side of her head, trickling down the front of her neck.

She grabbed with both hands. Her left hand slapped her neck, bringing a torrent of dirt onto her chest. Her right hand struck a floor support beam on the way. A cloud of dust struck the flooring and rained grime down on her face.

It was in her nose and mouth. She snorted and spat. The grime assaulted her nasal passages, her throat, her teeth, and her tongue.

Her eyes were the worst. She bent her elbows and rubbed them with the back of her hands, smearing more dirt across her face.

I detest this.

It's the human condition to be dirty, GG.

No, it's not. It may be a legacy thrust upon us, but it's not our condition. I refuse to believe that. Who would choose this?

Do you think Charles thinks you're dirty?

Look who's equivocating now, Ms. Logic. Julia cracked a grin, into which a dirt clod entered her mouth. She spit it out.

Her eyes grew resolute in the darkness. She pressed on toward her goal, the traumatic memory receding. Thanks, though, she said.

My pleasure, GG.

• • •

"I'll take your hand," Charles said to Mrs. Cleveland. "You take your daughter's. We are going to walk quickly, but we are not going to act like we are in a hurry. Got it?"

Mrs. Cleveland nodded. Her daughter nodded. As tough as Cleveland, Charles thought.

So far, so good. The alarms were howling like a pack of hounds and the doors were still open. Julia had outdone herself, and the reverend had pressed the button at just the right time.

"Who are you?" Mrs. Cleveland asked as they walked.

"I'm not always sure," Charles said.

Charles led them out the doorway of cell number 46 and took a right toward the end of the cellblock. The general mayhem of the cellblock thrived. Most of the inmates charged toward the front door of the cellblock where Charles had entered or were crowded around the cell where the two guards remained holed up. One of the inmates had been shot trying to rush the guards. He lay at the cell door.

Several of the inmates milled around the back door of the cellblock. Charles wondered how he would get them out of his way.

He led Mrs. Cleveland and her daughter through to the door. The dark man had been right, as usual. In the flashing red light, the blue of Charles's uniform pants seemed purple. Shirtless, he could pass for a prisoner.

"Where y'all goin'?" one of the prisoners asked.

"Out," Charles said. He pushed through the crowd of inmates, dragging the Clevelands like a pull-toy. Two shots rang out from behind. Another inmate fell in front of cell 43.

Charles yanked at the door leading out of the cellblock. It opened, revealing another hall like the one he'd entered through. The hallway was dark, with a single flashing red light halfway down the hall. Thirty seconds before the guards came pouring in from the opposite end, he figured.

Charles stepped through the door. He felt a firm hand on his arm.

"You're takin' us with you," a voice said.

Charles looked down at the hand and then up to its owner. It was one of the inmates. Several more crowded around him.

"Can you run?" Charles asked.

"You betcha." The hand released.

Charles pulled the Clevelands and sprinted down the hall, followed by a horde of inmates. He felt the wood-block pieces rattling in his pocket. The pounding of all those feet thundered like a stampede in the cramped hallway, but it was audible only during the breaks of the intermittent game show siren.

They were under the lone flashing red light at the center of the hall when the portal at the far end slid open. The light from the portal revealed a troop of armed guards in riot gear. They poured into the hallway.

The siren desisted. In its place, a voice came over the loud-speaker. It filled the air with authority. "Lie on the floor immediately with your hands on your head. Those who fail to comply will be shot."

Most of the horde at Charles's back hit the floor faster than a marine giving his sergeant twenty. Charles saw the guns at the end of the hall lowering. Judging from the reports of gun-shots behind him, gunfire had already started at the other end of the cellblock.

Charles felt the wood-block pieces rattle again. The dark man screamed. *Left! Now! Left!*

Charles struck a door on his left on the run. The door pushed inward, and Charles hit the opening in stride, slinging the Clevelands through with him. Cleveland's daughter slammed her shoulder into the door frame but entered ahead of a rain of bullets whizzing through the air. Charles realized that if he'd had to pull the door open instead of pushing it, they would be dead.

The horde following Charles was either on the floor in a submissive position or rendered submissive on the floor by the bullets. The man who had grabbed his arm was dead at the doorway. His body lay halfway through the doorway, preventing the door from closing.

Charles knew this meant he had mere seconds. They were standing in a featureless hallway that would soon become a labyrinth if he didn't get his bearings. He searched his mind for the reclamation center schematics Julia had provided him. There were several doors down this hall. Which was the right one?

Between the sound of sporadic gunfire and wailing prisoners, he could hear the footsteps of guards behind them.

Third on the right, the dark man said.

Charles hit this door on the run as well. With the Clevelands safely inside, he stopped and shut the door. Maybe there was enough time to get away, maybe not. They had gotten in before guards had seen what door they'd gone through, but there were only a handful of doors for them to check.

Charles examined the door handle. It was a metal latch extending out from the metal door in a one-inch by three-inch L-shape.

He pulled one of the dark man's eyes from his pocket. He compared it with the handle. I think I could wedge it in tight enough, but that would mean leaving part of him here.

Try your heel, the dark man said.

Charles ripped his left shoe off and wedged it in the door handle. "It might hold for a minute." He put the puzzle piece back in his pocket.

The room they'd entered opened to another hallway with three more doors. Charles ran to the last one, the Clevelands in tow. He pushed the door open. It led to a stairwell leading up. A single red light lit each landing above them. The alarm blared, echoing through the stairwell.

The door, Charles, the dark man said.

Charles pulled the Clevelands in, shut the stairwell door, and removed his right shoe. He wedged it into the latch. As he did, he heard the first door give way.

"It's a footrace now," Charles said.

Charles grabbed Mrs. Cleveland and headed up the stairs. Cleveland's daughter followed.

They paused on the fourth floor landing, sucking air. Banging from the first floor door echoed through the stairwell.

"We're not going to make it," Charles said.

Mrs. Cleveland let loose of Charles's hand. She tore her shirt off. Charles turned his head.

"We ain't got time for that," Mrs. Cleveland said. "Help me."

Charles turned back around and saw Mrs. Cleveland with the fourth floor door propped open, stuffing her shirt into the doorframe by the lower hinge.

It might work in this bad light, Charles thought. He passed through the doorway and tugged on the shirt from the back side. He reentered the stairwell and they let the door close. It stopped inches from the doorjamb.

"It'll do," Mrs. Cleveland said. "Now, where you takin' us?"

"C'mon," Charles said.

He heard the first floor stairwell door give way.

When the door of the cab opened, Cotton Graves awoke. A smell of stale beer and smoke flooded the cab. Cotton focused his eyes on the two men who stood outside his car. One positioned himself between the open door and the cab's chassis.

The men were oversized. Bouncers, perhaps. The one inside the door wore a sleeveless leather vest. A tattoo of a whale ran along his right arm from shoulder to elbow.

"I was just leaving," Cotton said. He flashed his greasiest politician's grin.

"You was just sleepin'," the bouncer said. "You a pervert?"

Cotton assessed his politician's snake oil routine and determined it was not working. "I needed a nap, fellas. I'm on the road. Got a long trip ahead of me. Let me go. It's the last you'll see of me. That's for certain."

The bouncer leaned in. "You're familiar." He addressed his accomplice. "Buck, who's he look like to you?"

The bouncer's accomplice shrugged.

"Get out of the car."

"Let me—"

The hand that grabbed Cotton's hair was a no-doubter. It felt as big as a catcher's mitt. The bouncer lifted him out of the cab, bumping his head as he pulled him out. He held Cotton to his face. Cotton's feet dangled a foot from the ground. "Who are you?"

"Frank Cotton Graves, U.S. Senator." Cotton hoped there was some respect for the office in these primates.

"I see it," the bouncer said. "Shore do." He set Cotton down and brushed him off.

Cotton flashed the politician's grin. "You fellas voters?"

"Yeah, right. But our boss is. What do you say we go inside, have us a drink, and get you acquainted with him? I bet he'd like to meet you."

"I don't drink," Cotton said.

"No worries, mate. I can scare up some ginger ale, I reckon."

"I'd rather get on my way, if you don't mind."

The bouncer placed his hand on the back of Cotton's neck. "I can carry you in, you know."

"Not much doubt about that, my very large friend."

Cotton and the bouncer walked into the club as if they were old friends, arm in arm, telling jokes, carousing. The bouncer's accomplice followed.

"Did you say something about a drink?" Cotton said.

NINETEEN

Julia considered her location under the house and estimated it was close to the right spot. She clicked the flashlight on and glanced around the crawlspace. Now she was glad she had left the light off coming in. It was nastier than she imagined.

Julia stuck the end of the flashlight in her mouth and removed the laser from her pocket. Picking a spot between two of the floorboard supports, she activated the laser. It knifed through the flooring with ease.

Julia kept the laser moving across the flooring to prevent it from puncturing into the room above. If she happened to be right under Charles's mother's bed, the quick movement would prevent the laser from harming her.

Julia cut threes sides of a three-foot square and deactivated the laser. She pressed up on the flooring, finding two places where the wood was not completely severed. She reactivated the laser and touched up her makeshift carpentry.

The flooring sagged about an inch from the severed end of the square. Julia pressed up on it, checking for weight. She determined no furniture or bed frame was on top of her incision.

She cut the final section of the square with her free hand supporting the detached flooring. As soon as it released, she deactivated the laser, dropped it in the crawlspace, and held the flooring with both hands. It felt like a bag of ready-mix cement.

Julia strained to bench-press the flooring. She ended up moving no more than a side of the square over the edge. But this allowed her enough leverage to push the flooring up into the house. It scraped against the hardwood floor as it entered in the interior of the house, crashing down with a bang when Julia could no longer control its weight.

The house awoke as if it were alive and reacting to the pain of the laceration. Footfalls reverberated on the flooring from different parts of the house. Voices cried out—not excited yet, but curious.

She navigated the hole, managing to elevate herself by pulling against the edges. Julia entered a dark, modest bedroom with a bookcase, a dresser, a desk, and a door leading to the rest of the house. Charles mother appeared to be asleep in a bed in a corner opposite from the door. No one else was in the room. She debated whether to go to Charles's mother first or check the door of the room to make sure it was locked.

She chose Charles's mother. The bang from the flooring had stirred her. She rustled in the bed sheets and switched to an upright position, one arm propping her up on the bed. It seemed to Julia she was trying to acclimate herself to the idea of a sound in her room.

Julia placed a hand over Teresa Graves's mouth and an arm around her chest. She whispered in her ear, "Your son sent me. Charles. Charles sent me to get you. I'm a friend. I'm here to get you out. Don't make a sound."

Julia sensed she understood. There was no resistance, no struggle, barely an elevated heartbeat. She removed her hand from the woman's mouth. "You're pretty calm. Better than I was expecting."

"Kill me or rescue me," Charles's mother said. "Either way, I'm free of this place."

"I just figured you'd at least be startled when a complete stranger busted through your floor. It's not really natural how you acted." Julia said. She kept an eye on the door.

"You sounded like a rhinoceros coming through the floor. I've been sitting here watching you." Charles's mother put a hand over Julia's. "What else was I supposed to think? That my own guards, who all carry keys, were breaking in through the floor?"

Julia considered this.

"You're right though, dear. It's not natural," Charles's mother said. "I've been praying for Charles. I knew he'd remember."

Julia released Charles's mother and moved to the door. It was locked from the outside. Julia sighed. "You're going to have to follow me through the hole."

Julia entered the crawlspace head first. She scraped her head on the flooring going in. She found the laser and pocketed it, then crawled ahead three feet to make room for Charles's mother.

She didn't come. Had Julia been outfoxed? If she—

But then Charles's mother's body appeared through the hole. They crawled.

They were halfway through the crawlspace when someone began knocking at the door to Teresa's room. The knocking escalated into pounding. Men called Teresa's name. When Julia reached the edge of the house, the door to Teresa's room opened. She heard the floorboards squeaking as they entered.

Julia exited the crawlspace. It was more liberating than bra-burning. She rolled over and looked back in. Charles's mother was three feet away. A guard's flashlight shone into the hole. Then his head was in the hole. The flashlight scanned the crawlspace. After a couple of passes he spotted them.

Julia stood. "Teresa, hurry. They're coming."

Julia felt for the pistol. It was still in her belt. Teresa emerged from the crawlspace, pulling at the grass. Julia bent down, grabbed her hands, and pulled. Teresa came out as if Julia were coiling loose rope. The ease of the lift sent Julia and Teresa sprawling onto the grass.

Teresa's nightgown was soiled. Her face was grimy, legs and feet bare. Julia reached over and hugged her.

"Thank you," Teresa said. "Thank you."

"Don't thank me yet," Julia said.

The front door to the house slammed open.

The two women jumped to their feet. Julia pointed to the hole in the fence. They ran.

Ten feet from the fence Julia turned, drew her pistol, and put two shots in the side of the house as the guards were coming around the corner. They dove for cover back around the side of the house, then returned fire.

Julia caught Teresa at the fence line and motioned her through. Julia followed.

Teresa pulled up at the wall of weeds.

The guards emerged from behind the corner of the house. They fired another salvo.

"The weeds will cover us," Julia said. She grabbed Teresa's hand and pulled her in alongside her.

Teresa howled with the pain of her bare feet in the field. Three feet in it was obvious she would never make it.

"Hop on," Julia said. She offered Teresa a piggyback.

Julia had forged five feet into the weeds when she heard the guards at the fence. With Teresa on her back, they would never make it, even if they did find the car without getting lost.

The laser, GG. Use it.

Are you sure?

Yes.

Julia pulled the laser from her pocket, aimed it as far away as she could by lifting it over her head, and activated it. The weeds smoldered. Julia kept the laser trained on the weeds. They burst into flame.

The heat sucked Julia's breath away. She turned and sprinted as fast as possible with the extra weight, weeds slapping her face. The weeds swarmed her, destroying her sense of direction. Behind her the fire raged. It sailed through the weeds like wind.

If she became lost, they would soon be surrounded by flames.

Charles and the Clevelands raced up the stairs. The stairway terminated at the sixth floor landing. The door was marked "Rooftop Access."

The guards rushed up the stairwell below. He figured their subterfuge at the fourth floor doorway might gain them a minute or two, if it worked at all.

"Where you takin' us?" Mrs. Cleveland said.

Charles did not have time to respond. As he reached the sixth floor landing, the door flew open and a guard charged in from the roof. The guard was armed with an assault rifle.

Charles sprung forward from the last stair step, grabbed the guard's gun, and used the guard's forward momentum to sling him downward. The guard hovered as he clasped his gun, teetered, and then lost his grip and sailed down the stairwell. He flailed at the Clevelands as he fell but came up empty. He landed with a thud at the bottom of the stairwell.

Charles reacted in time to confront the second guard at the door. He brought the butt of the first guard's assault rifle down on the second guard's wrist. The guard howled and dropped his rifle. Mrs. Cleveland dove for it.

Charles swung again, but the guard stepped inside the arc of the gun, which blunted the force of the blow and left the two of them locked in a strange dance on the landing. They crashed into the wall above the stairway. Charles felt the guard's strength was superior to his own. However, the blow to the wrist had disabled him, leaving the guard and Charles at even odds.

Using the wall as leverage, the guard managed to push Charles backward two feet. He flanked Charles's left, trying to get behind him. The guard's quickness surprised Charles.

The guard's maneuver would've worked, except for the stair. His right foot slipped off the landing and dangled in midair. He balanced on his left, twirling his arms.

What Charles saw was not the guard. It was his brother Stephen struggling to maintain his balance on the top step of the staircase of Graves Mansion

His brother held out his hands to Charles, his face pleading. "Charles, no! Charles, don't let me fall! Charles!"

His brother fell, toppling down like the toy cars they rocketed down the staircase when their mother wasn't watching. All the way down his arms remained outstretched as if he still expected Charles to catch him. When Stephen's head hit the floor, it sounded like someone flattening out a pillow.

Charles snapped back to the sound of Mrs. Cleveland connecting the butt of an assault rifle to the guard's face. The guard plummeted down the stairs and landed next to his partner. They did not appear badly injured, but it did seem the fight was gone out of them.

"You all right, honey?" Mrs. Cleveland said. "You were gone there for a while."

"I do that sometimes." Charles averted his eyes from her near-nakedness. He ran down the stairway, listening for more guards. He heard nothing. He pulled the jacket off of the second guard, who relinquished it without incident. He rushed back up the stairs. Now the guards below were starting up the stairway again.

He tossed the jacket to Mrs. Cleveland. "Put this on."

She shook her head and put it on. "You're a strange one. I bet you and James get along fine."

Charles led the two women out the door and onto a flat roof partially obscured by a maintenance room in front of the door. A twelve-foot wall in which the roof access door was encased led in both directions to the sides of the roof, forming the base of a control tower. There were ladders running to the top at intervals along the wall. He paused, took the rifle from Mrs. Cleveland, and tried to wedge it into the stairwell door latch. It fell to the ground.

"Follow me," he said.

"Don't we need that rifle?"

"I have a better one," Charles said.

He led them along the passageway created by the wall and the maintenance room and took a right at the corner where the maintenance room ended. The roof opened before them.

Thirty yards away was the first of two reclamation center gunships sitting on the roof's heliport. The helicopter gunship resembled a B-2 bomber with rotors. It was sleek, with black armor plating, flak cannons, radar deflective contouring, jet engines, bulletproof glass, retractable skids, and missiles.

Mrs. Cleveland traced her hand along the metal. "What is the reclamation center doing with military gunboats?"

"This ain't your daddy's police force." Charles ran to the fuselage and popped the hatch. The canopy opened and Charles loaded the Clevelands in. He entered the helicopter just as the guards burst onto the roof and appeared from behind the maintenance room. Getting in the gunship was like putting on a Darth Vader helmet. It was compact, black everywhere, full of electronics. The darkly tinted windshield was split down the middle, like eyes.

Charles closed the hatch and dropped into the pilot seat. He noticed a quizzical look on Mrs. Cleveland's face. "Standard Agency training," he said.

She curled her lips.

The guards lifted their weapons and commanded Charles to exit the vehicle.

Time for one last miracle, Julia. Charles spoke an access code to the gunship. The instrument panel illuminated and shot a red beam into his left eye, scanning his retina. The gunship confirmed him as "Charles Graves, authorized pilot." Unbelievable. I've got to marry that girl.

The guards opened fire. Bullets rattled against the armor plating and bulletproof glass like pea-sized hail.

"Arm," Charles said. A quarter of the instrument panel turned red. "Flak cannons." A red X appeared on the windshield. It followed the line of sight created by Charles's left eye.

On the sides of the gunship, the flak cannons, about the size of a grown man with an aperture facing forward, skewed around based on the tracking of Charles's eyes. The flak cannons' movement created a shrill whine, like hydraulic motors straining under an enormous load.

The guards got the message. The rifles fell silent and they scurried for the cover of the maintenance room.

"Watch this," Charles said to the Clevelands, who were spectating from the back. "Infrared."

The windshield lit up in an aurora-like transparent fog. The heat signatures of the guards were visible behind the maintenance room wall.

Charles targeted the portion of the wall to the right of the maintenance room, where no heat signature appeared. "Ten foot square dispersal pattern, five second duration. Engage."

The flak cannons roared like jet engines. The sheer power of the cannons shook the gunship and coursed through Charles down to his bones. It reminded him of the night he and Julia had lain on the hood of the car watching the airplanes pass overhead. The heat signatures of the guards fled down the stairwell.

The cannons ejected superheated metal particles at an extreme velocity. It was as if the cannons had released a plague of alien locusts on the wall. The infrared picked up the heated particles as one-foot-wide cylindrical tracers. After five seconds the cannons fell silent. When the dust settled, Charles could see a ten-foot square cavern in the wall.

"Flight ready," he said.

The gunship whirred, buzzed, and flashed. The rotors spun, the jet engines ignited. The windshield displayed flight information.

"You guys better strap in back there," Charles said. He followed his own advice in the pilot's seat. "Infrared off. Lift to one thousand feet."

The gunship lurched into the air as if it were God's yo-yo. It retracted its skids and hovered at one thousand feet.

"Missiles," Charles said. The gunship whirred again. Charles targeted the other gunship on the reclamation center roof. "Two missiles, simultaneous strike pattern, dorsal impact. Engage."

The missiles fired from the gunship's sides. The jet engines kicked in with the precise force necessary to counterbalance the missiles' takeoff. The helicopter remained motionless in the sky.

The missiles struck the other gunship with dead aim. The roof of the reclamation center erupted and a one hundred foot ball of flame leapt into the night sky.

The armored gunship absorbed most of the shock, leaving the roof damaged but intact. The gunship was destroyed.

"Disarm," Charles said. The gunship powered down its weapons systems. "Coordinates." Charles read in a predetermined set of GPS coordinates given to him by Julia. "Hang on back there." He formed a takeoff gesture with his hand. "Go to top speed."

Julia didn't think she could outrun the flames. Teresa was feeling heavier with each step. Julia's thighs were starting to burn. Soon they would be screaming at her.

Even if she did outrun the flames, she figured she might miss the car and end up on the opposite side of the field in her headlong flight. Cleveland would be forced to evacuate on account of the fire. That would leave her stranded. Stranded equated with caught. Caught or burned. Even if she found Cleveland on the road, given she could progress that far, they would be apprehended in the open without a good head start.

Julia attempted to maintain a 45-degree heading to the left, judging on where she had exited the fence. How many steps had she counted to get to the fence? She couldn't remember. Thirty-something.

That show had made the Approved TV List.

Concentrate, GG, or you won't make it.

The flames kept good pace with her. Julia figured the flames' legs were not tiring. They threatened to outflank her on the left. If that happened, she wouldn't make it to the car. She trudged along, one agonizing step at a time.

I hate to use a cliché, but getting away from those guards was an out of the frying pan and into the fire decision.

Concentrate, GG.

I can't make it. I don't even know how far I've gone.

About twenty-four steps. Keep moving.

My thighs are killing me.

Don't you think I feel them too?

You're noted for logic, not feeling.

Touché. But try this . . .

Julia let go of one of Teresa's legs. Teresa's weight shifted to one side. Julia strained to keep her balance with the displaced weight.

She reached to her belt and pulled out the pistol. She pointed it up and squeezed off two shots. Julia adjusted Teresa's weight and took a couple more steps. She fired another shot into the air. It gave away her position to the guards, but maybe it would do something else.

The fire roared closer. The smoke had now outpaced the fire and was beginning to fill the weeds around her. Julia coughed.

Up ahead, the horn rang out. Cleveland blared the horn in a three short, one long pattern. The sound came from a spot ahead and to the right.

Julia adjusted her track toward the horn. She fired another shot into the air. The horn stopped, then resumed its pattern as if to acknowledge the gunshot.

The new direction afforded Julia space from the flames, but the flames rallied, diminishing the difference. Julia's thighs shrieked with pain.

Over the roar of the fire, the horn grew louder. She gambled. With her remaining thigh power, she ran. It was excruciating, but she gritted her teeth and ran toward the increasing volume of the horn. She burst through a stand of weeds and ran headlong into the hood of the station wagon, just ahead of the encroaching flames.

She poured Teresa onto the hood of the car. Her thighs worshipped her for the relief. Cleveland's eyes were wide as he stared at her through the windshield. Julia clawed herself onto the hood and held on. She beat on the hood, motioning for Cleveland to go.

He started the car and veered to the left, away from the flames. Weeds whipped Julia and Teresa across the hood.

The wagon bumped over the uneven field, flopping Teresa and Julia. At a reasonable distance from the flames, Cleveland stopped the wagon, then backed across its track through the weeds.

He jumped out of the car and ran to the front of the wagon. "You all right?"

"My legs," Julia said.

Cleveland lifted her off the hood and carried her to the backseat of the station wagon. Without setting her down, he opened the door and deposited her in the car.

"Get Teresa," Julia said.

Cleveland nodded. He ran, eyeing the flames as he executed the U-turn around the front of the wagon. "You all right?"

"My feet," Teresa said. They were covered with blood.

He lifted her off the hood and inserted her into the front seat. Teresa landed on the laptop, slamming it shut.

Cleveland completed a reverse U-turn around the front of the wagon. The flames were within ten feet. "Hold on." He put the wagon in drive and whipped the car around.

The flames had cut the field in half. Cleveland drove along the fire line, veering to the right.

Julia sat up in the backseat. "Not too fast. You'll blow a tire."

"Doin' the best I can, ma'am."

"You're doin' fine, sir," Teresa said.

The calmness in Teresa's voice amazed Julia. Teresa reached over, wiped Cleveland's brow, and kissed it.

Visibility in the weeds was poor, even with the car mowing a trail through them. The glow from the fire rose to their left. The station wagon puttered along. Julia thought of her night at Old Bones Lane again.

"You remind me of a man I saw on TV once." Teresa wiped Cleveland's brow again.

"Could be, ma'am," he said. "Pirate TV, I imagine."

"More than likely."

In the ghostly haze of the field, a haunting melody escaped her lips. She was singing? Julia wondered about this woman. Broken out of her captivity, roused from a deep sleep, forced to crawl through dirt in the dark, running from guards, avoiding gunshots, impaling her feet, and now riding through Sleepy Hollow with complete strangers. It's not logical.

"It led me down a lonesome road," Teresa sang. "A road that's paved with sin."

Cleveland chimed in. "I traveled down that road so long, I never thought I'd come back, come back again." He flashed the pastor's eyes at Teresa.

She grabbed his shoulder and backed his melody with an alto. "But when the Spirit touched my heart, and I called Jesus' name, He saved the soul of a man in the sinners' hall of fame."

In the middle of this field of weeds, with the fires of hell raging around them and hellhounds on their trail, Julia thought she had never heard anything so captivating.

TWENTY

Julia shouted as the station wagon burst from the weeds without warning.

Cleveland swerved to try to get onto the road, but struck a barbed-wire fence, a section of which got busy wrapping itself around the wagon's grill. A rotted fencepost was attached to the barbed-wire.

The wagon hit a shallow ditch between the field and the road and slammed against the far side of the ditch, catapulting it up onto the road. Julia, Cleveland, and Teresa all hit their heads on the roof and flopped around the wagon's interior.

Julia looked around to get her bearings. They had exited the field a mile from where Julia and Cleveland had entered. Behind them, the field was in full blaze. A truck, possibly dispatched from Teresa's prison home, was racing ahead of the flames, patrolling near where they exited. It trained its searchlight on the station wagon and swerved in their direction.

Cleveland jammed the gas pedal and the station wagon fishtailed onto the road ahead of the truck. He overcorrected and the wagon fishtailed in the opposite direction, then he got it straightened out.

The truck accelerated. It was about two hundred yards behind the car. It kept its spotlight trained on the back of the wagon.

Cleveland accelerated up to ninety. They were still dragging the fencepost. It worked its way under the wagon and beat up and down on the dark road behind the car. The truck kept pace behind them. Teresa kept up her song, wiping sweat from Cleveland's brow the entire time.

Cleveland had the car up to 110 miles per hour when Julia saw flashing lights ahead. Multiple cruisers blockaded the road about two miles up. Cleveland slowed. The truck gained from behind.

"You two may want to get down," Cleveland said. "I think they mean to shoot us if we don't stop."

Julia saw Cleveland's eyes dart back and forth from the road to the rearview mirror. They didn't seem like pastor's eyes. The truck was close now. The blockade was about a mile ahead.

"Hold on." Cleveland hit the gas.

Julia and Teresa braced themselves.

About a half mile from the roadblock, Cleveland slowed again. The truck behind was close, but not too close.

Then Cleveland stood on the brake pedal. The wagon screeched. Cleveland allowed it to veer left.

Behind them, the truck locked its brakes as well. The time differential and the truck's added weight sent it skidding toward the wagon.

Cleveland cut the steering wheel hard over and the car u-turned so it faced the skidding truck. The barbed wire snapped, sending the fencepost skidding down the road toward the blockade. Cleveland jammed the gas.

The truck missed by two feet, close enough for Julia to notice the driver's mustache as he passed by.

Cleveland had the station wagon going the opposite direction. They were heading away from the blockade, but away from the main highway as well.

The cruisers were sluggish in reacting to Cleveland's ploy. By the time the cruisers got going, navigated around the truck, and joined the chase, Cleveland had the wagon a mile down the road.

A strange grating came from the underside of the car. The barbed wire that had been snarled in the grill of the wagon came loose. It scraped the undercarriage of the car and was almost free when it wrapped around the rear axle. One end snaked around and caught one of the back wheels. It coiled up around the tire. The tire blew.

The wagon shimmied back and forth. Cleveland let the wagon slow on its own accord. At a safe speed he applied the brakes, stopped the wagon, and put it in park. He lit up the interior lights. "Well," he said, "that's that." He turned to look at Teresa and Julia. "Put your hands up, ladies, and maybe they won't shoot you. I'll get out and try to stop them."

"Let me do it," Julia said. "I'm one of them."

Cleveland turned to Julia. The pastor's eyes were back. Julia melted—for what she figured was the last time.

"No, child," Cleveland said. "You're one of us."

Julia grabbed his hand and squeezed. "Thanks. I want you to know, Reverend, that—"

"This ain't over yet, sweetheart."

"Yes, it is." Julia removed the pistol from her belt and loaded a fresh clip into it. It snapped into place with a raspy click.

"I'll try to get most of them before they get me. If I can cause enough commotion, maybe you can get to one of their cars or overpower the one or two left. Or you can get to the fields and hide. Take your choice."

Cleveland's face clouded. "We don't do things that way, Julia. Give me the gun."

"It's the logical way."

Teresa grabbed Julia's hand. "God did not bring me out here to abandon me in the street."

"He's abandoned you for twenty years. Why should this be any different?" Julia stepped out of the car and surveyed the dark field. Then she leaned her head back in. "Forgive me, Teresa. That was a rotten thing to say."

"I understand, dear."

Julia noticed the lights were almost up to the car. "Reverend, I'll make you a deal. If I get out of this alive, we'll have a long talk about your electricity. But really, this is good-bye. If you see him again, tell Charles I love him."

Julia saw Teresa's face light up before she shut the door. She walked behind the wagon into the middle of the road. She slid the gun into her belt, behind her back, and raised her hands into the air.

The cruisers halted a hundred yards from the wagon, spotlights trained on Julia. She walked into the blinding light, arms raised.

Now that he was on the inside of it, Cotton Graves saw that La Rosa Blanca was not the hole he'd expected. He sidled up to the bar with his arm around his new friend's shoulder.

A soca band was going strong and fifty people were dancing on a dance floor to Cotton's right. There was an upper level overlooking the dance floor with tables along a balcony, serviced by a recessed bar. Along the other side of the dance floor sprawled a massive rose garden encased in bamboo. The aroma of the roses overpowered the cloud of smoke that hung in the room like fog.

"Give this man anything he wants," the bouncer said. He flipped his accomplice some cash. "See to him while I run down the boss."

The bouncer high-fived Cotton. He exited the main room of the club through a doorway behind the bar. The doorway was covered with hippie beads.

Cotton surveyed his surroundings, devising an exit strategy should one be necessary. As this was shaping up, he might be able to cultivate some allies in this place.

Cotton saw the bouncer's arm emerge from the hippie-bead hallway. His hand beckoned Cotton. Cotton and the bouncer's accomplice pushed through the beads. The hallway they stepped into was stained yellow, smelled of beer and urine, and supported a thriving insect community. They exited the hallway, crossed over an open porch, and entered a back room behind the club.

The room closed in on Cotton at once. It was covered with plush red carpet, including the walls and ceiling. Cardboard boxes occupied most of the furniture. A pool table lamp with a green shade hung from the middle of the room.

At a desk in the back right corner of the room sat a man with oversized gray sideburns.

The four men consumed most of the room's available space. The bouncer removed a box from a chair in front of the desk.

He motioned for Cotton to sit. Cotton complied, engaging the senator's smile. The bouncer and accomplice retreated to a back wall.

"Frank Cotton Graves," the man with the sideburns said. "What a pleasure."

"Mr. Fah-reese. Mr. Fah-reese."

Farris winced from nasal pain. Light invaded the pitch dark of his office. From his couch, he saw a silhouette standing in the half open doorway. He flopped his head back and shut his eyes.

"What is it, Keesma?"

"Louis asked me to give you an update on Cotton Graves. He left the cab with two men, entered the bar, and went to a back room."

"Tell Louis to get a brain transplant. And tell him not to wake me up again unless something happens."

"Yes, sir." Keesma left, closing the door behind him. The office faded to black.

Farris embraced the darkness like an addict embraces an exotic nepenthe. He sensed a reckoning approaching. He settled further into his mind, searching for Charles's intent. *What are you doing, my old friend? You sent your father to La Rosa, but why? You don't trust him enough to set him up as a front man.* The thoughts fragmented as Farris slipped back to sleep.

A knock at the door jerked Farris out his doze like a perch on the end of a cane pole.

"What?" he said.

"Mr. Fah-reese." It was Louis. "You need to come now. We got a report that Reclamation Center Three is under attack."

"Lights," Farris said. His office illuminated. "Video. Current reports."

Farris's office video lit up, scrolling the latest posts of agency data. Farris attempted to adjust his eyes and read the posts simultaneously. He read portions of the scroll aloud, trying to transfer the developing situation to his brain.

"Hundred foot fireball . . . Firebird X-18 gunship stolen . . . Computer malfunction."

"Mr. Fah—"

"Shut up, Louis!" Farris said. "High speed chase . . . Farm to market road."

Farris entered a trance-like state as he processed the information. He was now fully awake, adrenaline flooding his veins. It felt much better than the darkness and sleep. His brain raced through event permutations. "Get out, Louis!"

Louis left, shutting the door.

"Computer!"

"Yes, Mr. Fah-reese."

"Top secret file database. Give me the agency holding nearest the high speed chase reported on the scroll."

The computer reported matter-of-factly. "Fah-reese, Richard. Top secret clearance approved. Transmitting. Basil's farm. Currently maintained as holding station for Teresa Graves. Status: Alarm."

"Alarm? Translate."

"Break-in reported. Gunshots fired. Occupant escaped. High-speed pursuit engaged."

Teresa Graves? Why didn't Ingraham tell me? Perhaps he didn't know. Could Graves have kept this a secret all these years? Not likely. No, not at all. Must have a deal with Ingraham.

"Okay, give me all current inmates at Reclamation Center Three. Sort by Graves, Cleveland, and Jenkins."

The computer reported. "Cleveland, Maggie, 62. Cleveland, Elizabeth, 35. Cell 46."

"Computer off." Farris allowed the information to set in. He walked to the office door, twirling an imaginary watch chain in his right hand. "I got to hand it to you, old friend."

Farris opened the door and called for Louis. Both Louis and Keesma answered.

"Get Ellington to scramble every available Air Force fighter down 45 South. Tell them to request direction from us when they are in the air. And get me a gunship on the ground here ASAP."

Louis and Keesma hustled to comply.

Not bad, Charles. A simultaneous suicide raid. Not bad. Nothing like going down in flames.

Julia felt the muzzle of her gun pressing against her back as she walked into the spotlights. She figured she'd need a second and a half to reach back, grab it, and bring it out firing. She might drop three before they could react. After the first three shots, she would need to roll to evade the retaliatory shots. But her opposition would be in relative cover behind the cruisers.

Her single biggest disadvantage was the light. How was she supposed to shoot what she could not see? Ahead was blinding light against the dim backdrop of the cruisers. And behind that—darkness. The irony of the situation struck her.

She was an atheist who was about to die approaching a tunnel of light.

A command blared over a loudspeaker. *"On the ground. Now!"*

There were still seventy-five yards of narrow highway between her and the cruisers. She needed to be closer to have a chance. She took another couple of steps, arms still reaching for the sky. She concentrated on the double yellow lines under her feet to keep from blinding herself in the light.

Girly-Girl, listen. If you run to your right, you could be under cover in that field before they could react. It would give you a chance. It would even the odds some.

I can't leave Cleveland out here alone to die.

That is exactly what you will accomplish if you try this in the middle of the street. If you do what I say, you might entice them into the field where you could pick them off one or two at a time. It could work. Besides, Cleveland and Teresa are not your responsibility. You gave it your best shot, GG. It's time for you to think about yourself and disappear into the field.

What's the point? Then what?

You could start over.

Maybe. But I am jealous of Charles's mother. I said a horrible thing back there, and she forgave me faster than I could apologize. I'm not sure she was even hurt by what I said. And the way Cleveland is.

A crutch, GG. Don't be sold on Cleveland. You'll notice he is still in the wagon.

"On the ground. This is your last warning."

Julia believed the loudspeaker voice meant what it said. It was now time to dance. The gap between her and the cruisers had been reduced to fifty yards. The field seemed like the best option. Julia took another step toward the cruisers.

She felt a shock. She wavered on her feet, then fell to her knees, straddling the double yellow lines. Am I shot? She lifted her head and gazed into the spotlights.

Blinded, Julia closed her eyes. She lifted one hand off the pavement of the farm to market road and kept herself propped up on her knees with the other. She groped for the gun in her belt. She found the butt of the gun and brought it out. Disoriented, she pointed in the general direction of the spotlights. She squeezed off three rounds.

Another shock pulsed through her body. Julia collapsed to the pavement.

Farris instructed Keesma and Louis to remain at headquarters. He drained a cup of coffee, savoring the burning sensation in his throat. In a way, it soothed the pain in his nose—much like pinching an ear when your foot hurts.

Farris hit his office door on the run, making for the stairwell. Four minutes later, he was out the back door of the agency watching the gunship descend out of the darkness and land on the back lawn.

Farris ran to the gunship, not concerned with ducking the rotors. He sprang into pilot's seat and strapped in on the double.

"Get this thing in the air," he said to the co-pilot. "Reclamation Center Three."

The co-pilot nodded and spoke the command to the computer. The gunship sailed into the air in backward trajectory, rolling over as it climbed. The jets kicked in, hurtling it across Houston.

Farris assumed control of the gunship and connected with Louis. "Link my com to those Air Force fighters." Farris saw the lights of I-45 below. He activated the gunship's tracking module. The fighters were making a pass around the reclamation center.

"Richard Fah-reese, Gunship 1," he said. "Come in, fighters."

"USAF Alpha, Bravo, and Charlie," a voice responded.

"Lock in our signature so you don't shoot down the good guys," Farris said. "We've got a renegade gunship in the air. Any sign of it on your scope?"

"None."

Farris passed over the reclamation center. It was surrounded by the flashing lights of emergency vehicles and police cruisers. A fire crew was mopping up the mangled wreck of an agency gunship. Searchlights scanned in random directions. No sign of Charles and the other gunship.

"Quadrant search pattern, fifty mile radius," he said. "We'll take south. Maintain contact on this frequency. If you confirm sighting, buzz the coordinates and heading, then shoot it down."

Farris saw the fighters in the tracking monitor. One zoomed north toward downtown. The other two split east and west. If they did not spot Charles's gunship on the way out, they would split the vectors on the way in. It should work.

"Louis," Farris said, "get me a tracking and attack satellite online. I want that gunship found."

The gunship was over Galveston in under a minute. Far off on his left Farris saw the causeway leading to the mainland.

Charles isn't fleeing yet. Farris wondered how he could be so obtuse.

"Alpha," he said, "converge on these coordinates." Farris read the coordinates. On the tracking module, the fighters began to change direction.

Farris whipped the gunship around.

There was still time to intercept Charles at Basil's farm.

Julia raised her head from the farm to market road and saw two fireballs climbing into the night behind the police blockade. In front of her was an inexplicable black phantom hovering over the road. A shrill whine arose from the phantom. It pointed at the blockade with two nasty overgrown fingers.

Julia felt hands on her back. Someone was touching her. Another phantom?

No. It was Cleveland.

"Get up," he said.

Teresa rode on Cleveland's back. The reverend's pull on Julia was weak, but it was enough to get her upright.

"What's happening?" she said.

"Your boyfriend came a callin'," Cleveland said.

Julia holstered her gun with one hand and felt her chest with the other, expecting to discover splotches of blood. All she found was grime from her trek through the crawlspace.

"Those explosions knocked you down," Cleveland said. "I think they knocked most of them silly too, because they missed you. I started runnin' to you when I saw the flames. They were shootin' all over the place. Looks like your boyfriend ain't done yet, either."

"My boyfriend . . . ?"

A roar erupted from the phantom. Julia spun to look, just as flak hurled through the air over the blockade and then arced slowly downward. Lights on the cruisers' roofs disintegrated. Agents dove for the ditch. The blockade shattered before the onslaught of the flak cannons. Glass shattered. Metal sheared off the cruisers in corrugated chunks. The impenetrable wall of death that had stood before her seconds ago now had four thousand holes in it.

The phantom—which, in the firelight, Julia could now see was some kind of helicopter, dropped to the pavement between the ruined blockade and Julia, Cleveland, and Teresa. A hatch lowered automatically, beckoning them.

They rushed for the gunship. The hatch opened fully and they climbed in. Cleveland, in last, shut the hatch behind them.

The gunship shot up into the night sky.

"USAF Alpha."

"Go," Farris said.

"Visual on the gunship. Coordinates entered. Heading: east, 250 mph."

"All units converge on Alpha's coordinates. Don't lose that gunship."

"Infrared satellite tracking locked."

"Engage."

"Please confirm. Hostile will be over Texas City in five seconds."

"Don't use missiles then. Engage with 30 millimeter."

"Roger. Coming around for pursuit."

Farris banked his gunship around, heading for Texas City, which glowed like a nightlight in Houston's bedroom.

TWENTY-ONE

Charles refused to look in the back of the gunship. He couldn't dare look to see if she was really there, after all these years. He kept his eyes on the navigation data projected on the gunship windshield.

Julia climbed into the co-pilot seat. "Charles—"

"I can't right now. This is our most vulnerable time. If we're lucky."

Without looking, Charles knew that in the rear of the gunship, Cleveland embraced his wife and daughter. "'Though he slay me, yet will I trust in him.'" Charles heard the rustle of movement and figured Cleveland was holding his wife and daughter close. "I love you two so much," Cleveland said. "Give me a second."

Charles sensed Cleveland moving up behind him in the pilot's chair. He reached over the seat and placed two hands on Charles's shoulder. "Charles, thank you. I don't know—"

"Don't thank me yet," Charles said. "We've got thirty miles of bad road ahead first."

The ravenous industrial complex of Texas City appeared below, lit in orange halogen lamps that turned the night amber. Charles slowed the gunship and scanned across the city-sized refinery that bordered state highway 146. He centered the gunship's targeting reticle on an open section amidst the jumble of tanks and piping.

"Hover there," he said. "Thirty feet." The gunship dove toward the plant.

They reached the coordinates and the gunship went into hover mode. Two bright flares burned above the gunship from 100-foot towers. They reminded Charles of birthday candles for a two-year-old giant.

"Why are you stopping?" Cleveland said.

Julia answered for Charles. "They'll be searching for us with infrared satellites. Here, we're invisible to them."

"She's right, as usual," Charles said. "Plus, I want to see if they have visual contact with us yet. No telling how many interceptors they launched to shoot us down."

Cleveland deflated like a kid given an extra chore when he thought he was finished working and could go out and play. "So we're not out of this?"

"Do you hear the roar from those flares?" Charles asked.

Cleveland nodded.

"If they are searching for us here," Charles said, "you will hear an occasional roar cross overhead sideways." Charles was holding one arm upright and demonstrating the sound from a jet with a crossing motion with his other hand. "When that happens, we will get a blip on the tracking module as the belly of the plane is exposed to us."

Charles held one finger up, cueing them all to listen. At the same time, he strained his ears to hear any sign of someone else in the gunship fuselage behind him.

As if to provide an audio/visual aid to Charles's demonstration, he heard a subtle roar. It was dissonant with the sound of the flares. The sound rose and waned. Charles watched the tracking module carefully. Nothing happened.

"Hmm," he said. "Well, maybe that wasn't a plane."

"Sure it was," Julia said. "Depending on the plane's speed and height, you might need to look for the blip first, then listen for the sound."

"She's a genius," Charles said.

Julia grabbed Charles's head and forced it away from the tracking module. "I know you know more about planes than that." She kissed him.

"Great job on those computers," Charles said. "Perfect. Four for four." Charles really wanted to look behind him. He fought hard to keep his head staring in Julia's direction. Finally, he swallowed and asked, "Is she here?"

"She is," Julia said.

Charles felt warm hands on his neck. His eyes shut. He knew the warmth of those hands. He thought of being tucked in bed as a child. He thought of walks in the woods out behind Graves Mansion. He thought of how long he had missed his mother.

She spoke in his ear over the back of the pilot seat. "It's okay, Charles," she said. "You get us home first. Then we can have all the time we need."

Charles's head dropped to his chest with enough force to ram his chin into his breastbone. He convulsed, dry heaving like a child who has cried so much his tear reservoir is empty.

Cleveland placed his hand on his mother's, which were still on Charles's neck.

Behind them, Cleveland began to pray. Charles comprehended the introduction to the prayer, but then Cleveland's words became jumbled and nonsensical to him. He was sobbing. Charles rubbed his eyes and tried to concentrate on their tactical situation. When his eyes cleared, there were multiple blips on the tracking module.

She's a liar, the dark man said. His face appeared in the tracking module, the product of the multiple blips.

Charles turned his gaze from the tracking module to the windshield. A full-sized dark man awaited him in the reflection there. Charles fumbled with the blocks in his pocket.

She's the reason for all your trouble, the dark man said, pointing a finger at Charles's mother. We've been through this a thousand times. When are you going to get it?

She's my *mother*!

She's a killer. Or have you forgotten?

She told me to remember, Charles said, and I have.

Oh, yeah, that. Notice who she always wants you to forget: Stephen. He'd be here if it weren't for her. He was a child, Charles, a child.

So was I.

But you are not anymore. So quit acting like one.

Julia told me the truth is more complex than that . . . than the way you are making it out to be, Charles said.

She doesn't know what happened, though, does she?

Cleveland told me we can all be forgiven.

He doesn't know either, does he?

So what do you want from me? Do you want me to kill myself?

Of course not, you buffoon. Then I'd be dead too. I want you to think about yourself. Only yourself. These people are no good for you. Take a look at your life.

Images of Farris, Julia, Pete, Stephen, his father, Cleveland, and his mother flashed across the gunship windshield. Some irritated him, like Farris's nose over his pompous sneer. Others were sweet, like the image of Julia watching the airplanes land.

The dark man exited to the right, returning with an old-fashioned balancing scale that covered most of the windshield. The dark man encapsulated the images and set them on one end of the scale. Their weight tipped the scale. The end they were on sank to the bottom of the screen while lifting the other side to the top of the windshield. The dark man pulled himself up onto the opposite side of the scale. The side the dark man was on sank about two feet.

The dark man produced a poster board and a marker. On the poster board he wrote: What could have been.

The words comprised characters composed of some chemical substance. The longer he stared at them, the fuzzier they became. Then they disappeared altogether. In their place, colors began to form. The poster board flashed to life, depicting scenes from Charles's life as they could have been. In the scenes, Charles was complete. He was successful. He was unburdened with the cares of his present life. He had a Lotus and a posh downtown loft instead of a van and a house on Old Bones Lane.

The scale began to tip to the dark man's side. It was now evenly balanced with the side holding Julia, his mother, and the others. The scale teetered back and forth, much like Stephen had on the third level of the cellblock.

The dark man produced a second poster board and wrote: What still could be.

A scene developed on the poster board screen. It pictured Charles as a hero. He was congratulated by Ingraham. The agency opened its arms to him. He saw himself rearranging things in Cotton Graves's suite at headquarters. He threw his dad's nameplate in the trash and replaced it with his own. He searched the suite on the poster board image for Sheila's desk. Would she still be there?

The image panned around the suite to the entrance. Sheila was not there. The image grew fuzzy as if it were trying to make up its mind. When the image clarified, Julia was sitting in Sheila's spot.

It's possible, the dark man said, if we work hard enough. We can pin some of the failure on Farris, which is an added bonus in itself. No one knows what happened in that office when Julia hit him.

What would I have to give up? Charles asked.

Cleveland. His whole affiliation. Perhaps your dad, the dark man said. We can find a way for your mother to live comfortably. Throw in the terrorists as well, and you'll be a hero. I will see to it.

The dark man's side of the scale sank to the bottom of the windshield.

Charles considered the scale. He felt the weight of events and choices pressing down on him. On the right side of the scale, he saw Cleveland and his family. Could he give them up? How well did he know Cleveland after all? What did he owe him?

The answer came in a flash of light that appeared on Cleveland's side of the scale. Voices came out of the light. It was

Charles and Cleveland studying the Bible at Lasanya's house. It seemed like ages had passed since that night.

Charles saw the Gospel of John. Cleveland's voice spoke the words:

"'These things have I spoken unto you, that my joy might remain in you, and that your joy might be full. This is my commandment, That ye love one another, as I have loved you. Greater love hath no man than this, that a man lay down his life for his friends. Ye are my friends, if ye do whatsoever I command you. Henceforth I call you not servants; for the servant knoweth not what his lord doeth: but I have called you friends; for all things that I have heard of my Father I have made known unto you. Ye have not chosen me, but I have chosen you, and ordained you, that ye should go and bring forth fruit, and that your fruit should remain; that whatsoever ye shall ask of the Father in my name, he may give it you.'"

The scale whined with the sound of straining metal. It writhed under the pressure of Charles's impending decision. Finally, the right side of the scale slammed down as if struck, catapulting the dark man off the other side. He flew out of view, cursing Charles for his stupidity. As Charles came to, Cleveland was still praying for him.

Cleveland ended his prayer. Charles sought his mother's hands. He found them.

"Get us home," she said.

Charles released her hands and cemented his attention on the windshield and tracking module. "How many do you think, Julia?"

"I count three."

Charles turned to Cleveland. "Can I shoot them down?"

Cleveland stammered. "Is there any other way?"

"Not if they get a fix on us, which they will once we leave here."

"Can't we just get out and try to find a ride back to town?"

"I think they know we are in the area. Farris probably has half the agency on the way."

"Are you sure it's the only way?"

"It's the only one I can think of," Charles said. "If it makes you feel any better about it, the pilots survive 90 percent of the time."

"Are you certain you won't shoot down commercial aircraft?"

"These targets will be moving much faster than commercial planes, and their signatures on the module will be different," Julia said.

Cleveland stole a glance at his daughter. "Do what you need to do."

Charles armed the gunship's weapon system.

"So you're on your way to Mexico?" Gurdy Morrison asked.

Cotton did not flinch. "Thinkin' about it. Some good weather down there." He flashed the smile.

"Were you doing some Mexican research here at La Rosa?"

"Nah. Stopped for a breather."

"That right? The missus givin' you trouble at home? All the hotels booked up? Nowhere else to stop on the way to Mexico?"

"I thought maybe I might stop in for a drink."

"Hmm."

Gurdy sat behind his desk facing Cotton, who sat in a chair under the green pool table lamp. The two bouncers stood against the red carpeted wall, close to the door.

"Where do you live, Cotton?" Gurdy asked. "You live at the agency, don't you?"

"That's right."

"Wasn't there somewhere closer to go? La Rosa is not even in the general vicinity. Come to think of it, it is not exactly the cultural center of town either." Gurdy and the two bouncers laughed. "It doesn't fit a man of your . . . how should I say it? Status."

Cotton leaned forward. "I haven't been a senator this long for nothing. Get on with it."

"I reckon you ain't." Gurdy leaned forward to match Cotton. "What are you doing here, Senator?"

"I stopped for rest, maybe a drink. La Rosa's out of the way." Cotton leaned back. "I'll level with you. I'm on the lam. La Rosa is not the kind of place they would predict me to be."

"Now we're gettin' somewhere. What'd you do?"

"You wouldn't be interested."

"Try me."

Cotton gestured like he was giving a speech. "My son works for the agency—"

"Charles Graves, right. What's he look like? I mean, what's he *really* look like?"

"No one is certain," Cotton said. "Depends on the day, I guess. He got into some trouble and I broke out from house arrest, figuring I at least stood a chance on the outside."

"You might've figured wrong."

"Maybe. But what's your interest in me?"

Gurdy opened a desk drawer and removed a small safe. "Come on, Graves. You've got to be smarter than this if you're a senator."

"You seen Congress lately?" Cotton laced his fingers behind his bald spot.

"Bring in the dog," Gurdy said. The two bouncers left the room.

Gurdy punched in a code on the faceplate of the safe. A green light lit up. Gurdy punched in another code. The safe opened. "Insurance, senator. That's all senators are good for these days. I want to show you something, so if and when I need you for insurance, you'll be able to help me—in a very sober and convincing manner."

The bouncers returned with a golden retriever in a sizeable cage, which they placed on Gurdy's desk. The dog was wagging its tail, frisky and playful. It had big brown eyes. Cotton thought the dog was smiling—expecting a walk, perhaps, or a swim, or a chance to chase a ball.

Gurdy threw it a piece of cheese through the cage. The dog slurped up the cheese with one bite, and looked around eagerly for more.

"This oughta make you see things from our perspective, Senator." Gurdy reached in his desk and pulled out a set of neoprene gloves.

Cotton reached over the desk to pet the dog through the cage. It licked his hand. "Whatever you're about to do, Gur—"

"Shut up, Graves. And you might want to move back some." Gurdy put the gloves on and then removed from the open safe something that looked like an asthma puffer. The puffer had a spout that tapered to a point like an ear-dropper.

Gurdy called the dog. It responded faithfully to him, inching up to the front of the cage. Gurdy stuck the spout in the dog's nostril and engaged the puffer.

Gurdy palmed the puffer and pulled one of the gloves off over it. He pulled the other glove off and dropped both into a plastic bag, which he handed to one of the bouncers. "Burn it," he said.

The bouncer left with the bag.

Cotton watched the dog. At first it remained the tail-wagging, happy golden retriever. Then it looked at Cotton and whimpered. The dog backed up in the cage and sat down.

Its eyes pleaded with Cotton, then they began to boil. The dog shrieked like a spanked puppy. It lurched back against the back of the cage, neck craning forward, smoke billowing out of its nose.

The dog fell to the floor of the cage and convulsed. Cotton could see its insides rippling. The whole time the dog's eyes pleaded with Cotton.

The dog let out a final whine and died.

Cotton leapt over the desk at Gurdy and managed to get a hold of one of Gurdy's sideburns before a bouncer pulled him off. The bouncer forced Cotton back into the chair. Cotton was pleased to notice a small clump of hair in one hand. He dropped it to the floor. "Why did you do that?"

"That was one part per million," Gurdy said, rubbing his cheek. "It'll go in through the skin or through the lungs. Nasty stuff, wouldn't you say?"

Cotton said nothing.

"I've got a whole drum full of that stuff." Gurdy reached under the desk and brought out a metal case, fastened with clamps. He popped the clamps open, rotated the case, and displayed the contents.

The bomb looked real enough to Cotton.

"I place that drum anywhere within a city block of this," Gurdy said, indicating the bomb, "and we've got a major disaster on our hands."

"If and when the time comes, you play along, Senator. Remember: insurance."

Cotton looked back at the dog's body. What was left of the dog's eyes were still trained on Cotton. "Why?"

"Don't worry about that." Gurdy motioned for the bouncer. "Run him through the scanner again and make sure he ain't bugged. Then check his car for anything interesting. After you're done, get rid of the car. Lock him in the back room closet."

Cotton searched deep inside and found the fortitude to summon the senator's smile. "You realize what a senator is, don't you?"

"Beyond insurance, I don't really care." He shrugged. "I didn't vote for you."

Charles kissed Julia's hand, never taking his eyes off the tracking module. Cleveland retreated back to his family. They huddled in the back of the gunship. Charles's mother kept a hand on Charles's shoulder.

The gunship's interior grew quiet—with the exception of Teresa's muted singing. Charles worried about fuel. Two blips appeared on the module. Two of the fighters were overhead.

"Arm missiles," Charles said. "Lock on and fire."

The gunship heaved itself upward. The ship's bow rose at a 45-degree angle. Four air-to-air missiles launched from their gunship. The missiles left tracers of exhaust as they climbed into the night sky.

"Manual steering," Charles said. "Ahead full." The gunship roared. Charles banked the craft between the flares.

In a minute, they crossed the Texas City dike and zoomed out over Galveston Bay. Charles dropped the gunship to an altitude of ten feet. The gunship created a wake in the bay water as it cruised.

The Houston Ship Channel ran down the center of Galveston Bay and then cut a winding, watery path through miles and miles of industrial refineries and factories on the mainland, ending near downtown Houston. At night, the refineries on the mainland would be a supercluster of electric light. Every tower, tank, and pipe would be lit.

Charles guided the gunship north over the ship channel, aiming for the spot where the channel cut into the mainland. He banked left in front of a tanker heading south out of Galveston Bay on its way to the Gulf of Mexico. Charles could see into the bridge of the tanker as he flew by. When the tanker passed, he settled the gunship back in over the channel.

"We got a little over twenty miles to the mainland," Charles informed his passengers. "I figure about six to seven minutes to get there. Even if they spot us, they can't execute a satellite strike within that time frame. But it's still going to be close if those fighters know where we are."

Cleveland spoke quietly to Charles. "They would use attack satellites on us?"

Charles looked at Julia, whose expression was probably what caused Cleveland to launch into prayer again.

"But we're not going to give them that chance," Charles said.

The gunship sped across the water. Charles saw the lights from another tanker up ahead.

"Um, Charles," Julia said, "I think they know we're here. I see two fast-movers approaching on the module. Looks like a fighter up high and a gunship trailing on the deck."

"Ready countermeasures," Charles said to the weapons computer. Two flaps in the rear of the gunship opened.

"They launched. Two missiles approaching," Julia said with practiced calmness. "Impact in twenty seconds."

"No place to hide," Charles said. He kept the gunship on its heading for the mainland.

"Two more launched," Julia said. "We're not going to make it, are we?"

Charles leaned forward, bearing down on the gunship controls as if he were willing the ship to fly faster. The open waters of the bay might have been a mistake. He had figured the ship channel might prevent the use of missiles, but even here they could have been taken down with conventional fire.

Teresa's humming increased to singing: "When the Spirit touched my heart, and I called Jesus' name."

Charles felt her hand press harder on his neck.

"Ten seconds," Julia said.

"Release countermeasures," Charles said.

The gunship lurched. A rushing noise came from the rear. A million heated particles rose into the air behind the gunship like a cloud of locusts. The missiles, on a path for the gunship, entered the cloud and exploded.

The gunship barely reacted to the explosion. Charles kept it on its heading.

"Eight seconds on the remaining two," Julia said.

"You can start praying now," Charles said.

"Are you going to release more countermeasures?" Julia asked.

"Takes at least fifteen seconds to get them ready," Charles said.

"Five seconds," Julia said.

The tanker was still ahead in the distance. Charles saw it lumbering through the channel heading for the mainland, but Charles's gunship was closing fast on it.

What had been a ring of lights and a lumbering blob in the dark ahead of them was now forming features. Charles saw water churning in the wake of the ship. He saw the great hull, the white superstructure of the bridge, the flat deck. Oil. Of all things, it had to be oil.

Charles was unsure of the morality of this gambit. It wasn't his fault that Farris, or whoever was behind them, had authorized the use of missiles in the middle of a commercial shipping lane. And it wasn't as if Charles had intentionally created the opportunity he was about to seize. Yet he knew he could avert this if he chose. Cleveland was on board too. What would he say? Come to think of it, what did God think about all of this? Where was He?

"Everybody hold on. Mom, get strapped in now!"

The hull of the tanker before them was now visible in full detail, despite the darkness. The aft loomed up in the windshield.

"Two seconds," Julia said.

Charles yanked back the yoke at the last possible moment before impact with the hull. The words *Dutchman's Pride, Rotterdam* appeared across the stern. With a roar and the pull of two Gs the gunship zoomed over the hull with mere feet to spare.

The missiles could not change course so suddenly.

The first impact obliterated the stern of the ship, catapulting the double-walled hull of the tanker in all directions, wrinkling the keel a hundred feet into the ship.

Almost instantly, a second explosion rang out, hurtling flaming metal through the air. Charles felt the shrapnel clanking against the underbelly of the gunship as he accelerated away.

The blast illuminated the fuselage of the gunship. Charles saw Julia clutching the co-pilot's seat in a death grip. His mother's hands returned to his neck, caressing him gently. She was the opposite of what the dark man had predicted.

A third and final concussion broke the tanker in half. The fireball, now below and behind them, ascended like a colossal bronze eyeball escaping from a shadowy socket.

Charles dipped the nose of the gunship. It raced toward the water, leveling out at ten feet. The mainland ship channel appeared in the distance.

"Prometheus would be proud," Julia said. "Though I doubt he stole that much fire from the gods."

"The devil would be proud too," Charles said. "I'm sure I made the headlines. Outlaw Charles Graves targets supertanker."

Charles saw the lights of Morgan's Point and Barbours Cut ahead on the left, the lights of Baytown on the right. The desolate Atkinson and Hogg islands were dead ahead. Atkinson Island was four miles long and two thousand feet across on average. It shimmied liked a noodle in the glare of the fireball. If he followed the islands, they would feed him into the mainland section of the ship channel. The supercluster of light from the refineries might expose the gunship, but there would be flares—lots of flares.

Charles lifted the gunship ten feet at the foot of Atkinson. The gunship brought a wake of water with it as it crossed over the land.

"The fighter tailed off," Julia said, monitoring the tracking module.

"The fighter won't target us in the refinery district," Charles said to Julia. "If you think the tanker explosion was bad—"

Charles cut off short when Julia flashed him a *You think I don't know that?* look. Charles shrugged. "I was informing the others."

"The gunship is still on our tail," Julia said.

Charles seized the opportunity to return the *You think I don't know that?* look.

The lights of the Fred Hartman Bridge appeared on their left as the gunship reached the northern edge of Atkinson Island. Charles veered toward the cable-stayed bridge that spanned the ship channel.

The gunship zoomed under the bridge to the right of an exiting tanker. Charles checked the fuel. There was enough.

Minutes later, Charles hovered the gunship between a clump of trees near the edge of the ship channel and the flares of the Exxon refinery that rose like torches of the gods.

Farris, if that's you in that gunship, come and get me.

TWENTY-TWO

As he navigated his gunship under the Fred Hartman Bridge, Farris watched Charles's gunship disappear from the satellite infrared image.

It was a nice attempt, my old friend.

"Louis. Get the ground response units mobilized along both sides of the channel. I want them ready to converge on my command. Graves has ducked into another refinery within three minutes' flight time of the Fred Hartman."

Farris slowed the gunship. Ahead of him was a sea of lights. The tangled mass of piping combined with the lights was an eerie combination. It looked like an alien world or a base on some desolate alien planet.

Farris cruised over the channel, scanning the shoreline for a hint of Charles. The tanker explosion was trouble enough, but on top of that was the theft of one agency gunship, the destruction of another, two fighters downed, the riot at Reclamation

Center Three, the loss of Cleveland's wife and daughter, and the escape of Teresa Graves. He needed Graves back—or dead. This was not the time to miss.

"All units approaching," Louis said over Farris's gunship's speaker.

Now all I need to do is to find you, Charles.

It seemed like a daunting task, yet there were not many places to hide within the radius of how far they could've gotten after disappearing off the screen. They couldn't penetrate too far within the plant or they would risk detection from workers. And since the whole area was one integrated organism of refineries, that meant Charles had probably stayed near the edges of the channel. Probably.

Farris considered Charles's propensity for concealing himself in wide open places. Not only could he disappear into crowds, he was even a ghost at the agency. Farris remembered their training days. They had been recruited in the same agency class—Charles, because of Cotton's influence. Himself, on the basis of merit.

It had quickly become apparent what Charles's gift was. Within weeks, the class began utilizing Charles in training. They would try to pick a disguised Charles out of a lineup. They identified him less often than averages would predict. They were guessing, and they were unlucky guessers. Farris attributed this not to bad luck but to Charles's skill.

Charles was also adept at concealing himself in the outdoors. Another training exercise had evolved, featuring Charles hiding in the agency back lot. The cadets formed a search line and hunted Charles down. If he could make it back to headquarters undetected, he won.

They never succeeded in catching him. The first time he was ten paces from the back door in open grass. They walked right past him. Other times, Charles would pelt his fellow cadets with rocks from his hiding places in order to taunt them. It was uncanny. Charles was a specter.

But not this time, my old friend. I don't think you can hide a gunship.

Still, part of Farris believed he could. He slowed the gunship down even more, marking every foot of the shoreline on both sides.

An alarm blared in the gunship. Someone had targeted Farris.

"*Full ahead!*" Farris urged the gunship to climb.

On his right he saw bursts from flak cannons from about two hundred yards. Charles had the drop on him.

Farris evaded the flak and figured Charles did not want to risk missiles. Yet Charles was on his tail. Farris was now the prey.

"USAF Charlie. Return to my position, lock on, and stand by."

Farris received confirmation from the fighter pilot. He waited to see Charles's next move. Would Charles shoot him down? Of course, with pleasure. He had nothing to lose.

Farris leveled out. He banked right, seeking the safety of the refineries. He was pretty sure Charles would not risk hitting them by accident. Farris flew his gunship erratically, trying to stay out of missile lock.

The blip that was Charles's gunship returned to Farris's tracking module. As Farris dove for the cover of the refinery, he noticed something strange: Charles's blip was crossing the channel. Away from Farris.

Charles was fleeing.

That rat always has a new angle. Farris whipped his gunship up and around. Helped by the refinery lights, he gained a visual on Charles on the far side of the channel. Charles banked right and accelerated inward along the channel, scant yards above the refinery towers.

Farris saw the outline of Charles's gunship against the refinery lights. The ghost was now a shadow crossing a galaxy of lights. Farris took an angle across the ship channel to cut the distance between them. He zoomed over the deck of a seagoing tug on his route across the channel.

Farris's angle achieved his objective. He was almost in weapons range.

Charles's gunship banked left and inward over the last refinery before the San Jacinto Monument Park. Now Farris wished he had crossed straight over the channel. Charles would not have risked the wide open space of the state park. Even staying in the channel didn't protect him though. The waterway bent left in a 90-degree arc around the park before being surrounded again by industry.

Charles was over Battleground Road and the heart of industry before Farris could target a shot. Farris adjusted his course left, settling in behind Charles. It was only a matter of time now.

"Charlie, mark current tracking coordinates," Farris said.

The San Jacinto Battleground Monument rose like a monolith to Farris's right. The white spire reminded him of his loft and the headquarters' tower. His stock was rising too, supertanker fireball or not.

Charles's gunship crossed the land beneath the dogleg in the channel and soared over the water. The gunship sailed above the ships transporting goods in the channel. Farris had a visual on Charles and was tracking him on the module. Charles's game was almost out of time.

Farris cut the dogleg as well and saw the lights of the tollway bridge ahead. Charles's gunship rocketed under the bridge. Farris edged closer to Charles, settling on his tail about three-quarters of a mile back. Farris roared under the tollway bridge.

"Louis, stand down the ground units at the mouth of the channel and ready teams from downtown out, five miles along the channel, ready to close on my orders."

Farris waited a few seconds for the response. What was keeping the oaf?

"Ready," Louis said.

Up ahead, Charles cut another dogleg in the channel, crossing over land and reemerging over the ship channel above the Washburn tunnel. He was closing on the Loop 610 ship channel bridge.

Farris followed Charles's lead, content to let the chase play out to its logical conclusion. Based on his own fuel, Charles couldn't go much farther. Farris crossed over the tunnel on Charles's heels.

Farris had calculated correctly. Charles's gunship slowed as it approached the ship channel bridge. The bridge grew in the distance. It spanned a mile from side to side, ten lanes wide, but was low enough for the occasional tanker to run into.

Farris slowed in concert with Charles. By the time Charles was under the bridge he was almost hovering. His gunship accomplished a perfect turn to the left.

"Louis. Now! All available units: 610 bridge."

Farris slowed to a hover, three hundred yards out, taking cover behind a slight bend in the channel. Still have missiles, Charles? Know I'm here, Charles?

Charles's gunship landed underneath one of the trestles supporting the bridge on either side. The trestles stood like two open hands of a giant, holding the bridge up from the sides of the channel.

"West side, Louis, under the bridge. Suspects will be on foot. Look for a getaway car."

"Roger," Louis said.

He'd called in the troops. They would arrive soon. But Farris had a more final solution in mind. He commanded his gunship to lift fifty feet into the air. Farris targeted Charles through the windshield and unleashed two missiles.

The missiles struck in seconds. Farris watched Charles's gunship shatter. The impact lifted the gunship several feet into the air.

It slammed back down to the ground in a tangled heap of twisted metal. The tail rotor jettisoned off the gunship and lodged like a splinter into one of the giant's fingers.

Farris pushed forward to examine the blast, hovering over the scene.

No sign of survivors. Louis's crew would be here in minutes to mop up. It was a hit. When had Richard Farris ever been known to miss?

Minutes before closing time, Gurdy motioned in the general direction of a closet to the right of his desk in the back room of La Rosa Blanca. "Is the good senator locked up tight?" Gurdy dimmed the green pool light. In the dim light, the red carpet of the back room appeared brown.

The bouncer nodded.

"Good. Make sure. I reckon the agency knows we are here. Why they would send him, though? It don't make sense. Somethin' ain't right. Got any ideas?"

The bouncer sat down at the desk. "Not sure, boss. But I kinda like the guy. Maybe he's telling the truth?"

"A senator tell the truth? Did you notice how he kept that greasy politician smile on him all the way to the end? Those guys are unbelievable."

"Boss, remember that guy we saw at Cleveland's?"

Gurdy tossed a pencil upward. The lead smashed against the ceiling and the pencil fell back to the floor. "I think you're onto it," Gurdy said. "That was the senator's son we saw, I'll bet. The one who used to be the agency's number one or two agent. The agency wouldn't send a senator over here to sit in our back parking lot, but maybe his son would. And since his son is on the outs with the agency, maybe our friend the senator is telling the truth about that part of it. He might really be on the run, but maybe he's working with his son."

"That means Cleveland and his group are keeping tabs on us," the bouncer said.

"You got it. And those Graves bozos might have tipped the agency off to us with this stunt. For all we know, they are casing La Rosa as we speak. Here's the plan then. Spread the word we are on verbal communication only. No phones. Also, get in touch with our agency man and confirm the senator is on the run. We go forward with our project as planned, but instead of targeting the agency, now we target Cleveland's next meeting. With an explosion that big, and with the nasty stuff it releases, it won't matter where we set it off."

"You think we can make it happen in two days, boss?"

"Sure, and this will make it easier. We have the senator as a bargaining chip or a decoy." Gurdy chuckled. "Old Rev. Cleveland wants to stop us, but he will never guess that it will be at his meeting."

The bouncer straightened up in his chair. "Are you sure you want to take Cleveland out?"

"I don't like the way he talks to me," Gurdy said. "I don't like the way he looks at me. We need the underground to rise up, not stay in hiding. He is the unofficial leader and a stabilizing force. Since he won't join us, having him out of the way is the next best thing. We will fill the void and create the anarchy needed to topple the agency."

"Sounds like it could work."

"His meeting is downtown too. It'll work."

It was deep into the night, so quiet the squeaking of the garage door opening seemed loud and invasive. The garage light activated, lighting the front yard. A car pulled into the driveway, crackling gravel under its tires. A dog began to bark across the street.

The car's brake lights lit up, then off, and the car pulled forward another few feet. The brake lights went on again. The headlights went off.

Six people sat in the car, three in the front and three in the back. There were two men and four women. They were laughing.

• • •

"I still can't believe Farris fell for that," Julia said. "I thought he was smarter."

Charles couldn't resist a pun. "He doesn't have much of a nose for detective work."

Cleveland's daughter spoke her first words to the group since they'd left Reclamation Center Three. "I don't understand what happened."

Charles turned toward the backseat. "When Farris came around the bend, I attacked with the flak cannon. I knew that would make him turn away. While he was evading the fire, I touched down and gave the gunship some instructions. That's when we all hopped out and hid in the trees. I programmed the gunship to take off and go land underneath the ship channel bridge on autopilot. Farris took the bait and trailed our empty gunship."

He tapped the ceiling of the car they were in. "We'd planted this car in the tree line on Bayway Drive before we left as part of the getaway plan. I never thought it would work, but it was the only thing I could come up with on short notice."

"It worked, though," Cleveland's daughter said. "Thank you so much."

"You're welcome. I just wish our escape hadn't been at the expense of a few sailors."

The laughing stopped. Cleveland offered a prayer for their safe return and for the sailors and their families.

Cleveland pulled the car into the garage next to Charles's white van, cut the motor, and instructed the door to close. Charles opened the car door too quickly, putting a ding in his van. He felt like he had slapped his best friend in the face.

Julia followed Charles out of the car and spoke into his ear across his back. "I know you need some time with your mom.

Come and find me when you're done." She traced her finger down the back of his neck, sidled past him, and walked into the house.

Cleveland helped his daughter and wife out of the backseat of the car. Charles sensed a joy from the Clevelands. It lingered in the garage air even after they'd entered the house.

Charles took a second to transfer the two puzzle pieces from his pocket into the van. Then he walked around the open door and reached in for his mother. She reached up for him. Charles lifted her out of the car.

"Are you too tired to spend some time with me?" she asked.

"Tired's got nothin' to do with it," Charles said. He carried her into the house.

For the first time, Chares saw lines on his mother's face. He had to force himself to acknowledge them. In his memories, she was a young woman. She was his mother, married to Cotton Graves, living in Graves Mansion.

But this was better than memories. Wrinkles meant the real thing, and the real thing was better than a thousand recollections, especially if some of his memories factored into the equation.

They sat on an L-shaped sofa in the living room of the safe house. Charles sat on the long side of the L, his mother sat on the short. They were as close to the turn of the L as possible. The lights were dimmed. Each had a second cup of coffee on a table in front of the couch. Charles thought he heard Cleveland emit a snore from one of the back rooms where the rest of the crew was fast asleep.

As they'd talked, Charles noticed they'd been dancing around a couple of memories in particular. There'd been no mention of an ASL unit shattering across the white marble, and no mention of Louis- and Keesma-like figures at the front door. There had also been no mention of a second memory, one only Charles had: Stephen teetering along the edge of the Graves Mansion staircase before cascading down and shattering on the white marble floor.

"But I don't hold too much against him, Charles," his mother said.

"I don't see how. He had you put away."

"No, that's not how it was. If anything, your father saved me. He used his influence to have my life spared. They originally took me straight to a reclamation center, did you know that?"

The words hit Charles like a baseball bat. "Wait, I thought he'd been the one to have you hauled off. You mean, he didn't call the agency?"

"No, I don't think so. I think someone else made the call. I do believe one of his connections tipped him off at the last minute, but I don't think he made the call. I was . . . I had gone off the deep end back then, Charles. I was actively involved with some subversive elements that arose when the world began to turn over. I had lots of connections and influence as a senator's wife, and I was fomenting rebellion behind your father's back. It wasn't just the Christianity that came between us. And I hid it all from him on purpose. The less he knew, the less trouble he could get into and the less he would feel he had to hide. It seemed better that way."

Charles shook his head. "Why didn't he ever tell me this?"

His mother took his hand. "I made him promise not to. He used to come and visit me quite a bit, you know. Especially at first."

"At a reclamation center?"

"No, at Basil's farm.

Charles felt his face flush with anger. He reached for his coffee cup. "You'd think he might've mentioned that."

"I wouldn't let him, Charles. I told him not to."

Charles blinked at her, tears brimming in his eyes. "But why? Don't you know what it did to me thinking you were gone? And all this time you were right there?"

"I figured you already had so much going against you," she said. "I didn't see any way for that to help matters."

"But I could have come to visit."

"As it turned out, no." his mother said. "They played ball with your father. He was high profile with a lot more influence back then. The world had turned, and the agency thought it was in their best interests to placate him. But not you. You they considered the next generation. They would not have allowed it."

"So you thought it was better that I thought you were dead? It doesn't make sense. You told me to *remember*!"

"I longed for you every day, Charles, like any mother would. It was worse for me than the thousands of other mothers who were reclaimed back then. They got off easy—no endless nights of crying, no wondering how their kids were doing in school, no imagining what their sons were like as men. Their executions were a relief to them."

Charles set his cup back on the table. He felt her hand tracing the scar that ran across his cheek.

"Not now, Mom," he said. "Not now."

She retracted her hand. "Let me ask you this, then. Has your faith come far enough along to let you see God's hand in all of this? It looks like you remembered after all."

"I don't know," Charles said. "Everything happened so fast. One day I was lying on a street downtown, disguised as a bum, infiltrating the lair of an enemy of the state. The next thing I know, I am saved and on this wild adventure. Now you're here—back from the dead for me—and Dad is on the loose somewhere. I can't process it all."

"I asked you how your faith was."

"I trust Cleveland for some reason."

"He's a good man, Charles. I remember seeing him on TV way back when. But that's not what I am asking."

Charles cracked his knuckles. "Something happened to me that night Cleveland was preaching. That's the one thing I am sure of. It's weird. My whole life I have been unsure of everything, especially myself. But that night . . . It was strange. I felt even more unsure of myself and who I was, but at the same time it was clearer to me than ever before. It was like I found myself by losing myself." He considered telling her about the dark man but decided against it. "So, to answer your question, I guess God is up to something here and I need to follow it through."

"Sure seems like it, Charles," she said. "By the way, I like your girl."

"Julia's the best," Charles said. "By the way, what do you think about Mexico?"

"I think it's a country south of here, but that's not important right now." His mother smiled sagely. "Do you think that's God's plan?"

"I don't know. We have a minor problem to take care of here, then we're planning to go to Mexico. You want to come with us?"

"If that's how it works out, sure. Is Cleveland going?"

"I don't know. He's pretty stubborn." Charles thought about the call from Cotton. "Oh yeah, one other thing: Dad's on the run. We might have one big family reunion." Charles stammered when he realized what he had done. "Well, I mean, except for . . . " He tried to apologize.

His mother stopped him. "It's okay, Charles. We can live with what happened. We have to. Your brother was always a challenging boy, to say the least. I love him. I miss him. I—"

"Not now, mother. Please, not now."

She took Charles in her arms. He fought it at first, but then he relaxed. His mind traveled back in time to when she'd used to hold him as a child. A part of Charles loved this embrace. Another part of him began to resent it.

Oh, the power of a mother over a son, the dark man said. Some things are as sure as the sun.

Not now, Charles thought. Yes, you did well tonight getting us out of that mess. Thank you. But not now. Please. This is our time.

You need me right now. Maybe more than you needed me earlier tonight. She's breaking you down, Charles. Slowly, yes, but methodically, like a sculptor.

Maybe the dark man was right. It had been twenty years, yet it could have been twenty minutes the way she was in control. But what was wrong with that? She was his mother.

I'll tell you what's wrong with it. We have spent all this time working on your identity. I didn't mind the girl much, but then Cleveland came and tore you in two. Now *she* is here trying to grind the pieces into a fine powder. No time for all this, Charles. You will have plenty of time in Mexico to hash all this out. And there you can do it with a cold one in your hand. Much better odds that way. Trust me.

The thought of booze, even if it was only beer, caused Charles's fingers itch. The dark man had a least one argument on his side: what Charles knew for certain about his mother could fit on a postcard.

That's it, pal, take it slow, the dark man said.

"Shut up," Charles said.

"What?"

"Nothing, Mom. Talking to myself. Hey, how about some sleep? I've got so many more things to say to you and ask you, but I am worn out."

"We've got plenty of time, Charles. Take it slow. And I love you. Remember that."

"I did, Mom. I remembered. And I love you too."

TWENTY-THREE

"So the cleanup crews found no sign of Graves and the others?" Ingraham tilted his head in the monitor. "Why am I trusting you with this operation, Farris?"

"Because I am the best you have and you know it." Farris sensed it was time to go on the offensive. Besides, it was true. He was the best.

Farris propped his feet on the edge of his tub. The loft finally felt like home again after the intrusion by Charles and Julia. Ingraham, Louis, and Keesma were patched in through the phone. Farris teased up a bubble and blew it into the air, watching it meander over the side of the tub and into the bathroom.

"You need to remember something, Mr. Ingraham." Farris inflected his voice to soften the blow of the words. "I ventured out on what amounts to a mop-up mission after your folks blew it at the reclamation center. Charles single-handedly infiltrating that center and escaping with two captives in an agency gunship." He shrugged. "And Julia Jenkins breaking Teresa Graves out of a hold-house with a preacher as the get-away driver. You've got to be kidding. And I almost got them, even with them having an insurmountable head start."

"It's unheard of," Ingraham said, conceding the point. "We are reviewing the performance of all involved and making roster decisions accordingly. This meeting is a segment of that review."

Farris detected a hint of weakness and decided to press his advantage. "Who authorized Teresa Graves to be in solitary, anyway? And in such secrecy? That's hardly agency protocol." Farris paused to gauge the effectiveness of the push.

Ingraham broke first. "You're too young to understand, Farris. I'll handle that end. What concerns me is the super-tanker. That's not what I would characterize as 'almost getting them.'"

Last-ditch effort, old man. Not bad, but not good enough either. "We have the story going strong on the approved news. Ongoing investigation. Unknown causes at this time. Charles Graves suspected." Farris stretched in the water. "It would be child's play if he hadn't been in your gunship. As it is, we'll get by with it."

Ingraham put his line on hold.

The line remained dead until Louis broke the silence. "Boss—"

"Shut up, Louis." Farris let himself sink until the water engulfed him. It was hot to his face, but the pain on his nose was therapeutic.

Farris marveled at his ability to handle Ingraham. You gotta beat the best to be the best, and Ingraham was number one, for the time being. There was only one source of true competition,

Charles Graves. And that match was coming to a close. Farris fantasized that a new Charles Graves would emerge once in a while in the future to keep things interesting.

Farris came up from the water in time to hear Ingraham return to the line. Farris squeegeed his face with his hands and wrung his hair out against the side of his head. The water splashed in the tub.

"What are you doing, Farris?" Ingraham asked.

"Waiting on you." Farris purposely splashed more.

"Any news on Cotton Graves?"

"We are positive he is still at La Rosa Blanca," Farris said. "We think he is either complicit in their activities or being held against his will. The latter is more likely."

"Your rationale?" Ingraham said.

"It's readily apparent," Farris said. "Cotton Graves hasn't been within twelve miles of La Rosa his entire life. His connections are major players, not the types who frequent the underground. Moreover, we believe he contacted Charles upon his escape and that Charles sent him there on some form of mission." None of that was readily apparent, but Farris knew it didn't matter.

"What's the go-forward plan?"

The go-forward plan. What a fool. "We have doubled the stakeout at La Rosa. This is the lynch pin to the operation. Cotton will be moving soon, and this will break the whole situation wide open."

"The entire agency is at your disposal, Farris. Let us know what you need. And good luck. You're number one in Houston now, son. Ingraham out."

Once again, no value added, Ingraham. "Louis," Farris said, "is Cotton still locked in the back room?"

"Yes, sir, Mr. Fah-reese."

"I want to know the second that changes. Fah-reese out."

Farris ordered the tub to reheat the water. He ordered jets and bubbles. The tub was good. The loft was better. Cotton Graves's agency tower suite was the best.

Number one. Hadn't taken that long. Ingraham's position was next. That wouldn't take too long either. The only thing in his way was Charles Graves.

What are you up to, Graves?

Farris slid into the water again, enjoying the healing pain on his nose. In his mind's eye, he saw Charles trying to carry Cleveland, Julia, his mother, and Cleveland's wife and daughter. It's too much weight, my old friend.

The monotone voice of an anchorman from the Approved Evening News program filled the living room when Charles awoke. He imagined everyone gathered around the screen watching themselves being portrayed as murderous outlaws to an unforgiving nation. He figured he needed to get out there and salvage what morale remained.

But the group that greeted him in the living room was surprisingly upbeat. The twin tower of faith combination that was Cleveland and his mother even had Julia in a positive frame of mind. Charles's stomach growled as he saw a table of food in the kitchen. He spent the next thirty minutes eating.

After dinner, Charles, Julia, his mother, and the Clevelands sat together on the L-shaped couch. Cleveland wrapped his arms around his wife and daughter on one branch of the L. Charles sat with his arms around Julia and his mother on the other.

"Lots of decisions to make here tonight," Cleveland said. "Best done after prayer." Cleveland bowed his head and led in prayer. At the end of it, Charles's mother let loose a hearty amen.

Julia broke the post-prayer silence. "Forgive me for hijacking the meeting, but the first priority is to corral those nutcases before they strike."

Cleveland smiled the pastor's smile. "God, family, and church come first, Miss Julia. It may be that this threat intersects with God, family, and the church and forces us into action, but until then—"

"I saw their eyes," Julia said. "You don't know what they are capable of."

"I'm very aware of their capabilities," Cleveland said. "They used to attend my church. Let me put it a different way: these folk are dangerous. The threat is real. That's why we need to get our families to safety first. Then we can focus all our attention on the threat. That's all I am saying."

"What about my dad?" Charles stood, then sat back down.

"What is it, Charles?" his mother said.

"I forgot all about him." Charles said. "And I haven't heard from him. That can't be good. Something's wrong. James, do you have that secure phone?"

"You can't use it here, Charles. You know that."

"Let's go then. I have to call him."

"Okay, but first let's finish what we are doing here," Cleveland said.

Charles started to argue but was interrupted by Julia. "He's right, Charles. If your dad is in trouble, they took his phone, so you won't be able to reach him. If not, there's no need to worry."

"He could be in a ditch with a broken leg."

"Then he would have called Cleveland's secure line," Julia said.

"I'll give you five minutes," Charles said. "Then we drive and call."

"Fair enough," Cleveland said. "I propose we send everyone on the way to Mexico tomorrow. Charles, you disguise the van for the trip. It should get you to the border, where you can cross on foot. I'll finish the church's business before joinin' you across the border."

"If we all leave, it gives those terrorists a free pass to do whatever it is they have planned," Julia said. "We're the only ones who know they're up to something big and bad. We can't leave. The plan is unacceptable."

Charles noticed how beautiful Julia was when she cared for something, which was most of the time. "Julia," he said, "those guys are the agency's problem. Let them deal with it. You and I both know Farris is very capable. The part of the plan I object to is Cleveland staying behind alone. He belongs with his family. Doesn't family come before church, my good reverend?"

"Did those words come out of your mouth?" Julia said. "We can't let those guys kill innocent people."

"We can tip off the agency tomorrow morning," Cleveland said. "Or even tonight, if we get in touch with Charles's dad. It'll work, Julia. I promise."

One of Julia's eyebrows rose. It was a decent Spock impersonation. Charles knew she wasn't convinced.

"I'll make a deal with you, Julia," Cleveland said. "If we make sure that the threat is handled, will you escort everyone here to Mexico?

"Easy. Done. Let's get started."

"I don't agree," Charles said to Cleveland. He felt his mother squeeze his hand. "You cannot stay back alone. I can't see it working out that way."

Cleveland shook his head. "You belong with Julia and your mother."

"You belong with your wife and daughter."

"And my church. I am also a pastor. And as *your* pastor, I am telling you this is the way it has to be. You are all going to Mexico together tomorrow, and I'm staying."

Charles felt the dark man surfacing. "We'll see. Your five minutes are almost up."

"Yes, they are," Cleveland said. "But let me use the rest of my time to say this. Charles and Julia, this is for you. I want you to remember one thing: don't forget to remember the last few days when you think about the next few days. Didn't I tell you there was electricity goin' on? And see what happened. You tellin' me that we broke into two jails, got out, flew away from jets and a gunship, and got back here safe all on our own? It ain't like that."

Cleveland stood. His presence in the room grew. "It ain't like that. God is at work here. There's electricity. Everything will work out for the best. Charles, your young faith needs to latch on to that and grow. Julia, you need to see that and get some faith. This is God's game, not ours."

Charles saw himself in the forgotten maintenance room staring into the effulgent glory of God. Everything from that point on had been by faith. He had remembered, and his faith had grown. His mother had been given back to him. Julia was his. They had pulled off an impossible rescue and escape. Surely there was something bigger than man and chance at work here.

And now, in the midst of Cleveland's exhortation, his fledging faith deepened its roots. It roared like falls of living water in his soul, louder than jet airplanes landing.

Loud enough to drown out the dark man, who was screaming at Charles at the top of his lungs.

Charles, Julia, and Cleveland had driven ten miles away from the safe house before Cleveland would allow the phone to be used. All three sat in the front seat, with Cleveland driving in random patterns through town. Charles dialed Cotton's number. There was no answer. He dialed again. It buzzed three times before a voice came on the line. It was a voice Charles did not recognize.

"Who is this?" the voice asked.

"Will Rogers." Charles forced out a chuckle. "Put Steve on."

"You ain't foolin' nobody," the voice said. "I got your dad, Graves. Now shut up and listen. This is Graves, ain't it?"

"Yeah. Who am I speaking with?"

"Cleveland will explain it to you. First, though, pay attention. I got your dad and he ain't hurt. Keep it that way, Graves. Don't try nothin' stupid. There's at least two agency squads outside and they're listening in on this call, so watch what you say. You ain't got a chance sneakin' in here with all them outside, so don't try. That'll get your dad hurt. Put Cleveland on."

"He isn't here." Charles sought Cleveland's approval and was denied.

"Boy, I ain't playin'. Put him on."

"Let me talk to my dad first."

"Don't say nothin' stupid. The walls got ears."

There was some fumbling in the background. Someone was muffling the phone. The receiver scratched a few times, then his dad's voice came on the line.

"Charles?"

"Dad, are you all right?"

"Doing very well, Charles. Don't worry about me."

"Pretty hard not to, under the circumstances."

"I was worried about you. You've gotten into some more trouble, if one can believe Authorized TV."

"You know how that is," Charles said. "I got her, Dad. Safe and sound. Wanted you to know."

There was dead silence on the line. "You mean her, her?" Cotton said. "You're kidding."

"No, sir. And I am coming for you next."

"Not a good idea, Charles," Cotton said. "You heard the man. Lay off for a while. And tell her I love her."

"I think she knows, Dad," Charles said. "And . . . I think I owe you—"

"The only thing you owe me is to care for her as best you can. I—"

"Fun time's over, boys," the other voice said. "Put Cleveland on the line. Now."

Charles debated with himself, then handed the phone to Cleveland.

Cleveland took the phone while slowing to a stoplight. He brought the car to a full stop before speaking. "Gurdy, what are you doing?"

Charles listened to Cleveland spit out a load of uh-huh's and nuh-uhs. Cleveland drove again, but without conviction. The voice on the other end of the line seemed to be in control.

Charles couldn't remember a time he had seen Cleveland on the losing end of a conversation.

Cleveland broke in. "That will not help anything, Gurdy. That's trouble for all of us."

Charles listened to another ten minutes of back and forth between Cleveland and Gurdy, while Cleveland drove the city in aimless patterns. An absurd thought passed through Charles's head. What if they were pulled over right now? What a way for it all to come crashing down. He reached out for Julia. She was there, sitting in the front seat between Charles and Cleveland.

Julia put hear head on Charles's shoulder, her hands in his. "It's going to be fine, Charles."

"With you here it is." He felt her press closer against him. He wished he could pull her inside him.

Cleveland shut the phone off and tossed it onto the dash. He took a left turn in the general direction of the safe house.

"What happened?" Charles said.

"Some good, some bad," Cleveland said. "I got him to promise your dad would not be hurt if we stayed away from the La Rosa. Also, he said if we alerted the agency and they stormed the place, they would use him as a hostage."

"Mostly bad so far," Charles said.

"Mostly," Cleveland said, "but they said they would let him go after they finished their operation. Until then, they needed him as protection."

"Do they think I couldn't get into La Rosa?" Charles said.

"I think they do believe it. That's why they are holding your dad."

"But if they let him go I wouldn't be after them," Charles said.

"Listen to yourself," Cleveland said. "Of course you would. Julia wouldn't stand for it if you didn't try to stop them."

Julia nudged Charles in the ribs.

"I forgot myself," Charles said. He watched Cleveland execute another left turn. "So what's the plan?"

"They insist that you be out of town and out of the way by tomorrow morning. You and Julia both."

"Unacceptable," Julia said, straightening up.

"Hang on, J," Charles said. "Why do they want us out of town?"

"I've known Gurdy a long time," Cleveland said. "He's not afraid of anything. He's not afraid of me, and I don't think he's afraid of the agency. But I believe you unnerve him, Charles. I noticed it that day at Lasanya's. He must be afraid of ghosts because you are one thing he fears. At least he fears you might be able to stop him."

Charles tried to bite back the words, but they came out anyway. "Did you just tell me Gurdy said that to get me to leave?"

Cleveland did not speak. He didn't have to. The pastor's eyes became possessed with rage. It was a righteous rage, Charles sensed, but rage nonetheless. Charles apologized and the eyes reverted to pastor's eyes. Like a block puzzle.

"I can't leave you here to handle this alone," Charles said.

"And I don't have any deal to honor with those guys still on the loose," Julia said.

"You gotta trust me on this one," Cleveland said. "I know it's hard, but I insist that you trust me. You two both have to leave for the border tomorrow and let me handle this. It's the only way."

• • •

Cleveland pulled the car back into the garage at the safe house. Cleveland shut the car down. Charles, Julia, and Cleveland sat in the car as the garage door closed behind them. When the door finished closing, the garage lights shut off. They sat in the dark.

"I'm not sure about this," Charles said.

"Me, either," Julia said. She pronounced either with a long I.

Charles took a second to study her face. "Either" with a long I? This is getting serious.

"Tomorrow you two are taking my family to safety," Cleveland said. "Teresa too. That's it. Let's go to bed. It's going to be a long day tomorrow."

Charles and Julia exited the passenger side. Julia slammed the door shut. Cleveland held the door open for them. Julia entered without a word, brushing past.

Cleveland whispered to Charles as he entered. "You know I'm right, Charles."

"Yeah, I do. Leave Julia to me."

His mother and Cleveland's daughter and wife were already in bed. Julia threw herself down on the couch with her hands over her head.

Charles leaned over the back of the couch and kissed her on the forehead. "I'll be back in a minute."

Charles followed Cleveland down the hall, watching him disappear into his wife's room. Charles nudged the door across the hall open.

"I'm awake, Charles," his mother said. "Come in."

Charles tiptoed through the dark to the edge of the bed, where he sat down.

His mother sat up and gave him a hug. "You upset, baby?"

"Is it obvious?" Charles rubbed his eyes. "I don't know what to do."

"Some things are hard, son," his mother said. "Did you want to tell me what's bothering you?"

"It's a bad spot, Mom. Cleveland is insisting Julia and I get you and his family out of town first thing tomorrow morning. That part is fine, except he wants to stay behind a day and perform a church service tomorrow afternoon. That's okay too, I guess. And I think I should stay behind also and try to rescue Dad."

"James doesn't trust Julia to get us out?"

"I'm sure he thinks that if I stay, Julia will stay, and there will be no one to escort you guys to the border. And even if I do leave, I am not sure Julia will leave. She's dead set on catching these terrorists."

"What makes you think I would leave without you? I could stay and help."

"You're leaving," Charles said.

"Why can't we wait and leave after tomorrow? What's the rush?"

"We thought at first these guys had a nerve agent they wanted to release downtown. We think it might be tomorrow or the next day. Now Cleveland seems to think it is something much worse than nerve gas." Charles felt his mother tense up. "Yeah, that much worse. So, you guys have to be well out of the area."

"Why can't we all leave? Cleveland too."

"He won't leave his church. And someone has to try and save Dad. It's not likely, but there's a chance."

"So you are caught between wanting to save me and Julia and the Cleveland women, and your desire to save Dad and catch these criminals?"

"Pretty close. Cleveland too, though I think he is underestimating these guys."

"Or overestimating his faith, perhaps. God has been known to let saints die."

Her words lodged in his mind. It was a concept he had never considered. Come to think of it, he thought God maybe had let some saints die before they thought they would. He thought again of Pastor Dean and the Creekside deacons.

"You're right, son. It's a tough one," she said. "I only want you to know I'm with you either way. And another thing: if you ask me to go, I won't make this harder on you by trying to stay. You've got enough to worry about."

One problem solved at least, Charles thought. "Thanks, Mom. That helps. A lot."

"Charles," she said, "all these years gone by and all those times I wasn't there to help you with stuff like this. All that time I wasn't there to be a mother."

Charles tried to get a vantage point over the parade of thoughts and memories passing through his mind. "I remembered, though, Mom. For that, you were always there, and better than a thousand mothers, even though we were apart. And we are not apart now."

She used Charles's sleeve to wipe her eyes. "I know, Charles, and I praise God. But with the world being turned over, who knows how long we have? Promise me you will always remember, until the time comes when we no longer have to remember."

"I can do that, Mom," Charles said. "Now go to sleep and *you* remember something: I always loved you and will always love you. No son ever loved his mother more."

"Thank you, son."

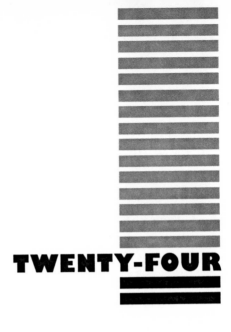

TWENTY-FOUR

Charles heard the signature Cleveland snore on his way back to the living room. He found Julia still on the couch. Charles cut the lights in the living room and sat with her on the couch. He snuggled in behind her, one hand around her waist, the other in her hair. She pressed back against him.

"You alright, J?" he asked.

"I guess."

He spent ten minutes caressing her. Then he whispered to her. "What are we going to do?"

Julia rotated her body to face him. "I am not happy with the way you and Cleveland are planning this out."

Charles studied the outline of her face in the dark. With her this close, he found he was having trouble concentrating on her words. "I wish I had studied art," he said, "so I would have something beautiful to compare to you."

"That doesn't work on me," Julia said. "When did you become the romantic type? I thought your idea of a romantic date was whizzing a girl through the sky in a gunship."

"Or watching planes land."

"I'll never forget that night," Julia said. "Not in all our nights to come."

Charles propped himself on an elbow. "I like the sound of that."

"Charles," Julia said, "I am not happy with it, but if you want me to, I'll go. We will go."

"Just like that?"

"I guess," Julia said. "As long as Cleveland promises to take care of things, I'll trust him."

"Really?"

Julia looked away a moment before answering. "Charles, when we were caught out on the highway by the agency, Cleveland stayed in the car with your mother. He did it because I told him I was the right one to go out. You should have seen his eyes, Charles. He didn't want to let me go, but he did it. He forced himself to. Now he is telling me he has to go out, because he is the right one to do it. I am having trouble getting past that. But I can, for his sake."

Julia leaned into Charles and gave him a long kiss. "There's another thing bothering me," she said. "The last thing I said to him before getting out was if we survived, I would talk to him about that electricity thing. It's been so crazy since then that there has not been time." Julia paused. "Don't call me crazy, but in some weird way, maybe this is his way of showing me the electricity. What do you think?"

Charles kissed her again. "I think," he said at length, "that there is more than one thing to accomplish here, and we can't all do all of them. If they have a bomb, we need to get my mother and the Clevelands out of town. I would also prefer it if you were safe as well. I also have my dad to think about, but I don't see any good endgame scenario for him."

"You don't know that."

"Julia, assessing situations like this is what I do." He smiled sadly. "Besides, it's not like I haven't been separated from my parents before. All this time I hardly knew my dad."

"Hey. Don't feel so bad. I don't have any family."

"I've always wondered about that. Why aren't you as screwed up as I am?"

"Maybe because I didn't have a brother die young." She dropped her eyes. "Or maybe you think I'm okay because you can't hear this constant conversation that goes on in my head."

"Do you think you have a dark girl?"

Julia hesitated. "Do you really want to discuss metaphysics, Charles? Why don't you hold me instead?"

Charles grabbed a pillow from the end of the couch and put it under her head. He spent thirty minutes holding her, thinking about Julia in her cube at headquarters with those eyes, Julia holding him on the ledge outside Farris's loft, Julia and airplanes, Julia and her leaving everything for him, and how much he loved her. He did not forget to tell her how much.

"Charles," she said, "maybe we should take this chance to get out. I mean, maybe we should."

"We already got out, J. Getting away is the trick now. Whatever happens—remember, okay? Promise me you will remember."

"I will," Julia said, "but nothing bad is going to happen."

Charles held her, whispering his love for her, until she fell asleep.

• • •

Charles turned the light on in the garage. His van sat under the light as if it were being interrogated. He approached it like a forgotten friend. The hood was cool to the touch. He wondered if his old partner was jealous of Julia.

If they were going to make a trip the length they were contemplating, he needed to do something with the outside appearance of the van. A description of the van was no doubt posted all across the state.

He walked to the rear of the van and opened the back doors. He rummaged through a compartment on his left, which held an assortment of dummy license plates and assorted tricks of the trade.

The plates would be easy enough to solve. The outside appearance of the van was trickier. He had enough paint, but he couldn't do an acceptable job with such limited time. Perhaps a different type of illusion was in order this time.

Somewhere he remembered hearing a principle that one way to remain inconspicuous was to be conspicuous. He stepped into the van. Charles searched around in several compartments and stepped out of the van holding two paint sets like they were pizza boxes. He set them on the hood of Cleveland's car.

He took out a roller brush, mixed a vibrant green into a pan, and created an undulating swath across the midsection of the van with curls on both ends. Charles painted musical notes, brass horns, and some random dabbing that mimicked confetti. He mixed a bright red and wrote letters above the green swath. It read "South Padre Party Patrol."

Corny, but it would work. He repeated his artwork on the opposite side. You know, Charles, when you move to

Mexico with Julia and your mom you could make a living as an artist.

Chares was about to pack the paint set away when a mood struck him. He mixed a palate of blacks, blues, and purples and set to work painting a wizard on the side of the van. The wizard stood along the advertisement, near the tail end of the green swath undergirding the display.

The van's faded white paint lent a pale skin tone for the wizard's face. The wizard was dressed in rippling black robes. In his right hand he held a polished onyx staff, topped off with the silver head of a wolf. The wolf had ruby eyes and was snarling. The wizard had hollow eyes and appeared indifferent to the South Padre Party Patrol.

Charles studied the wizard for a moment and concluded the old guy was capable of getting them to Mexico.

Charles packed his paints. He climbed into the back of the van and stowed them away in their compartment. He meant to exit out the back of the van, close the doors, and head off to bed. Something stopped him.

He noticed the two wooden blocks he'd carried in his pocket during the rescue operation. Charles crept to the front seats and picked them up. They seemed orphaned from the rest of the puzzle.

Charles felt around the front seat and found the puzzle. It was warm to the touch. He took it and the two pieces with him to the rear of the van. He pulled the rear doors shut and sat Indian-style on the floor of the van, the puzzle in front of him.

He dumped the puzzle pieces onto the floor of the van. They rattled and rolled around the metal floor as if they were at a block party. So to speak. One spun like a top, coming to rest with the dark man's eye staring up. Charles flipped it over.

One of the blocks scooted through a space between two of the van's compartments. A muted clank sounded from inside the space. He leaned over and reached inside the void for the block. He found it without hassle. It was a mouth piece. He placed it in the puzzle.

Charles's hand grazed against the source of the clank. He reached back in the space and felt something cool and glassy. Even before he'd slid it out of the space and knew for sure what it was, his fingers were already itching.

It was a nearly full fifth of whiskey. Charles was not surprised he'd left it there. Drunks were known to have stashes. He wasn't surprised to find himself salivating, either.

One swallow wouldn't hurt. The liquid glistened in the bottle. Charles twirled the bottle in front of his face, watching the booze undulate in waves of sparkling forgetfulness.

He didn't need to worry about tomorrow. His role was to help Julia escort Teresa and the Clevelands out of town. One swallow wouldn't hurt. He had Julia, the rock, to hold on to. He unscrewed the cap and hit the bottle as fluidly as Paganini's fingers down a violin. It was the ultimate sweet and sour sauce, the sweetness of the whiskey veiled by the bite and sting of the alcohol. Charles held the fumes in as long as he could.

He took another swallow and set the bottle by the puzzle. Already his fingers felt less itchy. He rubbed his fingertips against his thumbs.

One by one, Charles placed blocks into the puzzle. A face began to appear in the frame. It was a young face. Stephen. When the last block slid into place, his brother's face came alive. The lines formed by the spaces between the blocks faded away.

Charles's surroundings faded away as well. Instead of sitting on the floor of the van, Charles found himself sitting on the balcony of Graves Mansion, playing with the wood-block puzzle.

Charles realized there was a shadow over his puzzle. Stephen stood over him. Stephen kicked the puzzle. It sailed, slamming into the wall behind them. Stephen told Charles puzzles were for babies.

Charles stood, still in the shadow of his brother. He still held one of the blocks, his hand squeezing it as if he were trying to pulverize it. He was so mad he swung the hand with the block at his brother.

The upward arc of his fist arrived uncontested on Stephen's chin. The block acted like a plug, increasing the force of Charles's fist. Stephen staggered back against the wall, right above the first step of the staircase. A metallic object flew from his hand.

Charles was on him in a flash. The brothers wrestled along the top step. Charles's surprise attack and intensity balanced Stephen's size and strength.

Then Stephen began to overpower Charles. Charles knew a beating was coming—but then Stephen's foot slipped off the balcony.

Stephen teetered, staring at Charles.

He flailed his arms like he was attempting to fly, but he was trying not to fall.

Stephen reached out for Charles with his right hand, fish-hooking Charles with his thumb in Charles's mouth and his fingers along his cheek.

Stephen squeezed his grip like a hydraulic press, his finger-nails burrowing deep into Charles's flesh. Charles's cheek felt like it had been stamped with a branding iron.

Stephen's weight committed him to falling, despite his hold on Charles. He drew Charles forward, threatening to bring

Charles with him down the stairs. Charles leaned out over the top stair, trying to brace himself with his hands on his knees.

Stephen's arm was fully extended. His body formed a 90-degree angle, his back and rear leaning out over the staircase.

The brothers' eyes met for the last time. Stephen's look pleaded with Charles to pull him back up. Charles's mouth flooded with blood.

Charles pulled back with all his strength on his knees. Stephen rose somewhat. He could pull him up!

Then Charles's cheek gave way.

Stephen launched down the stairway in a backward somersault. He turned over and over and over.

Charles's mind returned to the van and the wood-block puzzle before he had to hear the sickening thud of his brother hitting the marble.

The scar in his cheek throbbed. He yelled at his brother to go away. Charles upended the puzzle, scattering the blocks.

The itchy feeling in his fingers returned. He took a sip from the bottle and began replacing blocks. This time his dad appeared.

"I was wrong about you, Dad."

The image responded from the puzzle. "It's okay, son. It wasn't your fault. We hid it from you. We're gonna make this all right. Don't worry." The image came complete with the senatorial smile.

Charles conferred with his father for some time about the past. The pain in his cheek subsided. When he'd said all he could think of to say, he spilled his dad's image onto the floor of the van and replaced the puzzle pieces.

This time it was Cleveland who appeared. Charles didn't remember that any of the puzzle pieces had had Cleveland's skin tone, but there was Cleveland just the same.

Cleveland did all the talking. "Your faith is real, Charles. I seen enough fake ones to know. You trust in it now, ya hear, and everything will turn out the way it's supposed to. It don't matter that the world is turned over. It's still God's world, and it still has electricity in it. Thanks for saving my family. Charles, I want you to know you're the best thing that's happened for my faith in quite some time. I was about to give up before you came along. Did you know that? Wouldn't that have been a thing? God bless you, Charles. I'll see you in Mexico."

His mother was next. He listened to her tell wonderful stories about his dad, Stephen, their family when Charles was young, Graves Mansion, vacations they had taken to Grandfather Mountain before the world had turned over.

"I love you, Mom." Charles traced his fingertips over her features.

He took another swig from the bottle, then tipped over the puzzle and started to replace the pieces. The dark man was back.

"You're pathetic and weak," the dark man said. "I think that is why Cleveland was praising your faith a minute ago. He's trying to inoculate you. What he doesn't get is that he would be more effective if he listened to me."

"You believe all that, don't you?" Charles asked.

"It's what I do," the dark man said, cutting his eyes at the bottle. "Don't you feel like another swig?"

Charles took another drink. "Tell you what, this is the last time."

He dumped the pieces out onto the floor of the van. The dark man's head shattered. Charles replaced the pieces, forming a portrait of Julia Jenkins.

"I love you more than you will ever know. This will prove it." Charles removed a tube of glue from his art compartment and squeezed it over the puzzle. He worked the glue into the cracks between the pieces and along the border between the puzzle and the raised sides of the oaken frame.

He finished rubbing the glue in, leaving a portrait of Julia Jenkins enshrined in his wood-block puzzle.

Cotton Graves saw a thin point of light. Someone was opening the closet he was locked inside. As the door opened, the light became a shaft, then a bar, then a band. Finally, it shone over him like a radiating, cyclopean eye. Once his pupils adjusted, the bar's back room came into view. It seemed to be daytime. The bouncer and Gurdy appeared in the doorway of the closet.

"Get up," Gurdy said. "You don't give us no trouble and you're likely as not to make it out of this."

Cotton debated the truth of Gurdy's claim before getting up. And then getting up proved a task. His joints moved like a rusty pump handle, and a thousand points of numbness were assaulted by a thousand needles. Must have been in that closet a while.

Cotton's face was not numb. He kept it senatorial as he rose to face Gurdy and the bouncer. "Don't start none, won't be none."

A grunt rumbled its way up from somewhere deep down in Gurdy's abdomen. "I'd hate to kill you, Cotton. I kinda like you. Nothin' like a greasy politician for a few laughs. Speakin' of greasy, there's a burger on the table if you want one for the road."

"Where are we going?" Cotton asked.

Gurdy and the bouncer laughed. Cotton joined in. He managed to check his watch during the frivolity. Almost noon. Cotton realized how long he had been in the closet and stretched again.

The bouncer strolled to the center of La Rosa Blanca's back room and removed a square of carpet from the floor. He tossed the square aside. Where the carpet had been was a trap door.

Here we go again, Cotton thought.

The bouncer twisted a metal latch on the trap door, which disengaged two bolts locking the door to the floor. The bouncer lifted the door, which creaked but opened.

Gurdy was the first into the hole. He was followed by Cotton, who grabbed the burger on the way. The bouncer entered the hole last, pulling the door closed behind him. Cotton saw about ten feet of well-constructed tunnel running into the darkness before the bouncer shut the door.

"Quick," Gurdy said. He lit a flashlight and started off down the tunnel.

Gurdy moved well considering his awkward frame. Cotton started down the tunnel in his footsteps, after a prod from the bouncer, who followed closely. The tunnel resembled a mineshaft, with railroad ties bracing the walls and ceiling.

Cotton scraped against the narrow walls several times and twice rammed a support brace with his shoulder. The three men pushed through three hundred yards by the light of Gurdy's flashlight before Cotton noticed the tunnel floor beginning to incline. The angle of inclination increased over the last fifty feet before Cotton saw a ladder in the light of the flashlight.

Gurdy needed only one rung to reach the top of the tunnel. He pushed open a hatch, letting in dim illumination, and climbed through.

Cotton followed with the bouncer behind. Cotton found himself in what appeared to be the back room of an abandoned gas station. Through a doorway, he saw a garage with two vehicles parked. The cars were parked in what used to be a service center. There were lifts, hydraulic jacks, old tires, and a host of dust and trash. Through the windows on the garage doors, he saw the awning for the discarded gas pumps. The sun was out and it was hot in the station.

"Quick, the doors." Gurdy was already climbing into one of the cars, a poorly restored Dodge Charger.

Based on how out of breath Cotton was after their walk, he developed an appreciation for Gurdy's conditioning.

The bouncer threw the garage doors up. They rolled up with enough force to crash against the ends of their rails.

"You know what to do," Gurdy said to the bouncer.

Cotton didn't like the sound of that.

Gurdy fired up the Charger and sped out of the garage. He took a right out of the garage and another right out onto the street.

The bouncer motioned for Cotton to get in the other car. Cotton knew what would happen if he got in. He considered making a final stand in the garage. Then he thought better of it.

Cotton slinked into the car. The bouncer, waiting for him to get in, followed. He fired the car. The bouncer drove straight out from the garage, took a right into the street, and then a quick left.

Things seemed to be coming to a head, Cotton thought.

• • •

Louis stormed into Farris's office like headquarters was on fire.

How many times have I told that idiot not to crash in here like this, Farris thought.

"Senator Graves is on the move!" Louis said.

Farris jerked his feet from the desk. "Get us airborne."

Louis vanished from the office.

Farris loaded a set of pistol clips into his jacket. He straightened his coat by standing and pulling on the arms of his jacket and the tips of the collar. He removed a vanity mirror from the desk drawer. He held it up to each side of his face, then to his hair. Only one hair seemed out of place. He coaxed it into line.

Farris exited the office and stepped into the cubicle bullpen area. Louis was busy in a cube on the right, issuing orders over the phone to a gunship to fire up and meet them out back behind the agency. Keesma was bent over a monitor to his left. "Where is he?" Farris asked.

"His GPS disappeared for about five minutes. It showed up again a couple blocks away," Keesma said. "We—"

"I asked you where he is right now."

Keesma stared at the screen. "Moving along the outskirts of downtown. Maybe headed for Allen Parkway."

"How many in the car?"

"Two."

Farris did some math. Two didn't figure. Should be at least three based on their observations at La Rosa, unless one of them had stayed behind. "We got a tail on him?"

"Yes, sir."

"Tell them not to be seen. Get a crew inside La Rosa immediately. I want to know everything now, real-time feed."

Farris concentrated. Five minutes out of sight. They knew we were there then, or suspected. Did they split up, maybe?

"Keesma, get another crew to the exit point where Cotton's GPS came online again."

"Done."

"Blades spinnin' on that gunship yet, Louis?"

"Five minutes, boss," Louis said.

Ten minutes later Farris and Louis were in the air. Farris set his face toward downtown. He thought he saw his loft and imagined the bust of Caesar urging him on.

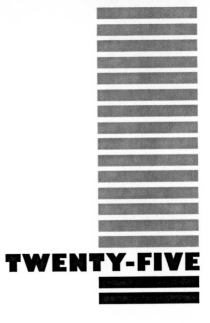

TWENTY-FIVE

"Where are we headed?" Cotton asked.

The bouncer drove on the outskirts of downtown and was approaching Allen Parkway, which would put them near Graves Mansion if they kept driving. From the passenger seat, Cotton kept an eye on the side mirror.

"Best you don't know," the bouncer said.

Cotton watched Buffalo Bayou go by on his right. He remembered walking along that path with Charles, Stephen, and their Great Dane. He'd let Charles and Stephen roll down the grassy hill sloping from the street to the bayou below.

Cotton saw no one following them. The bouncer slowed for the traffic light at Allen Parkway and Taft, but crossed the intersection under a yellow light. The old Graves Mansion was just up ahead now.

"Can I take a leak?" Cotton asked. "I was locked up all that time, you know."

"When we get there," the bouncer said.

"Can't wait."

"See if there is a can or something in the floorboard."

Cotton unfastened his seat belt. He twirled, got up on his knees, and draped himself over the seat.

In the back floorboard was a general assortment of trash. Cotton rummaged through papers, plastic soda bottles, pop-top cans, pens . . . nothing. Then his hand felt something promising. He pulled out a drinking glass.

Cotton felt the car coming to a stop as he returned to his sitting position. They stopped at a red light. Cotton ventured a glance at the side mirror. Still no one following. Cotton unzipped his pants.

"Do you mind?" Cotton flashed the senator smile.

"Oh," the bouncer said. He turned his head forward.

Cotton swung the glass at the bridge of the bouncer's nose. The base of the glass struck the bouncer in the mouth instead.

The bouncer reacted without hesitation. His darted inside his jacket to the hilt of his gun.

Cotton recognized the threat and caught the bouncer's hand while it was still inside his coat. Cotton held the bouncer's hand inside the coat with his left hand on the lapel of the coat. He felt his grip on the bouncer's hand slipping away through the jacket.

Cotton rotated the glass in his right hand. He slapped the top of the glass against the steering wheel. It shattered. Glass ricocheted off the windshield and rattled around on the dashboard. It reminded Cotton of dice inside a Yahtzee shaker.

Cotton held the base of the glass, which was now like the bottom jaw of an alligator. He pressed it against the bouncer's neck.

The bouncer grabbed Cotton's hand holding the glass. He succeeded in moving it. Cotton pressed harder. The combination of the two efforts brought a trickle of blood from the bouncer's neck.

"I'll kill you if I have to," Cotton said. The senator's smile was gone. He felt the bouncer's hand give, then all the pressure was gone. "Let go of the gun."

The bouncer withdrew his hand. Cotton reached into the bouncer's jacket with his left hand and extracted the gun. Cotton slumped back in his seat and pointed the gun at the bouncer.

"Sorry I had to do that, man," Cotton said. "Start driving."

"How bad's the cut?" The bouncer wiped his neck with his hand. His hand came back red.

Cotton saw a two-inch laceration. "About an inch from you being dead. Now, where you taking me?"

"Like I said, it's better if you don't know. Why don't I get you out of here?"

"Pull into that hotel parking lot." Cotton pointed across the street with the gun.

The bouncer drove across the street and pulled into a parking space on the side of the hotel. He looked over at Cotton.

Cotton smashed the butt of the gun against the bridge of the bouncer's nose. This time he did not miss. Cotton felt a crack reverberate through the gun metal.

The bouncer threw both hands at his face, then jerked them away. Pockets developed under his eyes. His nose swelled. The blood from his hand smeared across his cheek.

"You're starting to look like a cut tomato," Cotton said. "Where are we going?"

"Gurdy will kill me," the bouncer said.

Cotton marveled at the bouncer's toughness. "He won't get the chance."

"But you're a senator."

"And you trusted a politician?" Cotton held the bloody glass up. He twirled it in the sunlight.

"All right, all right. Gurdy told me to get you out of town and to wait for him there. We weren't gonna do nothin' bad to you. He said we wanted you for insurance."

"Where's he at?"

"I can't tell you."

Cotton held the butt of the gun up next to the glass. "I'll pretend I didn't hear that."

"You heard it."

Cotton brought the butt of the gun down like a hammer on the bouncer's kneecap. This time a gurgling sound escaped the bouncer's mouth.

"Am I still pretending?" Cotton held the gun back up with the glass.

The bouncer forced a jet of air through his teeth. "Yep."

"I do like you, though," Cotton said. He placed the muzzle of the gun an inch or two above the bouncer's kneecap and pulled the trigger. The sound of the report in the confined space was eardrum-rattling. The bullet passed through the bouncer's knee into the floorboard. Cotton checked his surroundings. No one was near them in the parking lot.

This time the bouncer howled, clutching his knee. Cotton gave him some time to get his bearings then held the gun up again.

The bouncer spat out choppy words and phrases. "Gurdy . . . has . . . bomb. Cleveland's church . . . today. Hour or so. Big bomb."

"Where's Cleveland's church at?"

"You know . . . Graves. You can—"

Cotton moved the butt of the gun over the bouncer's knee. The bouncer held his hands out, pleading. He gave Cotton garbled directions to the church.

Cotton exited the car and walked around the hood to the driver's side. "Move over."

The bouncer's eyes pleaded with Cotton. Cotton opened the driver's door. "It'll hurt for a second, but then you'll be all right. Big, strappin' tough guy like you. No problem."

The bouncer pushed off the floorboard with his good foot and shoved himself over to the passenger's seat with a grunt. His cell phone rang.

"No, you don't," Cotton said. "Give me that." Cotton took the cell phone and put it in his pocket.

Five minutes later Cotton pulled up in front of a hospital emergency room. "Get out."

The bouncer opened the door and grabbed the top of the car. Before lifting himself out onto his good leg, he paused. "Why did you do this for me?"

"I told you I liked you," Cotton said. "Go get fixed up. I'll tell the agency I dropped you on the side of the road back near downtown."

"Thanks, man," the bouncer said. "I told you the truth about Gurdy and the church."

"I know," Cotton said. This time the senator's smile was authentic.

● ● ●

Julia awoke on the couch at Cleveland's safe house where she'd fallen asleep after talking to Charles. Cleveland was shaking her. Her eyes took awhile to adjust.

"We overslept," Cleveland said. "Gotta move. No time to spare. I'll get the others."

Julia sat up and tried to collect her thoughts. *I guess I got too much sleep after not having slept a lot lately.* She tried to shake the grogginess out of her head. She would pay plenty to be able to lie back down.

Rustling arose from the back rooms and she thought she heard Cleveland dart from Teresa's room to his wife and daughter's room. She swung her feet to the carpet and put her head in her hands.

Cleveland came from the back rooms. "I've got the rest of them up. Come on. There's something I have to show you."

Those "pastor's eyes" were not to be found. Now what? Julia thought. *After all we've been through, I didn't think there were any surprises left.*

Cleveland took her hand and led her into the garage. He pointed out Charles's artwork on the way to the back doors of the van. Cleveland swung the doors open. Before he let her look, he spoke directly to her. "Don't be mad."

Julia took her time getting around the corner. She saw clutter on the floor of the van. Paints and brushes, it appeared. Then she saw Charles.

He was wedged between the wall of the van and the back of the driver's seat. His mouth was gaping. One hand held an empty whiskey bottle. The other arm clutched his wood-block puzzle.

The van smelled like spring break. Julia tweaked her nose. "He's drunk." She sat on the van's bumper, facing Cleveland. "I don't believe it. He's drunk."

"Flat out snockered," Cleveland said. "I tried to wake him, but he's good and out. Mumbled about the dark man when I rubbed his face with a wet rag, but that's about it."

"What a time to pick—"

"No time for all that," Cleveland said. "I am relying on you now to get everyone out of here. There's no time left. I need you two hours' down the road if things don't go right, and you only have an hour to get there. Get moving."

Julia took a look back at Charles. Why now, Charles?

The voice kicked in. Girly-Girl, it's on you now. Cleveland needs you. Charles does too. Get moving. Now.

But I am so tired.

We all are, but the finish line is in sight. Get up.

Julia stood up. "Get them loaded, James. I'll tend to Charles."

"I've got him fixed up as good as can be," Cleveland said. "He'll be fine. I need your help getting my wife and daughter into the van. They are going to try and stay with me. I can't allow that to happen."

Cleveland grabbed Julia by the arm. She could sense the growing tension in him as he hurried her inside.

Teresa was standing by the couch, waiting, holding a packed bag. "Anything the matter?"

"Everything's just right," Julia said. "Couldn't be better." She twirled both her index fingers in the air.

Cleveland spun her toward him, a hand on each shoulder. "Get my family. Get them in the van. Now!" Cleveland released Julia and grabbed Teresa. "Come on." They walked into the garage.

Quit worrying about him, GG. You can save yourself, Charles, Teresa, and Cleveland's wife and daughter. It's the best play you can make. Cleveland is a grown man and can fend for himself.

I doubt he can handle this one.

It doesn't matter at this point. Do what you can. If you don't do this, they all might die.

I can't believe Charles copped out and left me to handle this. I'll never forgive him for this.

He needs you yet again. Right now, GG.

He's so weak, though. Do I want to be with a man like him?

GG, think back on the last week and tell me how weak you think he is.

Good point.

I know. I've got a quiver full of them.

Julia rushed into the back room. She found Cleveland's wife and daughter arguing. "Shut up. You are not staying. We risked too much to let you stay now. Get your stuff. We're leaving."

Julia pushed Cleveland's wife out of the room. She assumed the daughter would follow. She was correct.

She herded Mrs. Cleveland into the garage. Cleveland already had Teresa in the passenger seat of the van. He motioned for Julia to put his wife and daughter in the back. Julia guided them to the back. She felt the wizard's eyes following her as she passed.

Julia took the Clevelands' bags and threw them in the back of the van. One of them crashed next to Charles. He did not respond.

"It stinks back there, I know," Julia said. "I'll open the windows when we get going."

"What's wrong with him?" Cleveland's daughter asked.

"Never mind," Julia said. "Get in."

The Clevelands hopped in and tried to find a comfortable seating arrangement around Charles. Julia shut the doors behind them.

Cleveland opened the garage door from a remote by the door when Julia came back around the side of the van toward the driver's door. The garage door rattled and screeched as it opened.

Julia opened the driver's door and hopped in. She hollered out at Cleveland. "I forgot my bag. It's by the couch."

Cleveland disappeared through the door. Julia started the van, adjusted the mirrors, and checked with Teresa to make sure she was settled in. Cleveland returned to the van with Julia's bag.

"Get out of here before you change your mind," Cleveland said. "And thanks, Julia." Cleveland caressed the back of Julia's head.

"I'm trusting you, James." Julia put the van in reverse.

Cleveland reached through the window for his wife and daughter. "I love you," he said. "I love you so much."

His wife and daughter began to wail. They started for the back of the van. Julia heard a "*No!*" from Cleveland's wife.

"This is why I need you and why it had to be this way, Julia," Cleveland said. "Now get going. And remember, always remember, that no matter what happens, I love you."

Julia instructed the van to lock the rear doors. The Clevelands pounded on the back doors, one with her feet, the other with her fists.

Julia backed out. "Get the electricity going, James. You still owe me a sit-down, remember?"

"Of course I do. I'll see you in Fort Stockton around three a.m. I love all of you."

Julia backed the van out of the garage before the Cleveland women could think of a way out.

Cleveland set his face toward downtown. This was not the worst position he had been in since the world had turned over. There was that sticky situation with the elders of the South Houston Church of New Hope, for one, and he had dealt with folks as bad as Gurdy before. Worse than Gurdy for that matter.

Cleveland had entered downtown in time to make the service, he figured, but he was pushing it. To make it on time, he would have to take some chances around Johnny Taco's, but so be it. This would be the last time, and—God willing and the electricity don't get shut off—it would work out.

Cleveland parallel parked the car on Main. After inserting city tokens into a parking meter, he merged into a crowd walking by. He crossed Main at the first light, watching to see if he was being followed. It did not appear so.

He took the chance. Cleveland ducked into the underground stairway leading to the food court.

Cotton Graves stood next to the dark hallway past Johnny Taco's. To his right he saw a man resembling a young Johnny Carson ordering two taco specials for him and his son. Across the food court, the afternoon crowd created a soft hum that buzzed over the sounds and smells of fast-food preparation.

Why would Cleveland hold church here? It didn't make any sense. Still, this was where the bouncer said it was, so here he stood.

Cotton slid a step or two toward the hall. He felt invisible to the crowd. A police officer in the center of the court walked in a wide circle. Cotton waited for his back to turn. He faded into the dark.

He felt his way along the hallway. Halfway down, he removed his phone from his pocket and flipped it on. The phone's luminescence lighted his way. He hoped the light was too faint to be seen from the court.

Cotton found his way to the end of the hall. The door was right where the bouncer said it would be. He placed his hand on the door.

He paused, staring down at the light of the phone. He whispered Charles's name into the phone. It rang. Cotton squatted against the wall at the end of the hallway.

"Answer the phone, Charles."

Julia had the van thirty miles west down Interstate 10 when Charles's phone announced Cotton's call. The phone spoke from the floor of the van. Cleveland's daughter found it in a space between two of the compartments. She answered the phone and handed it to Julia.

Julia pressed the phone to her ear, releasing foot pressure on the accelerator. It was Cotton's voice.

"Yes, I know where he is, and no, he won't be there to help you," Julia said, glancing in the rearview mirror at Charles's sleeping form. "He's dead drunk."

Julia thumped harder on the steering wheel with every mile. She knew a country pond further up the road where she could sober Charles up fast.

"Cleveland should be there. Look for him." Julia concealed her voice from the Clevelands in the back of the van. She listened to Cotton speak and then winced. "Don't say that over the air, Cotton."

The van passed a field of cows on the side of the interstate. It reminded Julia of her getaway from the agency with Charles and Cleveland. "Cotton," she said, "You and Cleveland must prevent Gurdy from detonating. Promise me."

She waited for the response. Cotton and Cleveland. At least Cleveland knew Gurdy. That might give them an advantage. She noticed another field of cows approaching. I'm not in the cube anymore. That's something to be thankful for.

"Thanks, Cotton."

Julia thought about phoning Farris. She tossed the phone on the dashboard instead.

TWENTY-SIX

Cotton flipped the phone off. The hallway went dark. He pursed his lips and blew out. Time to go in.

At the food court end of the hall, Cotton saw the frame of a man entering the hallway. Cotton pressed himself as far back into the darkness as possible.

The silhouette glided through the darkness of the hallway like a phantom. Cotton could not see its feet, nor did they make any sound. He tried to imagine sound coming from the footsteps. He tried to imagine the sounds of the food court, people talking, babies crying, the sounds of life. Nothing came.

The phantom kept coming. Its bulk eclipsed the light from the end of the hall. Cotton was not sure if he was terrified or was feeling the presence of the numinous, or both.

The phantom swelled until it filled the hallway. Then the hallway disappeared. The phantom was all that was.

The phantom developed into a whirlwind a hundred stories high. Cotton found himself outside of Graves Mansion, watching the impending doom approaching. The cloud was all-consuming and moving toward him. It was black as night and eclipsed the sun. It was as wide as his field of vision. In its wake, everything seemed to be engulfed into the darkness of the cloud. Time itself seemed to be sucked into the vortex.

The winds were not swirling, though. Cotton thought the thing behaved more like a blob than a tornado, yet it was a windy cloud. He watched his neighbor's house and yard vanish under the cloud's onslaught. The cloud was earsplitting.

Graves Mansion was next. Cotton rushed inside the mansion, with the cloud not two minutes behind. Cotton dashed through the house, wondering what one thing was most important to him. He would save something.

The house was empty. Cotton rushed up the staircase to the boys' rooms. The doors were locked. He beat on the first door until it collapsed. There was nothing behind the door. It fell off into darkness.

The swirling of the wind now surrounded the mansion. Cotton sailed down the staircase. He crossed the marble floor toward the back door. His last thought before plowing into the backyard was how desolate the mansion was, as if no one had been there for years.

He crossed the manicured portion of the backyard in seconds, reaching what amounted to a forest in the Graves Mansion backyard. He plunged into the trees. After a hundred feet or so, he fell against a live oak, one so big it had collapsed under its own weight. Cotton pressed his back against the fallen tree, which, even on its side, reached above his head.

He felt the gathering gloom obscure his house. Cotton closed his eyes. Seconds later, the noise ceased.

Cotton opened his eyes with the strange feeling he was on an island of existence in the middle of nowhere, or perhaps no-thing.

He pushed himself to his feet and walked through the trees. He crossed the manicured potion of the back lawn to where the house had been. All that remained was the marble floor, the staircase, and the balcony. It was a peninsula over a gulf of non-being.

Cotton walked onto the marble, his feet clacking in the sudden silence left by the storm's departure. The sound from his feet was sharp when it left the marble but seemed to be absorbed into the nothingness and became a gentle thud.

He saw something in the middle of the marble floor. He bent down and picked it up. It was a shattered remote control.

Why would this be the only thing left? He threw the remote into the nothing. It seemed to hang on the edge of existence before dissolving, random fractals of existence devolving into scattered pixels of nothingness.

Cotton began a slow march up the staircase. He took his time, noting each step. At the top of the stair, he sat. He sat long enough to realize why he had been brought here. He had forgotten.

"What are you doing?"

Cotton's vision was sucked down the hallway. He saw what remained of Graves Mansion first, followed by the manicured lawn and trailed by the trees. It funneled out the opening of the hallway into the food court, where it took a right and sailed off in front of Johnny Taco's. Gone.

The last thing to vanish was the forest behind the mansion. The fallen oak caught on the hallway opening, holding the rest of the vision with it. The tree trunk cracked under the pressure of the escaping vision, and the whole procession disappeared around the corner.

Cotton heard the voice again. It sounded familiar.

"What are you doing?" it asked.

It was Cleveland. Cleveland stuck out a hand. Cotton took it and pulled himself to his feet.

Now Cotton was back in the food court. The phantom had turned into Cleveland, and someone was about to set off a bomb.

"Glad to see you," Cotton said.

"You ready for this?"

"Yeah." Cotton told Cleveland about Gurdy, the bouncer, and the bomb.

"Do you know where the bomb is?" Cleveland asked.

"No. It slipped my mind to ask." Cotton leaned against the wall. "I am so tired, Reverend."

"We all are, but hang on. It's almost over." Cleveland leaned against the wall next to Cotton.

"Did you know we've been after you since the world turned over?" Cotton said. "Now you're standing right next to me after all this time, and all I want to do is help you. Kinda ironic, don't ya think?"

"In more ways than you know," Cleveland said. "Did you ever consider the Gospel of Jesus Christ, Senator?"

"Considered it in gruesome detail when it destroyed my family."

"I don't think that's how it happened," Cleveland said.

"How would you know? You weren't there."

"Sure I was."

Cotton saw Cleveland's mouth speaking the words, but they didn't make sense. Do all preachers think they can know things when they weren't there? Is it some esoteric knowledge they get directly from God?

"I got Mom out of town. That's one less thing we have to worry about."

Cotton blinked at Cleveland. Mom? Wait a minute.

Suddenly he realized he'd been had. Charles was way better than he'd ever imagined, even if he did have the advantage of the dark hallway. Cotton figured he would have been fooled in broad daylight.

"Charles!" Cotton embraced Charles like the prodigal son. "After everything you've been through too. You've turned out so well. I'm proud of you, son."

"I love you too, Dad. And I want you to know I was unfair to you all these years. I didn't know any better. Mom told me a lot."

"She's good for that. You said she was safe."

"Yep. Out of town."

"Where?" Cotton released Charles from the hug. He watched Charles's eyes. He knew this was a big step for Charles.

"Safe," Charles said, "with Julia."

Cotton saw Charles squirming. "If you don't want to tell me, don't."

Charles grabbed his father by the shoulders. "It was us who tore the family apart. All four of us. The Gospel put us back together. Took some time, but that's because we had ripped it wide open. Filleted it. "

"You ain't lyin', son."

"Mom's with Julia and the Clevelands. They're headed to Mexico. If we do this right, we can join them."

"Wait a minute," Cotton said. "Julia said you're dead drunk. She said you weren't coming to help me. She said Cleveland would be here." He looked askance at Charles. "What have you done?"

"What I had to do."

Cotton held Charles's hands on top of his shoulders. "I doubt I can go to Mexico with you. But let's worry about that if we get out of this." He pointed to the door with his thumb. "Charles, it's very probable that Gurdy has a bomb in there. A big one with enough killer gas hidden somewhere that he could take out everyone within miles. The stuff's horrid. I saw it in action."

Charles leaned against the side of the hallway. "That certainly complicates things."

Cotton saw Charles's eyes go hollow.

"I think I know where it might be." Charles said. "If I could follow in behind you, I might be able to get to it without being noticed. I doubt I can disable it, but you never know. Let's at least try."

"As good a plan as any," Cotton said.

"Okay," Charles said, "before we go in, one more thing. I need to give you this list. Work through the crowd and get these five people out before anything else. Definitely before we do anything with Gurdy."

"Who are they?"

"Don't worry who they are, Dad." Charles took a breath. "Don't let Gurdy see you removing these people, if you can help it. Once the five are out, work your way in behind him. After I disable the bomb—if I disable the bomb—I'll work my way back up front and call him out. Then make your move. I'll also arrange help for you once we are inside."

"Sounds like a plan," Cotton said.

"And if you see him move for the door, tackle him," Charles said. "I don't think he will set anything off while he's here. I hope not. He's probably here to pressure Cleveland one last time. I'll bet he tries to leave after the service begins." Charles put his hand on his father's shoulder. "I want to repeat one more thing before we go in."

"Wha—"

"Listen," Charles said, "I am ashamed of the way I thought of you for so long, Dad. I even hated you sometimes. And now I found out you had done right by Mom and even by me. I hate myself sometimes over it."

Cotton reached for the back of Charles head. "I was the adult, Charles. The blame is on me. I should have done better. There are so many different things I could have done. It's my fault. Forgive me, please."

"And Stephen," Charles said. "I want to tell you about Steph—"

"Now's not the time. Let's go in . . . Reverend." Cotton embraced his son one more time before they opened the door. It seemed like the first time.

The makeshift sanctuary in the abandoned maintenance room was packed when they entered. Charles figured that would be to their advantage. The room was darkened save for the bright light shining from behind the podium, as it had been the night Charles was saved.

The crowd and the light combined to allow Charles and Cotton to enter undetected. Cotton slinked along the wall toward the back. Charles stooped a bit and followed Cotton closely. When Cotton reached the back of the crowd, Charles peeled off and slinked into the darkness behind the crowd.

He slipped behind the old air conditioner condenser unit where he had been his first night in church. It was dark, but there was just enough light filtering back from the front of the room for Charles's eyes to adjust.

His lifelong companion greeted him. You gonna thank me for telling you where the bomb is? the dark man said.

How do you know it's here? Charles rummaged through the trash behind the condenser. There's other places for it to be.

The dark man sighed. All this time and you still don't know me. It's destiny, Charles. It's balance. It's symmetry. It's there.

Charles felt around the condenser and discovered a hatch. He opened it and reached into the hole. He felt a cool metallic case. He pulled it out.

Thank you. Thank you very much, the dark man said as if to a cheering audience.

Charles balanced the case on a cardboard box. He closed his eyes and popped the clasps on the front of the case. He looked inside.

It appeared to be a rudimentary explosive device—no apparent balance detectors, no fail-safes, no booby traps. Just a simple detonator connected to a receiver.

Unfortunately, the agency never trained me how to actually disarm one.

But I know, said the dark man. Time to trust your old friend.

Charles looked around the wall of trash, trying to determine where Gurdy might be, where Cotton was, and how much time he might have. It seemed the crowd was growing restless. Must be close to time.

The light caught Charles's eyes. It was just like the night he was saved. This time, though, the light didn't beckon him. It reassured him.

The light was his only comfort in life and death. It was a deep-rooted assurance. It was faith, full grown.

Charles looked back at the bomb. Two wires. Difficult to see any color in the sparse light.

Trust me, Charles, the dark man said. Trust me.

You're right, my old man. This is balance. Charles smiled. This is where I got saved. This is where my faith is cemented.

The dark man's voice quavered. Don't do it, Charles. You'll kill us both. We can still be heroes. Call Farris. Stop Gurdy. They'll forgive the whole thing. We'll be set. Think about Julia.

I am thinking about Julia. And one other thing.

What's that? the dark man said.

You're the one that's going to die in the dark. I choose the light.

With that, Charles reached his hand into the bomb case, grabbed both wires barehanded, and ripped them out.

The congregation was singing. Their voices floated through the air like confetti. Charles snuck up to the front of the room and positioned himself in a front corner off to the side of the stage, hidden from view, but with an eye on Cotton.

The singing stopped and an elder rose to pray. The man finished praying. He assisted a young woman, who was apparently blind, to the front of the room. A guitar was strapped around her neck and shoulder. The woman slung the guitar around and began to play.

The melody was haunting. It reminded Charles of a day long past and a life long lived. She sang:

When I was young, I was taught the things
    To make me grow up good
But as I got so much older
    I took a path my momma never understood.
It took me down a lonesome road
    A road that's paved with sin
I traveled down that road so long
    I never thought I'd come back, come back again.
But when the Spirit touched my heart
    And I called Jesus' name,
He saved the soul of a man
    In the sinners' hall of fame.
So take my picture off the wall.
    And mark right through my name.
God saved the soul
    Of a man
In the sinners' hall of fame.

The song caught Charles off-guard. It resonated deep within his soul. Half of him cried with joy. The other half mourned a wasted life.

Charles saw five men leave through the door. Three of the men were accompanied by women. Charles figured Cotton was on to step two.

Something welled up in Charles. Electricity, maybe. To his left the light seemed even brighter than it had been when he had come in. It seemed even brighter than the night he was saved.

It was time to preach.

• • •

A moan came from the back of the van. Julia had been thinking of how to tear into Charles and now she was finally going
to get her chance.

But the moan was followed by a shriek. Julia pulled the van
over on the side of Interstate 10, halfway to San Antonio.

She turned to Teresa. "If anything looks funny outside, get
behind the wheel and drive."

Teresa nodded.

Julia climbed out, shut the driver's door, and walked to the
rear of the van. The wizard's eyes followed her. She opened the
back doors.

Charles was stirring. But why were the Clevelands hugging
him? They would always be grateful for him, but this seemed
overdone.

Julia hopped in. "Is he awake?"

"He's coming to," Mrs. Cleveland said. She had a finger
on her chin and the corners of her lips curled around an open
mouth. "Sit down, Julia."

"What do you mean, sit down? What is going on?"

"This isn't going to be easy."

"What isn't? Spit it out."

Julia studied Mrs. Cleveland's face. Her mind calculated
logical permutations at an accelerated rate. Charles is having
a heart attack? Not logical. He's fighting because he realized
what he's done and wants to go back? Logical, but not in accor-
dance with observation. He's still too groggy. He doesn't love
me anymore? Nah.

"Julia," Mrs. Cleveland said, "Charles—"

Julia never heard the words. He's doubting this whole faith
thing and his abandonment of duty? Possibly.

Another voice spoke in her head. Disguises, Girly-Girl. That's what Charles does. Charles is not here.

Then who's here?

She saw the Clevelands staring back at her. She saw Charles muttering. She saw the facial features. She saw the hair. She saw the clothes. It looked like him.

Julia crawled across the floor of the van, banging her knees. She reached out for his face.

It was a fake.

"James?" she said. She sought Mrs. Cleveland.

Mrs. Cleveland's eyes said all that needed to be said.

Julia shook the Charles-who-was-Cleveland back and forth. Mrs. Cleveland reached for her, but Julia fended her off with an elbow. Cleveland muttered something and grabbed his forehead.

The shaking dislodged something from Cleveland's shirt pocket. A white corner of paper stuck out enough to catch Julia's eye.

Julia reached for it as if it were covered with thorns. She grasped the corner of the paper and pulled.

It was a syringe taped to a note. The note read: "Tell Reverend Cleveland I'm sorry. It was the only way. Tell him it was electricity."

Julia collapsed on the floor. Mrs. Cleveland held her and stroked the back of her head. Julia had a blurred sensation that the van was moving.

Farris circled downtown in an agency gunship, waiting on Keesma to report.

Finally, Keesma's voice crackled over the gunship speakers. "Mr. Fah-reese."

"What do you have, Keesma?"

"Our agent trailing Mr. Graves says he followed him into the Main Street food court. Mr. Graves disappeared at the end of the court past a restaurant called Johnny Taco's. The agent said Graves went down a dead-end hallway. He's still there."

"Tell him to monitor the hallway and wait for reinforcements."

"There's something else, Mr.Fah-reese," Keesma said. "A man fitting the description of James Cleveland followed not long after. Disappeared down the same hall."

"Get me a schematic of the food court area," Farris said.

Farris waited thirty seconds for the schematic, which appeared on the gunship monitor. It showed the layout of the food court. The hallway led nowhere. A mystery, it seemed, but there did not appear to be a back way out.

"Keesma, have all units close in now," Farris said. "We're going in."

Farris banked the gunship hard right and downward. He saw his loft in the corner of his left eye. This close all the time.

Agency ground units converged along Main Street heading toward the underground food court.

The street approached rapidly on Farris's wild descent in the gunship. He leveled out ten feet above the ground.

Farris set the gunship down in the middle of Main Street, lifting the nose of the craft up once to allow a car to pass under the skids. Traffic screeched to a halt on all sides. The gunship thumped onto the pavement. What an entrance.

He popped the hatch and hit the pavement running, intent on beating the rest of the force to the scene. Farris's pearl necklace flapped around his neck, pounding his chest and circling around his neck. He chambered a bullet in his pistol as he hit the stairs leading down into the food court. He had a fifty-foot advantage on the nearest agent and was gaining ground.

His nose felt much better.

TWENTY-SEVEN

Charles's throat tightened as if an invisible pair of hands were squeezing it. He sucked as much air as he could into his lungs and held it. He imagined squeezing the air through his stomach in an attempt to force the butterflies out. His stomach bulged into the podium.

The light beamed from behind his head. It afforded him a fair view of the room. The two hundred or so faces of God's people were like huddled masses cloistered away from the world in the abandoned maintenance room.

One woman held a baby to her cheek. Another woman sat with an arm around a son. A man in a wheelchair quivered in the front row. Charles saw many nervous glances toward the door. A man in the back stood with eyes closed and hands raised. His lips were moving.

The crushing responsibility. Charles realized he was not worthy to be in the same room with Cleveland, much less at his pulpit. The uncertainty of this life and the certain hope of God emerged from the crowd and pounced on him like a tiger.

His old friend stood against the back wall, still by the condenser.

So, the dark man said, the indistinguishable man goes big time. The man who would be others takes center stage. Bravo. What existential irony. Feeling the eyes on you yet?

No one in the crowd turned toward the dark man. Charles saw Cotton sidle up next to him and wave his hands. Cotton did not seem to notice the dark man. Instead, he pointed at a man sitting in front of him.

Charles performed an OK gesture. Cotton gestured back.

Is that the best you can think of? the dark man said. Why don't you broadcast it to Gurdy he's been tagged?

"Okay," Charles said in Cleveland's voice. He performed the OK gesture again for emphasis. "I want everyone to turn to someone and make sure they are okay."

A murmur rose through the room as the crowd followed Charles's instructions. Gurdy did not move.

"But we are not okay," Charles said. "The world has turned over. I can see it on your faces. The worry, the despair, the hopelessness, as if Christ Himself has turned over. But we know there is no shadow of turning in Him."

Charles kept an eye on Gurdy and Cotton. No movement yet.

It was becoming difficult to concentrate on Gurdy. Charles felt a presence welling up inside him. It grew in strength and intensity. The room faded, until all he saw was the light. It was much like the night he was saved, but it was stronger.

Charles raised the pitch and volume of his tone to match Cleveland's. "In these perilous times, we must be Christ to each other."

The dark man's voice was as a whisper in the light. It's time to quit now, Charles. Look at these folks. Are you going to throw our life away for them? Do you think you can represent Christ to them? Julia is expecting you. How do you think she is going to feel when she discovers what you did to her?

Charles could no longer see the dark man, nor was he sure who the voice belonged to. The voice was an impotent interloper, barely intruding into the light. Charles thought at first it was vaguely familiar, though he could not place it. Now, it was as bland as an Approved TV commercial announcer's voice. He wondered why it was even addressing him.

"In these dark times . . . " Charles paused, unconsciously mimicking Cleveland's delivery. "We must shine the light of Christ to our neighbor."

The light was now all-consuming. It was ten times more luminous than the night he'd been saved, even though it now shone from behind him. Charles heard a scratching sound. It was soft, like the scratching and popping at the end of a vinyl record from the old days, with the record being played in another room.

The scratching refined itself into the nondescript interloper's voice one last time. He sensed the man was screaming. He didn't know why, nor did he care. The voice hardly registered. It was the voice of a dream he could not remember upon waking.

Don't do this, Charles! Come back! Come back now! I'm the one. I'm the one! I'm—

Charles roared from the podium. "This light is the most precious thing in the world. It is a pearl of great price. A pearl of such value that any man would sell all he has to own it once he has found it. The ASL cannot drown out this light. Approved TV cannot obscure it. Though the world turns over a thousand times, it cannot eclipse this light. You are the keepers of the light in this dark world. Christ has spoken: 'This is my commandment, that ye love one another, as I have loved you.'"

The light opened up to Charles. He preached, but it was the Spirit preaching through him. Charles lost touch with the sound of his voice. The light was all there was. He saw himself embrace the light the night he was saved. He saw his mother telling him to remember. He saw Stephen smile. The light was beautiful.

Farris hit the hallway past Johnny Taco's on the run. Fifty agents sprinted on his heels, in full riot gear with guns drawn. His eyes adjusted to the reduced light. His footsteps echoed through the hallway and were joined by the first of the agents entering behind him.

Farris found the end of the passage. A strange thought passed through his mind. Perhaps there is a God who works miracles after all. He brushed the thought off like a mosquito.

Farris felt around the end of the hall first, working his way up the sides of the hall. The guards behind him piled up in the hallway, obscuring all the available light from the food court.

Farris's fingers hit on the cracks of the door. He forced the door open and burst into the room, gun drawn.

He rushed to the left, knocking a man down. Farris screamed. "On the floor. Now! Everyone. Now!"

Agents flowed in behind him, fighting for space. They pushed in to the right, working their way around the side and back of the room.

Farris felt like his face had been hit with liquid nitrogen. He expected the room to explode with chaos, for these mullets to squirm and flop every which way to avoid capture.

Not a word was spoken, except for Cleveland's continual ranting about Jesus and the light. The crowd in the room moved to their knees as if they were competing in a synchronized swimming contest. They raised their hands in unison. Surrendering? Not a punch was thrown, not a scream was released, not a face displayed anger or fear. Farris suspected the mullets were praying for him.

The light from the front of the room gave Farris a good view of the action. To his left, Cleveland carried on. The rest of the room was on the floor and silent. At the back, he noticed a flurry of activity.

Cleveland's voice thundered. "I say it again: this is my commandment, that ye love one another, as I have loved you."

"*Shut up!*" Farris screamed.

Cleveland continued. The praying of the crowd developed into a low hum. Farris witnessed a brawl at the back of the room.

Cotton Graves was fighting with a man with oversized sideburns. They grappled forward into the kneeling crowd, knocking over a row of prayers. The kneeling crowd pushed back, sending them careening back against the wall in a violent tango. Cotton held the man's right arm in a death grip with both his hands. The man held something in the hand Cotton seemed to be devoting all his energy to.

"Help me!" Cotton screamed.

Three agents behind the crowd leapt at the pair of grappling men. The man with the sideburns twisted Cotton toward the agents. They impacted Cotton full on in their charge, sending Cotton to the floor. The other man broke free.

Cleveland's ranting was at fever pitch. The humming of the crowd sounded like a beehive. Farris saw his agents sprawled on top of Cotton Graves. Farris felt like a he-goat was ramming around the inside of his skull.

Farris raised his pistol, drew a bead on the man with the sideburns, and fired. He staggered and fell face-first into the crowd.

Cleveland roared again. "Obedience to God in these dark days is your calling, my friends. There is no higher calling."

Farris wheeled on Cleveland. "*Silence!*"

Cleveland pressed forward against the podium. Farris had never seen an expression like the one crossing Cleveland's face.

Cleveland's voice subsided. "You have to be Jesus to one another," he said. "Love one another, and this world's turning will seem like a child's merry-go-round."

The he-goat slammed into Farris's skull with added force. "*Shut up!*"

"Greater love hath no man than this," Cleveland said, his voice suddenly going peaceful, "that a man lay down his life for his friends."

Farris squeezed the trigger. The bullet struck Cleveland in the chest.

He staggered back against the wall, balanced against the wall for a second, and slid down to the floor.

The room hung in silence. Farris pushed his way up to the altar. From the back of the room Farris heard Cotton's voice. It was wailing.

Cotton Graves forced his way through the kneeling crowd, jumping over some, stepping on others. He reached the front row, where he used someone's wheelchair as a fulcrum to propel himself to the altar. He flung himself at Cleveland, embracing him.

"I love you, son," he said.

"I love you too, Dad."

What? Farris stepped up onto the altar, holstered his gun, and walked to Cleveland. He bent down next to Cotton. Cotton's head was on Cleveland's chest. The tears from Cotton's eyes mixed with the blood on Cleveland's shirt. Farris leaned in to Cleveland's face.

The longer he stared, the less the face looked like Cleveland's, and the more it looked like Charles's.

"I asked you to shut up." Farris's voice cracked. "I asked you."

Charles rolled his eyes up at Farris. "You were after Cleveland." He coughed once and produced a smile and two words. "You missed." Charles's eyes rolled back up into his head.

Farris fell back against the wall, next to father and son.

Three days later, Farris lounged in his tub, entertaining a call from Ingraham. He pressed back against the jets and rubbed his toes across the rough flooring of the tub.

"A satisfactory conclusion," Ingraham said. "I was pleased when the headlines came out up here: 'Federal agent thwarts terrorist plot. Recovers bomb and drum of nerve agent.' 'Rogue agent responsible for tanker explosion killed in agency raid.' All in all, not bad."

"It's better than not bad," Farris said. "Charles was the main domino. The rest will fall now that he's out of the way. I'll give him this though: he was always the best—besides me. That's why the operation stretched out as long as it did."

Farris popped a bubble perched on the palm of his hand. He needed to pop Ingraham next.

"With Cleveland on the loose, we cannot close Operation Belt Buckle," Ingraham said. "Technically, it's a failure thus far. That Jenkins girl is out there too. She worries me."

You're always too worried, old man. You've lost the edge. That's why you're about to fall.

"She's nothing without Charles. I wouldn't be half surprised if she comes to see me at headquarters now that Charles is gone." Farris decided to push Ingraham further. "Cleveland will be easy now as well. We sent two hundred of his followers to the reclamation center after the raid. He's all alone now."

Ingraham snorted. "If Cleveland's so easy, why is he still on the loose after two decades?"

You are losing it, old man. "Because you waited too long to put me on the case. By the way, the headlines down here say 'Richard Fah-reese spoils terrorist plot.' Your neck of the woods will catch up soon, I'm sure."

Farris let the silence linger. The first man to talk next would lose control of the conversation. The first man to speak would lose control of the relationship.

Ingraham broke the silence. "Your promotion is on my desk for signature. Congratulations, Richard. You may occupy Cotton Graves's suite."

"I already did," Farris said. "Thanks, though."

"What are you going to do with Cotton?"

"He wormed his way well with the media," Farris said. "He's got friends over there. He convinced them he was instrumental in foiling the terrorist plot."

"I guess he is right in a roundabout way."

"Yeah, but not the way he tells it. He's spun it as though he volunteered to go undercover. He's become almost a folk hero down here. He's untouchable, for right now, at any rate. That'll change."

"Why?" Ingraham asked.

"I don't think he will ever forgive me for shooting Charles. He is playing it close to the vest, but I know he is waiting for a chance for revenge."

"Could be," Ingraham said. "Cotton was always to be reckoned with. But I guess that's your problem."

"I'm in the problem-solving business," Farris said. It was time to seal the deal. "Anything else? I gotta go."

"Nothing. Ingraham out"

"You're out, all right," Farris said. The loft and the suite were now his. Southeast Texas was his. But as big as Texas was, it wasn't big enough.

Farris slinked under the water. Today was a good day to shop for a new suit.

EPILOGUE

"You could have picked the beach for this, Charles." Julia picked her way through the woods behind Graves Mansion. It reminded her of Old Bones Lane. "You could have done a lot of things differently."

The woods were in their summertime lush phase. The undergrowth was waist-high, the trees were full and green, and wild bushes fighting for space impeded her progress. She pried in through the foliage. The afternoon air was humid and stifling.

Julia brushed sweat from her forehead, hoping she wasn't spreading poison oak like facial cream. The underbrush triggered appreciation for her jeans, but the heat made her wish she had worn shorts.

The scrub gave way to a clearing created by a fallen live oak tree. Julia entered the clearing. Teresa and Cotton Graves already stood next to the oak.

"You guys made it," Julia said.

Teresa and Cotton did not speak. They embraced Julia. Without introduction, Teresa fell into prayer. When she finished, Julia thought she heard Teresa singing, but she couldn't be certain.

Julia took at deep breath. "The Clevelands are safe for now." Julia swallowed, then continued. "The note I found in Charles's van said something was buried directly beneath a mark cut into the side of the oak."

"Did the note say anything else?" Cotton asked.

"Yeah," Julia said, "the note was taped to a closed envelope. It said to open the envelope after digging below the mark at the fallen oak."

"This must be it." Teresa pointed at a six-inch-long cut into the side of the tree. The cut appeared too deep and too straight to be naturally occurring.

Julia fell to her knees in front of the gash in the oak. She removed a buck knife from a scabbard on her belt. She held the knife up with both hands. It lingered in front of her face. She plunged it into the ground.

Julia ripped back and forth, up and down, with the knife. She tossed the knife to her side and began to pull away at the loose earth with her hands.

She felt something in the hole. It was cool to the touch. It felt metallic. Julia grabbed it and pulled it out of the ground.

She held it up for Cotton and Teresa to see. It was worn and rusty, with the appearance of age and exposure. It was a handgun.

"It's my old Colt 45," Cotton said, taking it from Julia with two fingers. "I lost it years ago. Decades ago."

Julia opened the letter. She read aloud:

"'The gun. I don't know how to say it. Never have been able to say it. Julia, you will have to tell them for me.

"'I planted the gun out behind Graves Mansion under this oak when I was eight years old. I kept it hidden in a board game at the back of my closet for months. But then I couldn't stand it any longer. It called to me during the night from the closet. It was threatening me.

"'The dark man helped me get through those nights. He convinced me to bury the gun. I know it sounds crazy—the dark man, not the gun calling, although I guess you might think the gun calling me is crazy too—but that's how it happened. The dark man led me out here one night when everyone one was asleep. I buried it and came back later to carve the gash in the oak. I don't know why I did that. I probably wanted to remember. I always wanted to remember.

"'Anyway, the dark man was right. It worked. The gun didn't call for me anymore. Stephen quit calling for me for a while as well. And this is what I want you to tell them, Julia.

"'I think Stephen stole the gun from Dad's room and was planning to shoot Dad with it. I was never sure why. I believe to this day that he thought he was doing the right thing, like Dad was going to hurt Mom and he was going to be her protector. I don't know. He never told me. The first time I saw him with the gun was when he brought it out of his room to use it.

"'I was playing on the balcony with my wood-block puzzle when he came out of his room with the gun. It was the first time I saw him with it. I swear. You have to believe me and you have to make them understand.

"'Mom and Dad were fighting below. When Stephen held that gun he wasn't my older brother anymore. He was more like a little child. I didn't know what to do. Maybe I should have yelled when I saw him come out with it that day, but I don't think that would have changed anything. There was too much noise below, and if I had been heard, Stephen would have shot Dad coming up the stairs. At least that's how I saw it at the time.

"'Forgive me—I was a kid. Please make then understand that, Julia. I am counting on you. Of all the people in this world, you seem to get me, so do your best.

"'I stood up and tried to stop Stephen. We wrestled. He dropped the gun. He fell. You know the rest.

"'I picked up the gun and hid it in my room while Mom and Dad were at the foot of the stairs with Stephen. They never suspected. They assumed the blood trail into my room from my lacerated cheek meant that I had tried to hide after the accident. The lacerated cheek was bad enough to leave the scar. It is the one thing that saved me. It made it believable, my story that it was all just an accident. They have always believed we were just having a brotherly spat that turned into a horrible tragedy. In a way, they were right, but it was more than that, as you now know. I thought I was saving Dad.

"'Julia, please make them know that I have carried the awful sight of Stephen teetering in midair before he fell for my entire life since that day. The look on his face was horrible. I am so sorry. No one could feel worse for what happened. Please do your best to make them understand. You are a master of logic, after all. Use all your skills.

"'There are only a few times when I have been able to escape that look on his face. One is the night I was saved in Cleveland's church. Coming into that light eased the pain of Stephen's death. It did not erase the memory, but maybe it changed the perspective of the event. It also gave me a great hope that since God was there, somehow Stephen's death could make sense one day. God is something else, huh? I have been terrified of stairways my whole life, and He showed me Jacob's ladder through Cleveland. Redeemed stairs for me, you know?

"'The other main way of escaping it has been your loving face. You are the most beautiful person to me, Julia. In your presence, the world seems right, no matter how many times it has turned over.

"'You will never know how much I love you. If your reading this letter means what I think it means, you will never get to know how much I love you. I am so sorry I will not be there to show you how much.

"'I am sorry for ruining your life and not being there to put it back together. Do me a favor and listen to what Cleveland has to say about electricity. He's a good man, Julia. Trust him, but more importantly, trust in the One he follows. If you do this, you will find that your life has actually been saved, not ruined.

"'Now that I think about it, giving you those pearls was kinda stupid. But ask Cleveland about pearls when you get a chance. He'll know what I mean. It's not what I meant when I gave them to you, but maybe they won't seem so stupid if you think of them that way.

"'Tell Cleveland everything. Tell him not to give up. Tell my mom and dad that I love them and that I am sorry. Tell my mom I remembered.

"'I love you, Julia.

"'Charles Graves.'"

Julia dropped the note. She fell to the ground on her back and stared up at the sky through the clearing. Somehow the world seemed an unearthly, nether region. Her vision melted as if she were looking at the sky and the top of the trees through a fish tank of tears. She was aware of Cotton and Teresa at her side, but she couldn't hear their words.

A faint roar of jet engines called in the distance. The roar grew until the jet engines were as loud as the crashing sea. As loud as a Galveston hurricane. Or the protesting of her mind. The jetliner passed over overhead and was gone.

Julia wept.

Be sure to catch all three
Second List Titles

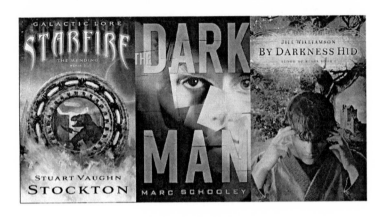

from

Marcher Lord Press

order online at
www.marcherlordpress.com

LaVergne, TN USA
04 September 2009
157071LV00002BA/1/P